PELICAN BOOKS

Pelican Library of Business and Management
Editor: T. Kempner

AN INSIGHT INTO
MANAGEMENT ACCOUNTING

Professor John Sizer was born in Grimsby, Lincolnshire, in 1938. After leaving school in 1954 he worked for companies in the trawling, frozen food and dairy industries. During this period he studied for the examinations of the Institute of Cost and Management Accountants, of which he is now an associate member, and in 1961 he was awarded their Leverhulme Prize. He read Industrial Economics at Nottingham University from 1961 to 1964. After graduating he spent a year in the Group Controller's Department at Guest, Keen and Nettlefolds Ltd. In 1965 he became Teaching Fellow and subsequently lecturer in management accountancy in the Department of Business Studies at Edinburgh University. He moved to the London Graduate School of Business Studies as Senior Lecturer in Accounting in 1968, and became Assistant Academic Dean (Post Graduate Studies) in July 1969. Since 1970 he has been Professor of Financial Management at Loughborough University of Technology, where he is now Head of the Department of Management Studies. John Sizer, a bronze and silver medallionist of the Royal Society of Arts, frequently contributes to the leading British accounting and management journals. He is a member of the American Accounting Association and a director of Loughborough Consultants Ltd. He has also undertaken consulting work and conducted seminars for a number of companies and the National Economic Development Office.

AN INSIGHT INTO
MANAGEMENT ACCOUNTING

JOHN SIZER

PENGUIN BOOKS

Penguin Books Ltd, Harmondsworth, Middlesex, England
Penguin Books Inc., 7110 Ambassador Road, Baltimore, Maryland 21207, U.S.A.
Penguin Books Australia Ltd, Ringwood, Victoria, Australia

—

First published 1969
Reprinted 1970, 1972, 1973

—

Copyright © John Sizer, 1969

—

Made and printed in Great Britain by
C. Nicholls & Company Ltd
Set in Monotype Times

To my parents

Contents

Preface

THERE are a large number of very weighty cost and management accountancy textbooks containing detailed descriptions of various accounting techniques. These books are primarily aimed at students preparing for the examinations of professional accountancy bodies. The questions set by these bodies frequently require complex calculations without any discussion of the limitations of the techniques employed. Many of these textbooks are inevitably technique-oriented and do not fully examine the role of the modern management accountant in the firm. At the other extreme some books on accountancy for managers treat the subject matter superficially. These books tend to assume that the reader has had no previous contact with accounting information. However, most managers have received financial data of one kind or another for a number of years. They require to know how the data is prepared and how to make maximum use of it. The objective has been to produce a book which falls between these two extremes and meets the needs of present and future managers.

It was my former colleague, Professor Edward Stamp, Professor of Accounting and Business Method at the University of Edinburgh, who brought to my attention Elbert Hubbard's description of a typical accountant:

A man past middle age, spare, wrinkled, intelligent, cold, passive, non-committal, with eyes like a codfish; polite in contact but at the same time unresponsive, calm and damnably composed as a concrete post or a plaster of Paris cast; a petrification with a heart of feldspar and without charm of the friendly germ, minus bowels, passion or a sense of humour. Happily they never reproduce and all of them finally go to Hell.

In Professor Stamp's opinion accountants don't have to be like this, even if most of them are. Certainly, Hubbard's description is still representative of many managers' images of their accountants. One of my objects has been to break down this nineteenth-century image. The modern management accountant was recently described by Joseph R. Dugan as:

A highly skilled technician – well educated, complex, confident, intelligent, optimistic – who abhors detailed direction. He expects to be influenced, persuaded and enlightened. He wants to be confronted with choices and alternatives, demanding freedom to structure his work, select his alternatives, present his solutions and speak for himself. He refuses to be considered an automaton who is supposed to respond eagerly to orders, edicts and ultimatums.

The book is concerned with the world of Dugan's modern management accountant not Hubbard's typical nineteenth-century accountant.

An Insight into Management Accounting should provide executives in general management and in other management specialisms with an insight into the financial aspects of management and the techniques available to the management accountant. It is concerned with the information the accountant should provide management to assist in planning, decision-making and control. A detailed explanation of the mechanics of the techniques is not appropriate, but an adequate description is provided to form the basis for a critical examination of their strengths and weaknesses. Throughout the subject matter is considered in the context of the environment of the firm. It is hoped that the book will encourage readers to ask their accountants the right questions. It is felt that some accountants, particularly in small and medium-sized firms, are not up-to-date in their thinking because they are not kept on their toes by management. The accounting techniques employed are all too often wrapped up in an aura of mystique.

As well as meeting the needs of managers, *An Insight into Management Accounting* is designed as an introductory text for post-graduate management students, and could also form the basis for a one-term course in management accounting for science or engineering students. Students preparing for the examinations of professional accountancy bodies will find the book integrates much of the material presented in the technique-oriented textbooks and relates it to other relevant disciplines, such as managerial economics, human relations, and operational research. It is hoped that the book will also be of interest to many qualified accountants, particularly those with a professional background, who wish to bring their thinking on management accounting up to date. While the book is primarily directed at general and specialist managers and management students, intelligent lay readers requiring an insight into management accounting will certainly not find the material beyond their comprehension.

A number of authors and publishers willingly gave permission to quote from their publications. In particular, parts of Chapters 8, 9, and 10 appeared originally in articles I wrote for *Accountancy, The Accountant*, the *Accountants Magazine* and the *Journal of Management Studies*.

The book is based on lectures given to post-graduate, post-experience, and in-plant management accountancy courses for management students and experienced managers during the three years I was a member of the Department of Business Studies at the University of Edinburgh. The participants on these courses constantly stimulated my thinking with their pointed questions. The lectures were, in part, based on my previous industrial experience. I am indebted to my former colleagues in industry who shared their experiences, in particular to Hugh Webster who guided my development as an accountancy student. Ninety-five per cent of the book was written during my last year at the University of Edinburgh, and I benefited considerably from the interaction with my colleagues in the Department of Business Studies. In particular, my thanks are due to Professor Norman Hunt, Michael Knowles, Tom Milne and Howard Thomas, who gave advice on particular points falling within their specialist fields. David Tweedie read the manuscript from the point of view of the potential reader and provided some useful comments. I am deeply indebted to my wife who has been a constant source of encouragement during the writing of this book and has helped in its preparation whenever possible.

Carpenders Park, Watford   John Sizer
December 1968

CHAPTER 1

What Is Management Accounting?

THIS book is concerned with management accounting. What is management accounting? In the broadest sense all accounting is management accounting. All financial and cost information generated by accountants is of some interest to management. But, in practice, where management accounting differs from financial accounting, cost accounting, budgetary control, and financial planning, is in the emphasis upon *purpose* rather than upon techniques. Management accounting may be defined as the application of accounting techniques to the provision of information designed to assist all levels of management in *planning* and *controlling* the activities of the firm. The management accountant employs the techniques of financial accounting, cost accounting, budgetary control and many others. Thus, management accounting has been defined by H.M. Treasury, in its *Glossary of Management Techniques*, as: 'The application of accounting knowledge to the *purpose* of producing and of interpreting accounting and statistical information designed to assist management in its functions of promoting maximum efficiency and in formulating and coordinating future plans and subsequently in measuring their execution.'

The term 'management accounting' came into use when accountants added to their existing functions – 1. correctly determining a firm's profit or loss for a period and evaluating its assets and liabilities on the last day of the period; 2. generating information for controlling operations to maximize efficiency – a third function: assisting management in planning and decision-making. Management accounting became fashionable in Britain following the visit of the Anglo-American Council of Productivity Management Accounting Team to the United States during April, May and June 1950. In the introduction to its report, entitled *Management Accounting* and published in November 1950, the team stated: 'Management accountancy is the presentation of accounting information in such a way as to assist management in the creation of policy and in the day-to-day operation of an undertaking.' They recommended that industrial accountants should make greater efforts to acquaint themselves with the problems of management and the technical processes in their industry, and concentrate their efforts towards producing information which will serve as a guide to policy and action. Shortly after the publication of the report of the management accounting team, the Institute of Cost and Works Accountants decided in future to award its Fellowship (F.C.W.A.) on the basis of an examination in management accountancy, and offered the Fellowship as a post-experience qualification to members of other professional accounting bodies in Great Britain. Today these examinations are part of the Institute's Associateship examinations. A Joint Diploma in Management Accounting Services (J.Dip.M.A.) is offered as the highest award available to qualified accountants in Great Britain jointly by the Institute of Chartered Accountants in England and Wales, the Institute of Chartered Accountants in Ireland, the Institute of Chartered Accountants of Scotland, the Institute of Cost and Works Accountants, and the Association of Certified and Corporate Accountants.

During the last fifteen years the term 'management accounting' has come into wide use. Many firms advertised for a cost accountant fifteen years ago; today they advertise for a management accountant. The journal of the Institute of Cost and Works Accountants, first published in June 1931, was called *The Cost Accountant* until January 1965, when it became *Management Accounting*. In a statement on the new name the President of the Institute pointed out: 'Cost and works accountancy, as practised by members of the Institute with their practical experience of costing in industry and their ability to see figures in terms of real things and real happenings, is the very stuff of management accounting.' Of course, many cost accountants would argue that they had always provided management with information to assist in planning and decision-making. They might suggest that 'management accountant' is a more impressive and glamorous title than 'cost accountant', but that the job content is much the same. Professor Lloyd R. Amey has pointed out that to inform and guide management has always been a function of accounting at least as important as external reporting, and that this function has become relatively more important with the passage of time. Amey argues that while management accounting is the newest accounting term, it refers to what is, in industrialized communities at least, probably the oldest function of accounting. 'The 19th-century entrepreneur or owner manager probably found it much more necessary to keep accounts to inform *himself* on all matters concerning the internal operations of his business – its asset balance, liquidity, profitability, and so on – than he did for the benefit of outside parties.'[1] However, while management accounting may not be altogether new, it is reasonable to argue that significant changes have taken place both in the role of the accountant in industry, and in the techniques employed by the accountant to provide management with information to assist in planning, decision-making, and control. While Professor Amey has suggested there is nothing new in the purpose of management accounting, he also states: 'It is undoubtedly in the provision of information for decision problems – strategically the most vital task of all – that the accountant is weakest.'[2] In recent years the accountant has developed new techniques for producing information for decision-making, although these techniques may not be new to the economist. This book is concerned with the information the accountant should provide management to assist in planning, decision-making, and control. It is also concerned with the techniques the accountant should employ to generate this information.

While accountancy provides the essential financial information system of business, the language of business, economists would argue that they provide its underlying logic. Therefore, it is useful to develop a classification of accountancy which makes the relationship between accountancy and economics clearer. A distinction can be made between:

Stewardship (including tax accounting), e.g. profit-and-loss accounts and balance sheets;

1. Lloyd R. Amey, 'Accounting as a Tool of Management', *District Bank Review*, December 1964, p. 26.
2. op. cit., p. 35.

Decision accounting, e.g. estimates of costs and revenues associated with particular alternatives; and

Control accounting, e.g. information to assist management in maximizing efficiency.

Financial accounting, the principal interest of most professional accountants, is concerned with stewardship. The task of the financial accountants is to produce profit-and-loss accounts and balance sheets that are fair to the shareholders and meet the requirements of the law. Professional accountants in practice are concerned with the auditing of these financial accounts. Financial accountants are employed in industry and commerce to classify, record, and interpret, in terms of money, transactions and events of a financial character. They prepare periodic accounting reports for individual companies and consolidated accounts for holding companies with one or more subsidiaries. Whilst a knowledge of financial accounting is an essential prerequisite of any discussion of management accounting techniques, the management accountant is primarily concerned with decision accounting and control accounting. However, it is extremely important that the concepts underlying the preparation of company profit-and-loss accounts and balance sheets are understood. Financial accounting is the subject of Chapter 2, and emphasis is placed in this chapter on these basic concepts. While disclosure in company accounts is also an important topic, it is beyond the scope of this book. A specialized aspect of financial accounting is company taxation, both the computation of taxation payable and the management of the company's affairs to legally minimize taxation payable. The management accountant must take taxation into account when evaluating alternatives and preparing long-term and short-term financial plans. Many companies employ taxation specialists, and the management accountant will consult the specialist on taxation aspects of his work.

The management accountant is primarily concerned with *decision accounting* and *control accounting*. The questions considered by the accountant under these headings are also of interest to the behavioural scientist, the managerial economist, and the operational researcher. It is important that the management accountant should be familiar with these disciplines. He must remember at all times that a business is a human/organizational system, and that management involves people. People are subject to complex motives and attitudes. The management information system must take account of the human element; it must not simply be seen as something mechanistic. The management accountant must have some insights into human relations. He must know when to seek the advice of the industrial psychologist. Similarly, an appreciation of managerial economics is essential. He should also be familiar with operational research techniques and know when to seek the advice of an operational research team. He must work with these and other specialists in the design and implementation of integrated management information systems.

Decision accounting is mainly concerned with '*ad hoc*' decisions. These '*ad hoc*' decisions require the analysis of the profitability of various allocations of resources. While these decisions may be repeated at intervals, it will probably be at irregular intervals. The task of *control accounting* is to produce data at regular intervals in a standard form, so that the firm's actual performance can be compared with plans and budgets and differences analysed by causes. Control accounting, by making such comparisons of planned and actual performance possible, enables a 'feedback' process to operate and guides the progress of the firm. The managerial economist is more likely to be interested in decision accounting than in control accounting. He will obviously appreciate that control accounting is important. He will be particularly interested in pricing, marketing, and investment decisions. To the operational researcher there are no such things as operational research problems, there are just problems. He will be interested in the appraisal of all types of decisions and in the establishment of management information systems. The behavioural scientist, on the other hand, will probably be more interested in control accounting. For example, the motivational aspects of establishing standards and budgets are within his sphere of interest.

Before an examination can be made of control and decision accounting techniques, some understanding of basic cost accounting is necessary. Basic cost accounting is the subject of

Chapter 3. Much of the cost information used by the management accountant flows from the cost accounting system. In Chapter 3 an insight is given into cost classification, overhead absorption, costing systems, and historical and standard costs. In particular, the uses which can be made of cost data are critically examined. Certain limitations are pointed out and these are further examined in subsequent chapters.

CONTROL ACCOUNTING

One definition of control is the guidance of the internal operations of the business to produce the most satisfactory profit at the lowest cost. Planning is the basis for control, because the essential nature of control is not simply the correcting of past mistakes but the directing of current and future operations in such a manner as to ensure the realization of management plans. The control process involves three aspects:

To *communicate* information about proposed plans;
To *motivate* people to achieve the plans;
To *report* performance.
So, while planning is the basis for control, information is the guide for control, and action is the essence of control.

It is suggested that management must plan in both the long term and the short term. Before management can plan the future it must have some assessment of its present position and its past performance. 'Profitability – Measurement and Control' is the subject of Chapter 4. The use of accounting ratios in the measurement of past performance, the diagnosis of the present position, and the establishment of profitability objectives are considered in this chapter. The establishment of profitability objectives leads into a discussion of long-range planning and, in particular, financial planning in Chapter 5. Financial planning is an integral part of long-range planning. Therefore, prior to the consideration of financial planning, the establishment of corporate objectives and the development of a strategy to achieve the agreed objectives is briefly examined. Long-range planning gives rise to the need to appraise capital expenditure decisions and to plan in the short term. Capital expenditure appraisal is the subject of

Chapter 6. Budgetary control, which is concerned with planning in the short term, is considered in Chapter 7. Within the framework of the financial plan, a budgetary control system should be operated to ensure that detailed budgets are prepared for the current year of the financial plan. These budgets normally form the basis for subsequent control. Motivating people to achieve plans, the reporting of performance, the significance of variances from budget, and the need for separate budgets for planning and control are considered in Chapter 7.

DECISION ACCOUNTING

Decision accounting and control accounting are closely inter-related. While planning is the basis for control, the preparation of plans involves the consideration of alternatives, and decision accounting is concerned with the evaluation of alternatives. The formulation of long-range and short-term plans and the appraisal of decisions, which provide the basis for subsequent control, are concerned with the future and involve the choice between alternatives. The decision under consideration may involve investment in additional buildings, the introduction of a new product, the choice between two contracts when there is limited plant capacity, the altering of a selling price, or some similar decision. However, regardless of the nature of the decision, the problem is basically the same. Management requires an answer to the question: 'Which is the most worthwhile alternative, alternative A, B, C, ...?' Management requires a measure of 'worthwhileness'.

In developing costs for decision-making a distinction must be drawn between short-run and long-run decisions. The essence of the distinction is *time*. Where, in choosing between alternative courses of action, the time factor is important, and carries a cost or interest with it, the problem is of an *investment* nature. In appraising investment decisions discounting techniques must be employed. Investment decisions and discounting techniques are considered in Chapter 6. Costs for short-run decision-making are considered in Chapter 8. The determination of selling prices is a major policy decision in many companies, and the whole of Chapter 9 is devoted to an examination of the accountant's contribution to the pricing decision. In employing flexible budgets for cost control purposes in Chapter 7, and in developing costs for decision-making in Chapters 8 and 9, the segregation of costs into fixed and variable categories is of critical importance. In Chapter 10 the determination of fixed and variable costs is considered in detail.

Inevitably, in an introductory text of this length, which aims at giving an insight into management accounting, it is not possible to develop at length many aspects of particular topics. The number of illustrations of the application of techniques to practical problems is also limited for the same reason. In order to minimize these two limitations, at the end of each chapter a list of recommended readings is provided. The readings are of two types:

1. Articles and texts which examine in greater detail the topics considered in the chapter;

2. Managerial applications of techniques considered in the chapter.

SUMMARY OF CHAPTER

It has been emphasized that management accounting is concerned with the *purpose* of accounting rather than with techniques. The management accountant should employ planning, control, and decision-making techniques to provide information to assist all levels of management in planning and controlling the activities of the firm. The management accountant has traditionally been at his strongest when producing information for control purposes. The management accountant of the future must also have an understanding of the nature of decision problems and the information needed to solve them. He must understand the background of modern business, and appreciate that any business is a complex of interlocking sets of 'systems'. In addition to the economic/financial set of systems, there are the human/organizational and technical sets of systems. With the rapid introduction of computers these sub-systems are being integrated into unified computer-based management information systems. All this implies that a management accountant, in addition to his specialized training in accounting and financial management, must have a fairly thorough understanding of the basic subjects like mathematics, statistics, economics, psychology, etc. He must have sufficient insight into these basic subjects to be able to work with the operational research worker, the industrial psychologist, the managerial economist, the systems analyst, and other specialists in the management team.

CHAPTER 2

Basic Financial Accounting

FINANCIAL accounting is concerned with the *external* requirements of creditors, shareholders, prospective investors, the
Registrar of Companies, the Inspector of Taxes, and persons
outside the management, as well as with the *internal* requirements
of the management. Financial accountants record the revenue
received and expenditure incurred by the company so that its
o*erall* trading position can be ascertained at any point in time.
The financial accounting system classifies, records, and interprets,
in terms of money, transactions and events of a financial character. These facts and figures are summarized and presented to
management and outside parties in the form of periodic accounting reports. The following periodic accounting reports will
normally be prepared for the management of a manufacturing
company:

Manufacturing and trading accounts;
Profit-and-loss account;
Profit-and-loss appropriation account;
Balance sheet; and possibly
Cash flow or funds flow statement.

These statements are illustrated in Tables 2.1, 2.2, 2.3 and 2.4.

The *manufacturing and trading accounts* (Table 2.1) show the
cost of goods manufactured during the period of the account, the
cost of goods sold during the period of the account, the sales for
the period, and the gross profit, i.e. sales minus cost of goods
sold. The gross profit is transferred to the *profit-and-loss account*
(Table 2.2), which shows the profit or loss for the period before
taxation, i.e. gross profit minus selling and distribution costs and
administration expenses for the period. The profit or loss
minus the taxation payable on the profits, if any, gives the net
profit or loss for the period. The *profit-and-loss appropriation
account* (Table 2.2) indicates the profit available for appropriation

Table 2.1

THE E. D. COMPANY LTD
Manufacturing and Trading Accounts for the year
ended 31 December 1966

	£	£		£
Raw Materials				
Opening Stock		42,000	Finished Goods	
Purchases		250,307	Transferred to	
		———	Warehouse	732,431
		292,307		
Less Closing Stock		30,000		
		———		
Costs of Materials Consumed		262,307		
Production Wages		220,000		
		———		
Prime Cost of Production		482,307		
Factory Overhead:				
Packing Wages	10,000			
Factory Rates	435			
Factory Insurance	895			
Packing Materials	13,600			
Factory Repairs	7,020			
Factory Gas, Water				
and Electricity	6,556			
Non-productive				
Wages	180,458			
Works Salaries	33,140			
Depreciation of:				
Plant and				
Machinery	15,224			
Fixtures and				
Fittings	532			
Freehold Premises	4,784			
	———			
		272,644		
		———		
		754,951		
Less Increase in Work in Progress		2,520		
		———		
Factory Costs of Production		752,431		
Less Stock of Finished Goods				
in Factory		20,000		
		———		
Cost of Goods to Warehouse		£732,431		£732,431

Table 2.1 – cont.	£			£
Finished Goods in Warehouse				
Opening Stock	65,000		Sales	855,716
Factory Production				
Transferred	732,431			
	797,431			
Less Closing Stock	45.000			
Cost of Sales	752,431			
Gross Profit to Profit-and-				
loss A/c	103,285			
	£855,716			£855,716

Table 2.2

THE E. D. COMPANY LTD

Profit-and-loss and Profit-and-loss Appropriation Accounts
for the year ended 31 December 1966

	£	£		£
Selling and Distribution Cost			Gross Profit b/d	103,285
Carriage Outwards	14,300			
Salesmen's Travelling			Discounts Received	2,030
Expenses	1,763			
Sales Office Salaries	2,000			
Salesmen's Commission	10,620			
		28,683		
Advertising		2,075		
General Expenses		2,012		
Administration Expenses				
Office Salaries		17,005		
Depreciation:				
Freehold Premises	252			
Fixtures and Fittings	532			
Cars	300			
		1,084		
Directors' Fees		3,000		
Audit Fees		500		
Provision for Bad Debts		2,765		
Bank Interest		2,427		

Table 2.2 – cont.

	£		£
	59,551		
Net Profit before Taxation c/d	45,764		
	£105,315		£105,315
Provision for Taxation	18,000	Net Profit before Taxation b/d	45,764
Net Profit for Year c/d	27,764		
	£45,764		£45,764
Transfer to General Reserve	20,000	Balance brought down from previous year	20,517
Proposed Dividend at 5%	15,000		
Balance carried forward to next year	13,281	Net Profit for year b/d	27,764
	£48,281		£48,281

to shareholders in the form of dividends, for transfer to reserves, and for carrying forward to the next account. The profit available for appropriation is represented by the balance brought forward from the previous account plus or minus the net profit or loss for the period transferred from the profit-and-loss account.

The *balance sheet* (Table 2.3) is a statement, *not* an account, and shows:

1. The *assets* or *resources* of the company on the last day of the period, e.g. fixed assets such as buildings, plant and machinery, vehicles, etc., and current assets such as stocks, debtors, cash, etc. Fixed assets have a long but nevertheless limited life, and current assets are changing from day to day.

2. The *liabilities* or *obligations* of the company on the last day of the accounting period, e.g. long-term liabilities such as debentures and future taxation, and current liabilities such as creditors, current taxation, proposed dividends, etc.

3. The *share capital and reserves* or *shareholders' investment* in the company on the last day of the accounting period, e.g. ordinary share capital, preference share capital (if any), capital reserves, and revenue reserves.

Table 2.3

THE E. D. COMPANY LTD

Balance Sheet as at 31 December 1966

	£	£		£	£	£
			Fixed Assets		*Accumulated*	
				Cost	Depreciation	
Authorized Capital			Freehold Land	25,000	–	25,000
500,000 Ordinary Shares	500,000		Freehold Buildings	125,725	30,253	95,472
of £1 each			Plant and Machinery	172,240	95,368	76,872
			Fixtures and Fittings	10,640	5,614	5,026
Issued Capital			Motor Cars	1,200	1,000	200
300,000 Ordinary Shares		300,000		£334,805	£132,235	202,570
of £1 each fully paid						

Revenue Reserves		
General Reserve	20,000	
Profit and Loss A/c	13,281	33,281
Total Shareholders' Interests		333,281
Reserve for Future Taxation (1)		18,000
Capital Employed		351,281
Current Liabilities		
Sundry Creditors	100,578	
Current Taxation (2)	15,000	
Proposed Dividend	15,000	130,578
		£481,859

Current Assets		
Stocks in Hand and Work in Progress	165,560	
Sundry Debtors	97,855	
Tax Reserve Certificates	10,000	
Cash at Bank	5,874	279,289
		£481,859

(1) Payable 1 January 1968
(2) Payable 1 January 1967

In the balance sheet the company's assets are equal to liabilities plus share capital and reserves. The reason for this is explained later in this chapter.

The manufacturing, trading, and profit-and-loss accounts summarize the income received and expenses incurred during an accounting period. The *cash flow or funds flow statement* (Table 2.4) summarizes the events of the period from another standpoint;

Table 2.4

THE E.D. COMPANY LTD

Sources and Uses of Funds Statement for the year
ended 31 December 1966

	£
Internal Sources of Funds	
Profit before Taxation	45,764
Add: Depreciation	21,624
Profit before Taxation and Depreciation	67,388
Decrease in Stocks	9,480
Sales of Fixed Assets	1,200
	£78,068
Disposition of Funds	
Expenditure on Fixed Assets	57,358
Increase in Debtors less Creditors	5,000
Taxation paid	17,000
Dividends paid	12,000
	£91,358
Deficiency of Internally Generated Funds	(13,290)
External Sources of Funds	
Increase in Ordinary Share Capital	100,000
Variation in Liquid Resources	86,710
Bank Overdraft at commencement of period	(80,836)
Cash at Bank at end of period	£5,874

it describes the sources from which additional cash (funds) was derived and the uses to which this cash (funds) was put. A distinction is made in this statement between *internal sources* of funds generated by the company such as profit before depreciation and taxation, and *external sources* of funds raised from outside the company such as share capital and debenture loans.

Companies are required to prepare a summarized profit-and-loss account, a profit-and-loss appropriation account, and a balance sheet in accordance with the requirements of the Companies Acts of 1948 and 1967. Disclosure in company reports has received considerable attention in recent years. The main concern of this chapter is an examination of financial accounting principles and concepts. This knowledge is an essential prerequisite of any discussion of management accounting techniques such as financial planning, budgetary control, rate of return on capital employed, and ratio analysis. It is particularly important that readers should fully appreciate the concepts underlying the preparation of company profit-and-loss accounts and balance sheets. While disclosure in company accounts is an important topic, it is beyond the scope of a book on management accountancy. A full discussion of this topic will be found in Selected Readings 5, 7 and 12 (see p. 48). Readers are also advised to study the annual report and accounts of a public company, preferably a company which has received 'The Accountant's Award' for the best annual report and accounts published during a particular year. Two such companies are Ross Group Ltd and Guest, Keen & Nettlefolds Ltd.

DOUBLE-ENTRY ACCOUNTING

To build up the trading and profit-and-loss accounts and the balance sheet, the financial accounting department classifies and records receipts and payments, assets and liabilities, and debtors and creditors in ledgers using a *double-entry* accounting system. To fully understand financial accounting concepts and principles the double-entry system must be mastered.

The resources owned by a business are called *assets*, and the claims of various parties against these assets are either liabilities or capital. *Liabilities* are claims of creditors, every one other than the owners of the business. *Capital* is the claim of the owners of the business and represents their investment in the business. A company has a legal identity separate from that of its shareholders, and the shareholders' investment in the company represents a potential claim on the company. Since all the assets of a company are claimed by someone (either by the shareholders or by the creditors), and since these claims cannot exceed the amount of assets available to be claimed, it follows that ASSETS = CAPITAL + LIABILITIES and CAPITAL = ASSETS − LIABILITIES. Therefore, any change in one of these items must result in an equal change in one of the others. For example, if assets are increased by the introduction of £1,000 additional cash from shareholders, then capital must increase by an equal amount. Accounting systems are designed to record the two aspects of every event (transaction) of a financial character in the activities of the company, i.e. changes in assets and changes in liabilities or capital. It follows that every event that is recorded in the ledgers affects at least two items; there is no conceivable way of making a single item change in the accounts. Accounting is therefore called a double-entry system. In this system one entry is the creditor or *credit entry* and the other the debtor or *debit entry*. In any transaction the creditor *gives* and the debtor *receives*. Thus, in the introduction of further capital the shareholders *give* £1,000 and the cash account *receives* £1,000. This transaction is recorded in the ledger as follows:

Dr.	*Share Capital Account*		Cr.
		Cash	£1,000

	Cash Account	
Share Capital	£1,000	

It will be seen that any increase in capital or liabilities is recorded with a credit entry, any increase in assets with a debit entry, and with a decrease the entries are reversed. In addition to assets and liabilities a company has expenses and revenue. If £100 wages are paid by cash, cash *gives* and wages *receives*, and the entries in the ledger would be:

Dr.		*Cash Account*	Cr.
		Wages	£100

	Wages Account	
Cash	£100	

In the case of sales for cash the entry would be the opposite, sales *gives* (credit entry) and cash *receives* (debit entry). It follows then that expenses are debit entries and revenues are credit entries. In summary, increases in assets, decreases in liabilities or capital, and expenses appear as debit entries; increases in liabilities or capital, decreases in assets, and sales appear as *credit entries.*

A SIMPLE ILLUSTRATION

A. Trader & Co. Ltd commenced business on 1 September with the issue of 750 £1 shares for cash. The company's transactions for the month of September are summarized in Table 2.5. It will be seen that for the first ten transactions the account that *receives* (the debit entry) and the account that *gives* (the credit entry) are indicated. Readers are invited to complete columns four and five. Each transaction has been numbered to enable the reader to trace the double entry for each transaction in the ledger accounts (Table 2.6). The reader's completion of Table 2.5 can also be checked. Having traced each transaction into the ledger accounts, the next stage is to prepare the trading account and the profit-and-loss account.[1] The balances of expense and revenue accounts have to be transferred to the trading and profit-and-loss accounts for September, that is sales, purchases, and wages. Gross profit is determined by deducting from sales the cost of goods sold. In order to arrive at the cost of goods sold, it is necessary to deduct from the purchases during

1. In practice, before the trading account and profit-and-loss account are prepared, a trial balance would be taken out to ensure the transactions have been correctly entered in the ledgers, and the total of the debit entries equals the total of the credit entries.

Table 2.5

A. TRADER & CO. LTD

Transactions – September

Date	Transaction	£	Receives (*Debit*)	Gives (*Credit*)	No.
1st	Issued 750 £1 shares for cash	750	Cash	Share Capital	1
2nd	Purchased goods from A. Peters on credit	250	Purchases	A. Peters	2
3rd	Purchased second-hand van for cash	100	Motor Vehicles	Cash	3
4th	Purchased goods for cash	27	Purchases	Cash	4
5th	Sold goods for cash	25	Cash	Sales	5
8th	Sold goods to W. Trainer on credit	50	W. Trainer	Sales	6
9th	Sold goods to R. Roberts on credit	27	R. Roberts	Sales	7
11th	Purchased goods from H. Morton on credit	100	Purchases	H.Morton	8
12th	Paid A. Peters cash	150	A. Peters	Cash	9
15th	Received cash from W. Trainer	30	Cash	W.Trainer	10
18th	Bought goods from A. Peters on credit	50			11
19th	Received cash from R. Roberts	17			12
23rd	Sold goods to W. Trainer for cash	125			13
25th	Sent cash to A. Peters	100			14
26th	Paid wages	37			15
30th	Paid cash to H. Morton	50			16

September the stock on hand at 30 September of £290. How does this appear in the ledger ? Stock is an asset and the stock account must therefore be debited and the trading account credited (shown by a deduction on the debit side). The entry is therefore:

	Dr.	Cr.
Stock Account	£290	
Trading Account		£290

Stock on Hand at 30 September

It will be seen that the balance of the stock account is carried down to become the opening stock of the next period.

The second-hand van has a long but nevertheless limited life, and the cost of the van must be systematically reduced over its life by the process called *depreciation*. The purpose of the depreciation process is gradually to remove the cost of the asset from the motor vehicles account and show it as an expense. The depreciation charge on the van for September is £5 and is recorded in the ledger with the following entry:

	Dr.	Cr.
Provision for Depreciation	£5	
Motor Vehicles Account		£5

Motor Vehicle Depreciation for September

The balance of the provision for depreciation account is then transferred to the profit-and-loss account like any other expense. It is important to appreciate that the provision for depreciation does not provide a fund to replace the asset at the end of its life. No cash is involved in accounting for depreciation, merely book entries. However, it does reduce the profit available for distribution to shareholders, and, therefore, the potential outflow of cash from the business in the form of dividends.

The balance of the profit-and-loss account represents the profit for the period, and it will be seen that it is a *credit* balance.

Table 2.6

A. TRADER & CO. LTD
Ledger

Dr.						Cr.
			Share Capital A/c			
		£				£
Sept. 30 Balance	c/d	750	Sept. 1 Cash	(1)	750
			Oct. 1 Balance	b/d	750

Table 2.6 – cont.

Dr.   Cr.

Motor Vehicles A/c

		£			£
Sept. 3 Cash	(3)	100	Sept. 30 Provision for Depreciation		5
			30 Balance	c/d	95
		£100			£100
Oct. 1 Balance	b/d	95			

Cash A/c

		£			£
Sept. 1 Share Capital	(1)	750	Sept. 3 Motor Vehicles	(3)	100
5 Sales	(5)	25	4 Purchases	(4)	27
15 W. Trainer	(10)	30	12 A. Peters	(9)	150
19 R. Roberts	(12)	17	25 "	(14)	100
23 Sales	(13)	125	26 Wages	(15)	37
			30 H. Morton	(16)	50
			30 Balance	c/d	483
		£947			£947
Oct. 1 Balance	b/d	483			

Stock A/c

		£			£
Sept. 30 Trading A/c		290	Sept. 30 Balance	c/d	290
Oct. 1 Balance	b/d	290			

Sales A/c

		£			£
Sept. 30 Trading A/c		227	Sept. 5 Cash	(5)	25
			8 W. Trainer	(6)	50
			9 R. Roberts	(7)	27
			23 Cash	(13)	125
		£227			£227

Table 2.6 – cont.

Dr.   Cr.

Purchases A/c

		£			£
Sept. 2	A. Peters	(2) 250	Sept. 30	Trading A/c	427
4	Cash	(4) 27			
11	H. Morton	(8) 100			
18	A. Peters	(11) 50			
		£427			£427

Wages A/c

		£			£
Sept. 26	Cash	(15) 37	Sept. 30	Profit-and-loss A/c	37

Provision for Depreciation A/c

		£			£
Sept. 30	Motor Vehicles	5	Sept. 30	Profit-and-loss A/c	5

DEBTORS   *W. Trainer A/c*

		£				£
Sept. 8	Sales	(6) 50	Sept. 15	Cash	(10)	30
			30	Balance	c/d	20
		£50				£50
Oct. 1	Balance	b/d 20				

Dr.   Cr.

R. Roberts A/c

		£				£
Sept. 9	Sales	(7) 27	Sept. 19	Cash	(12)	17
			30	Balance	c/d	10
		£27				£27
Oct. 1	Balance	b/d 10				

Table 2.6 – cont.

Dr.   Cr.

CREDITORS   A. Peters A/c

		£			£
Sept. 12 Cash	(9)	150	Sept. 2 Purchases	(2)	250
25 Cash	(14)	100	18 Purchases	(11)	50
30 Balance	c/d	50			
		£300			£300
			Oct. 1 Balance	b/d	50

H. Morton A/c

		£			£
Sept. 30 Cash	(16)	50	Sept. 11 Purchases	(8)	100
30 Balance	c/d	50			
		£100			£100
			Oct. 1 Balance	b/d	50

Trading and Profit-and-loss Accounts – September

		£			£
Purchases		427	Sales		227
Less Closing Stock		290			
Cost of Goods Sold		137			
Gross Profit	c/d	90			
		£227			£227
Wages		37	Gross Profit	b/d	90
Depreciation		5			
Net Profit	c/d	48			
		£90			£90
			Oct. 1 Balance	b/d	48

Profit is net revenue and revenue is a credit entry. Profit earned is payable to shareholders and any profit retained in the business represents an additional investment in the company by the shareholders. Thus, retained profit forms part of the capital of the company and increases in capital appear as credit entries. The other capital, liability, and asset accounts are now balanced. The balances are carried down to the next period because they represent the capital, liabilities and assets at the commencement of the next period. The balance sheet (Table 2.7), which is a *statement* of the company's assets, liabilities, and capital on the last day of the period, is then prepared.

Table 2.7

A. TRADER & CO. LTD

Balance Sheet as at 30 September 19 . .

	£			£
Capital and Reserves		*Fixed Assets*		
750 £1 Ordinary Shares	750	Motor Vehicles at cost		100
		Less Provision for		
		Depreciation		5
Profit and loss Account	48	Written Down Value		95
	798			
Current Liabilities		*Current Assets*	£	£
Sundry Creditors £		Stocks		290
A. Peters 50		Sundry Debtors		
H. Morton 50	100	W. Trainer	20	
		R. Roberts	10	30
		Cash on hand		483 803
	£898			£898

It will be appreciated that this is a very simple illustration, but by systematically working through the entries in the ledger accounts the reader should be able to grasp the principles of double-entry accounting.

ACCRUALS AND PREPAYMENTS

In the A. Trader & Co. Ltd illustration it was assumed that all expenses for the period had been paid when the trading and Profit-and-loss accounts for September were prepared, and also that no expenses had been paid in advance. In a normal business at the end of the accounting period some expenses have not been paid and have to be *accrued*, and others have been paid in advance and have to be treated as *prepayments*. How are accruals and prepayments handled in double-entry accounting?

Accruals are liabilities which have become due or are accruing at the end of the accounting period but have not been recorded in the ledger accounts. These may include such items as charges for gas, water, electricity or telephone, or similar items consumed or incurred during the period, for which no invoice has yet been received. For example, if the electricity account of a manufacturing concern has a balance of £1,250 at the end of the accounting period (31 December) and there is an outstanding electricity charge of £150 for December, the amount to be transferred to the profit-and-loss account is £1,400. The balance of the electricity account is carried down to the next period as a liability in the same way as a balance due to a creditor. The electricity account would appear as follows:

Dr.			*Electricity Account*		Cr.
		£			£
Dec. 31	Expenses paid (detailed)	1,250	Dec. 31	Profit-and-loss Account	1,400
31	Balance: December charge outstanding c/d	150			
		£1,400			£1,400
Jan. 15	Expense paid	150	Jan. 1	Balance b/d	150

The credit balance on 31 December would appear in the balance sheet as an accrued charge under current liabilities. Frequently, accrued charges are lumped in the balance sheet with sundry creditors as sundry creditors and accrued charges. When the outstanding amount is paid in January it cancels out the accrued charge.

Prepayments arise when payments for expenses such as rent, rates, insurances, etc. made during an accounting period refer wholly or partly to a succeeding period. The treatment is similar to that for accruals. For example, if the rent and rates account of a manufacturing concern has a balance of £1,000 at the end of the accounting period (31 December), and the sum of £80 for local rates for the half-year ending 31 March following was paid on 1 December, the amount to be transferred to the profit-and-loss account is £960 (i.e. £1,000 minus £40 rates paid in advance). The balance of the rent and rates account is carried down to the next period, in the same way as a balance due to a debtor, and would appear in the balance sheet as a payment in advance under the heading of current assets. The ledger account would appear as follows:

Dr.				Rent and Rates Account		Cr.
		£				£
Dec. 31	Expenses paid (detailed)	1,000	Dec. 31	Balance: one quarter's rates paid in advance c/d		40
			31	Profit-and-loss Account		960
		£1,000				£1,000
Jan. 1	Balance b/d	40				

The prepayment of one period becomes an expense of the next period.

FINANCIAL ACCOUNTING CONCEPTS

Financial accounting is based upon a number of basic concepts. In presenting accounting statements to management many accountants do not fully explain these concepts. An understanding of the concepts is a basic prerequisite for any discussion of management accounting techniques.

1. *The Money Measurement Concept.* In accounting a record is made only of those facts and events that can be expressed in monetary terms. This concept imposes severe limitations on the scope of accounting statements. The accounts of A. Trader & Co. Ltd do not reveal, for example, that a competitor has introduced an improved service to customers. The money measurement concept is a common denominator concept and is clearly an essential one. While money is probably the only practical denominator, the use of money implies homogeneity, a basic similarity between £1 and another. In periods of inflation or

deflation this homogeneity may not in fact exist. This problem is considered later in this chapter.

2. *The Business Entity Concept*. Accounts are maintained for business entities as distinct from the persons who own them, operate them, or are otherwise associated with the business. There follows from this distinction between the business entity and the outside world the idea that an important function of financial accounting is *stewardship*. The directors of a company are entrusted with the finance supplied by the shareholders, debenture-holders, banks, and creditors. Financial accounting systems are in part designed to produce reports to indicate how effectively this responsibility, or stewardship, has been undertaken.

3. *The Going Concern Concept*. Accounting assumes that the business will continue to operate for an indefinitely long period in the future. Accounting does *not* attempt to measure at all times what the business is currently worth to a potential buyer. Accounting does *not* produce balance sheets which show the value of the assets of the company if it went into voluntary liquidation. If the E. D. Company Ltd (Table 2.3) had offered its assets for sale on 31 December 1966 the fixed assets would not have realized £202,570 nor the current assets £279,289. A business is viewed as an economic/financial system for adding value to the resources it uses, and its success is measured by comparing the value of its output with the cost of the resources used in producing that output. The difference between the value of its output and the costs of the resources it uses is called profit. Resources which have been acquired but not yet employed in producing output are called assets. They are shown in the accounting records *not* at their current value to an outside buyer, but rather at their cost. The current value may be above or below the cost shown in the accounting records. This concept is clearly illustrated by the following extract from the estimated statement of affairs[1] of Planet Productions Ltd at 31 March 1967. Planet Productions Ltd is the owner of Radio Caroline, the pirate radio illegal under the Marine Etc. Broadcasting (Offences) Act, 1967.

1. For the complete statement of affairs, see *The Accountant*, 30 September 1967, pp. 428–31.

PLANET PRODUCTIONS LTD

(Subject to Audit)

Estimated Statement of Affairs as at 31 March 1967

Notes on Accounts

1. *Fixed Assets*

Cost	£
Office Furniture, Fixtures and Equipment	15,010
Technical Equipment	23,605
Studio Erection and Equipment	60,006
Motor Vehicles	325
	98,946
Less Depreciation written off	19,268
	£79,678

Note: In the event of forced closure by the Government, the Assets would only realize approximately 10% of their net value.

4. *The Cost Concept.* Resources owned by a business are called in accounting terminology, assets. A fundamental concept of accounting, closely related to the going concern concept, is that an asset is ordinarily entered in the accounting records at the price paid to acquire the asset, and that cost is the basis of all subsequent accounting for the asset. The accounting measurement of assets does *not* normally reflect the worth of assets except at the moment they are acquired. The going-concern concept and the cost concept may result in the production of accounting reports which make it difficult to measure how efficiently the directors have carried out their stewardship function. The measurement of profitability, using rate of return on capital employed as a measure of efficiency, is considered in Chapter 4.

The cost concept does not mean that all assets remain in the accounting records at their original cost for as long as the company own them. The cost of a fixed asset, such as a boiler, that has a long but nevertheless limited life is systematically reduced over the life of the asset by the process of *depreciation*. The purpose of depreciation is gradually to remove the cost of the asset from the accounting records by showing it as a cost of operations in the profit-and-loss account. It is important to appreciate that the depreciation process does *not* provide a fund to replace the asset at the end of its useful life. It does reduce the profit available for distribution to shareholders and, therefore, the potential outflow of cash from the business in the form of dividends to shareholders. The depreciation process has no clear relationship to changes in the market value of the asset or its real worth to the company. It has no clear relationship with the cost of the replacement asset at the end of the asset's useful life.

Another important consequence of the cost concept is that if the company pays nothing for an item it acquires, this item will usually not appear in the accounting records as an asset. The knowledge, skill and expertise of an electronic company's research and development team does not appear in the company's balance sheet as an asset.

THE PROBLEM OF INFLATION

Since the end of the Second World War accountants have become increasingly aware of the problems and impact of changing price levels on accounting records and statements. Accountants measure profit by finding the difference between net assets at the beginning and end of the accounting period. They match the *actual* revenues of the period with the *actual* expenses of the period, and, to the extent that revenue exceeds expenses, there is a profit. However, the matching process may be of revenue of the period with costs of an earlier period; they do not necessarily match current values. This particularly applies to the depreciation of fixed assets on a historical cost basis. An overstatement of profit will occur in times of rising prices if any input costs of one date are matched with output revenues of a later date. Part of what the accountants calculate as profit will be required to maintain the capital of the business intact. Part of the profit will be required to cover the increased cost of replacing plant acquired at prices considerably lower than those now ruling.

The effects of inflation on taxation must also be considered. If as a result of inflation profit is seriously overstated, the burden of taxation on the business will be greater than that implied by the nominal rate of taxation. If reported profits which result from merely a change in the value of money, or capital gains arising for the same reason, are taxed as if they were real income to the business, then the ability of the company to maintain the capital of the business intact and sustain real growth will be diminished.

Certain steps can be taken to allow for inflation. For example, the British Transport Docks Board and Guest, Keen & Nettle-folds both allow for the effects of inflation when computing annual depreciation charges. The next step would be to make a correction for inflation in the balance sheet statements of assets. G.K.N. recognizes the problem in its internal accounts and corrects the net valuation of fixed assets for inflation. Other companies periodically revalue assets. Imperial Chemical Industries revalued their assets and recalculated depreciation in 1950 and 1958. Philips Electrical Industries are one of the few companies which account for changing price levels in a fully integrated fashion. They report fixed assets, depreciation, investments, and stocks at current price levels. They charge the loss of purchasing power of cash assets in the profit-and-loss account. The difference between historical cost profit and pur-chasing power profit for Philips in 1968 amounted to over $13 million and 10 per cent of historical cost profit.

Clearly, great care must be taken in interpreting profit-and-loss accounts and balance sheets prepared on a historical cost basis and which take no account of the impact of inflation. The use of rates of return on capital employed to measure efficiency, for the discernment of trends in performance, and for both internal and external comparisons can be hindered by the effects of accounting conventions used in the preparation of financial accounts. In particular, the problem of changing price levels has to be recog-nized in rate of return on capital employed calculations, and is further considered in Chapter 4.

A SIMPLE ILLUSTRATION OF THE
INFLATION PROBLEM

In order to illustrate how inflation can lead to an overstatement of profits, assume a company operating in a tax-free world with a share capital of £100. The company's only asset is a machine purchased at the commencement of Year 1 for £100. It was estimated that the machine would have a ten-year life and no residual value. The machine was depreciated at the rate of 10 per cent per annum of original cost, i.e. £10 per annum. The company generated a profit before depreciation, i.e. cash flow, in Year 1 of £30. Assume that the company distributed all its profits to shareholders in the form of dividends on the last day of the year. All costs and prices, and therefore profits, increased at an annual rate of 3 per cent per annum, i.e. there was a rate of inflation of 3 per cent per annum.

The company's balance sheet at the commencement of Year 1 was:

	£		£
Share Capital	100	Machine – Cost	100

The profit for Year 1 distributed to shareholders was:

	£
Profit before depreciation	30
Less Depreciation	10
Profit paid as dividend	£20

The balance sheet at the end of Year 1, assuming the dividend had been paid to the shareholders, was:

	£		£
Share Capital	100	Machine – Cost	100
		Less Depreciation	10
		Written Down Value	90
		Cash	10
	£100		£100

The £10 cash in the balance sheet is the difference between the cash flow for the year and the dividend paid to shareholders.

The profits for Years 2–10, assuming 3-per-cent annual inflation, were:

	2	3	4	5 – – – – – – – –10
	£	£	£	£ £
Profit before depreciation	31	32	33	34 · · · 39
Less Depreciation	10	10	10	10 · · · 10
Profit paid as dividend	£21	£22	£23	£24 · · · £29

Because depreciation was based on the *original cost* of the asset, the depreciation charge remained constant over the period. Each year £10 of the cash flow was retained in the business. The cash flow and, therefore, the profit paid as dividends increased with the inflation. The dividend increased at a rate in excess of 4 per cent per annum because the depreciation charge was based on the original cost of the asset. Over the ten-year period the share capital remained constant at £100 and the asset side of the balance sheets for Years 2–10 appeared as follows:

	2	3	4	5 – – – – – 10
	£	£	£	£ £
Machine – Cost	100	100	100	100 · · · 100
Less Depreciation	20	30	40	50 · · · 100
Written Down Value	80	70	60	50 · · · —
Cash	20	30	40	50 · · · 100
	£100	£100	£100	£100 · · · £100

At the end of Year 10 the machine is written down to nil, it is completely worn out, and it is decided to replace it. £100 is available in the bank to replace the machine, i.e. the internally generated cash flow not distributed to the shareholders. An identical machine can be purchased, but, because of the 3-per-cent inflation during the period, its cost has risen to £134. Thus, part of the profit distributed to shareholders should have been retained in the business in order to replace the machine. Part of the distributed profit was required to maintain the capital of the business intact.

If the depreciation charge had been calculated on the basis of the *assumed current cost* of the machine, the annual depreciation charges would have been:

	1	2	3	4	5----	10
Assumed Current Cost	£103	£106	£109	£113	£116	£134
Accumulated Depreciation:						
%	10%	20%	30%	40%	50%	100%
Amount	£10	£21	£33	£45	£58	£134
Annual Depreciation	£10	£11	£12	£12	£13	£17

Using these depreciation figures the profit-and-loss accounts for
Years 2–10 would have been:

	2	3	4	5--------	10
	£	£	£	£	£
Profit before depreciation	31	32	33	34	39
Less Depreciation	11	12	12	13	17
Profit paid as dividend	20	20	21	21	22

The cash flow retained in the business, i.e. the depreciation charge
would have been higher, and the asset side of the balance sheets
would have shown cash balances equivalent to the accumulated
depreciation. £134 would have been available in cash to replace
the machine at the end of Year 10. With this approach the
depreciation in excess of that based on original cost (£34) would
be shown in the balance sheet under capital reserves. The balance
sheet at the end of Year 10 would appear as follows:

	£		£
Share Capital	100	Machine – Cost	100
		Less Depreciation	100
Replacement Reserve	34	*Written Down Value*	—
Total Shareholders' Interest	134	Cash	134
	£134		£134

Thus, by basing depreciation on the assumed current cost of the
machine, the dividend paid to shareholders would have been
lower, and the cash would have been available to replace the
machine. The capital of the business would have been maintained
intact.

SUMMARY OF CHAPTER

Financial accounting is concerned with the external requirements of persons outside the firm as well as with the internal requirements of the management. A number of periodic accounting reports are prepared for management and summarized annual reports are prepared for outside parties. Accounting systems employ the double-entry accounting principle recognizing that every event of a financial character in the activities of a business has two aspects. In any transaction one account gives (the credit entry) and the other receives (the debit entry). At the end of the accounting period accruals and prepayments have to be taken into consideration. There are a number of basic concepts employed in financial accounting, including money measurement, business entity, going concern, and cost. The impact of price-level changes on accounting profits and asset values is a difficult problem which has attracted increasing attention in recent years. If depreciation is based on the original cost of assets there is a danger that the capital of the business will *not* be maintained intact.

SELECTED READINGS

1. Robert N. Anthony, *Management Accounting: Text and Cases*, Irwin, Homewood, Illinois, 1970.
2. Harold Bierman, Jr, *Financial Accounting Theory*, Macmillan, New York, 1965.
3. Raymond J. Chambers, *Accounting Evaluation and Economic Behavior*, Prentice-Hall, Englewood Cliffs, 1966.
4. Harold C. Edey, *Introduction to Accounting*, Hutchinson, London, 1963.
5. General Educational Trust of the Institute of Chartered Accountants in England and Wales, *Guide to the Accounting Requirements of the Companies Acts 1948–1967*, Gee & Co., London, 1967.
6. Myron J. Gordon and Gordon Shillinglaw, *Accounting: A Management Approach*, Irwin, Homewood, Illinois, 1964.
7. T. S. Gynther, *Accounting for Price Level Changes: Theory and Practice*, Pergamon, London, 1966.
8. Institute of Chartered Accountants of Scotland, *The Companies Act 1967*, Edinburgh, 1967.
9. Frank H. Jones, *Guide to Company Balance Sheets and Profit and Loss Accounts*, Heffer, Cambridge, 1970.
10. Russell Mathews, *Accounting for Economists*, Cheshire, Melbourne, 1965.
11. F. Clive de Paula, 'Balance Sheet Fiction', *Management Today*, March 1967.
12. Harold Rose, *Disclosure in Company Accounts*, Eaton Paper No. 1, Institute of Economic Affairs, London, 1965.
13. E. E. Spicer and E. C. Pegler, *Book-Keeping and Accounts*, H.F.L., London, 1963.
14. F. Wood and J. Townsley, *Accounting: A Programmed Text*, Polytech Publishers, Manchester, 1970.

CHAPTER 3

Basic Cost Accounting

COST accounting is primarily concerned with meeting the cost information requirements of management. The cost accountant classifies, records, allocates, summarizes, and reports to management on current and future costs. The following activities are usually the responsibility of the cost accountant:

1. The design and operation of cost systems and procedures.

2. The determination of costs by departments, functions, responsibilities, activities, products, geographical areas, periods, and other cost centres and cost units. The costs may be historical or actual costs, or future or standard costs.

3. The comparison of costs of different periods, of actual costs with estimated and standard costs, and costs of different alternatives.

4. The presentation and interpretation of costing information as an aid to management in controlling the current and future operations of a company.

Three main purposes for which cost data may be useful in the *control* of current operations are:

As a communication device;

As a device for motivation;

As an appraisal device.

As a *communication* device, cost data assists management in directing individuals within an organization to carry out plans, including the objectives the management wishes to achieve, the methods to be used to achieve these objectives, and the limitations to which the organization is expected to adhere. As a device for *motivation*, if cost data is properly constructed and is accompanied by proper management action and attitudes, it may serve as a significant incentive for attaining planned objectives. It should improve both the direction and strength of employee motivation. As an *appraisal* device, two types of preparation of costs for control purposes can be distinguished: *before* the fact (standards and/or budgets), and *after* the fact (performance reports). While performance reports are useful to avoid repeating previous mistakes, the knowledge that appraisals are being made may provide a strong incentive for good performance. This belief is based on the view that targets (standards and/or budgets) agreed by a manager and his subordinates are in themselves an incentive to good performance, and that they form a yardstick against which performance can be measured. This type of accounting, *responsibility accounting*, is considered in Chapter 7.

Cost data is also essential for planning purposes, both for period planning and for project planning. *Period planning* is the process whereby management systematically develops an acceptable set of plans for the total future activities of the firm, or some sub-division thereof, for a specified period of time. Long-term period planning is considered in Chapter 5 and short-term period planning, i.e. budgetary control, is the subject for Chapter 7. *Project planning* on the other hand, is the process whereby management, confronted by a specific problem, evaluates each alternative in order to arrive at a decision as to the course of future action. The appraisal of capital expenditure projects is considered in Chapter 6.

THE CLASSIFICATION OF COSTS

The classification of costs is the basis of all cost accounting systems. Classification of costs is the identification of each item of cost and the systematic placement of like items of cost together according to their common characteristics. The classification of costs is an essential step in the summarization of detailed costs.

Costs are classified by *functions*: production, selling, distribution, research and development, and administration. Within functions, costs are collected by cost centres and cost units. A *cost centre* is a location, person, or item of equipment (or group of these) for which costs may be ascertained for purposes of cost control. A *cost unit* is a unit of product, service, or time (or combination of these) in relation to which costs may be ascertained or expressed. The cost unit may be a job, batch, contract, or product group depending upon the nature of the production in which the firm is engaged. Ultimately all cost centre costs are allocated to, apportioned to, or absorbed by cost units. Costs are first classified to cost centres for purposes of cost control.

Within cost centres and cost units costs are further classified into *cost elements*:

MATERIAL COST, which is the cost of commodities supplied to an undertaking.

LABOUR COST, which is the cost of remuneration (wages, salaries, bonuses, commissions, etc.) of the employees of an undertaking.

EXPENSES, which are the cost of services provided to an undertaking, such as water and electricity, and the notional cost of the use of owned assets, such as depreciation of plant and machinery.

These cost elements are classified according to whether they are direct costs or indirect costs, i.e. direct or indirect material, direct or indirect labour, and direct or indirect expense.

A *direct* cost is one which can be allocated directly as a whole item to a cost centre or a cost unit. The cost can be directly associated with the production of a cost unit or with the activity of a cost centre. Cost allocation is, therefore, defined as the allotment of whole items of cost to cost centres or cost units. An *indirect* cost cannot be directly associated with the production of a cost unit or with the activity of a cost centre, but has to be apportioned to the cost centre or cost unit on a suitable basis. Thus, one *allocates* direct expenditure which can be directly identified with a cost centre or cost unit, but one *apportions* indirect expenditure. For example, materials used in the production of a cost unit can be allocated directly to that cost unit, but the rent of factory premises is apportioned amongst cost centres using some suitable basis.

Direct materials, direct labour, and direct expenses are *prime expenses*, and are traceable directly to the production of a cost unit or the activity of a cost centre. The sum of these direct costs for the production of a cost unit or the total production for a period is called the prime cost of production. The indirect costs of production, and all selling costs, distribution costs, research and development costs, and administration expenses are called *overheads.* Ultimately all overheads that have been apportioned to cost centres have to be absorbed by cost units. Overhead *absorption* is usually achieved by the use of one or a combination of overhead rates, for example, labour hour rate, machine hour rate, direct material cost percentage.

Individual overhead costs may be either fixed costs or variable costs, though some have fixed and variable elements and are called semi-variable. *Fixed costs* are costs of *time* in that they accumulate with the passage of time irrespective of the volume of output, e.g. rent and rates, office salaries, insurance, etc. This does not mean that a fixed cost is always fixed in amount for there are other forces, such as price level changes, market shortages, etc., which can cause fixed costs to change in amount from period to period. Of course, if a sufficiently long time period is considered, almost all costs become variable through changes in the scale of the company's operations. For decision-making purposes whether a cost is fixed or variable will depend upon the decision under consideration. A *variable overhead cost* is one which tends to vary with variations in the volume of output, but which cannot be allocated directly to a cost unit and has to be absorbed on a suitable basis. It will be appreciated that, in theory, all prime costs are variable costs because their distinguishing characteristic is the very fact that they can be associated with particular cost units. In practice, this may not necessarily be the case when classifying costs for decision-making purposes. The classification of costs as fixed and variable is given detailed consideration in Chapter 10.

Total cost is the sum of prime costs and overheads attributable to the cost unit under consideration. The unit may be the whole undertaking, a job, batch, contract, or product group; it may be a process or a service. The cost classification, which has been outlined above, makes up total cost as follows:

DIRECT COSTS	£	£
Direct Material	5	
Direct Labour	6	
Direct Expense	1	
	—	
Prime Cost		12

OVERHEAD COSTS[1]

Production Overheads:

Indirect Material	1	
Indirect Labour	1	
Indirect Expense	3	
	—	5
		—
Cost of Production		17
Selling and Distribution Cost	2	
Research and Development Cost	1	
Administration Expenses	1	
	—	4
		—
TOTAL COST		£21

AN ILLUSTRATION – COST CLASSIFICATION

The classification of costs is best understood by a simple illustration. The costs incurred by the Odd Job Engineering Company during the year ended 31 December 1967 are listed in Table 3.1. Readers are invited to complete the column headed 'Classification', indicating whether an item of cost is direct material, direct labour, or indirect expense, etc. The reader's classification of the costs can be checked in Table 3.2.

1. Individual items of overhead cost may be either fixed, variable, or semi-variable in nature.

Table 3.1

ODD JOB ENGINEERING COMPANY

Costs for the year ended 31 December 1967

Cost	£	Classification
Wages traceable to jobs	45,500	Direct Labour
Wages paid to maintenance men	12,250	
General Manager's Car Expenses	150	
Hire of cranes for Jobs 530–531	50	
Power for Factory	5,200	
Materials used on jobs	47,350	
Lighting (factory)	600	
Salesmen's Salaries	3,500	
Office Expenses	570	
Rent, Rates and Taxes (Factory)	2,200	
Oils for lubricating machines	150	
Machinery Depreciation	6,520	
Office Wages and Salaries	2,450	
Machinery Repairs	725	
Lighting (Office)	25	
Maintenance Materials	600	
Storekeepers' Wages	1,200	
Factory Management Salaries	5,300	
Delivery Costs	330	
Office Rent	150	
Advertising	220	
Depreciation of General Manager's Car	80	
Salesmen's Travelling Expenses	170	
General Manager's Salary	2,400	
Special tools for Jobs 527–528	75	
Factory Premises Depreciation	270	
Agents' Commission	55	
Office Cleaning	200	

Table 3.2

ODD JOB ENGINEERING COMPANY

Classification of Costs for the year ended
31 December 1967

	£	£	£
Direct Materials			47,350
Direct Labour			45,500
Direct Expenses			
Hire of Cranes		50	
Special tools		75	
		—	125
PRIME COST			92,975
Production Overheads			
Indirect Material			
Lubricating Oils	150		
Maintenance Materials	600		
	—	750	
Indirect Labour			
Maintenance Wages	12,250		
Storekeepers' Wages	1,200		
Factory Management Salaries	5,300		
		18,750	
Indirect Expenses			
Factory Power	5,200		
Factory Lighting	600		
Factory Rent, Rates and Taxes	2,200		
Machinery Depreciation	6,520		
Machinery Repairs	725		
Factory Premises Depreciation	270		
		15,515	
Total Production Overheads			35,015
COST OF PRODUCTION			127,990

Table 3.2 – cont.

	£	£
Selling and Distribution Costs		
Salesmen's Salaries	3,500	
Salesmen's Travelling Expenses	170	
Agents' Commission	55	
Advertising	220	
Delivery Costs	330	
		4,275
Administration Expenses		
General Manager's Salary	2,400	
General Manager's Car Depreciation	80	
General Manager's Car Expenses	150	
Office Wages and Salaries	2,450	
Office Expenses	570	
Office Lighting	25	
Office Rent	150	
Office Cleaning	200	
		6,025
TOTAL COST		£138,290

AN ILLUSTRATION – OVERHEAD ABSORPTION RATES

Bang-Bang Manufacturing Ltd operates a factory whose annual budget includes the budgeted trading account shown in Table 3.3.

Table 3.3

BANG-BANG MANUFACTURING LTD

Budgeted Trading Account for the year ended
31 March 1968

	£	£
SELLING VALUE OF GOODS PRODUCED		300,000
Cost of Production:		
Direct Wages		70,000
Direct Materials		90,000
PRIME COST		£160,000

56

Table 3.3 – cont.

	£	£
Indirect Wages and Supervision		
Machine dept A	3,800	
Machine dept B	4,350	
Assembly dept	4,125	
Packing dept	2,300	
Maintenance dept	2,250	
Stores	1,150	
General dept	2,425	
		20,400
Maintenance Wages		
Machine dept A	1,000	
Machine dept B	2,000	
Assembly dept	500	
Packing dept	500	
Maintenance dept	500	
Stores	250	
General dept	450	
		5,200
Indirect Materials		
Machine dept A	2,700	
Machine dept B	3,600	
Assembly dept	1,800	
Packing dept	2,700	
Maintenance dept	900	
Stores	675	
General dept	400	
		12,775
Power		6,000
Rent and Rates		8,000
Lighting and Heating		2,000
Insurance		1,000
Depreciation		20,000
PRODUCTION OVERHEADS		£75,375
COST OF PRODUCTION		£235,375
BUDGETED FACTORY PROFIT		£64,625

The following operating information is also available:

Departments	Effective h.p.	Area occupied (sq. ft)	Book value of machin- ery and equip- ment	Productive capacity (normal)		
				Direct Labour Hours	Cost	Machine hours
			£		£	
Productive						
Machine A	40	1,000	30,000	100,000	28,000	50,000
Machine B	40	750	40,000	75,000	21,000	60,000
Assembly	—	1,500	5,000	75,000	14,000	
Packing	10	750	5,000	50,000	7,000	
Service						
Maintenance	10	300	15,000			
Stores		500	2,500			
General		200	2,500			
		5,000	£100,000			

The general department consists of the factory manager and general clerical and wages personnel.

It will be seen that the production costs are analysed into direct costs and production overheads. The direct costs can be charged directly to cost units as they arise, but the production overheads will have to be absorbed by cost units using some suitable basis of absorption. There are three stages in the calculation of hourly cost rates of overhead absorption for each productive department:

1. The various production overheads are first analysed to the seven cost centres, i.e. four productive departments and three service departments. The first stage is shown in the top third of Table 3.4. It will be seen that for some costs the figures for each department are shown separately in the budget and for other costs some suitable basis of apportionment has to be used. For example, power has been apportioned to departments on the basis of effective horse power available in each department.

Table 3.4

BANG-BANG MANUFACTURING LTD
Overhead Analysis for the year ended 31 March 1968

Expense	Basis	Total	Productive Departments				Service Departments		
			Machine A	Machine B	Assembly	Packing	Maintenance	Stores	General
Indirect Wages and Supervision	Actual	20,400	3,800	4,350	4,125	2,300	2,250	1,150	2,425
Maintenance Wages	Actual	5,200	1,000	2,000	500	500	500	250	450
Indirect Materials	Actual	12,775	2,700	3,600	1,800	2,700	900	675	400
Power	Effective h.p.	6,000	2,400	2,400	—	600	600	—	—
Rent and Rates	Area Occupied	8,000	1,600	1,200	2,400	1,200	480	800	320
Lighting and Heating	Area Occupied	2,000	400	300	600	300	120	200	80
Insurance	Book Values	1,000	300	400	50	50	150	25	25
Depreciation	Actual	20,000	6,000	8,000	1,000	1,000	3,000	500	500
TOTAL		£75,375	£18,200	£22,250	£10,475	£8,650	£8,000	£3,600	£4,200

Apportionment of Service Departments

Service Department	Basis	Total	Machine A	Machine B	Assembly	Packing
				Productive Departments		
Maintenance	Maintenance Wages	8,000	2,000	4,000	1,000	1,000
Stores	Indirect Materials	3,600	900	1,200	600	900
General	Direct Labour Hours	4,200	1,400	1,050	1,050	700
		15,800	4,300	6,250	2,650	2,600
Add. Total from above		59,575	18,200	22,250	10,475	8,650
Production Department Totals		£75,375	£22,500	£28,500	£13,125	£11,250

Hourly Cost Rates

Machine A $\dfrac{£22,500 \times 20}{50,000}$ = 9s. 0d. per machine hour

Machine B $\dfrac{£28,500 \times 20}{60,000}$ = 9s. 6d. per machine hour

Assembly $\dfrac{£13,125 \times 20}{75,000}$ = 3s. 6d. per direct labour hour

Packing $\dfrac{£11,250 \times 20}{50,000}$ = 4s. 6d. per direct labour hour

2. The costs of each service department are apportioned to the productive departments using some suitable basis. For example, the maintenance department costs have been apportioned to the four productive departments on the basis of the maintenance wages budgeted for each department.[1]

3. Having apportioned the total production overheads to the four productive departments, the final stage is the calculation of separate hourly cost rates of overhead absorption for each productive department. The calculation appears in the third part of Table 3.4. It will be seen that in the case of machine departments A and B, machine hour rates have been calculated by dividing the overhead cost by the normal productive capacity of the departments (normal capacity being defined as full capacity less normal unavoidable idle time). Similarly, direct labour hour rates have been calculated for the assembly and packing departments.

It is important to appreciate that *there is no one way of apportioning overhead costs and calculating overhead absorption rates.* There are a number of possible bases and the cost accountant has to decide which is the most suitable in the circumstances. It is quite possible for two equally competent accountants to arrive at different overhead absorption rates from the same basic data.

When these hourly overhead absorption rates have been calculated, how are they used by the cost accountant? They have a number of uses:

1. They are used for charging overhead costs to operations, processes, or products when *absorption costing* is employed, i.e. the practice of charging all costs, both fixed and variable, to operations, processes, or products. The overhead which, by means of rates of overhead absorption, is charged to cost units is called *absorbed overhead.* The difference between the amount of overhead absorbed during a period and the actual overhead incurred during a period is called *under- or over-absorbed overhead.* For example, if 48,000 machine hours' production for machine department A was charged to cost units during the year

---

1. To simplify the illustration the apportionment of service department costs among service departments has been ignored. In practice, this simplification may not be justified.

ending 31 March 1968, the absorbed overhead for the department would be £21,600, i.e. 48,000 × 9s. If the actual overhead incurred during this period amounted to £23,000, then the overheads for machine department A would be under-absorbed by £1,400. Normally, if actual production is *less* than normal capacity there will be *under-absorption*, and if actual production is *greater* than normal capacity there will be *over-absorption*. Certain overheads are fixed in nature and others variable and, therefore, the total production overhead does not change in proportion with changes in the level of production. Thus, because certain of machine department A's costs are fixed, the overhead absorption rate per machine hour is *only valid for normal capacity machine hours*. In particular, it is unsuitable for cost control purposes and flexible budgets should be used, i.e. a series of static budgets for various forecast levels of activity. Flexible budgets are explained in Chapter 7 on budgetary control.

2. Overhead absorption rates are also used for valuing work-in-progress and finished stocks. For stock valuation purposes, overheads are usually charged to production on the basis of normal capacity. For example, product A may be valued for stock purposes as follows:

		£ s. d.	£ s. d.
Direct Material			5 10 0
Direct Labour			5 0 0
Production Overhead:			
Machine dept A	2 hrs at 9/–	18 0	
Machine dept B	2 hrs at 9/6	19 0	
Assembly	2 hrs at 3/6	7 0	
Packing	1 hr at 4/6	4 6	
			2 8 6
Cost of Production			£12 18 6

3. In many instances the overhead absorption rates are used in developing costs for pricing decisions, though this may not be the most suitable form of cost information for this purpose. The whole question of costs for pricing purposes is considered in

Chapter 9. However, it is important to appreciate that overhead absorption rates are *not* suitable for calculating the effects of changes in volume and type of output, because they are only valid for normal capacity output. They do not represent the *incremental* overhead costs of increasing or decreasing production by one unit. If one more unit of product A is produced the cost of production will *not* be £12 18s. 6d., because the production overhead in the above calculation includes fixed costs which will not change with changes in the volume of production in the short run. If one additional unit is produced the factory rent and rates will not increase, because rent and rates are a fixed cost. Marginal costs not absorption costs are required for this purpose and are considered in Chapter 8.

COSTING SYSTEMS

The problems faced by management differ from industry to industry and within industries from company to company. The costing system employed by a particular company must be designed to provide the management with the information required to solve its particular problems. The two basic costing systems are *job costing* and *process costing*, and the system used will depend upon a number of factors. Some manufacturing companies produce one or more standard products for stock. Their manufacturing processes are firmly established, and work flows continuously through the processes. Such companies wish to know the production costs for each process. They employ a *process costing* system to generate this information. Other manufacturing companies are not engaged in producing goods for stock; they are employed in production only when they receive an order from a customer. No two orders are necessarily alike, nor do all orders pass through the same manufacturing processes. Consequently, cost information must be accumulated for each order or job. The system of accounting that provides information in this way is called a job order cost system or *job costing*. There is an exception to the foregoing. Some companies produce standard products but manufacture their products in separate, clearly distinguishable, batches or lots. When the cost of producing each batch is important to management, the company may decide to employ a job costing system as the most satisfactory means of obtaining such information on batches and lots.

Job Costing

When job costing is employed, costs are compiled for a specific quantity of product, equipment, repair, or other service. The cost unit, i.e. the specific quantity of product, etc., remains an identifiable unit as it passes through the production departments, and costs directly associated with the production of that job, and usually a calculated portion of overheads, are charged to the job. The important consideration, therefore, for the use of a job costing system is that individual jobs or batches can be separately identified in the operating departments. Among the industries using job costing are construction, printing, heavy engineering, and ship-building.

The principal advantage of a job costing system is that it compiles data in a manner that is most useful in the administration of certain kinds of business. However, it is an expensive system to operate because it involves considerable detailed clerical work. It is important that job costing is only used in situations where it is needed.

AN ILLUSTRATION OF JOB COSTING. The following figures have been extracted from the budget of the Smalltown Engineering Company for 1968. All jobs pass through the company's two departments:

	Machining Dept	Finishing Dept
Materials Used	£6,000	£500
Direct Labour	£3,000	£1,500
Factory Overheads	£1,800	£1,200
Direct Labour Hours	12,000	5,000
Machine Hours	10,000	2,000

The following information relates to job A100:

	Machining Dept	Finishing Dept
Materials Used	£120	£10
Direct Labour	£65	£25
Direct Labour Hours	265	70
Machine Hours	255	25

You are required to prepare a statement showing the different cost results for job A100 using the following methods of absorbing factory overheads by jobs, with separate rates for each department:

1. Factory Overhead as a % of Direct Material;
2. Factory Overhead as a % of Direct Labour;
3. Factory Overhead per Direct Labour Hour; and
4. Factory Overhead per Machine Hour.

The various factory overhead absorption rates are as follows:

	Machining Dept	Finishing Dept
1. % of Direct Material	30%	240%
2. % of Direct Labour	60%	80%
3. Direct Labour Hour rate	3s. per hr.	4.8s. per hr.
4. Machine Hour Rate	3.6s. per hr.	12s. per hr.

The cost of job A100 can now be calculated using the various factory overhead absorption rates:

Cost of Job A100

	Machining Dept £	Finishing Dept £	Total £
Material	120	10	130
Direct Labour	65	25	90
Prime Cost	185	35	220
Factory Overhead:			
Method 1	36	24	60
Method 2	39	20	59
Method 3	39.75	16.8	56.55
Method 4	45.9	15	60.9

Total Cost

Method 1	221	59	280
Method 2	224	55	279
Method 3	224.75	51.8	276.55
Method 4	230.9	50	280.9

It will be seen that the total cost of job A100 varies according to the method of absorbing factory overheads. It has already been emphasized that there are a number of possible methods of absorbing overheads and that the cost accountant must decide which is the most appropriate in the circumstances. For example, he may decide a machine hour rate is most suitable for the machining department and a direct labour hour rate for the finishing department.

Process Costing

Process costing is used in those industries where large quantities of homogeneous or very similar units of product are produced by continuous or mass production methods. In such industries it is not possible to identify the successive jobs or batches of production for cost accounting purposes. Unlike job costing, where costs are recorded separately for each job or order going through the plant, the emphasis in process costing is on the accumulation of costs for all work units during a given period of time. At the end of each period the cost per unit of goods produced is determined as an *average* unit cost for the period. The average cost per unit is used to value completed units and work-in-progress. The conditions for the use of process costing are continuous or mass production, loss of identity of individual items or lots, and complete standardization of product or process. Manufacturers using process costing may be classified as follows:

1. Production of a single product, e.g. cement or sugar;
2. Production of a variety of products using some basic production facilities, e.g. brick, tile and ceramic products;
3. Production of a variety of products using separate facilities, that is a separate plant for each product (e.g. a dairy firm may have separate milk, orange drink, and cream bottling lines).

The chief advantages of a process cost system are:

1. Costs are computed periodically, usually at the end of the month;

2. Average costs are calculated easily, provided the product is homogeneous; and

3. Less clerical effort and expense are involved than in job costing.

However, there are problems and disadvantages, including:

1. Where the process costs are historical costs (see below) they are not determined until after the end of the cost period;

2. Average costs are not always accurate because the units are not fully homogeneous; and

3. Where different products are manufactured, the proration of joint costs is necessary and the computation is made more difficult, often extremely difficult.

AN ILLUSTRATION OF PROCESS COSTING. XYZ Ltd produces a single product and the costs incurred for the month of January for process 1 are as follows:

Process 1	£
Material	4,000
Labour	1,800
Overhead	1,700
	£7,500

Units Completed and Transferred	800 units
Work-in-progress 31 January	200 units

The production and costing departments estimate that the state of completion of the units in progress is:

1. Fully completed – material.
2. Half completed – labour.
3. Quarter completed – overhead.

There were no uncompleted units in progress at the beginning of the month.

You are required to calculate the transfer cost to process 2 and work-in-progress valuation at the end of the month.

To ascertain the transfer cost and work-in-progress valuation the uncompleted units must be converted into equivalent production in terms of finished units. Thus, the units of work in progress in terms of completed units will be as follows:

Material   = 200 (200 units completed)
Labour   = 100 (200 units half completed)
Overhead =   50 (200 units quarter completed)

If the equivalent production figures are added to the completed units and divided into the respective cost totals, the result will be an average unit cost in respect of materials, labour, and overhead costs. Thus:

	Per unit £
Materials (800 + 200) = 1,000 units which divided into £4,000	= 4
Labour (800 + 100) = 900 units which divided into £1,800	= 2
Overhead (800 + 50) = 850 units which divided into £1,700	= 2
Average unit cost for January	£8

The work-in-progress valuation may be calculated as follows:

	£
Material 200 × £4	800
Labour 100 × £2	200
Overhead 50 × £2	100
	£1,100

The transfer cost to process 2 may be calculated by multiplying the number of completed units by unit cost, i.e. 800 × £8 = £6,400. The transfer cost and the valuation of work in progress together equal the month's total cost £7,500. The process account in the cost ledger would appear as follows:

68

Process 1 Account

Dr.		£			Cr. £
Jan. 31.	Stores control account	4,000	Jan. 31.	Process 2 account	6,400
	Labour control account	1,800		Balance c/d	1,100
	Overhead control account	1,700			
		£7,500			£7,500
Feb. 1.	Balance b/d	1,100			

It will be seen that the cost of the completed units has been transferred to the process 2 account. In the final process the transfer is made to the finished goods account. Thus, the finished goods of one process become the raw materials of a later process. Many simplifying assumptions have been made in this example; by-products, units lost in process, wastage, etc. have been ignored.

Historical Costing

The job costs and process costs calculated may be either *historical* or *standard* costs. With a historical costing system, actual costs are accumulated *after* operations have taken place. Historical costs are ascertained after the costs are incurred; standard costs are calculated *before* the costs are incurred. Historical costs are of limited value in themselves but are an essential part of a standard costing system. The historical costs are compared with the predetermined standard costs and the differences are analysed for control purposes. The principal disadvantages of using historical costs in isolation are:

1. The accuracy of the costs is open to doubt, so limited reliance can be placed on them.

2. Sound interpretation of costs, because of all the 'unknowns', is virtually impossible.

3. There is no yardstick against which efficiency can be measured. For this purpose past actual costs are of limited value.

4. Delays in taking action are inevitable, so inefficiencies are not likely to be minimized.

Standard Costing

In a standard costing system *predetermined* costs are carefully computed and later contrasted with actual costs to aid in cost control. The differences between the actual costs and the predetermined standard costs are called *variances*. The cost accountant analyses these variances by causes, and inefficiencies are promptly notified to the persons responsible for them. For example, a *material cost variance*, i.e. the difference between standard material cost and actual material cost, may be analysed into a *material price variance* and a *material usage variance*. An unfavourable material cost variance may have arisen because the price paid for the material used was higher than the standard price, and/or because the quantity of material used was in excess of the standard quantity specified. A buyer may be responsible for a price variance and a departmental supervisor for a usage variance. Table 3.5 illustrates the calculation of these

Table 3.5

Computation of Material Variances

Material Cost Variance = Actual Cost − Standard Cost, i.e. standard quantity × standard price. May be analysed into:

1. *Material Price Variance* = actual quantity × actual price − actual quantity × standard price

or

actual quantity (actual price − standard price)

2. *Material Usage Variance* = actual quantity × standard price − standard quantity × standard price

or

standard price (actual quantity − standard quantity)

Example

The standard raw material mix for a ton of finished product is:

Material A 1,200 lb. at 3d. lb.
  ,,   B   500 lb. at 1s. lb.
  ,,   C   500 lb. at 6d. lb.
  ,,   D   100 lb. at 2s. 6d. lb.

Table 3.5 – cont.

Material used during an accounting period was as follows:

Material A 2,900 lb. at 3¼d. lb.
    „ B 1,300 lb. at 1s. 1d. lb.
    „ C 1,350 lb. at 5½d. lb.
    „ D   260 lb. at 2s. lb.

Production during the period was 5,600 lbs. Identify and calculate the material cost variances.

Material	STANDARD Quantity (a)	Price (b)	£ s. d. (c)	ACTUAL Quantity (d)	Price (e)	£ s. d. (f)
	lbs.	per lb.		lbs.	per lb.	
A	3,000	3d.	37 10 0	2,900	3¼d.	39 5 5
B	1,250	1s.	62 10 0	1,300	1s.1d.	70 8 4
C	1,250	6d.	31 5 0	1,350	5½d.	30 18 9
D	250	2s.6d.	31 5 0	260	2s.0d.	26 0 0
			£162 10 0			£166 12 6

VARIANCES Total c−f	Price d × (b−e)	Usage b × (a−d)
£ s. d.	£ s. d.	£ s. d.
(1 15 5)	(3 0 5)	1 5 0
(7 18 4)	(5 8 4)	(2 10 0)
6 3	2 16 3	(2 10 0)
5 5 0	6 10 0	(1 5 0)
(4 2 6)	17 6	(5 0 0)

Note: Brackets indicate variance is unfavourable.

material variances. In process industries the usage variance may be further analysed into a *mixture variance* and a *yield variance*. Similarly, a *direct wages variance*, i.e. the difference between actual direct wages and standard direct wages, may be analysed into a *wage rate variance* and a *labour efficiency variance*. Rates of pay above or below the standard rate may have been paid and/or the efficiency of the direct operatives may have been above or below standard efficiency. The computation of wages variances is illustrated in Table 3.6. A third group of variances is the *overhead variances*, i.e. the difference between the actual manufacturing overhead incurred and the standard overhead charged to production during the period. Overhead variances can be further

Table 3.6

Computation of Wages Variances

Wages Variance = Actual Cost − Standard Cost, i.e. standard hours × standard rate. May be analysed into:

1. *Wage Rate Variance* = actual hours × actual rate − actual hours × standard rate

or

actual hours (actual rate − standard rate)

2. *Labour Efficiency Variance* = actual hours × standard rate − standard hours × standard rate

or

standard rate (actual hours − standard hours)

Example

A company manufactures a standard model based on the following direct labour specification:

Standard direct labour hours   20
Standard direct labour hourly rate   5s.

During the month 250 models were produced, and direct labour amounted to £1,500 for 5,600 hours worked. Calculate the wages variances.

	£
1. *Wages Variance*	
Standard Cost (20 × 250 × 5s.)	1,250
Actual Cost	1,500
Variance (adverse)	(£250)

Table 3.6 – cont.

2. *Wage Rate Variance*

Standard Cost of Actual Hours 5,600 at 5s.	1,400
Actual Cost of Actual Hours	1,500
Variance (adverse)	(£100)

3. *Labour Efficiency Variance*

Standard Hours for Actual Production 250 × 20	5,000
Actual Hours for Actual Production	5,600
Variance (adverse)	(600)
at 5s. per hr	£(150)

Note: Brackets indicate variance is unfavourable.

analysed into *volume*, *cost*, and *efficiency variances*. The computation of these variances is considered in Chapter 7 following an explanation of fixed and flexible budgets. The principal cost variances calculated by comparing actual and standard costs are illustrated in Figure 1.

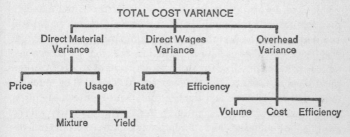

Figure 1. *Principal cost variances*

Standard costing may, therefore, be defined as: the preparation and use of standard costs, their comparison with actual costs and the analysis of variances to their causes and points of incidence. Standard costs are scientifically predetermined costs of materials, labour and overheads chargeable to a product or service. They represent a carefully planned method of producing a product or providing a service. With a standard costing system the standard costs are usually entered into the books of account to facilitate

73

the comparison with actual costs. Although standard costs are generally incorporated in the accounts, some concerns prefer to use them for statistical purposes only.

The meaning of the variances between standard costs and actual costs will be dependent upon the kind of costs with which actual costs are compared. Variances resulting from careless standards will not have the same significance as variances from vigorous or 'tight' standards. A loose standard, as an incentive to better performance, may be completely useless. On the other hand, an ideal standard which is attainable only under the most favourable conditions would be impossible to achieve. An ideal standard probably may not motivate employees to improve their performance. An expected standard which it is anticipated can be attained during a future specific period is usually set. Such a standard takes into account human rates of work, normal machine breakdowns, and other unavoidable inefficiencies. It is a consistent reliable standard, is attainable, and should provide an incentive to improve performance.

Assuming the existence of proper standard costs for the product of an operation, function, or department, the management can concentrate upon the discrepancies between actual and standard costs. The usefulness of this comparison between actual and standard costs is based upon the *principle of exceptions*, which makes it possible for the cost accountant to sift from the great mass of his cost data the essential facts needed by management. However, there is a danger that, with so much attention being focused on the 'exceptions', insufficient attention will be paid to the standards. The standards must never become out-of-date or unreliable so that they are not taken seriously by operating management. There must be confidence in the standards. The use of standard costing can develop into a ritual which loses sight of the problem at issue. The 'cost of costing' must always be borne in mind. While a sophisticated standard costing system may reveal large inefficiencies in the early years of its use, there is always the possibility that the variances will eventually become insignificant in relation to the cost of operating the system.

The cost accountant must promptly draw the attention of operating management to the existence of *controllable* variances from standard. This requires that where a significantly large cost variance arises, the cost accountant should be able to present an analysis to management making it possible to determine:

Where the variance occurred;

Who was responsible; and

Why it happened.

The cost accountant must be able to present reports to management which highlight the essentials and point out particular variances and possibilities for improvement. For example, reports to departmental supervisors should:

1. Show the supervisor what his costs should have been;

2. Show him how closely he came to meeting these costs;

3. Show him whether his performance in this respect is improving;

4. Explain the causes of variances so that the knowledge of their causes can be used to achieve improvements in his performance.

Standard costs and budgets complement each other in various ways. The development of standard costs will provide a sound basis for budgetary control. The use of standards will tend to enhance the accuracy of budgets and will facilitate their preparation. Ideally, standard costs should be made an integral part of the budgetary control system, both in the preparation of budgets and in their use as a control device. For this reason, accounting for control involving the use of standards and budgets is considered more fully in Chapter 7 under the title of Budgetary Control.

SUMMARY OF CHAPTER

Cost accounting is primarily concerned with meeting the information requirements of management for decision-making and control. The classification of costs is the basis of all cost accounting systems. Costs are classified by functions, within functions by cost elements, and within cost elements according to whether they are direct or indirect costs. Direct costs can be allocated directly to cost units; indirect costs have to be absorbed by cost units. There are a number of alternative methods of overhead absorption. Individual indirect costs may be variable, semivariable, or fixed in relation to short-run changes in volume.

There are two basic costing systems: job costing and process costing. The system employed will depend upon the type of production and the information requirements of management. Job costing is expensive to operate and should be used only when essential. Job costs and process costs calculated may be either historical or standard costs. Historical costs in isolation are of limited value, but are an essential part of a standard costing system. The principle of exceptions is utilized in a standard costing system, management's attention being focused on the variances from standard. Budgets and standards complement each other, and ideally standard costs should be an integral part of a budgetary control system.

SELECTED READINGS

1. R. N. Anthony, *Management Accounting*, Irwin, Homewood, Illinois, 1970.
2. J. Batty, *Standard Costing*, MacDonald & Evans, London, 1966.
3. J. G. Birnberg and N. Dopuch, *Cost Accounting: Accounting Data for Management Decisions*, Harcourt, Brace & World, New York, 1969.
4. C. I. Buyers and G. A. Holmes, *Principles of Cost Accounting*, Cassell, London, 1959.
5. R. I. Dickey (ed.), *Accountants' Cost Handbook*, Ronald Press, New York, 1960.
6. S. B. Henrici, *Standard Costs for Manufacturing*, McGraw-Hill, New York, 1960.
7. Charles T. Horngren, *Cost Accounting: A Managerial Emphasis*, Prentice-Hall, Englewood Cliffs, 1972.
8. Institute of Cost and Works Accountants, *Terminology of Cost Accountancy*, London, 1966.
9. Russell Mathews, *Accounting for Economists*, Cheshire, Melbourne, 1962.
10. Gordon Shillinglaw, *Cost Accounting: Analysis and Control*, Irwin, Homewood, Illinois, 1972.
11. D. Solomons (ed.), *Studies in Cost Analysis*, Sweet & Maxwell London, 1968.
12. Harold J. Wheldon, *Wheldon's Cost Accounting*, revised edition by L. W. J. Owler and J. C. Brown, MacDonald & Evans, London, 1965.

CHAPTER 4

Profitability – Measurement and Control

AMONG the characteristics of a successful business are expanding sales, respected 'household' name, accepted products, the Queen's Award for Industry, contented labour force, and many others. All of these are unquestionably desirable achievements and objectives, yet separately or together they are not enough to guarantee the continued existence and growth of a business.

The ultimate measure of the success of any business is whether or not it continues to exist and expand. To achieve this, whatever else a business does or aims to do, it must generate profits and generate them in perpetuity. Of the hundred largest corporations in the United States in 1909 only two remain in that category today. Managerial economists have shown that there is a significant relationship between the rate of profit and the rate of growth. That profits are necessary for growth and growth produces profits is an accepted maxim of modern business. In recent years the concept of 'profit maximization' has been extensively qualified by economic theorists to refer to the long run rather than the short run; to refer to management's rather than the shareholders' income; and to include non-financial income. They have made allowance for special considerations such as restraining competition, maintaining managerial control, and holding off wage demands. While the concept may have become 'so general and hazy that it seems to encompass most of man's aims in life',[1] and it is increasingly recognized that boards of directors try to 'saticfice' rather than maximize, the fact remains, profitability is the primary aim and best measure of efficiency in competitive business.

In his book *The Practice of Management*, Peter Drucker has pointed out that profit serves three purposes[2]:

1. Joel Dean, *Managerial Economics*, Prentice-Hall, Englewood Cliffs, 1951, London, 1962, p. 28.
2. Peter Drucker, *The Practice of Management*, Mercury Books, London, 1961, pp. 65–9.

1. It measures the net effectiveness and soundness of a business's effort.

2. It is the premium that covers the costs of staying in business – replacement, obsolescence, market and technical risk and uncertainty. Seen from this point of view it may be argued that there is no such thing as profit; there are only the costs of being and staying in business. The management of a business has to provide adequately for these costs by generating sufficient profit.

3. It ensures the supply of future capital for innovation and expansion, either directly, by providing the means of self-financing out of retained profits, or indirectly, through providing sufficient inducement for new outside capital in the form which will optimize the company's capital structure and minimize its cost of capital.

MEASUREMENT OF PROFITABILITY

It has been argued that profitability is the primary aim and the best measure of efficiency in competitive business. However, profits as such are meaningless unless related to the equity (ordinary) shareholders' investment in the business. The relationship between the capital invested in a business and the profits earned is the *rate of return on capital employed.* The ability to earn a satisfactory rate of return on equity shareholders' investment is the most important characteristic of the successful business. Increased sales volume is at best a short-term indication of successful growth, and, without additional information, must be viewed as such.

In the long run, increased sales volume may prove a deceptive guidepost if there is not a proper return on the capital necessary to support these sales. Real growth comes from the ability of management to employ successfully additional capital at a satisfactory rate of return. This is the final criterion of the soundness and strength of a company's growth, for in a competitive economy capital gravitates towards the more profitable enterprises. The company that is merely expanding sales at a declining rate of return on capital employed will eventually be unable to attract expansion capital. Thus any measurement of a company's effectiveness must be based on the successful employment of capital. It is vital that the long-run return on equity shareholders' investment should be sufficient to:

1. Give a fair return to shareholders in relation to the risk and uncertainty attached to their investments.

2. Provide for the normal expansion of the business.

3. Provide, in times of inflation, adequate reserves to maintain the real capital of the business intact.

4. Attract new external capital when required.

5. Satisfy creditors and employees of the likelihood of the continued existence and/or growth of the business.

The importance of (3) above will depend upon how return on capital employed is defined. The various definitions of return on capital employed are examined later in this chapter.

CONTROL OF PROFITABILITY

The rate of return on capital employed, as well as being the key measure of efficiency, provides a starting point from which to examine influences, make comparisons, and discern trends in the company's performance. It gives rise to a pyramid of subsidiary control ratios based on the factors affecting return on capital employed. These ratios permit a similar process of examination of more detailed aspects of a company's operations.

Rate of return on capital employed is the percentage profit to capital employed, and can be divided into (a) *percentage profit to sales* and (b) *sales to capital employed*, i.e. the rate of asset turnover. Thus:

$$\frac{\text{Profit}}{\text{Capital Employed}} = \frac{\text{Profit}}{\text{Sales}} \times \frac{\text{Sales}}{\text{Capital Employed}}$$

The essential idea of this division is that low return on capital employed is due to both/either falling profit margins and/or a low rate of asset turnover. There has been increasing pressure on profit margins in recent years. Stronger domestic and international competition, combined with the Government's prices and incomes policy, has made it increasingly difficult to pass on to customers increases in costs. If profit margins in relation to sales income are to assume a lower level than previously, how can earnings in relation to capital expenditure be maintained? Only by increasing the rate of asset turnover, only by increasing productivity.

To answer the question 'Why has the capital employed in the business not produced the desired level of sales?', or 'Why has the rate of asset turnover declined?', it is necessary to calculate a third tier of ratios. This is attained by splitting up the capital employed:

$$\frac{\text{Sales}}{\text{Fixed Assets}} \quad \text{and} \quad \frac{\text{Sales}}{\text{Working Capital}}$$

The working capital ratio can be further analysed into ratios for stocks, work-in-progress, debtors, etc.

Similarly, to answer the question 'Why has the profit margin on sales declined?', the ratio of profit to sales can be analysed into a third tier of cost ratios. Profit equals sales minus costs, and costs may be analysed as follows:

$$\frac{\text{Production Cost}}{\text{Sales}} \quad \frac{\text{Selling Cost}}{\text{Sales}} \quad \text{etc.}$$

The production cost ratio can be analysed into ratios for the various components of production cost, that is, materials, wages, and overheads. Because of the increasing pressure on profit margins, percentage profit to sales will be maintained only if management is cost-conscious, exercises cost control, and effects cost reductions.

The two sides of the pyramid of ratios are not, of course, independent of each other. For example, an increase in the sales of a company, without any increase in productive capacity or change in selling prices, would increase not only the rate of asset turnover but also the percentage profit to sales. A company has fixed, semi-variable, and variable costs, and an increase in sales would not result in a proportionate increase in costs.

The relationship between the various ratios is illustrated in Figure 2. The use of the pyramid of ratios in analysing a company's performance over a number of years is illustrated in Appendix A to this chapter. The profit-and-loss accounts and balance sheets of the Widget Manufacturing Company, a hypothetical engineering company, are analysed for the period 1960–66.

THE PROBLEM OF DEFINITIONS

The definition of rate of return on capital employed is arrived at by first defining its two components: *profit* and *capital*. Defining these two terms is not straightforward, but this is not the place for a detailed discussion of the problem. A general examination of the problem is made in this section. More detailed discussions will be found in Selected Readings 6, 11, 14 and 15 (see p. 102).

The definitions of the two components, profit and capital, are dependent on the use to which the ratio will be put. For example, the return to equity shareholders will need to be evaluated by taking comprehensive figures for both capital employed and profit. On the other hand, the return on the capital under the control of a factory manager could be assessed on the restricted basis of trading profit before investment income and corporation tax to tangible assets (fixed assets and stocks) under his control. The definition of profit for ratios appropriate to particular situations can often be established without too much difficulty, but the definition of capital employed in particular circumstances is a more complex and difficult matter.

It is important to recognize that different ratios are required for different purposes. In a large group of companies a clearly defined set of ratios which can be used over a long period is required. A large group of companies may require two key ratios:

1. A *comprehensive ratio* for use in assessing the performance of the group as a whole.

2. A *control ratio* for use in evaluating, comparing, and denoting trends in the performance of product groups, divisions, and companies within the group.

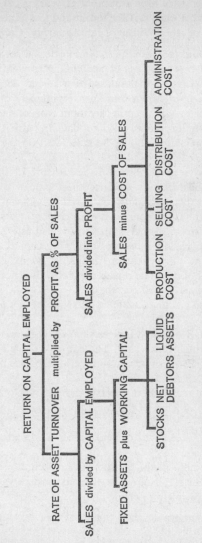

Figure 2. *Relationship of factors affecting return on capital employment*

DEPARTURE FROM THE HISTORICAL ACCOUNTS

The use of rates of return on capital employed for the discernment of trends, and for both internal and external comparisons, can be hindered by the effects of accounting conventions used over past years in the preparation of financial accounts. In Chapter 2 it was pointed out that an overstatement of profit in times of rising prices will occur if any input costs of one date are matched with output revenues of a later date. In particular, it was argued that depreciation should be calculated on the assumed current cost of fixed assets and not on the basis of historical cost. Similarly, to arrive at a more realistic measure of the capital employed in a business, the balance sheet statement of assets employed in the business must be corrected. Guest, Keen & Nettlefolds Ltd has recognized the problem in its internal accounts and corrects the net valuation of fixed assets for inflation, in order to permit a realistic return on capital employed comparison to be made between individual companies in the group. They do not calculate replacement cost; it is not possible. They calculate the assumed current cost.

Companies can calculate assumed current cost in a number of ways:

1. By the use of accepted indices such as those calculated by the Economist Intelligence Unit. These are available as a single index for industrial plant or in a number of separate indices for main groups of assets.

2. By a formal revaluation undertaken by professional valuers or by competent officials of the company at regular intervals of time.

3. By the substitution of current values as declared for fire insurance purposes.

Whilst none of these methods produces an accurate assessment of the current values of fixed assets, they do go some way towards recognizing the problem of changing price levels.[3]

3. A more accurate measure of the capital employed in a business would be the *present value* of all future net cash receipts of the firm. This would require an estimate of future cash flows and an appropriate rate of interest to discount them back to the present. This approach would recognize that

For the above reasons, certain departures from the financial accounts basis can be justified. The uplift of fixed assets to a basis of assumed current cost gives recognition to the influence of inflation, and at the same time gives a much greater degree of comparability. The omission of certain assets and liabilities can also be justified on grounds of simplicity. Nevertheless, the ratios used must be firmly linked with the financial accounts and such adjustments as are made must be seen to be soundly based.

COMPREHENSIVE RATIO

A comprehensive ratio which would measure the overall performance of a company or group of companies might be:

$$\frac{\text{Profit after corporation tax but before net payments of loan and debenture interest}}{\text{Total Net Assets Employed (irrespective of source of finance)}}$$

An associated ratio would be:

$$\frac{\text{Profit after corporation tax and interest, and after deduction of profit attributable to outside shareholders and preference shareholders}}{\text{Equity Capital}}$$

This ratio measures the return on the equity shareholders' investment in the company.

CONTROL RATIO

A control ratio for making internal comparisons within a company or group of companies might be:

$$\frac{\text{Trading Profit}}{\text{Net Trading Assets}}$$

the true value of the capital employed is dependent upon its future earning power. Unfortunately, at this point in time, it is extremely difficult to put this concept into practice. Assumed current cost is a practical compromise. Discounted cash flow is explained in Chapter 6.

In each of these ratios profits would preferably be after deducting depreciation based on the assumed current cost of fixed assets. Similarly, in the calculation of assets employed, fixed assets and accumulated depreciation should be valued in principle at assumed current cost. However, it must be recognized that many companies have neither the time nor the information to enable them to make these adjustments with any great accuracy. If these adjustments are not made, it should not be assumed too readily that a comparison of great accuracy can be made between different companies, factories, or divisions. Unadjusted accounting data is notoriously incomparable. This does not apply to the same degree to the comparison of a company's performance over a period of time, as will be shown in Appendix A to this chapter.

USING THE RATIOS

Having calculated your pyramid of control ratios, in what ways can you use the ratios to measure the efficiency of your business? You can compare your own results roughly or in detail with those of your competitors. You can keep an internal check on the trends of your own overall results. Internal comparisons can be made between one producing division (subsidiary or department) and another. They can provide an internal check on the comparative profitability of different products or product groups. If you prepare long-term plans or short-term budgets (and you should), you can compare actual and planned performance and analyse the variances.

EXTERNAL COMPARISONS

You can compare your own results roughly or in detail with those of your competitors. You can make the comparison with the performance of individual companies or with industry figures. Comparisons with financial accounts of individual companies drawn from the files of the Registrar of Companies may be of limited value for a number of reasons, including:

1. The accounts are prepared on a historical cost basis.

2. There are a number of permitted accounting rules for dealing with particular items of revenue, expenditure, assets and liabilities. As no two companies employ exactly the same set of accounting rules, the rates of return of any two companies may not be intrinsically comparable.

3. If a company is a subsidiary of a large group, it is often difficult to separate the financing of the subsidiary from its trading activities.

4. If the company is a member of a vertically integrated group of companies, where the end products of one company become the raw materials of another company, the *transfer prices* from one company to another may not be market prices and the profits of individual companies in the group may not be meaningful.

5. In a vertically integrated group of companies, one company in the group may accept an export order at a loss, but for the group as a whole the order may be profitable. A comparison with the company accepting the export order at a loss would be of limited value.

6. In a group of companies a single product line might be produced by several subsidiary companies, each of which also produces several other products, while the parent company absorbs all research and development costs.

7. If the competitor was an exempt private company under the Companies Act, 1948, there will be very little past information available.

A more valuable and meaningful method of comparing the performance of individual companies is to participate in an interfirm comparison scheme. Interfirm comparisons are discussed later in this chapter.

There are an increasing number of published sources of return on capital employed by industry groups. The Government publishes summarized profit-and-loss appropriation accounts, balance sheets, and sources and uses of capital funds statements under twenty-two industry groups quarterly in *Statistics on Incomes, Prices, Employment, and Production*. The triennial government publication, *Company Assets, Income and Finance*, gives the main figures for each individual large company. Return on capital employed statistics for these twenty-two industry groups are published at regular intervals in the *Board of Trade Journal* and *Economic Trends*. Business ratios for twenty-seven main industry groups are published in *Business Ratios* jointly by Dun & Bradstreet Ltd and Moodies Services Ltd. The ratios in this publication include profit to net assets, profit to sales, and sales to net assets. Quarterly figures analysed under twenty-three industrial groups are published by the *Economist*, and monthly figures appear in the *Financial Times* under thirty industrial groups. Individual company figures appear weekly in the *Investors Chronicle* and annually in *The Times*. Clearly, there is a vast amount of information available. However, at the present time, almost all the information available is based on the published accounts of quoted public companies and their subsidiaries. It may not, therefore, be representative of non-quoted private companies or of the unincorporated businesses. However, under the Companies Act, 1967, all companies are required to file accounts with the Registrar of Companies. In comparing company performance with these published sources particular attention must be paid to the definitions of profit and capital employed which vary considerably between sources.

TREND ANALYSIS

You can keep an internal check on the trends of your own overall results. By analysing the company's performance through time, it is possible to isolate causes of profit erosion or improvement. In particular, it is possible to diagnose long-term influences on the company's performance, such as continuing pressure on profit margins because of an inability to pass on wage increases by increasing selling prices. This type of analysis will be illustrated in Appendix A when the performance of the Widget Manufacturing Company is examined.

INTERNAL COMPARISONS

Internal comparisons can be made between one subsidiary and another, one producing division (or department) and another. Some companies also calculate and compare return on capital employed by product groups. Internal comparisons of this type can assist management in appraising the performance of individual companies in a group, divisions of a company, or product groups from year to year, i.e. by the comparison of performance through time. They will also assist in measuring the performance of decentralized management in the case of holding companies with a large number of autonomous operating subsidiaries; or individual factories, plants, or branches which operate as autonomous units within a large company.

Internal comparisons of this type may be of considerable value. However, it must be emphasized that the calculation of a separate rate of return for products, departments, divisions, or subsidiary companies frequently involves difficult questions of apportionment, in computing both capital employed and profit. The problem of transfer prices also occurs in many companies. It is important that management knows how to interpret the rates of return calculated. The case of Bang-Bang Manufacturing Ltd will illustrate the difficulties.

Bang-Bang Manufacturing Ltd manufactures and markets three separate groups of products, Product Groups A, B, C. For the year ending 31 December 1969, the forecast return on capital employed for the company is 15 per cent. Return on capital employed is defined by the company for this purpose as percentage trading profit to net trading assets employed in the business. The chief accountant is asked to calculate the forecast return on capital employed by product groups. The results of his calculations are shown in Table 4.1. It will be seen that Product Group B is expected to produce a return on capital employed of 7.6 per cent during 1969, and its performance in this respect has been consistently below that of Product Groups A and C. What exactly does this mean? How should this information be interpreted? It does *not* mean that:

1. If the company decided to cease manufacturing and marketing Product Group B, the company's capital employed would be reduced by £33,000 and trading profit by £2,500 in 1969.

2. £33,000 capital employed will be realized for investment if the company ceases manufacturing Product Group B.

It has been shown in Chapter 2 that a company's balance sheet

Table 4.1

BANG-BANG MANUFACTURING LTD

Forecast Return on Capital Employed for the year ended
31 December 1969

	Total	Product Groups			Service Depts	
		A	B	C	X	Y
	£	£	£	£	£	£
FIXED ASSETS						
Assumed Current Cost	210,000	120,000	20,000	50,000	15,000	5,000
Less Accumulated Depreciation	140,000	90,000	5,000	39,000	5,000	1,000
Written Down Value	£70,000	£30,000	£15,000	£11,000	£10,000	£4,000
NET CURRENT ASSETS						
Stocks	30,000	10,000	6,000	3,000	8,000	3,000
Trade Debtors	40,000	25,000	10,000	5,000	—	—
Less Trade Creditors	(20,000)	(9,000)	(4,000)	(2,000)	(3,000)	(2,000)
	£50,000	£26,000	£12,000	£6,000	£5,000	£1,000
NET TRADING ASSETS EMPLOYED	120,000	56,000	27,000	17,000	15,000	5,000
Apportionment of Service Departments	—	11,000	6,000	3,000	(15,000)	(5,000)
NET TRADING ASSETS EMPLOYED IN PRODUCT GROUPS	£120,000	£67,000	£33,000	£20,000		

Table 4.1 – cont.

	Total	Product Groups		
		A	B	
	£	£	£	£
SALES	173,000	100,000	33,000	40,000
Less Variable Cost of Sales	140,000	83,900	25,200	30,900
Total Contribution	33,000	16,100	7,800	9,100
Less Separable Fixed Costs	10,000	4,000	3,500	2,500
Direct Product Profits	23,000	12,100	4,300	6,600
Less Apportioned Common Fixed Costs	5,000	1,900	1,800	1,300
TRADING PROFIT	£18,000	£10,200	£2,500	£5,300
RETURN ON ASSETS EMPLOYED				
Forecast 1969	15%	15.2%	7.6%	26.5%
Actual 1968	16.3	15.0%	9.0%	25.0%
„ 1967	17.0%	14.5%	10.5%	25.3%

is prepared on the assumption that the company is a going concern and will continue trading. The balance sheet does *not* represent the realizable values of the assets. The company would not realize £120,000 if it went into voluntary liquidation. It must also be recognized, in relation to Product Group B, that it is not possible to allocate all the fixed costs of the business directly to product groups. Some of the fixed costs are clearly related to production and marketing of specific product groups, for example, product advertising and tooling costs. Other fixed costs are common to the whole organization and have to be apportioned to product groups. They would still be incurred if a product group was dropped: for example, the managing director's salary would not be reduced. Separable and common fixed costs are considered further in Chapter 8. Similarly, it is not possible to allocate all capital employed to product groups. Certain capital employed is common to all product groups, e.g. the capital employed in certain service and administration departments, the managing director's car, the company's computer installation, etc.

It will be seen in Table 4.1 that the fixed costs which are separable are shown separately from those which are common to the whole business. The capital employed can be analysed in the same way:

			Product Groups	
	Total	A	B	C
	£	£	£	£
Separable	68,000	37,000	19,000	12,000
Common	52,000	30,000	14,000	8,000
	£120,000	£67,000	£33,000	£20,000

It will now be appreciated that if, on the basis of the forecast return on capital employed of 7.6 per cent for Product Group B, the product group is dropped, the capital employed will be reduced by only £19,000. On the other hand, the trading profit will fall by £4,300, the direct product profit. This would mean that the company would be forgoing a return of 22.6 per cent on the *incremental* capital. In other words, the forecast return on the remaining capital employed must fall:

	£	£
Capital Employed:		
Separable		
Product Group A	37,000	
Product Group C	12,000	
		49,000
Common		52,000
Total		£101,000

Trading Profit:		
Direct Product Profits		
Product Group A	12,100	
Product Group C	6,600	
		18,700
Less Common Fixed Costs		5,000
		£13,700
Return on Capital Employed		13.6%

What then does the 7.6 per cent return on capital employed for Product Group B indicate? It indicates that the company is not making a satisfactory return on Product Group B in relation to the *total* capital employed in the business. However, unless the company has a better way of keeping the common capital resources employed, there is a case for retaining the product group. Thus, whether the product group should be retained or not depends upon the firm's alternative opportunities. It will be appreciated that return on capital employed by product groups must be interpreted with considerable caution. The same arguments apply whenever there is an apportionment of common fixed costs and capital employed.

INTERFIRM COMPARISONS

An external comparison of return on capital employed does not by itself tell the management any more than that in a particular year the firm's ratio was higher or lower than that of firms A, B, or C. As long as the comparison does not tell the management *why* the ratios of the firms differ, they have obtained neither a basis for judgement nor a guide for executive action. If it is to provide a basis for judgement, an external comparison between the returns on capital employed of firms should be planned in such a way that management is provided with adequate supporting data. They require a comparison of the detailed ratios in the lower part of the pyramid of control ratios.

The pyramid of control ratios provides the basis for the

interfirm comparisons undertaken by the Centre for Interfirm Comparisons and a number of trade associations, such as the British Federation of Master Printers.

Interfirm differences between the supporting pyramid ratios, which determine a firm's return on capital employed, can to a large extent be due to differences in the accounting treatment of the constituent parts. It is extremely important to ensure that the figures for all the firms in the comparison are calculated on the basis of the same definitions and valuation principles. If the data is not strictly comparable neither the comparison of the supporting pyramid ratios nor the overall return on capital employed will be useful.

It has been argued earlier in this chapter that published accounting data for individual firms can never be of more than very limited value for purposes of comparison. The only way to obtain accurate interfirm comparisons is for some central organization:

1. To establish detailed definitions and principles of valuation;
2. To agree with each participating company the methods for following them; and then
3. To collect and check the actual figures.

There are over sixty industries in Britain whose firms can obtain comparable ratios by participating in anonymous and absolutely confidential interfirm comparisons of selected ratios. The component figures of the ratios are based on uniform definitions and valuation principles developed in consultation with the firms concerned. The Centre for Interfirm Comparison provides participating firms with simple but detailed definitions of terms, and instructions on asset values. In particular, they show firms how, by using a price index, they can arive at comparable current values of plant and machinery.

After checking the accuracy and comparability of the figures contributed by participants, the Centre calculates the control ratios for each firm. The ratios are then tabulated and circulated to the participating firms, each firm being given a code number. The data appear in ratio, percentage, and similar statistical form (rather than absolute figures), which further reduces the possibility of identification. Each participating firm will also receive the Centre's observations on its ratios to help it in interpreting the differences between its ratios and those of others in the comparison. These observations will be made in the light of background information relating to the operating conditions of the industry and the firms in question. The comparative ratios of firms in the Centre's reports will not be the same as those that might be calculated from published accounts, because much of the information is not given in published accounts, and because the accounting information has been standardized. 'Those who attempt to draw conclusions from comparisons of figures which do not result from such organised schemes, but, for example, from published accounts, do so at their peril.'[4]

It is important to appreciate that it is *not* the object of interfirm comparisons to arrive at general conclusions about the industry. The aim is to provide the top management of each participating firm with a diagnostic tool which throws into sharp relief otherwise undetected weaknesses in the firm's operating policy and performance. The Centre's confidential reports will show the firm how well its overall performance compares with those of the other participants, and *why* it differs from theirs. The less efficient the firm the more it stands to gain from participating in an interfirm comparison scheme. However, the more efficient firms will derive much useful information from the comparison. 'There must always be some areas in which the most successful firm can strive to improve. The knowledge as to which these areas are is, I think, the most important justification for Interfirm Comparison.'[5] In Appendix B to this chapter the case of an efficient printing firm, Bigtown Printers, is examined.

It is important that, having participated in an interfirm comparison scheme, management fully utilize the information. Fred Catherwood, Director-General of the National Economic Development Office, has rightly pointed out, 'It is odd that some firms will spend thousands of pounds on a consultant's report and go through it with a fine tooth comb, especially the technical and

4. H. Ingham (Director, Centre for Interfirm Comparison), letter to *Financial Times*, 14 April 1966, p. 9.

5. Dr A. W. Clark, British Institute of Management National Conference, 1967, reported in *Management Today*, May 1967, pp. 123–4.

production matter, but the same firms will sometimes disregard an interfirm comparison that has cost them thirty guineas.' In some schemes, such as that operated by the British Federation of Master Printers, the participants do not automatically receive observations on their ratios. In these cases it is important that the company accountant not only understands the relationship between the ratios, but also explains the relationship to management. He should also prepare a detailed interpretation of the ratios. The author is familiar with a case similar to that suggested by Fred Catherwood. The interfirm comparison was disregarded because the directors neither understood the relationship between the ratios nor received any meaningful interpretation of the ratios. The accountant did not really understand the relationship between the ratios himself, and he never explained to the directors the pyramid of ratios. He merely circulated the ratios with short cryptic comments alongside each ratio.

It should not be assumed that interfirm comparison schemes overcome all the weaknesses of direct external comparisons. The uniform definitions and valuation problems may not, for example, overcome the *transfer price* problems if a participating company is a member of a vertically integrated group of companies, nor the problems of the company accepting an export order which is profitable for the group of companies but not for the company itself. No two companies are strictly comparable in that they market exactly the same products for the same markets. Interfirm comparison data produces a more realistic starting point in the analysis of a company's past performance in relation to that of its competitors than direct external comparisons with published accounts. Even after detailed analysis of the interfirm comparison data further studies will often be required before detailed recommendations for improving performance can be made. The interfirm comparison will enable the management to determine *where* and *why* its performance is better or worse than that of its competitors but it will not necessarily tell it *how* to improve it.

SETTING A STANDARD

Increasing emphasis on return on capital employed and attempts to improve it naturally lead to a number of questions. What rate of return on capital employed should be earned? Is there such a thing as a 'fair' rate of return? What should be regarded as a standard rate of return on capital employed? The establishment of a standard is a difficult and controversial matter and requires careful judgement. Important factors to be considered include:

1. The return on capital employed earned by other companies in the same industry, particularly some of the more successful ones.

2. The return earned by some successful companies in other industries, particularly industries in which the risk and uncertainty faced by the firms in the industry is similar or the skills required to be successful are similar.

3. The position of the company in the industry, and the competitive nature of the industry. Is the company a price-maker or a price-taker? What is the company's market share?

4. The likelihood of new companies being attracted into the industry by present high returns. How high are the barriers to new entry?

5. The risk and uncertainty faced by the firm and the industry. The higher the risk and the greater the uncertainty the higher the return on capital employed to be expected?

6. The return considered reasonable by crucial outsiders, i.e. the trade unions, the financial press, the investing public, potential competitors, the Monopolies Commission, the Restrictive Trade Practices Court, the Prices and Incomes Board, etc. The T.U.C. Wage Vetting Committee takes into account the profitability of individual concerns when examining wage claims. The Prices and Incomes Board has placed considerable importance on rate of return on capital employed in a number of its reports on proposed price increases.

The above factors confirm that setting a standard rate of return on capital employed is a difficult matter requiring considerable skill. They also suggest that a standard (or 'fair') rate of return on capital employed *cannot* be applied uniformly to all companies. Return on capital employed is an imperfect tool which must be interpreted against the background circumstances of each individual case. Although useful for the appraisal of long-term performance, profit potentialities and long-term plans, *standard* rates of return may not provide useful criteria for measuring short-term performance. Interfirm comparisons will be more useful for this purpose.

A standard rate of return could be established by the preparation of a business plan covering the normal cycle, for instance, five years, and reflecting the cyclical nature of earnings. The forecast rate of return for each year of the plan could become the standard for that period. This method would overcome many of the accounting difficulties of setting a standard, such as differences in the age of assets. It would also take into consideration such factors as the competitive position of the company, the cyclical nature of the industry, the risk and uncertainty faced by the industry, and the planned expansion of the company. Alternatively, the long-term plan may be based on objectives set by the management. This type of planning, *strategic planning*, is considered in Chapter 5. The basic steps in this type of long-range planning are:

1. *What kind of business should the company be in? What should the objectives of the firm be?* The company will have a whole hierarchy of objectives and constraints, company-wide economic and non-economic objectives, and individual economic and non-economic objectives. It will have short-term and long-term objectives, individual and institutional responsibilities and constraints. Peter Drucker considers that there are eight areas in which objectives of performance and results have to be set: market standing; innovation; productivity; physical and financial resources; profitability; manager performance and development; worker performance and attitude; and public responsibility.[6] Return on capital employed will form part of the economic or profitability objective of the firm. For example, the economic objectives of the firm may be:

6. Peter Drucker, *The Practice of Management*, Mercury Books, London, 1961, p. 53.

Return on Equity Shareholders' Investment
Short-term	10%
Long-term	15%

Equity Shareholders' Investment Growth Rate
Short-term	5%
Long-term	15%

Sales Growth Rate
Short-term	5%
Long-term	15%

An application of this thinking may be found in the Annual Report of Guest, Keen & Nettlefolds Ltd for 1966. 'After a year of unremitting pressure to improve our results, it is particularly disappointing to record a fall to a ratio (of profit to net assets employed) of 10.5% against 12.2% for 1965, an initial budget of 13% and a target rate of 15%.' Thus G.K.N. appears to set both a short-term and a long-term profit objective.

2. *How should the company pursue its objectives in each kind of business specified in (1)? What should be the company's competitive strategy?* The long-run sales growth objective of the firm may give rise to a sales gap and the management must determine its strategy to close the gap. However astutely management changes its day-to-day operating strategy there is usually an inevitable fall-off in the rate of growth of existing business, with the result that the company must introduce new products or enter new markets if it is to continue to grow. In order to achieve the desired rate of growth and fill the gap between the momentum line of its existing business and its long-term growth objective, the company must rethink its strategy and change its product-market scope. This means the company must do one or more of the following:

Sell existing products more effectively in existing markets (market penetration)

Sell existing products in new markets (market development)

Introduce new products in existing markets (product development)

Introduce new products in new markets (diversification)

The sales gap and ways of filling it are illustrated in Figure 3. The question of strategy is examined in more detail in Chapter 5.

3. *How should the events and activities required to accomplish*

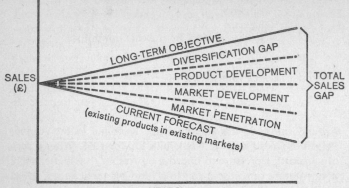

Figure 3. *Sales-gap filling*

the competitive strategy be programmed? What should the plan of action be? This step involves spelling out in detail a time-phased schedule of events and activities required to implement the competitive strategy.

4. *When and to what extent should the master plan be changed?* Feedback and reappraisal:

Is a new economic objective indicated?

Is a new competitive strategy indicated?

Is a new programme of action indicated?

Thus, a standard rate of return on capital employed may be the end result of the long-range planning process, or it may be part of the economic objective of the firm in strategic planning.

SUMMARY OF CHAPTER

Profitability is the primary aim and best measure of efficiency in competitive business. Rate of return on capital employed should be used to measure profitability. Rate of return on capital employed gives rise to a pyramid of subsidiary control ratios. Defining capital and profit for purposes of calculating return on capital employed is not straightforward. Certain departures from published financial accounts are justified and advisable. The ratios calculated can be used for external comparisons, trend analysis, and internal comparisons. Organized interfirm comparison schemes are the best form of external comparison. Internal comparisons of return on capital employed by product groups require careful interpretation. The establishment of a standard rate of return is a difficult and controversial matter. The standard may be the result of the long-range planning process or included in the economic objective of the firm.

SELECTED READINGS

1. R. Appelby, *Profitability and Productivity in the United Kingdom, 1954–1964*, British Institute of Management, London, 1967.
2. K. W. Bevan, *The use of ratios in the study of business fluctuations and trends*, General Educational Trust of the Institute of Chartered Accountants in England and Wales, London, 1966.
3. Centre for Interfirm Comparison, *Higher Profitability through I.F.C. – The Case of Firm D*, free from Management House, Parket Street, London WC2.
4. 'Interfirm Comparisons in the Engineering Industry', *The Accountant*, 3 October 1965.
5. John H. Dunning, 'U.S. Subsidiaries in Britain and Their U.K. Competitors – A Case Study in Business Ratios', *Business Ratios*, Autumn 1966.
6. Institute of Cost and Works Accountants, *The Profitable Use of Capital in Industry*, London, 1965.
7. H. W. G. Kendall, 'The Use of Ratios in the Printing Industry', *Business Ratios*, Summer 1967.
8. Robin L. Marris, 'Profitability and growth in the individual firm', *Business Ratios*, Spring 1967.
9. A. J. Merrett and Allen Sykes, 'Incomes Policy and Company Profitability', *District Bank Review*, September 1963.
10. A. J. Merrett and John Whittaker, 'The Profitability of British and American Industry', *Lloyds Bank Review*, January 1967.
11. National Association of Accountants, *Return on Capital as a Guide to Managerial Decisions*, Research Report No. 35, New York, 1959.
12. J. M. Samuels and D. J. Smyth, *Profit, Profits, Variability and Firm Size*, Graduate Centre for Management Studies, Birmingham, Discussion Paper No. 1, November 1966.
13. R. C. Skinner, 'Return on Capital Employed as a Measure of Efficiency', *Accountancy*, June 1965.
14. David Solomons, *Divisional Performance: Measurement and Control*, Financial Executives Research Foundation, New York, 1965.
15. L. Taylor Harrington, *Problems of using 'Return on Capital' as a measure of success*, Manchester Statistical Society, Manchester, March 1961.
16. Spencer A. Tucker, *Successful Managerial Control by Ratio Analysis*, McGraw-Hill, New York, 1961.

Appendix A

Widget Manufacturing Company Ltd

The Widget Manufacturing Company Ltd manufactures and markets a hypothetical engineering component, 'Widgets'. The company is a wholly owned subsidiary of an industrial investment company, All Purpose Investments Ltd, and was acquired on 1 January 1960. King Kong, the founder, chairman and managing director of All Purpose Investments, is not satisfied with the profit performance of Widget Manufacturing Company since the date of acquisition. On 30 April 1967, he writes to Tom Brain, Widget's managing director, requesting an analysis of Widget's financial performance since the date of acquisition. He receives from Tom Brain by return post the following statements:

Summarized trading and profit statements, and balance sheets for the years 1960 to 1966 (Tables 4A.1 and 4A.2).

A ratio analysis for the years 1960 to 1966 (Table 4A.3).

Table 4A.1

THE WIDGET MANUFACTURING COMPANY LTD

Trading and Profit-and-loss Statements, 1960–66

	1960 £	1961 £	1962 £	1963 £	1964 £	1965 £	1966 £
Turnover	251,460	238,120	245,572	275,541	338,109	360,509	362,157
Production Costs	160,616	156,505	158,745	183,809	234,465	248,212	250,107
Selling Costs	11,768	12,004	12,537	13,769	14,887	16,859	17,012
Distribution Costs	22,764	22,057	25,768	26,107	27,154	31,758	33,173
Administration Expenses	25,606	26,104	27,342	28,104	30,166	33,475	34,360
	220,754	216,770	224,392	251,789	306,672	330,304	334,652
Surplus on Trading	30,706	21,350	21,180	23,752	31,437	30,205	27,505

103

Table 4A.1 – cont.

Investment Income and Interest Receivable	958	1,394	1,119	779	307	325	582
Interest on Debentures	(782)	(506)	(431)	(583)	(634)	(628)	(1,184)
Profit before Taxation	30,882	22,238	21,868	23,948	31,110	29,902	26,903
Taxation	15,644	11,700	11,054	11,930	16,218	12,698	12,685
Net Profit for Year	15,238	10,538	10,814	12,018	14,892	17,204	14,218
Preference Dividends	358	363	368	368	371	372	633
Ordinary Dividends	6,120	6,120	6,120	6,120	6,120	8,749	10,261
Retained in Reserves	8,760	4,055	4,326	5,530	8,401	8,083	3,324
	15,238	10,538	10,814	12,018	14,892	17,204	14,218
Depreciation Charged	8,956	9,991	11,267	12,086	13,204	14,335	16,333

Table 4A.2

THE WIDGET MANUFACTURING COMPANY LTD

Balance Sheets, 1960–66

	1960 £	1961 £	1962 £	1963 £	1964 £	1965 £	1966 £
Fixed Assets							
Cost	167,340	181,963	202,275	220,324	236,384	249,021	293,755
Less							
Accumulated Depreciation	68,022	70,721	76,535	83,637	91,834	101,711	126,412
W.D.V.	99,318	111,242	125,740	136,687	144,550	147,310	167,343
Trade Investments	751	764	1,006	1,899	2,037	2,310	7,843

Table 4A.2 – cont.

Current Assets							
Stock in Trade	57,552	60,681	64,791	67,772	75,965	85,740	92,606
Debtors	46,144	46,628	43,947	45,049	58,411	70,280	75,808
Quoted Investments	3,000	6,000	5,000	4,000	—	—	—
Bank and Other Short-term Deposits	9,000	11,000	12,000	6,000	3,000	—	—
Cash at Bank	2,977	3,618	2,784	2,226	1,569	738	442
	118,673	127,927	128,522	125,047	138,945	156,758	168,856
Current Liabilities							
Sundry Creditors	29,743	32,174	33,261	34,736	38,717	40,275	46,953
Current Taxation	6,743	5,842	5,702	6,372	9,500	—	8,620
Proposed Final Dividend	3,875	3,875	3,875	3,875	3,875	6,596	6,596
	40,361	41,891	42,838	43,983	52,092	46,871	62,169
Net Current Assets	78,312	86,036	85,684	81,064	86,853	109,887	106,687
Net Assets Employed	178,381	198,042	212,430	218,650	233,440	259,507	281,873
Represented by:							
Ordinary Share Capital	42,900	46,500	48,400	49,000	75,000	75,000	75,000
Capital Reserves	21,097	22,703	24,206	25,347	27,106	28,295	28,790
Revenue Reserves	75,803	94,305	103,152	106,520	88,628	107,474	110,204
Equity Interest	139,800	163,508	175,758	180,867	190,734	210,769	213,994

Table 4A.2 – cont.

Preference Capital	7,647	7,847	7,847	7,847	8,047	8,047	8,047
Debenture Stock	11,558	8,863	10,950	10,720	11,529	12,626	30,626
Deferred Liabilities	10,570	11,830	13,020	14,509	15,703	14,539	14,105
Future Taxation	8,806	5,994	4,855	5,707	7,427	13,526	15,101
	178,381	198,042	212,430	219,650	233,440	259,507	281,873
Capital Expenditure during year	17,329	19,387	21,406	18,235	18,744	17,475	28,260

NOTES ON ACCOUNTS

1. Depreciation

The total depreciation charged against profits takes into account the reduced purchasing power of money. This is done by increasing the depreciation charge based on the original cost of the assets by varying percentages according to the class of asset. The assumed current cost of assets is not calculated. The amount provided in excess of that required to write off the original cost of fixed assets over their estimated life is transferred to capital reserves in the balance sheet.

For example:

	1964	1965	1966
	£	£	£
Written off Fixed Assets	11,606	12,324	13,883
Transferred to Capital Reserves	1,598	2,011	2,450
Depreciation charged against Profits	13,204	14,335	16,333

2. Taxation

The charge for taxation and subsequent after-tax figures for 1965 and 1966 are not comparable with previous years owing to changes introduced in the Finance Act, 1965. In arriving at the net profit for 1965 and 1966, the rate of U.K. corporation tax has been taken as 40 per cent compared with the combined rate of income tax and profits tax in earlier years (56¼ per cent in 1964).

3. Acquisition of Supplier

On 1 January 1966, the assets and current liabilities of a small component supplier were acquired and paid for by the issue of £18,000 debenture stock. For this reason the cost of fixed assets increased during 1966 by an amount in excess of the capital expenditure during the year.

Table 4A.3

THE WIDGET MANUFACTURING COMPANY LTD

Ratio Analysis 1960–66

	1960	*1961*	*1962*	*1963*	*1964*	*1965*	*1966*
1. Profitability Ratios							
1.1 Net Profit *less* Preference Dividends	14,880	10,175	10,466	11,650	14,521	16,832	13,585
Equity Interest	139,800	163,508	175,758	180,867	190,734	210,769	213,994
%	10.6%	6.2%	5.9%	6.4%	7.6%	8.0%	6.3%
1.2 Net Profit	15,238	10,538	10,814	12,018	14,892	17,204	14,218
Net Assets Employed	178,381	198,042	212,430	219,650	233,440	259,507	281,873
%	8.5%	5.3%	5.1%	5.5%	6.4%	6.6%	5.0%
1.3 Profit before Taxation and Debenture Interest	31,664	22,744	22,299	24,531	31,744	30,530	28,087
Net Assets Employed	178,381	198,042	212,430	219,650	233,440	259,507	281,873
%	17.8%	11.5%	10.5%	11.2%	13.6%	11.8%	10.0%
1.4 Surplus on Trading	30,706	21,350	21,180	23,752	31,437	30,205	27,505
Net Assets Employed in Business	176,248	189,995	204,001	216,998	241,778	263,793	289,246
%	17.4%	11.2%	10.4%	10.9%	13.0%	11.5%	9.5%
1.41 Surplus on Trading	30,706	21,350	21,180	23,752	31,437	30,205	27,505
Sales	251,460	238,120	245,572	275,541	338,109	360,509	362,157
%	12.2%	9.0%	8.6%	8.6%	9.3%	8.4%	7.6%
1.42 Sales	251,460	238,120	245,572	275,541	338,109	360,509	362,157

Table 4A.3 – cont.

Net Assets Employed in Business	176,248	189,995	204,001	216,998	241,778	263,793	289,246
Rate of Asset Turnover	1.43	1.25	1.20	1.27	1.40	1.37	1.25

% of Sales:	%	%	%	%	%	%	%
1.411 Production Costs	63.9	65.8	64.6	66.7	69.3	68.9	69.1
1.412 Selling Costs	4.7	5.0	5.1	5.0	4.4	4.6	4.7
1.413 Distribution Costs	9.0	9.3	10.5	9.5	8.1	8.8	9.1
1.414 Administration Expenses	10.2	10.9	11.2	10.2	8.9	9.3	9.5
Total Cost	87.8	91.0	91.4	91.4	90.7	91.6	92.4

Asset Turnover	Times	Times	Times	Times	Times	Times	Times
1.421 Fixed Assets	2.53	2.14	1.95	2.02	2.34	2.45	2.16
1.422 Stocks	4.37	3.92	3.79	4.07	4.45	4.20	3.91
1.423 % Net Debtors of Sales	6.5%	6.1%	4.4%	3.7%	5.8%	8.3%	8.0%
1.424 % Debtors of Sales	18.4%	19.6%	17.9%	16.3%	17.3%	19.5%	20.9%

King Kong has heard all about return on capital employed and ratio analysis, but has neither the time nor the expertise to interpret the information. He therefore instructs his financial analyst, A. Gnome, to prepare a brief interpretation of the ratios. Gnome's interpretation follows. Before you read it you might wish to make your own interpretation of the statements received from Tom Brain.

To: King Kong   Date: 15 May 1967

WIDGET MANUFACTURING COMPANY LTD
FINANCIAL ANALYSIS, 1960–66

[This interpretation should be read in conjunction with Tables 4A.1, 4A.2, and 4A.3.]

1. PROFITABILITY RATIOS

1.1. Percentage Net Profit less Preference Dividends to Equity Interest

This ratio indicates that the return earned on the equity shareholders' investment in the firm has steadily declined since 1960. There was some apparent recovery in 1965 and a further setback in 1966, but the 1965 and 1966 returns are distorted by the change to corporation tax in the United Kingdom and are not comparable with earlier years. The figures indicate that the management has earned an even lower rate of return on *incremental* equity investment, i.e. the additional equity investment in the form of retained earnings, new issues, etc.

1.2. Percentage Net Profit to Net Assets Employed

The same picture emerges from a study of the return on the total capital employed in the firm – steady decline since 1960, some recovery in 1964 and apparent recovery in 1965, with a further setback in 1966. However, these ratios are distorted by debenture interest being deducted as an expense in the calculation of net profit, but not being deducted as a liability in the calculation of capital employed. Similarly, the figures are distorted by the changeover to corporation tax in 1965 and tax rate changes in earlier years. It may be argued that taxation is not wholly within the control of the management.

1.3. Percentage Profit before Taxation and Debenture Interest to Net Assets Employed

This ratio looks at the position before charging debenture interest and tax in the calculation of profit. It shows that the apparent recovery in 1965 was a result of the change to corporation tax, and that there was a fall in the return in 1965 and a further serious decline in 1966.

Widget's performance must be related to the general economic situation in the United Kingdom during the period. Broadly speaking the first eighteen months of the three years 1960–62 were a period of expansion, and the second half a period when the effects of the restrictive measures taken in mid 1961 were holding the economy in check; although the reins had been considerably loosened by mid 1962. Company profits followed roughly the same trend, with high returns being made in 1960 and significantly lower returns in 1961 and 1962. Widget's performance followed much the same trend. Conditions improved steadily during 1963 and had become buoyant in the latter half of the year, and this improved situation continued throughout 1964. Again the improvement was reflected in company profits and in

Widget's performance. It was felt necessary to introduce deflationary measures in the 1965 Budget, and these measures noticeably began to take effect in the latter half of 1965 and continued into 1966. In July 1966, Prime Minister Harold Wilson announced further severe deflationary measures to correct the adverse balance of payments situation. Conditions declined further in the latter half of 1966, but there has been some easing of credit restrictions in 1967 with the reductions in the Bank Rate in January, March and May. The 1967 Budget was a standstill affair. Widget's performance continued to follow that of the economy with falling returns on capital employed in 1965 and 1966.

In a report prepared in October 1966, I emphasized that company profits improved in 1963 and 1964, but never recovered to 1960 levels of return on capital employed when the economic climate was similar. I suggested that 1961 was repeated in 1965 and questioned whether 1962 would be repeated in 1966, but starting from a lower level of profitability. It will be seen that Widget's return on capital employed falls below that of 1962 in ratios 1.2, 1.3 and 1.4. Professor A. J. Merrett and John Whittaker, writing in the January issue of *Lloyds Bank Review*[1], suggest that industrial profitability probably reached its lowest level since the war in 1966. They also suggest that 1967 may be as bad or worse. Clearly Widget's performance must be appraised in the light of the external economic environment.

1.4. Percentage Surplus on Trading to Net Assets Employed in Business

In using ratio analysis to examine the performance of Widget's management and answer the questions, 'Why did not profits recover to 1960 levels in 1963 and 1964, when the economic climate was favourable?', and 'Why has there been a further setback in 1966?', it is preferable to examine the assets employed in the business and controllable by the management. Ratio 1.4 excludes outside investments and

Table 4A.4

THE WIDGET MANUFACTURING COMPANY LTD
Net Assets Employed in Business, 1960–66

	1960 £	1961 £	1962 £	1963 £	1964 £	1965 £	1966 £
Fixed Assets	99,318	111,242	125,740	136,687	144,550	147,310	167,343
Stocks	57,552	60,681	64,791	67,772	75,965	85,740	92,606
Debtors	46,144	46,628	43,947	45,049	58,411	70,280	75,808

1. A. J. Merrett and John Whittaker, 'The Profitability of British and American Industry', *Lloyds Bank Review*, January 1967, p. 6.

Table 4A.4 – cont.

Less Creditors	(29,743)	(32,174)	(33,261)	(34,736)	(38,717)	(40,275)	(46,953)
Net Debtors	16,401	14,454	10,696	10,313	19,694	30,005	28,855
Cash at Bank	2,977	3,618	2,784	2,226	1,569	738	442
Net Assets Employed in Business	176,248	189,995	204,001	216,998	241,778	263,793	289,246

related income, and financial items such as current taxation and dividend provisions (see Table 4A.4). The ratio indicates that the more capital invested in the business the lower the return has become. This ratio is the apex of a pyramid of control ratios shown in Figure 4. The ratio is determined by percentage profit to sales (ratio 1.41) and the rate of asset turnover (ratio 1.42). The trend since 1960 of the three absolute measures that determine these ratios, net assets employed in business, surplus on trading, and sales, is shown graphically in Figure 5. It will be seen that net assets employed in business has risen steadily during the period, and sales have also climbed steadily since 1961. Surplus on trading has been consistently below the 1960 level, except for 1964.

1.41 and 1.42. Percentage Surplus on Trading to Sales and Rate of Asset Turnover

In 1964 Widget achieved a record sales level of £338,000, being 22.7 per cent up in value on 1963 and 34.5 per cent in value higher than 1960, but surplus on trading was only slightly higher than in 1960. As a result *percentage surplus on trading to sales* (ratio 1.41) only increased from 8.6 per cent to 9.3 per cent between 1963 and 1964, and fell well short of the 1960 level of 12.2 per cent, but with the substantial increase in sales there was an improvement in the *rate of asset turnover* (ratio 1.42). The rate of asset turnover improved in 1964 to 1.40 times and compared favourably with the 1960 rate of 1.43 times. Under buoyant conditions, as existed in 1964, one would normally expect percentage surplus on trading to sales to increase, in line with an improvement in the rate of asset turnover, for two reasons:

Costs do not normally increase proportionately with an increase in sales and capacity utilization;

It is easier to pass on increases in costs when there is a sellers' market.

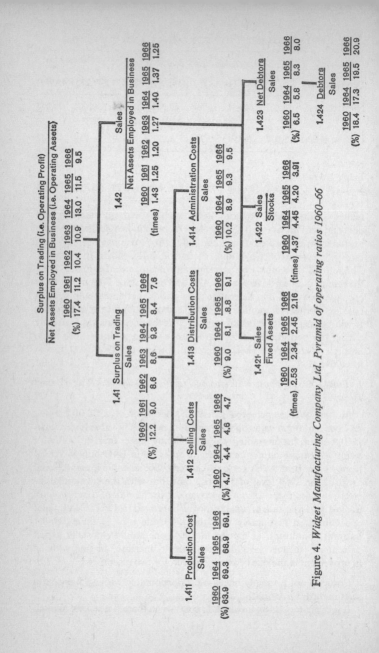

Figure 4. *Widget Manufacturing Company Ltd. Pyramid of operating ratios 1960–66*

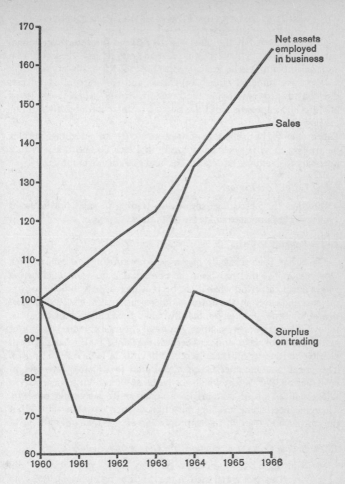

Figure 5. *Widget Manufacturing Company Ltd. Surplus on trading, sales, and net assets employed in business 1960–66.* (*1960 = 100*)

Since 1964 both percentage surplus on trading to sales and rate of asset turnover have declined in line with the Government's deflationary measures. Throughout the period the rate of asset turnover has moved more or less in line with the general economic conditions.

It would appear that profit margins will never recover to their pre-

1960 levels, and that the only way to achieve the return on capital employed earned in 1960 is to increase the rate of asset turnover. You will remember that in his annual report for 1965 Mr Brain stated:

'We have initiated closely organized and well integrated policies directed towards improving the rate of turnover to assets employed and are uncompromising in the pursuit of this vital objective to our earning power.'

Unfortunately, both the rate of asset turnover and percentage surplus on trading to sales declined seriously in 1966. To find out why it is necessary to examine the detailed cost and asset turnover ratios.

1.411–1.414. Cost Ratios

Why has the percentage surplus on trading to sales not achieved 1960 levels? We must examine the cost ratios:

1.411. Production Costs

There has been a steady increase in production costs since 1960. One reason for this has been the continual increase in engineering wages during a period when it has become increasingly difficult to pass on cost increases in the form of higher prices. In his 1965 annual report Mr Brain pointed out that there had been major increases in the following costs: wages, salaries, National Insurance, materials, power and bought-out parts and services. He explained that it has not been possible to recover all these increases in costs in higher selling prices. The prices and incomes freeze meant that inescapable increases in costs during 1966 again could not be passed on to customers. Given this situation, profit margins have come under increasing pressure. There has been some levelling out of production costs since 1964, but they form a considerably higher proportion of sales than in 1960.

1.412. Selling Costs, Distribution Costs and Administration Costs

Many of these costs are fixed costs; they do not vary with the level of activity. This fact is reflected in the ratios being higher in 1962 than in 1964. There has been some reduction in the level of administration costs during the last three years. Together these costs represented 23.9 per cent of sales in 1960 and 23.3 per cent of sales in 1966.

1.421–1.424. Asset Turnover Ratios

If the rate of asset turnover had not recovered with the improvement in the general economic climate in 1964, we could have answered the question 'Why?' by examining the asset turnover ratios. These ratios can also be examined to discover the reasons for the decline in the rate of asset turnover from 1.37 times in 1965 to 1.25 times in 1966. It will be seen that both the rate of fixed asset turnover and stock turnover fell in 1966. The decline in the rate of fixed asset turnover indicates that the company was not utilizing its capacity to the same extent as in 1965. In his 1966 annual report Tom Brain stated:

'The high level of activity in 1965 continued well into 1966, but the demand for Widgets by the motor industry was drastically reduced from September 1966 onwards. Strikes at certain of our customers' plants were also major aggravations.'

The decline in the rate of stock turnover may well indicate that the company continued to build up stocks when the level of demand declined from September 1966 onwards.

The ratio of net debtors to sales fell slightly in 1966, but is considerably higher than in the early 1960s. It would appear that the level of debtors has increased significantly during the last three years. This trend would appear to be in line with the recent findings of the Engineering Industries Association.[2] Their investigations have shown an upward trend in the length of credit terms taken as disclosed by the following percentage debtors to turnover for the preceding three months:

At 31 December 1961	78.0%
1962	75.6%
1963	73.9%
1964	81.3%
1965	85.9%
1966	89.0%

The upward trend was most marked with the smaller and medium-sized companies where the percentage as between 1965 and 1966 went up from 73.8 per cent to 80.1 per cent and 76.4 per cent to 82.8 per cent respectively. Widget's figures show a similar trend to the industry figures.

Summary

Widget's profit performance has declined significantly since 1960. There has been a serious erosion of the company's profit margins as a result in part of external economic factors. If the company is to im-

2. 'The Use of Extended Credit', *The Accountant*, 29 April 1967, pp. 544–5.

prove its return on capital employed, however defined, it must improve its rate of asset turnover, i.e., it must increase its productivity.

A. Gnome

Financial Analyst

Having read and digested Gnome's interpretation, King Kong sent the following brief letter to Tom Brain:

17 May 1967

Dear Brain,

I have studied carefully the financial information you sent me on Widget's financial performance since 1960. I am not satisfied with your profit performance; there has been a serious decline in your return on capital employed since 1960. It would appear that you will never be able to increase your profit margins on sales significantly. You must improve your rate of asset turnover to at least 1.5 times per annum. Would you prepare a report indicating how you propose to achieve this increase, and let me have it by 1 June 1967.

King Kong

QUESTIONS

1. Has A. Gnome placed too much emphasis on the general economic situation during the period in his analysis of Widget's performance? Should he have given more consideration to the industry performance during the period?

2. If you were King Kong would you have suggested to Brain that he will never be able to increase his profit margin on sales significantly and that he must improve his rate of asset turnover to 1.5 times? Would you have established a profitability objective for Widget Manufacturing Company of, say, 15 per cent surplus on trading to net assets employed in business and required Brain to prepare a long-term plan for the next five years?

3. 'The examination of accounting ratios is only a starting point in the analysis of a company's past performance and further detailed studies are required before recommendations to improve performance can be made.' Do you agree?

APPENDIX B

Bigtown Printers Ltd

Bigtown Printers Ltd is a medium-sized firm of general letter-press printers, with an annual turnover in excess of £300,000 and 117 employees. The company specializes in higher-quality products including calendars, company annual reports, advertising and travel brochures. The firm is a member of the Ruritanian Federation of Master Printers and participates in the Federation's Management Ratio Scheme. A summary of the ratios received from the Federation for 1964 is shown in Table 4B.1. A summary of the basic information used in the calculation of Bigtown Printers' ratios is shown in Table 4B.2.

The Ruritanian Federation of Master Printers does not supply an interpretation of the ratios. Bigtown Printers do not employ a qualified accountant, and the ratios are interpreted by the company secretary, William Biggs. Biggs has attended a number of courses on financial management at the local university. He is familiar with the pyramid of ratios, but is not quite sure how the ratios in the Federation's scheme are inter-related. He would also like a second opinion on his interpretation. He asks one of the university lecturers, Bernard Knowall, if he would prepare an interpretation of the ratios. Knowall's interpretation follows, but you may wish to make your own interpretation before you read it.

BIGTOWN PRINTERS LTD

Interfirm Comparison, 1964

I have constructed a pyramid showing the relationship between the various ratios provided in the Management Ratio Scheme. Some additional ratios have been deduced from the ratios provided. The pyramid is too large to show on one diagram; the apex of the pyramid is shown in Figure 6 and the two sides of the pyramid in Figures 7 and 8. You will see that I have entered on the pyramid the first quartile, median, and third quartile ratios together with Bigtown Printers' ratios. To interpret the information it is necessary to work systematically down each side of the pyramid in order to reveal the cause(s) of unsatisfactory ratios in the higher part of the pyramid. If my interpretation is read in conjunction with the pyramid of ratios, you will see how this systematic analysis is undertaken.

Assuming your firm is comparable with the other general printing–letterpress firms in the interfirm comparison, you would note from the table of ratios provided by the Ruritanian Federation of Master Printers:

1. Your *operating profit on operating capital* (ratio 1), indicating the earning power of the operations of your business, is above the median earned by general printing–letterpress firms, and compares favourably with that earned by the most profitable firms.

2. Your performance is below that of the third quartile firm because your *operating profit on net sales* (ratio 2) is 2 per cent below that of the third quartile firm. Your *turnover of operating capital* (ratio 8) compares very favourably with that of the third quartile firm.

Ratio 2, *operating profit on net sales*, shows what profit margin you have earned on sales, whilst ratio 8, *turnover of operating capital*, indicates how often with your operating assets you have been able to earn it in a year.

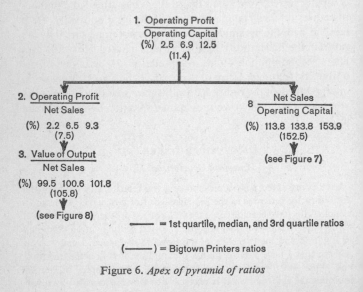

Figure 6. *Apex of pyramid of ratios*

118

Table 4B.1

RURITANIAN FEDERATION OF MASTER PRINTERS

General Printing Letterpress – 101 and over employees
35 firms (5,707 employees)

	Unit	Ratios 1964			
		1st Quartile	Median	3rd Quartile	Bigtown Printers
PRIMARY RATIOS					
1. Operating Profit / Operating Capital	%	2.5	6.9	12.5	11.4
Operating Cost Ratios					
2. Operating Profit / Net Sales	%	2.2	6.5	9.3	7.5
3. Value of Output / Net Sales	%	99.5	100.6	101.8	105.8
4. Production Cost (Gross) / Cost of Output	%	82.9	84.9	85.6	85.5
5. Distribution Cost / Cost of Output	%	1.1	1.4	2.0	1.6
6. Selling Cost / Cost of Output	%	3.3	4.0	5.4	5.2
7. Administration Cost / Cost of Output	%	8.4	9.9	11.1	7.7
Use of Capital Ratios					
8. Net Sales / Operating Capital	%	113.8	133.8	153.9	152.5
9. Fixed Assets / Operating Capital	%	52.2	58.7	66.9	53.9
10. Plant / Fixed Assets	%	78.6	83.9	93.2	92.6
11. Value added / Plant	%	148.6	204.8	242.9	189.0
12. Materials / Stock	Times per year	2.5	3.9	5.2	6.0

Table 4B.1 – cont.

			Ratios 1964		
	Unit	1st Quartile	Median	3rd Quartile	Bigtown Printers
13. Debtors Sales per Day	Days credit	51.2	59.7	68.3	58.5
SECONDARY RATIOS					
Production Costs					
14. Value Added Factory Employees	£ per employee	1,669.1	1,835.0	2,043.1	2,032.2
15. Value Added Factory Wages	per £	1.8	2.0	2.2	2.2
16. Production Cost (Net) Cost of Output	%	46.0	54.4	59.7	40.8
17. Factory Wages Production Cost (Net)	%	68.6	71.0	76.1	70.0
18. Factory Management Salaries Production Cost (Net)	%	4.4	6.4	7.8	8.0
19. Depreciation Production Cost (Net)	%	7.3	8.7	10.0	8.5
20. Other Factory Expenses Production Cost (Net)	%	10.2	12.0	15.3	13.4
21. Factory Wages Factory Employees	£ per capita	820.1	946.5	1,046.9	923.1
22. Male Factory Employees Factory Employees	%	67.8	78.7	83.5	74.2
23. Factory Management Salaries Factory Management Staff	£ per capita	1,408.0	1,651.1	1,939.9	1,429.7
24. Plant Factory Employees	£ per employee	732.7	940.1	1,126.1	1,075.3

Table 4B.1 – cont.

		Ratios 1964			
	Unit	1st Quartile	Median	3rd Quartile	Bigtown Printers
Selling Costs					
25. Sales Staff Remuneration / Sales Staff	£ per capita	1,318.7	1,794.9	2,203.5	1,847.8
Administration Costs					
26. Administration Expenses / Administration Cost	%	34.8	43.6	50.2	50.2
27. General Management Salaries / Administration Cost	%	6.8	10.7	14.6	17.9
28. Administrative Staff Salaries / Administration Cost	%	36.0	46.5	53.1	31.9
29. Administration Cost / Printing Jobs	£ per job	4.6	7.5	16.9	N.A.
30. General Management Salaries / General Management Staff	£ per capita	2,189.7	2,996.7	3,838.0	2,764.0
31. Administrative Staff Salaries / Administrative Staff	£ per capita	698.1	855.6	931.8	738.7
32. Male Administrative Staff / Administrative Staff	%	36.1	49.3	61.1	30.0

The three comparison ratios given provide an indication of the middle performance and range of results. For each ratio the figures are listed in order of size from the lowest to the highest. The median is the figure which comes half-way down the list. The first and third quartiles are the figures a quarter and three quarters down the list. The median and quartiles are therefore figures of actual firms, but it is very probable that they will be different firms for each ratio.

Table 4B.2

BIGTOWN PRINTERS LTD

Basic Interfirm Comparison Information, 1964

	£	£
OPERATING CAPITAL		
Fixed Assets at Current Values *less* Depreciation		
Plant, Machinery, Fixtures, and Fittings	100,000	
Metal and Type	4,500	
Cars	3,358	
Vans	133	
		107,991
Current Assets		
Loans to Employees, Sports Clubs, Employees' Housing Associations. etc.	—	
Stock of Materials/goods (average holding)	12,300	
Work-in-progress (average holding)	30,000	
Trade Debtors (average holding)	50,000	
Cash (at bank, in hand) (average holding)	80	
		92,380
		£200,371
OPERATING PROFIT		
GROSS SALES	312,272	
Less Purchase Tax	6,688	
Net Sales	305,584	
Add Closing Work-in-progress	41,069	
		346,653
Less Opening Work-in-progress		23.343
Value of Output		£323,310
Cost of Output		
Production Cost		
Factory Wages	85,848	
Factory Management Salaries	9,865	

Table 4B.2 – cont.

Depreciation	10,450	
Other Factory Expenses	16,468	
Production Cost (Net)	122,631	
Materials	73,527	
Outwork	60,792	
Production Cost (Gross)		256,950
Selling Cost		
Sales Staff Remuneration	8,500	
Selling Expenses	7,019	
		15,519
Distribution Cost		4,765
Administration Cost		
General Management Salaries	4,146	
Administrative Staff Salaries	7,387	
Administration Expenses	11,612	
		23,145
Cost of Output		£300,379
OPERATING PROFIT		£22,931

OTHER INFORMATION

Average Number of Employees	*Directors Apportioned*	*Male*	*Female*	*Total*
Factory	—	69	24	93
Factory Management	0.9	6	—	6.9
Selling	1.6	3	—	4.6
Distribution	—	1	—	1
General Management	1.5	—	—	1.5
Administration	—	3	7	10
Total	4	82	31	117

Shift Working Shift working is operated in certain departments.

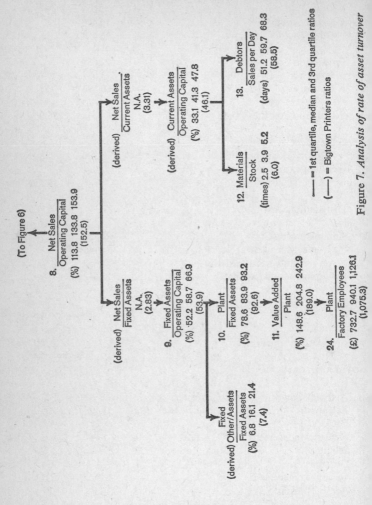

Figure 7. Analysis of rate of asset turnover

—— = 1st quartile, median and 3rd quartile ratios

( ) = Bigtown Printers ratios

(To Figure 6)

8. Net Sales / Operating Capital (%) 113.8 133.8 153.9 (152.5)

(derived) Net Sales / Fixed Assets N.A. (2.83)

(derived) Net Sales / Current Assets N.A. (3.31)

9. Fixed Assets / Operating Capital (%) 52.2 58.7 66.9 (53.9)

(derived) Current Assets / Operating Capital (%) 33.1 41.3 47.8 (46.1)

(derived) Fixed Other/Assets Fixed Assets (%) 6.8 16.1 21.4 (7.4)

10. Plant / Fixed Assets (%) 78.6 83.9 93.2 (92.6)

12. Materials Stock (times) 2.5 3.9 5.2 (6.0)

13. Debtors / Sales per Day (days) 51.2 59.7 68.3 (58.5)

11. Value Added / Plant (%) 148.6 204.8 242.9 (189.0)

24. Plant / Factory Employees (£) 732.7 940.1 1,126.1 (1,075.3)

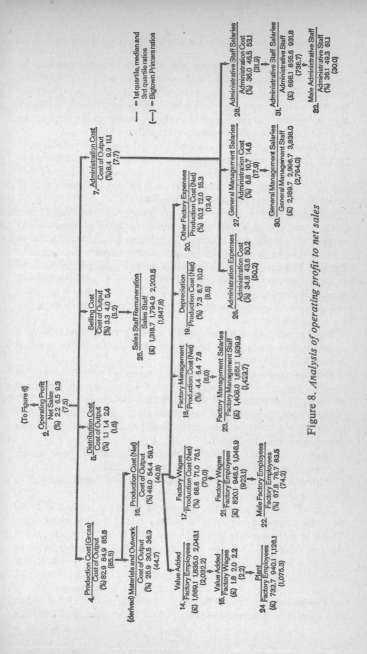

Figure 8. *Analysis of operating profit to net sales*

Ratio 3 shows the relationship between *value of output and value of sales* and indicates whether your work-in-progress has increased or decreased during the year. In your case value of output is higher than net sales and indicates that your work-in-progress increased considerably during the year, and more than three quarters of the firms in the comparison. This may be because you are shift working.

3. *Operating profit to net sales* (ratio 2) compares unfavourably with that of the third quartile firm because your *production cost (gross) to cost of output* (ratio 4) and *selling cost to cost of output* (ratio 6) are comparatively high. Your *distribution cost to cost of output* (ratio 5) is also slightly higher than that of the median firm.

4. *Production Costs* (ratios 4 and 16). Your *production costs (gross)* (ratio 4) are comparatively high because your ratio of *materials and outwork to cost of output* is considerably higher than that of the other firms in the comparison (44.7 per cent compared with third quartile figure of 36.9 per cent). This ratio is deduced by comparing the ratio of *production cost (gross) to cost of output* (ratio 4) with the ratio of *production cost (net) to cost of output* (ratio 16). Your ratio of *materials and outwork to cost of output* may be high for one or more of the following reasons:

You are printing a higher quality of work for different types of customer than many of the participants, but this should be reflected in your selling prices.

You put more work out than other firms in the comparison, either because you sub-contract specialist work or because you have not adequate capacity to cope with all the orders you receive.

Many of the firms in the comparison are larger than you and may benefit from quantity discounts on larger orders (the average number of employees per firm is 163).

Some of the participants may be members of integrated paper groups and can purchase their raw materials at a lower price.

Without a detailed knowledge of your firm's operations it is difficult to be precise on this point.

You will see that your ratio of *production cost (net) to cost of output* (ratio 16) compares extremely favourably with that of the other firms. This is in part caused by your high raw material and outwork costs in the cost of output, but also because your ratios of *factory wages to production costs (net)* (ratio 17) and *depreciation to production costs (net)* (ratio 19) compare favourably with that of the lowest-cost firms, i.e. the first quartile firms. On the other hand, your ratios of *factory management salaries to production costs (net)* (ratio 18) and *other factory expenses to production cost (net)* (ratio 20) are comparatively high.

Your ratio 17, *factory wages to production cost* (*net*), compares favourably because your *factory wages per employee* (ratio 21) is below that of the median firm. This is because you have a lower proportion of *male employees* (ratio 22) than the median firm. The *productivity* of your employees is also high. This conclusion is indicated by the fact that *your value added per factory employee* (ratio 14) and *value added per £ of factory wages* (ratio 15) compare favourably with the third quartile firms' ratios. One reason for your high level of employee productivity is that you are more capital-intensive than many of your competitors. You have more or newer *plant per factory employee* (ratio 24) despite the fact that you are on shift working. This conclusion is supported by your high ratio of *plant to fixed assets* (ratio 10).

Your ratio 18, *factory management to production cost* (*net*), is high despite the fact that your *average factory management salary* (ratio 23) is well below that of the median firm. This could indicate that you have more factory management staff than your competitors but that tehy are lower paid. You may require more detailed supervision for your quality of work, or it may be that you could increase your number of factory employees to that of the average firm without increasing your factory management staff. A high factory management cost is not, of course, necessarily a bad thing. It may well be that your factory wages are lower and value added per employee higher than most firms because you have a higher factory management cost. This may well be why your ratio 20, *other factory expenses to production cost* (*net*), is high. On the other hand, with shift working, you would expect your fixed management salaries and factory expenses to be spread over a greater volume of output.

5. *Other Costs*. Your ratio 6, *selling cost to cost of output*, is comparatively high. One reason for this is that your *sales staff remuneration* (ratio 25) is above that of the median firm. This is maybe necessary in marketing your type of printing, or you may be more market orientated than many of your competitors. However, this ratio may be high because of the way you have allocated directors' salaries; factory management salaries may be low for the same reason. I shall return to this point.

Your ratio 7, *administration cost to cost of output*, is below that of the first quartile firm. This ratio may be distorted by your high raw material content in *production cost* (*gross*) *to cost of output* (ratio 4). Your administrative costs would appear to be lower than average because your administrative staff salaries are lower than those of the median firm. This is reflected in your ratio of *administrative staff salaries to administration cost* (ratio 28), which is below that of the first quartile firm. Your *average administrative staff salary* (ratio 31) is well below that of the median firm. This is probably because you employ a lower proportion of *male administrative staff* (ratio 32) than most of the firms.

On the other hand, your ratio of *general management salaries to administrative cost* (ratio 27) is well above that of the third quartile firm. This is despite the fact that your *average general management salary* (ratio 30) is below that of the median firm, which indicates that you have more general management staff but that they are lower paid. However, this ratio is dependent on how you apportion your directors' salaries. Clearly the various management salary ratios cannot be considered in isolation. The various wage and salary ratios can be summarized as follows:

Type of wage or salary cost	Cost ratio	Average per employee	Proportion of males
Factory wages	Below median	Below median	Below median
Factory management	Above 3rd quartile	Near 1st quartile	—
Sales staff	—	Above median	—
Administration staff	Below 1st quartile	Near 1st quartile	Near 1st quartile
General management	Above 3rd quartile	Below median	—

It would appear from this summary that your total wage and salary costs compare favourably with other participating firms. You employ fewer male staff, you have a higher proportion of managerial staff, but you probably pay lower salaries.

6. *Turnover of operating capital* (ratio 8). Turning to the other side of the pyramid, you will see that your *rate of asset turnover* compares favourably with most of the participating firms, and is close to that of the third quartile firm. Your favourable rate of asset turnover will in part have resulted from the fact that you are on shift working. However, the analysis of this ratio does indicate some interesting points.

a) Despite the fact that you appear to be more capital–intensive than most of the other firms in the comparison, i.e. your ratio of *plant to factory employees* (ratio 24) is above average, your ratio of *fixed assets to operating capital* (ratio 9) is comparatively low. This indicates that your ratio of *current assets to operating capital* (derived) is comparatively high.

Your current assets are a high proportion of operating capital despite the fact that you *turnover stocks* (ratio 12) six times per year while the median firm turns stocks over only 3.9 times a year. Similarly, your *days' sales outstanding as debtors* (ratio 13) compares favourably with other participants. If the debtors and stock ratios compare favourably, why are the current assets high? It may well be that because you produce a higher quality product more working capital is required to support sales. You carry higher quality paper stocks rather than a higher quantity of stocks. The value of your production is higher and therefore debtors are higher. This conclusion is supported by your high added value per employee and material cost ratios. On the other hand it may be that your work-in-progress is high. It increased from £23,343 to £41,069 during the year. With shift working you would expect your work-in-progress to be higher than for firms who are not on shift working. Your high proportion of current assets may result in part from shift working, but you may have too high a level of partly finished work in your factory.

b) Returning to fixed assets you will see that you have a high ratio of *plant to fixed assets* (ratio 10) and more *plant per factory employee* (ratio 24) than most firms. However, your ratio of *value added to plant* (ratio 11) is below that of the median firm. This is despite the fact that you are on shift working, and this low ratio may indicate that you are not utilizing your plant capacity as effectively as other firms in the comparison. On the other hand it may simply result from the method of estimating current value of plant.

CONCLUSION

Your performance compares favourably with that of other participants in the comparison, and, therefore, you will not derive as much value from the comparison as a low performance firm. However, some further thought should be given to the following points:

Why are your raw material and outwork costs high?

Why are your current assets so high a proportion of operating capital? Is your work-in-progress too high?

Why is your value added per £ of plant below median? Are you underutilizing your capacity?

An interesting comparison may be made between your 1963 and 1964 ratios to find out why your performance improved. Was the improvement simply due to shift working?

University of Bigtown Bernard Knowall
March 1965

CHAPTER 5

Long-range Financial Planning

LONG-RANGE and short-term planning of all aspects of a business should be an integral part of the management of any business. There is nothing new in planning. The element of planning as a feature of the management process is almost always present. It has long been recognized that planning is the basis for control. Formalized long-range planning is relatively new. How is long-range planning distinguished from other forms of planning? Long-range planning has been defined as a systematic and formalized process for purposefully directing and controlling future operations towards desired objectives for periods extending beyond one year.[1] Long-range planning covers a time period which is long enough to provide management with an opportunity to anticipate future problems, and thus to have greater freedom of action to resolve them in an orderly manner. Management can establish its long-range objectives and then decide its strategy for achieving its objectives. This type of long-range planning has become known as *strategic planning*. Management has to translate the agreed strategy into detailed operational programmes for achieving the specified results. This type of planning is called *operations planning*. Long-range planning is essentially a formalized programme of inter-related actions to achieve desired results. It therefore rests upon the implicit assumption that some planning is better than no planning at all, and that the imposition of a predetermined programme of action upon the future development of the business will favourably influence the outcome of future operations. *Short-term planning*, on the other hand, must accept the environment of today, and the physical, human, and financial resources at present available to the firm. These are to a considerable extent determined by the quality of the firm's long-range planning efforts.

1. John D. Simmons, *Long Range Profit Planning*, Research Report No. 42, National Association of Accountants, New York, 1964, p. 4.

Since *financial planning* is an integral part of the long-range planning process, before an examination of financial planning can be made the long-range planning process must be briefly considered. Because of the increasing interest in strategic planning, discussion is concentrated on this topic rather than on detailed operations planning. The upsurge of interest in strategic planning stems primarily from the radical transformation in business environment that has taken place in recent years. The accelerating pace of technological change, changing end-use markets, intensified domestic and international competition allied to change in competitive structures, the growing scale and complexity of business, the need for longer lead times, the changing nature of labour cost from variable to fixed (considered in Chapter 10), and the shortage of skilled personnel: all these factors have materially changed the business environment. While the rate of change has accelerated, operations have become less flexible, and this calls for the introduction or improvement of long-range planning.

STRATEGIC PLANNING: DETERMINING THE LONG-RANGE OBJECTIVES AND STRATEGY

Long-range planning presupposes *objectives*. It commences with the specification of objectives towards which future operations should be directed. These long-range objectives will usually be formulated within the framework of a basic company philosophy or broad strategic goals, and are established to specify the results desired during the planning period. The company can then consider the strategic moves required if it is to achieve the desired objectives in the next five or ten years.

The basic company philosophy may be formulated in terms similar to those of Hewlett Packard[2]:

1. To recognize that *profit* is the best single measure of our contribution to society, and the ultimate source of corporate strength. We should attempt to achieve the maximum possible profit consistent with our other objectives.

2. Extracted from David Packard, *Statement of Corporate Objectives*, Hewlett Packard, 1 January 1966 (author's italics).

2. To strive for continued improvement in the quality, usefulness and value of the products and services we offer our *customers*.

3. To concentrate our efforts in the *field of instrumentation*, continually seeking new opportunities for growth but limiting our involvement to areas in which we have capability and can make a contribution.

4. To emphasize *growth* as a measure of strength and a requirement for survival.

5. To provide employment opportunities for *hp people* that include the opportunity to share in the company's success which they help make possible. To provide for them job security based on their performance, and to provide the opportunity for personal satisfaction that comes from a sense of accomplishment in their work.

6. To maintain an *organizational environment* which fosters individual motivation, initiative and creativity, and a wide latitude of freedom in working toward established objectives and goals.

7. To meet the obligations of good *citizenship* by making contributions to the community and to the institutions in our society which generate the environment in which we operate.

Objectives answer a number of fundamental questions about the company's future growth and development. For example:

1. What is the economic mission of the company?
   What kind of business should the company be in?
   What goods and services should be sold?
   What markets should be served?
   What share of the market is desired?

2. What rate of growth is required in sales, profit, assets, and value of equity shareholders' investment?

3. What are the profit objectives? (Considered in Chapter 4.) The establishment of these and other broad direction, growth, and profit objectives leads in turn to the establishment of a strategy to achieve these objectives. It will be appreciated that to some extent strategy flows from primary objectives, and also gives rise to subsidiary objectives.

However astutely management changes its strategy there is usually an inevitable fall-off in the rate of growth of existing business, with the result that a company must enter new fields if it is to achieve its growth and profitability objectives. In other words, if a business concentrates entirely upon its present products and markets, the company's rate of growth will eventually decline and possibly fall away completely. In order to achieve the desired rate of growth the company must change its product-market scope. It may:

1. Sell existing products in *new* markets (market development).

2. Develop *new* products for sale in existing markets (product development).

3. Develop *new* products for sale in *new* markets (diversification). The ability of management to recognize the need to change the product-market scope is vital. In an age of rapid technological change, it is the early recognition of the need to enter new fields that is critical, and this is one reason why companies introduce long-range planning.

Not only must companies recognize the predictable fall-off in the growth rate of their existing business and the need to enter new fields as the expansion of existing business slackens; they must be able to select these new fields correctly. In order to do this they must be able to evaluate correctly two questions:

1. How attractive are the economic characteristics and vitality of the particular field as compared to the existing business in which the company is engaged, especially in regard to the prospects for growth, stability, return on capital employed, degree of risk, and size and duration of financial commitment?

2. What marketing, manufacturing, technical, and/or financial know-how could existing management contribute to the new business?

An analysis of *corporate strengths and weaknesses* must be made before the second question can be correctly evaluated. The management must decide what resources and skills are required in each alternative new field, and which ones the company currently possesses. In other words, the management must, like the military commander, relate its strategy to its resources. It must answer the questions:

1. What are our critical resources?

2. Is the proposed strategy appropriate for available resources? Resources are those things that a company *is* or *has* and that help it to achieve its corporate objectives. The essential strategic attribute of resources is that they represent action potential.

Taken together, a company's resources represent its capacity to respond to threats and opportunities that may be perceived in the environment.

It is argued, therefore, that if companies are to maintain a satisfactory rate of growth they must select new fields of activity, which necessitates a creative search for investment opportunities. In order to select these new fields of activity, they must be aware of their own strengths and weaknesses. They must know their critical resources. Therefore, an analysis of corporate strengths and weaknesses is an essential step in long-range planning. It is necessary to develop a *capability profile*. A firm's capability profile is a statement in quantitative and qualitative terms of its resources; factors to be considered include physical facilities, organization, managerial and technical competence, human resources, financial resources, company reputation, and access to markets. An evaluation is also needed of the products and/or services offered by the company. The capability profile developed can be used:

1. To evaluate any internal strengths and weaknesses within the firm;

2. To derive characteristics which the firm can use in its search for opportunities; and

3. To measure the performance potential between the firm and a possible new field of activity.

INTERNAL APPRAISAL

The capability profile can be used to evaluate any internal strengths and weaknesses of the firm. One of the early stages of strategy formulation will be to assess the firm's capability to meet its objectives without any change in its existing strategy. In order to make this assessment a *competitive profile* can be constructed which presents the capability pattern of the most successful competitors in the industry. By comparing the firm's capability profile with the competitive profile it will be possible to determine the areas in which the firm is either outstanding or deficient. These are the strengths and weaknesses relative to the firm's present product-market posture. In the internal appraisal the firm's present products and/or services should be compared with competitors to determine product strengths and weaknesses.

EXTERNAL APPRAISAL

At a later stage of strategy formulation, after the internal appraisal has been made, a broad range of possible fields of activity should be considered, i.e. possible changes in the product-market scope will be examined. A part of the evaluation of the possible fields of activity will be concerned with determining the inherent potential. The *inherent potential* defines the extent to which a field of activity offers the possibility of achievement in critical performance areas, for example (a) growth – both rate of growth and outlook for continuance of growth; (b) flexibility in relation to the uncertainties of technological change; (c) stability in resisting major decline in economic conditions; and (d) return on capital employed. The performance of leading firms offers some indication of the potential inherent in the field.

A company must have performance potential to take advantage of the inherent potential. A second part of the evaluation measures the *performance potential* between the firm and the possible new field of activity. This requires a *normative capability profile* for each possible field of activity, i.e. a composite statement in quantitative and qualitative terms of what it takes to be successful in a particular field. A study of the capabilities and resources of strength of the leading firms in each field can provide a starting point in estimating requirements for success. Relating the firm's capability profile to the normative capability profile for each field of activity will serve to develop a *comparative profile*, which indicates how well the firm's capabilities match the requirements for success in each field. The firm's *performance potential* in each field may then be derived by matching the comparative capability profiles with the inherent potential in each field with respect to growth, flexibility, stability, and return on capital employed. The external appraisal procedure is summarized in Figure 9. Once the firm has decided which fields have the highest *performance potential*, the form of entry into the new field can be considered.

The strategic planning stage of long-range planning, when objectives are established and strategies determined, is similar to strategic military planning. The military commander has his objectives and he has his resources, men and equipment. He must

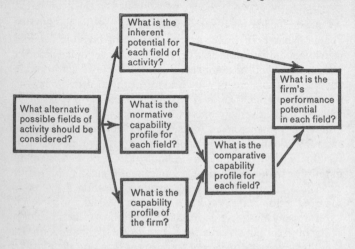

Figure 9. *External appraisal procedure*

decide the best strategy to achieve his objectives with the minimum loss of the resources he has available. Strategic planning, like strategic military planning, is followed by detailed operations planning. *Operations planning* comprises the supporting programmes of events and activities required for meeting the planned objectives and implementing the strategy. These detailed operations must be formulated in financial terms and translated into an overall financial plan. Since plans for developing new products, markets, production facilities, etc. will all require finance, there must be planning to determine where the necessary finance is to come from. Management also needs to know whether the plans will achieve the desired profit and growth objectives. The plans must therefore be translated into long-range profit and balance sheet forecasts.

FINANCIAL PLANNING

Financial planning is an integral part of the long-range planning process. Not only do plans have to be translated into financial terms; objectives have to be formulated in financial terms, historical financial information has to be provided, and alternatives have to be evaluated. In fact, the management accountant has a central role to play in the long-range planning process. His role has been defined by the National Association of Accountants of the United States in the following terms[3]:

1. Providing background information which serves as a prelude to planning. The accountant can make a valuable contribution in this area of planning by preparing studies covering past performance, product mix, physical facilities, and capital expenditures; and by analysing cost–volume–profit relationships (considered in Chapter 8), profit margins by product line, cash flows, etc.

2. Assisting management in the evaluation of alternatives and assessing the financial feasibility of proposed courses of action. Relevant data must be analysed and expressed in financial terms, and must constitute a reliable basis for guiding management decisions.

3. Assembling, integrating and coordinating detailed plans into a company-wide master plan.

4. Translating plans into overall schedules of cost, profit, and financial condition. These schedules subsequently become the basis for preparing the operating budgets (considered in Chapter 7).

5. Presenting anticipated results of plans for future operations in financial terms.

6. Assisting management in the review, critical appraisal, and revision of plans to ensure that they constitute a realistic basis for directing and controlling future operations.

7. Establishing and administering operational controls to help in attaining planned objectives. This vital phase of the planning process requires the integration of long- and short-range profit

3. John D. Simmons, *Long Range Profit Planning*. Research Report No. 42, National Association of Accountants, New York, 1964, pp. 44–5.

plans and involves the monitoring of performance against the long-range plans, and the preparation of reports to management.

Space does not permit a detailed examination and explanation of each of the above activities of the management accountant. The importance of financial information to the planning process, and the types of financial information presented in the plans, will be illustrated in the form of a memorandum to companies which are members of a group. The memorandum concerns the presentation of long-range plans to the group head office. In reading the memorandum it should be borne in mind that the ranking in importance of factors influencing the long-range plans may differ widely according to the nature of each company. It must be recognized that:

1. The planning system has to be tailored to the needs of the group and the individual companies in the group. These needs, in turn, should be derived from the opportunities, threats, and problems faced both by individual companies and the group as a whole.

2. Problems, threats, and opportunities differ from firm to firm depending on its industry, size, stage of growth, management, state of technology, etc. Therefore, each company will require a distinctive and different planning system.

3. On the other hand, there are enough similarities among companies within a group to make it possible to suggest a standard form of presentation which can be adapted to meet the requirements of individual situations.

Thus, the relative importance of different factors will be reflected in the plans produced, but they should adhere to the standard layout as far as possible. While the memorandum illustrates the importance of financial information in the planning process, it must be emphasized that planning is not simply an accounting exercise.

To: Managing Directors all Group Companies
From: Group Planning Department

LONG-RANGE PLANS

Submission

1. The Group Board of Directors will consider the Long-range Plans of companies annually in October. Plans should be submitted to Group Head Office not later than 30 September.

Period Covered

2. The Plan will normally forecast five years ahead. Because of the phasing of major developments or for other reasons, it may be appropriate for the future period covered in the Plan to be extended beyond five years.

3. Certain statistics to be provided in the Plan will require previous years' figures and, including forecasts, a total span of ten years is normally requested.

Form of Presentation

4. The Plan should be prefaced by a contents sheet and will usually comprise the following sections:

Introduction
Environmental Forecast
Objectives and Strategy
Summary
Product Division Plans (a section for each division)
General Services
Financial Implications
Appendices

Supplementary Information

5. Certain additional information is required to enable the derivation of figures in the Plan to be followed in detail. This will be required for Head Office use and will not normally be submitted to the Board of Directors.

Introduction

6. The introduction should briefly describe the recent history of the company, indicate the size and location of its main productive units, and define the purpose and scope of its business. In subsequent years the introduction should provide a link with the previous year's plan by comparing key figures and referring briefly to major developments

which have taken place in the interim. Comparison with the previous year's plan and reference to major developments should at this stage be confined to introductory remarks. Developments during the preceding year and such detailed comparisons with previous year's plans as are useful should be dealt with in the appropriate later section of the Plan.

Environmental Forecast

7. Companies should make an appraisal of the economic influences which affect their activities, including a forecast of the expected economic and socio-political environment during the next five years. Opportunities and competitive threats should be identified. It would be useful in dealing with the economic influences to make reference to statistics or projections issued by the government or other outside bodies covering the particular business activity. This should not imply that the companies' assessments need to be in conformity with the view of any outside body, but it would be helpful to establish some relationship between them.

Objectives and Strategy

8. The principal corporate goal of the Group is to earn an optimum return on capital employed. Companies should formulate objectives in terms of:

a) *Existing Business* – expected increased market penetration with existing product lines in existing markets.

b) *New Business* – general areas which the company expects to enter over the next five years and methods of accomplishing entry, distinguishing between market development, product development, and diversification.

c) *Return on Net Assets Employed* – expected return during the next five years.

d) *Growth* – expected company growth of turnover and net assets employed during next five years.

9. Strategies to be followed in accomplishing the objectives should be discussed in broad terms. An analysis of company strengths and weaknesses should be included, and the proposed strategy related to the analysis.

Summary

10. A table summarizing actual and forecast results for the company should be completed for the ten-year period and included in the narrative as follows:

Turnover, Assets Employed and Profits

Year	Turnover	Net Assets Employed in Business	Surplus on Trading	% Surplus to Turnover	Rate of Asset Turnover	% Surplus to Net Assets Employed
Actual	£	£	£	%	Times	%
19..						
19..						
19..						
19..						
19..						
Forecast						
19..						
19..						
19..						
19..						
19..						

Forecast Growth in Turnover 19.. to 19.. % per annum
Forecast Growth in Capital Employed 19.. to 19.. % per annum

11. A table summarizing actual and forecast capital expenditure and working capital requirements for the company should be completed for the ten-year period, and included in the narrative as follows:

Capital Expenditure and Working Capital

	Capital Expenditure			Working Capital		
Year	Total	Already Authorized	Not Yet Authorized	Total	Stocks	Debtors less Creditors

12. The table of Turnover, Assets Employed and Profits, and that summarizing Capital Expenditure and Working Capital should show total figures which will be supported by similar figures in tables for each of the main product divisions of the company appearing in the Plan. Observations on the summary tables should be made regarding trends and exceptional items which affect the company as a whole. Comparison between forecast profitability and growth and company objectives should be made. Limits of accuracy in the forecasts should be clearly indicated. Where necessary, brief references should also be made to trends and exceptional items within product divisions which will receive more detailed examination in the appropriate section.

Product Division Plans

13. A Plan for each product division should be produced which

141

should follow a similar sequence to the preceding introduction and summary for the company as a whole. It should commence with brief general and historical information, followed by a statement of the objectives and strategy for the product division, to provide a background leading to tables of actual and forecast figures for the ten-year period in identical form to the earlier summary tables, viz. turnover, assets employed and profits, and capital expenditure and working capital with limits of accuracy.

14. Explanations should be given of any trends or exceptional items apparent from the tables either at this point or in a later section where appropriate. Major capital expenditure schemes (approximately £200,000 or more) should be briefly described, with, if possible, an estimate of D. C. F. rate of return expected from the scheme.[4] The effect of capital expenditure schemes on net assets employed, their subsequent effect on profits and the interplay of these two factors on the return on net assets employed should be commented upon.

15. The factors influencing the plans of the product division should be discussed and sections dealing with the following matters should normally be provided.

a) MARKETS. Details should be given of market size, market growth rate, the division's share of the market, competitors and their share of the market, and market influences on prices and profit margins. Past, present and forecast future levels should be indicated, trends noted, and the expected impact of company strategy commented on. The level of inter-company sales should be stated and mention of special customers should be made. An account could also be given of any special feature of market research undertaken. Exports and the problems of exporting should be considered with particular mention of export markets, price policy and credit extended.

b) PRODUCT DEVELOPMENTS. For certain divisions the products and the product strategy may have been sufficiently described in the introduction of the Product Division Plan. More complex product groupings may need to be analysed to indicate their composition. Changes in the range of products, the introduction of new products, and improvements and withdrawals from the existing product range should be indicated and evaluated in terms of effect on turnover, profit levels, and return on net assets employed.

c) PRODUCTION FACILITIES. The nature, location, area in square feet, capacity in weight or units, utilization and shift working arrange-

4. Capital investment appraisal, including Discounted Cash Flow (D.C.F.) techniques, is considered in Chapter 6.

ment of production facilities, with mention of recent changes and contemplated changes to meet planned production requirements, should be included. The link between capacity usage and sales achievement, and between forecast sales and planned productive capacity should be made apparent. The extent to which productive equipment is obtained from Group sources should be mentioned.

d) TECHNICAL IMPROVEMENTS. Recent and likely future technological developments and technical improvements should be discussed with mention where appropriate of research and development, method study, operational research, etc.

e) PERSONNEL. The numbers of skilled and unskilled labour, managerial and clerical staff at present employed in the division, and planned future requirements should be stated. Any problems of labour supply existing or foreseen should be indicated. Management performance and development and relations with the labour force should also be considered.

f) MATERIALS. Where significant, the types, qualities, annual consumption and sources of materials should be stated and problems discussed, e.g. licensing and import controls. Purchases from Group suppliers in quantity and quality should be mentioned.

g) WORKING CAPITAL. The levels of stocks and net debtors should be examined with particular reference to their effect on net assets employed. Past and future trends should be commented upon where appropriate.

General Services

16. The extent to which general services such as toolroom, welfare facilities, etc. and administrative departments can be treated as part of product divisions will vary with circumstances. In certain cases it may be necessary to deal with them in a separate section. If so, a table of capital expenditure in identical form to that used for product divisions should be provided and the value of assets employed should normally be apportioned to the product divisions concerned, so that the figures shown of total net assets employed in the company will represent the sum of those of the product divisions.

Details of Capital Expenditure

17. Totals of capital expenditure for the company as a whole and for each product division will appear in the narrative of the plan. Appendices will be required to show analysis of these totals and it is possible that an appendix for each product division will be necessary in addition to an appendix summarizing expenditures for the company.

18. Forecast expenditure yet to be authorized should be analysed in a

suitable manner so that projects can be identified from an appendix to the narrative. The analysis should distinguish between projects for:

a) replacement, cost reduction and improving productivity;

b) expansion of business; and

c) facilities not directly profit-earning such as canteens.

Financial Implications

19. The financial implications of the Plan will need to be summarized so that the proposed disposition of funds in capital expenditure, additional working capital, taxation and dividend payments, etc. can be examined and set against the expected sources of funds. A standard layout of financial forecast in the form of a funds flow statement is shown as Pro forma A. After arriving at the excess or deficiency of funds internally generated and retained over requirements, provision is made for any expected additional sources of finance to be detailed to determine the variation in liquid resources and cumulative surplus or deficiency at the end of each year.

20. A narrative section is required in which the financial implications of the financial forecast should be discussed and related to the current financial structure of the company. Where appropriate present and future facilities available from banks and financial institutions should be stated. When additional long-term finance from Group sources is considered necessary this should be indicated.

21. A further standard form to be provided is Pro forma B, a forecast profits statement. This form provides a link between the trading surplus shown in the narrative of the Plan and the cash movements in the financial forecast.

22. Pro forma C, Forecast Trading Account, and Pro forma D, Forecast Balance Sheet, should be completed for each forecast year commencing with the current year. These statements serve the dual purpose of working papers and the provision of supplementary information. The marginal costing form of presentation[5] has been used in Pro forma C to enable variable expenses and fixed expenses to be forecast separately. The statements should not form part of the completed Plan and they will not be submitted to the Board of Directors. They should be submitted to the Group Planning Department to enable the Plan to be followed in detail and so that additional financial information is available to evaluate any proposal made, such as the provision of additional finance.

23. It is appreciated that in arriving at both surplus on trading and net assets employed for product divisions there may be difficulties

5. Marginal costing and the marginal costing form of presentation are considered in Chapter 8.

encountered where apportionments are required. These should be carried out on as realistic a basis as possible.[6]

24. The standard forms should be adhered to as far as possible as this will greatly reduce the number of queries likely to arise. Members of the Group Planning Department will be available to advise companies on all aspects of long-range planning.

A. Fortune-Teller

Head of Group Planning Department

Pro forma A

LONG-RANGE PLAN

Financial Forecast, 19.. to 19..

	19.. (Current year)	19..	19..	19..	19..	19..

Sources of funds
  Profit before taxation
  Depreciation
  Investment grants

—	—	—	—	—	—
—	—	—	—	—	—

Disposition of funds
  Capital expenditure
    already authorized
    not yet authorized
  Increase or decrease in stocks
  Increase or decrease in net
    debtors
  Taxation paid
  Dividend paid

—	—	—	—	—	—
—	—	—	—	—	—

6. The problems associated with apportioning costs and assets to product groups have been considered in Chapter 4 and are further examined in Chapter 8.

Pro forma A – *cont*.

Excess or deficiency of funds
  generated and retained over
  requirements

Other funds:

— — — — — —

Variation in liquid resources
Surplus or deficiency at
  commencement of period

— — — — — —

*Surplus or deficiency at
  end of period*

═ ═ ═ ═ ═ ═

Pro forma B

LONG-RANGE PLAN

Forecast of Profits, 19.. to 19..

	19.. (Current year)	19..	19..	19..	19..	19..
Surplus on trading after depreciation						
Bank overdraft interest						
Loan interest						
	—	—	—	—	—	—
Profit before Taxation						
Taxation provision						
Taxation equalization						
Exceptional income or changes						
	—	—	—	—	—	—
Available surplus						
	═	═	═	═	═	═
Dividends						
General reserve						
	—	—	—	—	—	—
	═	═	═	═	═	═

Pro forma C

LONG-RANGE PLAN

Forecast Trading Account, 19..

Product Division	Turn-over	Variable Cost of Sales	Separable Fixed Costs	Direct Product Profits	Apportioned Common Fixed Costs	Surplus on Trading
Total						

Pro forma D

LONG-RANGE PLAN
Forecast Balance Sheet, 19...

	Total	Product Division	Product Division	Product Division, etc.
Fixed Assets				
Cost				
Less Depreciation				
Written Down Value				
Current Assets				
Stocks				
Debtors				
Cash and Bank Balances				
Current Liabilities				
Creditors				
Current Taxation				
Dividend				
Net Current Assets				
Net Assets Employed in Business				
Investments				
Net Assets Employed				

Derived from:
Issued Share Capital
Capital Reserves
Revenue Reserves

Pro forma D – *cont.*

Debenture and Fixed Loans
Deferred Liabilities
Group Loan Account
Bank Overdraft

—————

═════

It will be appreciated that the financial evaluation of long-range plans involves the management accountant in some complex calculations. The financial evaluation of plans is extremely difficult. The plans are prepared against a background of economic uncertainty, and technological unknowns obscure the horizon. Yet, if management is to undertake long-range planning, financial estimates of profitability must be attached to proposals. Even when the profitability estimates are based on detailed economic forecasting, demand forecasting, and cost analysis, the resulting figures can only be regarded as broad estimates based upon many assumptions about the future environment. Many of these assumptions may be invalidated overnight. Yet, despite the apparent lack of certainty in the estimates, decisions are based on them, individuals and boards of directors are committed to courses of action, and reputations are at stake. The danger is that the company will become too rigid in its approach to the future and inflexible in its attitude to alternative developments. Sticking to the plan can become as meaningless as complying with obsolete rules or reading the news in last week's newspapers. If, in fact, the plans are incorrectly evaluated and the company does make a bad decision, the management may reject all forms of long-range planning and simply 'fly off the seat of its pants'. The management accountant must clearly indicate the limits of accuracy to be attached to the financial forecasts. Some form of decision theory or sensitivity analysis should be employed so that the management can exercise the right degree of caution and provide for flexibility. The plan must be used as a signpost not a straitjacket. Long-range planning must be dynamic not static; it must be flexible not inflexible. The plans require updating:

1. Whenever an event of significant impact takes place to necessitate a change in the company's strategy. The merger of two

major competitors, such as that of British Motor Holdings and Leyland, or a technological breakthrough by a competitor cannot be ignored. The takeover of Associated Electrical Industries Ltd by General Electric Company Ltd in November 1967 probably forced other electrical companies in Britain, and possibly in the rest of the world, to reappraise their strategy. In August 1968, Plessey made a bid for English Electric, who in turn agreed in September 1968 to merge with General Electric.

2. Annually, to take account of the company's actual progress.

3. Every five years or so, to redefine the basic objectives and to revise the strategy.

It must be emphasized that planning is not simply a logical straightforward exercise. It is not easy; it is extremely difficult to quantify alternative strategies. Financial evaluation of long-range plans stretches the management accountant to the limits of his ability.

Within the framework of the financial plan, a *budgetary control* system should be operated to ensure that detailed plans are prepared for each year of the financial plan when it becomes current. A budget is a management tool for controlling operations within the scope of the long-range plan. Budgetary control is concerned with short-term planning and control, and is the subject of Chapter 7. A system of budgetary control should ensure that throughout the period covered by the financial plan there are regular accountability budgets prepared to achieve the targets that have been laid down in the plan, including sales volume, price levels, costs, profit, capital expenditure, return on capital employed and other ratios of efficiency. The budgetary control system will add flexibility to the financial plan by making any changes appropriate to new circumstances at the time the detailed one-year plans are prepared.

An important part of the long-range planning process is the preparation of the *capital expenditure forecast*. Normally, acceptance of the long-range plan by the board of directors does not imply approval of individual capital expenditure projects in the capital expenditure forecast. It merely implies approval in principle, and does *not* constitute authority to proceed on projects or to expend funds. Projects will eventually be included in the annual capital expenditure budget, probably in a modified form to their original proposal in the long-range plan. At this stage projects can be submitted in detail for approval by the board of directors. The merits of the various proposals can be appraised in detail in the light of the current economic environment and the state of technology. The appraisal of capital expenditure decisions is given detailed consideration in Chapter 6.

FINANCING THE PLAN

Once a plan has been prepared and approved by the board of directors, the financing of the proposed expansion can be considered. It has been illustrated in Pro forma A how a long-term financial forecast can be prepared. For a group of companies the financial forecasts of individual companies must be consolidated to determine the requirement, if any, of additional finance for the whole group. The consolidated financial forecast may indicate that there will be no deficiency of funds generated and retained over planned requirements. Some companies follow a deliberate policy of limiting growth to the extent that it can be financed from internally generated funds. Where there is a forecast deficiency of internally generated and retained funds, but it is not substantial and is expected to disappear in the later years of the plan, the deficiency may be covered by raising additional short-term finance in the form of a bank overdraft. Bank overdraft finance is not expensive. The interest payable on the outstanding balance is allowable as a charge against profits for taxation purposes. In appraising credit worthiness of companies, the banks are primarily concerned with the *current ratio* (the ratio of current assets to current liabilities) and the *acid test ratio* (the ratio of liquid assets to current liabilities). These ratios are considered later in this section. Where a substantial overdraft is required, the bank will also require a detailed cash forecast indicating the rate and period of repayment. Where a substantial cash deficiency is forecast the company will probably have to raise additional long-term finance. The basic choice is between *debt* finance and *equity* finance. Decisions regarding the raising of additional long-term finance are not usually the responsibility of the management accountant. They are made by the finance director after consultations with the company's financial advisers. However, the nature of the financing decision is briefly considered.

There appears to be a general reluctance by public quoted companies in Britain to obtain outside finance, especially debt finance. This aversion to external financing stems to some extent from the fear of restrictions imposed by debt finance, the historical difficulty and cost of obtaining outside funds, and the fact that outside finance represents in some circumstances a threat to the existing management control of the company. In the past, the picture has been one of external financial conservatism departed from only with reluctance. However, the aversion to outside finance, particularly debt finance, has been influenced by the Finance Act, 1965.

The Finance Act, 1965, separates corporate taxation from individual taxation. Whereas previously a company paid income tax and profits tax on its profits, it now pays corporation tax on its profits and income tax on dividends and similar distributions to shareholders. The effect of this change on the ordinary large quoted trading company is that a company distributing slightly less than 40 per cent of its pre-tax profits by way of dividend will pay precisely the same amount in tax under the new tax structure as under the old.

Old System	£	£	*New System*	£	£
Profits		100,000	Profit		100,000
Less Income Tax at 8/3d. in £	41,250		*Less* Corporation Tax at 40%		40,000
Profits Tax at 15%	15,000	56,250			60,000
		43,750	*Less* Net Dividend	23,144	
Less Dividend (net)		23,144	Income Tax on Dividend	16,250	
					39,394
Retained		£20,606	*Retained*		£20,606

With corporation tax at 40 per cent, if a company distributes a proportion of its pre-tax profits greater than 40 per cent it will have to pay *more* tax than previously; if less it will pay *less* tax. Even though in the illustration the company is paying the same amount in tax both before and after the Finance Act, 1965, the cover for the dividend has been reduced from 1.9 times (£43,750 ÷ £23,144) to 1.5 times (£60,000 ÷ £39,394). The Act encourages companies to retain earnings rather than distribute them in the form of dividends.

Under the Finance Act, 1965, debt interest payments continue to be chargeable against profits as a cost for tax purposes, i.e. debt interest payments reduce the amount of corporation tax payable. On the other hand, profits distributed as dividends are, in effect, taxed more heavily, and so the cost advantage of loan capital is increased under the corporation tax arrangements. It has always had the advantage of requiring a lower interest because it has a prior call on profits and assets. Debt capital is now even cheaper to service when compared with ordinary shares than before the introduction of corporation tax. The costs of alternative sources of capital are further considered in Chapter 6.

There was a sharp increase in debt capital raised during 1965, both in amount and as a proportion of all new issues of capital by companies during 1965. It will be seen from Table 5.1 that this high proportion of debt capital issues was maintained during 1966 and 1967. Many companies raised debt capital for the first time and others converted preference share capital into debt capital.

Since loan capital tends to be far cheaper than equity capital, it will be to the equity shareholders' benefit if the company finances part of its growth with fixed interest loan capital. It will be to the equity shareholders' benefit if the company obtains some *gearing* in its balance sheet. The term 'gearing' is used to define the proportions of debt and equity capital in the balance sheet. High gearing indicates a high ratio of debt to equity capital and low gearing the opposite. However, the principal sources of loan capital are the institutional lenders, such as banks, insurance companies, pension funds, etc. These institutional lenders' sources of income must be free of risk to either capital or income.

Table 5.1
Types of Company Security*

	DEBT				CAPITAL				TOTAL
	Convertible £m.	Other £m.	Total £m.	% of total	Preference £m.	% of total	Ordinary £m.	% of total	£m.
1951			49.1	37.8	19.7	15.1	61.1	47.1	129.9
1952			36.7	28.6	4.1	3.1	87.8	68.3	128.6
1953			53.1	50.4	7.9	7.5	44.3	42.1	105.4
1954			101.0	49.9	28.3	14.0	73.0	36.1	202.3
1955			65.1	27.2	18.9	7.9	154.9	64.9	238.9
1956			76.0	33.8	3.1	1.4	145.7	64.8	224.7
1957			183.3	54.0	1.7	0.5	155.2	45.5	340.2
1958			95.2	50.4	1.0	0.5	92.6	49.1	188.8
1959			119.5	29.6	10.7	2.6	274.0	67.8	404.2
1960			121.8	25.5	10.4	2.2	345.5	72.3	477.7
1961	28.1	120.0	148.1	26.5	2.8	0.5	408.9	73.0	559.8
1962	41.0	132.8	173.8	42.1	5.3	1.3	233.9	56.6	413.0
1963	35.3	236.2	271.5	60.3	14.7	3.3	163.9	36.4	450.1
1964	60.2	173.8	234.0	56.6	10.7	2.6	168.9	40.8	413.6
1965	28.1	426.5	454.6	90.3	3.2	0.6	45.5	9.0	503.4
1966	38.4	441.0	479.5	75.1	16.4	2.6	142.5	22.3	638.4
1967	29.7	313.8	343.5	81.5	5.7	1.4	72.6	17.2	421.9

*Excluding railway, gas and water undertakings before 1961. Source: *Midland Bank Review*, February 1968.

They also receive a low rate of fixed interest after tax and the impact of inflation. The standards of credit worthiness are usually expressed in the form of certain financial ratios which firms are required to attain. The principal financial ratios considered by the institutional lenders are:

1. Ratios of Times Covered.
2. Ratio of Current Assets to Current Liabilities – Current Ratio.
3. Ratio of Long-term Debt to Net Worth.
4. Net Tangible Assets Ratio.

1) Ratio of Times Covered

This ratio indicates the amount of income cover available to meet long-term interest charges, preference dividends, etc. The Finance Act, 1965, has made preference capital very expensive relative to debt capital, and, as Table 5.1 illustrates, preference capital is now of limited importance. The ratio is of gross income available to the suppliers of long-term capital (both debt and equity) to the interest charges on long-term debt. Gross income is defined as profit *after* allowing for interest due to the suppliers of short-term credit but *before* corporation tax. Loan interest is chargeable as a cost for tax purposes, and the ratio is therefore best calculated gross of Income Tax. For example, if gross income is £100,000 and debt interest £10,000 the ratio of times covered is ten.

2) Current Ratio

The ratio of current assets to current liabilities is an indication of the cover available to short-term lenders of finance such as banks providing overdraft facilities. A current ratio of 2:1 would generally be considered satisfactory and 1.5:1 would be the normal acceptable minimum. The more liquid the current assets the more acceptable is the ratio. The Acid Test Ratio or Liquid Ratio, the ratio of liquid assets to current liabilities, is also applied as a test of liquidity. A liquid assets ratio of 1:1 is considered satisfactory.

3) Ratio of Long-term Debt to Net Worth

This ratio provides an indication of the extent to which the assets of a company could fail to realize their book value in the event of liquidation, but still realize in aggregate sufficient to meet outstanding debt capital. The Net Worth is the equity and preference shareholders' investment in the firm at book value, i.e. the total shareholders' interest. In the following balance sheet the ratio is $\frac{1}{4}$.

	£		£
Ordinary Share Capital	100,000	Fixed Assets	200,000
Preference Share Capital	25,000		
Capital and Revenue		Current Assets	100,000
Reserves	75,000		
			300,000
Total Shareholders'		*Less* Current	
Interest	200,000	Liabilities	50,000
Debenture Capital	50,000		
	£250,000		£250,000

It will be appreciated that the resulting ratio is dependent on the valuation of fixed assets, a problem which has already been considered in Chapter 2. Companies sometimes revalue their fixed assets prior to raising debt capital in order to improve their ratio of long-term debt to net worth.

4) *Net Tangible Assets Ratio*

This ratio of debt to net tangible assets is also employed to provide some indication of the asset cover available to debenture holders. In the above balance sheet the ratio is $\frac{1}{5}$. The maximum ratio of long-term debt to net worth it is commonly thought practical for a normal manufacturing or distributing company to maintain is about $\frac{1}{3}$ to $\frac{1}{2}$. Where this ratio is $\frac{1}{3}$ the net tangible asset ratio will be $\frac{1}{4}$, because

$$\frac{\text{Debt}}{\text{Net Tangible Assets}} = \frac{\text{Net Worth Ratio}}{1 + \text{Net Worth Ratio}}$$

Taking the above example:

$$\frac{50,000}{250,000} = \frac{\frac{1}{4}}{1+\frac{1}{4}} = \frac{1}{5}$$

The institutional lenders will appraise a firm's credit worthiness by considering the above financial ratios, together with an evaluation of the firm's past profit record and future prospects. Provided the ratio of debt to net worth did not exceed 1:2 and the income cover exceeded five or six times, the institutional lenders would probably find the company an acceptable investment. This statement is subject to the overriding factor that there is no significant element of risk attached to the type of business in which the company is engaged. A. J. Merrett and Allen Sykes showed in a study prior to the Finance Act, 1965, that the net worth, net tangible asset, current, and times covered ratios for the majority of large companies were well within the limits suggested. The issues of debt capital since 1965 have confirmed this view. Merrett and Sykes also suggested that asset cover is the principal limitation on the amount of debt raised.[7] However, while the raising of debt capital will provide a company with finance on terms cheaper than those required by the equity shareholders, some companies are still reluctant to raise this form of capital and introduce an element of gearing into their balance sheets.

SUMMARY OF CHAPTER

Planning is not new. Formalized long-range planning is relatively new. The long-range planning process consists of deciding what is to be planned, preparing plans, assuring their acceptance and implementation, and monitoring the firm and its environment for new planning needs. Objectives are established. An appraisal of corporate strengths and weaknesses and a forecast of the future environment are undertaken. Corporate strategies are developed to achieve the objectives, taking account of the available resources and the external environment. Operations planning is concerned

7. A. J. Merrett and Allen Sykes, *The Finance and Analysis of Capital Projects*, Longmans, London, 1963.

with the preparation of the supporting programme of events and activities required for meeting planned objectives and implementing strategy. Financial planning is an integral part of the long-range planning process. Plans must be translated into long-range profit, balance sheet, and financial forecasts. Historical information on past performance is required, alternative strategies have to be appraised in financial terms, etc. The financial evaluation of plans is difficult. The limits of accuracy to be attached to the financial forecasts must be clearly indicated. The plan must be used as a signpost not a straitjacket. Long-range planning must be flexible not inflexible. A budgetary control system (the subject of Chapter 7) should be operated to ensure that detailed plans are prepared for each year of the financial plan as it becomes current. Budgetary control adds flexibility to the financial plan. Acceptance of the long-range plans does not usually imply authorization of individual capital expenditure projects. They will have to be submitted for approval by the board of directors after detailed appraisal (the subject of Chapter 6). Acceptance of long-range plans leads to consideration of the financing of the plan. Bank overdrafts can be raised if limited finance is required for short periods. If a substantial deficiency is forecast additional long-term finance will have to be raised. The basic choice is between debt and equity finance. Debt is cheaper, but limits are set on the amount that can be raised by the standards of credit worthiness imposed by the institutional lenders. Some companies are reluctant to raise debt finance; others limit growth so that it can be financed by retained earnings. There is an implicit assumption in this chapter that some planning is better than 'flying off the seat of your pants'.

SELECTED READINGS

1. H. Igor Ansoff, *Corporate Strategy*, McGraw-Hill, New York, 1965; Penguin, Harmondsworth, 1968.

2. Association of Certified and Corporate Accountants, *The Sources of Capital*, London, 1966.

3. James Bates, *The Financing of Small Business*, Sweet & Maxwell, London, 1966.

4. Norman Berg, 'Strategic Planning in Conglomerate Companies', *Harvard Business Review*, May–June 1965.

5. Melville C. Branch, *The Corporate Planning Process*, American Management Association, New York, 1962.

6. G. P. E. Clarkson and B. J. Elliot, *Managing Money and Finance*, Gower Press, London, 1969.

7. Ernest Dale, *Long Range Planning*, British Institute of Management, London, 1967.

8. David W. Ewing (ed.), *Long-Range Planning for Management*, Harper, New York, 1964.

9. Roger Falk and Ian Clark, 'Planning for Growth', *Management Today*, June 1966.

10. Frank F. Gilmore and Richard G. Brandenburg, 'Anatomy of Corporate Planning', *Harvard Business Review*, November–December 1962.

11. Myles L. Mace, 'The President and Corporate Planning', *Harvard Business Review*, January–February 1965.

12. A. J. Merrett and Allen Sykes, *The Finance and Analysis of Capital Projects*, Longmans, London, 1963.

13. F. W. Paish, *Business Finance*, Pitman, London, 1965.

14. Millard H. Pryor, Jr, 'Planning in a Worldwide Business', *Harvard Business Review*, January–February 1965.

15. George A. Steiner (ed.), *Managerial Long-Range Planning*, McGraw-Hill, New York, 1963.

16. George A. Steiner, 'Approaches to Long-Range Planning for Small Business', *California Management Review*, February 1967.

17. John D. Simmons, *Long Range Profit Planning*, Research Report No. 42, National Association of Accountants, New York, 1964.

18. John Sizer, 'Strategic Planning and the Management Accountant', *Management Accounting*, March 1969.

19. Seymour Tilles, 'How to Evaluate Corporate Strategy', *Harvard Business Review*, July–August 1963.

20. E. Kirby Warren, *Long Range Planning: the Executive Viewpoint*, Prentice-Hall, Englewood Cliffs, 1966.

CHAPTER 6

Capital Investment Appraisal

CAPITAL investment appraisal and, in particular, discounted cash flow techniques have received considerable attention during recent years. However, at the outset of any discussion of capital investment appraisal techniques, it should be recognized that appraisal forms only one part of the capital budgeting procedure. The component parts of capital budgeting have been summarized by a leading managerial economist[1] as follows:

1. A creative *search* for investment opportunities.

2. Long-range *plans* and projections for the company's future development.

3. A short-range *budget* of supply of funds and demanded capital.

4. A correct yardstick of *economic worth*.

5. Realistic *estimation* of the economic worth of individual projects.

6. *Standards* for screening investment proposals that are geared to the company's economic circumstances.

7. *Expenditure controls* of outlays for facilities by comparison of authorizations and expenditures.

8. Candid and economically realistic *post-completion audits* of project earnings.

9. Investment analysis of facilities that are candidates for *disposal*.

10. *Forms and procedures* to insure smooth working of the system.

The main concern of this chapter is the determination of a 'correct yardstick of economic worth', and the 'realistic estimation of the economic worth of individual projects'. Reference to the other components of capital budgeting will be made throughout the chapter, but these will not be considered in detail.

1. Joel Dean, 'Controls for Capital Expenditure', Financial Management Series No. 105, American Management Association, 1953.

NATURE OF INVESTMENT DECISION

The evaluation of capital investment decisions raises problems which are different from the measurement of past performance. In reviewing (in Chapter 4) the past performance of a business it was found necessary to record the amount of *net assets employed* and *profits before and after tax* (using accounting conventions which combine cash transactions, provisions for depreciation, accruals and prepayments) for what is in effect the sum total of a vast number of past investment decisions each in a different stage of its life. Various ratios of profit to net assets employed and subsidiary pyramid ratios were calculated, and used to judge the past performance of the business. Whilst these features do not invalidate the return on capital employed concept for measuring past performance, they ignore several considerations which need to be taken into account in assessing future investments.

The basic object of any investment is that in return for paying out a given amount of cash today, a larger amount will be received back over a period of time. This larger amount should not only repay the original outlay, but also provide a minimum annual rate of interest on the outlay. If an individual invests £100 in a building society, he expects to receive back at some later date £100 plus compound interest on the period of his investment. If he borrows £100 from his bank at 6 per cent per annum to invest in shares, he expects to receive back, during the period he owns the shares and on sale, £100 and compound interest in excess of 6 per cent per annum.

When considering an investment decision by a firm, it does not matter whether the *cash* outlay is labelled for accounting purposes 'capital' or 'revenue', nor the *cash* inflows 'profit', 'depreciation', 'taxation allowances' or 'investment grants'. To obtain a true picture of the investment all *cash* outlays and inflows must be taken into account. Furthermore, the value of a cash payment or receipt must be related to the time when the transfer takes place. It must be recognized that £1 received today is worth more than £1 receivable at some future date, because £1 received today could earn in the intervening period; this is the *time value of money concept*. If £1 was invested today at 5 per cent per annum compound interest it would accumulate to £1.2763 in five years' time and £1.6289 in ten years' time. Therefore, if income received today could be invested at 5 per cent per annum, £1.2763 receivable in five years' time would be worth only £1 today. It must be *discounted* back to the present at a rate of 5 per cent per annum. Similarly, £1.6289 receivable in ten years' time would be worth £1 today. This statement assumes no inflation; with inflation £1 today would purchase more than £1 receivable in ten years' time, which reinforces the time value of money concept.

The cash and time value of money concepts, although simple in principle, may appear to be difficult to reduce to a single earnings rate for a complex investment project which can be compared with the target rate of earnings. *Discounted Cash Flow* (D.C.F.) produces this single earnings rate. Discounting is a simple concept, being the opposite of compounding. It is best explained by a simple illustration.

On 1 January, Year 1, James Brown borrows £1,000 from a moneylender. Brown repays the moneylender £600 at the end of Year 1, £500 at the end of Year 2, and £55 at the end of Year 3. The moneylender charged 10 per cent per annum interest on the outstanding balance. The transactions can be summarized as follows:

Year	Balance Outstanding 1 Jan.	Interest at 10%	Balance Outstanding 31 Dec.	Repayment 31 Dec.
	£	£	£	£
1	1,000	100	1,100	600
2	500	50	550	500
3	50	5	55	55
		£155		£1,155

Brown borrowed £1,000 and repaid £1,155 over three years. He paid 10 per cent per annum interest on the outstanding balance. What rate of interest did the moneylender earn on his investment? Clearly, he received 10 per cent per annum compound interest. D.C.F. is concerned with the determination of this 10 per cent.

Discounting is the opposite of compounding. Compounding is used to determine the *future value* of present cash flows; discounting is used to determine the *present value* of future cash flows.

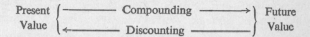

Present Value { Compounding → } Future Value
Discounting ←

Compound interest tables are calculated by the formula $(1+i)^n$ where i is the rate of interest and n the number of years, while discounting tables are calculated by the formula $\frac{1}{(1+i)^n}$. Discounting tables in the form of present value factors are provided in Tables 6.1 and 6.2.

The moneylender made a typical investment decision: he paid out £1,000 on 1 January, Year 1, in order to receive back £1,155 over a period of time. He knows he earned 10 per cent compound interest on his investment; the firm proposing an investment estimates the future cash flows and wishes to determine the rate of interest. How could the moneylender check that he has received 10 per cent compound interest? He could do so by discounting the cash flows as follows:

Years Outstanding	Cash Flow £	Discounted at 10% Factor	Present Value £
0	(1,000)	1.0000	(1,000)
1	600	.9091	545.46
2	500	.8264	413.20
3	55	.7513	41.32
			£(0.02)

It should be noted that cash outflows are indicated by brackets throughout this chapter. In the above calculation 10 per cent is the rate of interest which discounts the future cash inflows back

Table 6.1

Present Value Factors – Interest Rates (1% to 14%)

Years	1%	2%	3%	4%	5%	6%	7%	8%	9%	10%	11%	12%	13%	14%
1	.9901	.9804	.9709	.9615	.9524	.9434	.9346	.9259	.9174	.9091	.9009	.8929	.8850	.8772
2	.9803	.9612	.9426	.9246	.9070	.8900	.8734	.8573	.8417	.8264	.8116	.7972	.7831	.7695
3	.9706	.9423	.9151	.8890	.8638	.8396	.8163	.7938	.7722	.7513	.7312	.7118	.6931	.6750
4	.9610	.9238	.8885	.8548	.8227	.7921	.7629	.7350	.7084	.6830	.6587	.6355	.6133	.5921
5	.9515	.9057	.8626	.8219	.7835	.7473	.7130	.6806	.6499	.6209	.5935	.5674	.5428	.5194
6	.9420	.8880	.8375	.7903	.7462	.7050	.6663	.6302	.5963	.5645	.5346	.5066	.4803	.4556
7	.9327	.8706	.8131	.7599	.7107	.6651	.6227	.5835	.5470	.5132	.4817	.4523	.4251	.3996
8	.9235	.8535	.7894	.7307	.6768	.6274	.5820	.5403	.5019	.4665	.4339	.4039	.3762	.3506
9	.9143	.8368	.7664	.7026	.6446	.5919	.5439	.5002	.4604	.4241	.3909	.3606	.3329	.3075
10	.9053	.8203	.7441	.6756	.6139	.5584	.5083	.4632	.4224	.3855	.3522	.3220	.2946	.2679
11	.8963	.8043	.7224	.6496	.5847	.5268	.4751	.4289	.3875	.3505	.3173	.2875	.2607	.2366
12	.8874	.7885	.7014	.6246	.5568	.4970	.4440	.3971	.3555	.3186	.2855	.2567	.2307	.2076
13	.8787	.7730	.6810	.6006	.5303	.4688	.4150	.3677	.3262	.2897	.2575	.2292	.2042	.1821
14	.8700	.7579	.6611	.5775	.5051	.4423	.3878	.3405	.2992	.2633	.2320	.2046	.1807	.1597
15	.8613	.7430	.6419	.5553	.4810	.4173	.3624	.3152	.2745	.2394	.2090	.1827	.1599	.1401
16	.8528	.7284	.6232	.5339	.4581	.3936	.3387	.2919	.2519	.2176	.1883	.1631	.1415	.1229
17	.8444	.7142	.6050	.5134	.4363	.3714	.3166	.2703	.2311	.1978	.1696	.1456	.1252	.1078
18	.8360	.7002	.5874	.4936	.4155	.3503	.2959	.2502	.2120	.1799	.1528	.1300	.1108	.0946
19	.8277	.6864	.5703	.4746	.3957	.3305	.2765	.2317	.1945	.1635	.1377	.1161	.0981	.0829
20	.8195	.6730	.5537	.4564	.3769	.3118	.2584	.2145	.1784	.1486	.1240	.1037	.0868	.0728

Table 6.2
Present Value Factors – Interest Rates (15% to 50%)

Years	15%	16%	17%	18%	19%	20%	25%	30%	35%	40%	45%	50%
1	.8696	.8621	.8547	.8475	.8403	.8333	.8000	.7692	.7407	.7143	.6897	.6667
2	.7561	.7432	.7305	.7182	.7062	.6944	.6400	.5917	.5487	.5102	.4756	.4444
3	.6575	.6407	.6244	.6086	.5934	.5787	.5120	.4552	.4064	.3644	.3280	.2963
4	.5718	.5523	.5337	.5158	.4987	.4823	.4096	.3501	.3011	.2603	.2262	.1975
5	.4972	.4761	.4561	.4371	.4190	.4019	.3277	.2693	.2230	.1859	.1560	.1317
6	.4323	.4104	.3898	.3704	.3521	.3349	.2621	.2072	.1652	.1328	.1076	.0878
7	.3759	.3538	.3332	.3139	.2959	.2791	.2097	.1594	.1224	.0949	.0742	.0585
8	.3269	.3050	.2848	.2660	.2487	.2326	.1678	.1226	.0906	.0678	.0512	.0390
9	.2843	.2630	.2434	.2255	.2090	.1938	.1342	.0943	.0671	.0484	.0353	.0250
10	.2472	.2267	.2080	.1911	.1756	.1615	.1074	.0725	.0497	.0346	.0243	.0173
11	.2149	.1954	.1778	.1619	.1476	.1346	.0859	.0558	.0368	.0247	.0168	.0116
12	.1869	.1685	.1520	.1372	.1240	.1122	.0687	.0429	.0273	.0176	.0116	.0077
13	.1625	.1452	.1299	.1163	.1042	.0935	.0550	.0330	.0202	.0126	.0080	.0051
14	.1413	.1252	.1110	.0985	.0876	.0779	.0440	.0254	.0150	.0090	.0055	.0034
15	.1229	.1079	.0949	.0835	.0736	.0649	.0352	.0195	.0111	.0064	.0038	.0023
16	.1069	.0930	.0811	.0708	.0618	.0541	.0281	.0150	.0082	.0046	.0026	.0015
17	.0929	.0802	.0693	.0600	.0520	.0451	.0225	.0116	.0061	.0033	.0018	.0010
18	.0808	.0691	.0592	.0508	.0437	.0376	.0180	.0089	.0045	.0023	.0012	.0007
19	.0703	.0596	.0506	.0431	.0367	.0313	.0144	.0068	.0033	.0017	.0009	.0005
20	.0611	.0514	.0433	.0365	.0308	.0261	.0115	.0053	.0025	.0012	.0006	.0003

to the present cash outlay. The discounted cash flow (D.C.F.) rate of return is 10 per cent, because at this rate of interest the *present value* of the future cash inflows is equal to the cash outlay on 1 January, Year 1.

Had the above illustration represented an investment by a firm, the 10 per cent D.C.F. rate of return would have been determined by trial and error. If the cash flows had been discounted at 9 per cent or 11 per cent the result would have been:

Years Outstanding	Cash Flow £	Discounted at 9% Factor	Present Value £	Discounted at 11% Factor	Present Value £
0	(1,000)	1.0000	(1,000)	1.0000	(1,000)
1	600	.9174	550.44	.9009	540.54
2	500	.8417	420.85	.8116	405.80
3	55	.7722	42.47	.7312	40.22
	£155		N.P.V. = £13.76		N.P.V. = £(13.44)

Discounting at 9 per cent the net present value (N.P.V.) of the future cash flows is *positive*, which indicates that the rate of return is *greater* than 9 per cent, and discounting at 11 per cent it is *negative*, which indicates that the rate of interest is *less* than 11 per cent. By interpolation the correct rate of return (10 per cent) can be determined, i.e. $\left(9\% + \dfrac{13.76}{13.76+13.44} \times 2\% \right)$. The interpolation can be made graphically as in Figure 10. It will be noted that the discounting procedure gives greater weight to the cash flows in the early years, recognizing that money has a time value.

A MORE COMPLEX ILLUSTRATION

A more realistic investment decision is now considered. Traditional 'accounting' measures of profitability are computed and compared with the D.C.F. rate of return for the project.

The Widget Manufacturing Company has developed in its Research and Development Department a new product far in advance of existing products available to the market. It is proposed to manufacture and market the new product and this will require an investment of £150,000 in plant and machinery and revenue expenditure of £10,000 during 1967, and a further £40,000 of working capital in 1968. In pricing the new product advantage

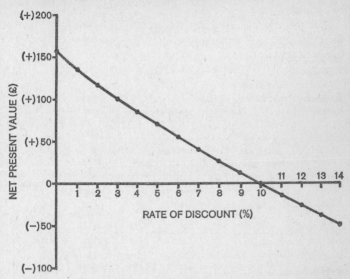

Figure 10. *Net present values at various rates of discount and D.C.F. rate of return by interpolation*

is to be taken of its high innovation value. Profits are expected to decline steadily from a maximum in 1968 as substitutes are marketed by competitors and as the product becomes technically obsolete. It is expected that the product will have a fourteen-year life. The plant and machinery will have an estimated residual value of £15,000 in 1981, and the investment in working capital (£40,000) will be recovered in cash in that year. The company accountant prepared in November 1966 the following schedules:

Table 6.3. Details of expected investment outlay and residual receipts, and investment grant and taxation allowances resulting from the investment.

Table 6.4. Estimated profits and corporation tax thereon.

Table 6.3

WIDGET MANUFACTURING COMPANY
New Product Decision

	Investment Outlay			Residual Receipts
	1967	1968	Total	1981
	£	£	£	£
	'000	'000	'000	'000
Plant and machinery	(150)	—	(150)	15
Working capital:				
Stocks	—	(25)	(25)	25
Debtors less creditors	—	(15)	(15)	15
Revenue expenditure	(10)	—	(10)	—
	£(160)	£(40)	£(200)	£55

Investment Grant and Taxation Allowance on
Plant and Machinery and Revenue Expenditure

Year		Investment Grant 25%	Annual Allowance at 15%	Revenue Expenditure 100%	Total Tax Allowance	Corporation Tax at 40%
		£	£	£	£	£
1967	1	—	16,875	10,000	26,875	—
1968	2	37,500	14,344		14,344	10,750
1969	3		12,192		12,192	5,738
1970	4		10,363		10,363	4,877
1971	5		8,809		8,809	4,145
1972	6		7,487		7,487	3,524
1973	7		6,364		6,364	2,995
1974	8		5,410		5,410	2,546
1975	9		4,599		4,599	2,164
1976	10		3,909		3,909	1,839
1977	11		3,322		3,322	1,563
1978	12		2,824		2,824	1,329
1979	13		2,400		2,400	1,129
1980	14		2,040		2,040	960
1981	15		(3,438)*		(3,438)	816
1982	16		—		—	(1,375)
		£37,500	£97,500	£10,000	£107,500	£43,000

*Balancing charge being difference between tax value of asset and realizable value.

Notes:

1. Annual allowances are calculated at a rate of 15% per annum reducing balance on the cost of plant and machinery *less* the investment grant, i.e. £150,000 − £37,500. The annual allowance for 1967 is 15% of £112,500, which is £16,875, and for 1968 15% of £95,625, which is £14,344.

2. It is assumed that all payments occur at year ends, and all taxation allowances on expenditure during 1967 reduce the amounts of corporation tax payable one year later. Therefore, it is further assumed in 1967 that sufficient profits are made by the company against which the total tax allowances can be offset.

In these tables cash outflows are indicated by brackets. All calculations are in *real* terms, i.e. the possible impact of inflation has been ignored.

The details of the proposed investment are shown graphically in Figure 11. It will be noted that the cash inflows are high in the

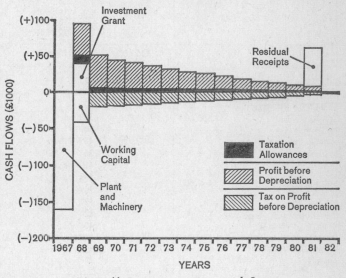

Figure 11. *Investment project – cash flows*

early years of the project's life. A method of investment appraisal is required that takes account of the pattern of the cash flows.

Table 6.4

WIDGET MANUFACTURING COMPANY
NEW PRODUCT DECISION
Profits and Corporation Tax

Year		Profit before Depreciation (£)	Corporation Tax at 40 %
1967	1	—	—
1968	2	43,800	—
1969	3	42,600	(17,520)
1970	4	39,400	(17,040)
1971	5	36,200	(15,760)
1972	6	33,000	(14,480)
1973	7	29,800	(13,200)
1974	8	26,600	(11,920)
1975	9	23,400	(10,640)
1976	10	20,200	(9,360)
1977	11	17,000	(8,080)
1978	12	13,800	(6,800)
1979	13	10,600	(5,520)
1980	14	8,400	(4,240)
1981	15	5,200	(3,360)
1982	16	—	(2,080)
		£350,000	£(140,000)

Less:

Depreciation	£135,000		
Initial Revenue Expenditure	£10,000	145,000	
Profit before taxation		205,000	
Taxation and Grant			
On Profits	140,000		
Less: Investment Grant (£37,500) and Allowances (£43,000)	80,500	59,500	
Profit after Taxation and Investment Grant		£145,500	

Note: All profits are assumed to generate at year ends and corporation tax payable on profits is paid one year later. Thus, all profit in 1968 occurs at end 1968, which is taken as Year 2, and corporation tax on profit in 1968 is payable at end 1969, as Year 3.

The firm's accountant has prepared the following measures of the project's profitability:

1. Average % profit *before depreciation* to additional
assets employed   12.5%
2. Average % profit *after depreciation* to additional
assets employed   7.3%
3. Average % profit *after depreciation, U.K. tax and
investment grant* to additional assets employed   5.2%
Pay-back periods:
4. before U.K. tax and investment grant   4   years
5. after U.K. tax and investment grant   3.4 years

The accountant's detailed calculations are shown in Table 6.5.

Table 6.5

WIDGET MANUFACTURING COMPANY
NEW PRODUCT DECISION
Accountant's Calculations

1. Average % profit *before depreciation* to additional assets employed

$$= \frac{£350,000}{14} \times \frac{1}{200,000} \times \frac{100}{1} = \underline{\underline{12.5\%}}$$

2. Average % profit *after depreciation* to additional assets employed.
    Total profit before depreciation (per Table 6.4)   £350,000
    less depreciation (cost less residual value,
    i.e. £150,000 − £15,000) and initial
    revenue expenditure (£10,000)   £145,000

    Total profit after depreciation (per Table 6.4)   £205,000

Average % profit after depreciation on additional assets employed

$$= \frac{£205,000}{14} \times \frac{1}{200,000} \times \frac{100}{1} = \underline{7.3\%}$$

3. Average % profit *after depreciation and U.K. tax and investment grant* to additional assets employed
    Total profit after depreciation (as above)   £205,000

less U.K. tax

On profits	£140,000	
Allowances and grants	(80,500)	
	————	59,500

Total profit after depreciation and U.K. tax and
   investment grant (per Table 6.4)   £145,500

Average % profit after depreciation and U.K. tax to additional assets employed

$$= \frac{£145,000}{14} \times \frac{1}{200,000} \times \frac{100}{1} = \underline{5.2\%}$$

4. Pay-back (before tax)   £'000
   Capital and revenue expenditure   £160.0

   Profit before depreciation (per Table 6.4)

1968	43.8
1969	42.6
1970	39.4
1971	36.2

   Pay-back for first four years   £162·0

   Pay-back (before tax)   =   4 years

5. Pay-back (after U.K. tax and investment grant)   £'000
   Capital and revenue expenditure   £160.0

   Cash inflows (columns, 3, 4 and 5 of Table 6.6)

1968	92.1
1969	30.8
1970	27.3
1971	24.6

   Pay-back for first four years   174·8

   Pay-back after U.K. tax   =   3.4 years

In weighing the financial considerations as an important part of the process of arriving at a decision on whether or not to recommend approval of the project, a board of directors would probably:

1. Have in mind a minimum rate of return required after having regard to the level of taxation, the risk and uncertainty attached to the project, past returns on capital employed or, possibly, the firm's cost of capital;

2. Realize that the different ratios calculated by the accountant are not inconsistent with each other but reflect different stages of profit.

Traditionally, many firms compared these 'accounting' rates of return with past performance for the firm as a whole. Fifteen per cent return before tax and 9 per cent after tax were frequently the criteria employed. On this basis the project under consideration would probably be rejected. If the firm calculates its cost of capital, it would probably be between 6 per cent and 11 per cent after tax in *real* terms for normal risk investments depending upon the methods of financing the firm. With 5.2 per cent 'accounting' return after depreciation, tax, and investment grant, the project would probably be rejected. The cost of capital concept is considered later in this chapter. The pay-back periods are relatively short and the project may be considered attractive for this reason. However, pay-back does *not* measure profitability; it merely indicates how quickly the initial investment will be repaid. Pay-back is a useful additional item of information but in isolation is not an adequate measure of profitability.[2]

In spite of the number of ratios calculated by the accountant, the true benefit of the investment grant and taxation allowances, which are largely received in the early years of the project's life, is not reflected. Nor do the ratios take into account the timing of the receipt of the profits, i.e. the earnings profile. The ratios have averaged the investment grant, taxation allowances, and profits over the life of the project. They are not based solely on cash flows in that depreciation has been included in the calculations.

The general effect of the investment grant and capital allowances is that 25 per cent grant (20 per cent after 1968) is received

2. A project with an infinite life and constant cash flows would have a D.C.F. rate of return exactly equal to its pay-back reciprocal. Pay-back reciprocal is a useful tool in quickly estimating the D.C.F. rate of return where the project life is at least *twice* the pay-back period and the cash inflows are *constant*. However, after taking account of corporation tax and the earnings profile, constant cash inflows are *not* common.

within one year of the expenditure taking place, and 75 per cent (80 per cent after 1968) of the cost of the machinery may be allowed for taxation at the ruling rate (at 40 per cent corporation tax) in the example. The payment of the grants is being progressively reduced to six months after the capital expenditure taking place. In Development Districts the grant is 45 per cent (40 per cent after 1968) and capital allowances 55 per cent (60 per cent after 1968). The bulk of the benefit of the grant and capital allowances is received in the early years of the project's life. This is clearly illustrated in Figure 11.

The D.C.F. approach is fundamentally different to the ratios calculated by the firm's accountant. Firstly, all *cash* outgoings and incomings are catalogued, and secondly, the cash flows are discounted at an annual rate of interest at which the present value of the future cash inflows equals the original outlay. The D.C.F. calculation is shown in detail in Table 6.6. It will be seen that the project promises a D.C.F. rate of return of 13 per cent after investment grant and tax, compared with an 'accounting' rate of return of 5.2 per cent after investment grant and tax. Why is there such a difference on the results shown for this example?

1. The 'after depreciation' and 'after depreciation, investment grant and tax' ratios are expressed on the original investment. The D.C.F. rate of return is calculated on the basis that the cash received each year must be apportioned into two parts:

(a) The amount required to be set aside to provide the given rate of return (in this example this is 13 per cent) on the amount of cash outlay outstanding.

(b) The balance applied to reduce progressively the original cash outlay.

Ultimately, the sum of all the apportionments under (b) will equal, and thus repay, the original cash outlay.

2. In the conventional ratios the effect of the investment grant and taxation allowances is *averaged* over the life of the project. The D.C.F. calculation correctly treats the allowances as reducing the actual amount of tax payable each year. The main benefits of the investment grant and taxation allowances are received in the early years of the asset's life when the discounting effect is slight.

Table 6.6
WIDGET MANUFACTURING COMPANY
New Product Decision
Discounted Cash Flow Calculation

1	2	3	4	5	6	7	8
Year	Invest-ment Outlay	Profit before Depre-ciation	U.K. Tax on Profit	U.K. Taxation Allow-ances and Invest-ment Grant	Net Cash Flows (cols. 3+5—2–4)	Dis-count-ing Factors at 13 %	Present Values of Net Cash Flows (cols. 6× 7)
Cash Flow	Out £'000	In £'000	Out £'000	In £'000	Net £'000		£'000
1967 1	(160.0)				(160.0)	1.0000	(160.0)
1968 2	(40.0)	43.8		48.3	52.1	.8850	46.1
1969 3		42.6	(17.5)	5.7	30.8	.7831	24.1
1970 4		39.4	(17.0)	4.9	27.3	.6931	18.9
1971 5		36.2	(15.8)	4.2	24.6	.6133	15.1
1972 6		33.0	(14.5)	3.5	22.0	.5428	11.9
1973 7		29.8	(13.2)	3.0	19.6	.4803	9.4
1974 8		26.6	(11.9)	2.5	17.2	.4251	7.3
1975 9		23.4	(10.6)	2.2	15.0	.3762	5.6
1976 10		20.2	(9.4)	1.8	12.6	.3329	4.2
1977 11		17.0	(8.1)	1.6	10.5	.2946	3.1
1978 12		13.8	(6.8)	1.3	8.3	.2607	2.2
1979 13		10.6	(5.5)	1.1	6.2	.2307	1.4
1980 14		8.4	(4.2)	1.0	5.2	.2042	1.1
1981 15	55.0	5.2	(3.4)	.8	57.6	.1807	10.4
1982 16			(2.1)	(1.4)	(3.5)	.1599	(0.6)
	(145.0)	350.0	(140.0)	80.5	145.5	N.P.V. = 0.2	

D.C.F. Rate of Return = 13%

Notes

1. All receipts and payments are assumed to occur at year ends. Thus, all expenditure and profit in 1967 occur at the end of 1967, which is taken as Year 1, and corporation tax on profit less capital allowances in 1967 occurs at the end of 1968, as Year 2.

2. The figures in columns 2 and 5 are transferred from Table 6.3, and in columns 3 and 4 from Table 6.4.

175

3. The D.C.F. calculation takes into account the fact that the profits are highest in the early years of the project's life by giving greater weight to these figures in the calculations.

The use of conventional ratios will in normal circumstances tend to show a lower rate of return, and this may give a wrong impression as to whether a particular project is acceptable or not. For example, in Figure 12 two simple investment projects are illustrated; both projects have the same initial capital expenditure, and both are expected to generate the same total cash inflow during the same period of time. However, Project I has high profits in the early years of its expected life and Project II high profits during the later years. The D.C.F. rate of returns for the two projects would reflect the pattern of the cash inflows. Project I would have a far higher return than Project II. 'Accounting' rates of return would be the same for both projects, because the initial expenditure and *average* profit are the same for both projects. Similarly, anyone who fully understands D.C.F. principles will also appreciate that if a project is delayed at the capital expenditure stage, for example, by a strike by the employees of a construction firm building a new factory, this delay will reduce the D.C.F. rate of return and possibly make a project unprofitable. Accounting rates of return are not sensitive to delays of this nature. Errors in estimating the amount and timing of initial capital expenditures are frequently made by optimistic executives.

NET PRESENT VALUE METHOD

An alternative application of the D.C.F. principle, which may be used in appraising capital investment projects, is the Net Present Value (N.P.V.) method. This is the converse of the D.C.F. rate of return. A minimum earnings rate is agreed, and this percentage used to discount separately cash inflows and cash outflows to present values. If the total present value of the inflows exceeds that of the outflows, the difference, the net present value, is a surplus yielded by the investment over the minimum earnings rate. Thus, if the Widget Manufacturing Company has a minimum required rate of return for the type of project under consideration of 8 per cent, the project would produce a N.P.V. of

£37,600. The project would be acceptable in that it promises a yield in excess of 8 per cent, but it may still have to compete with other projects.

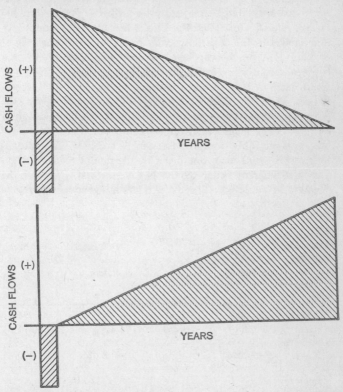

Figure 12. *Project I* (above): *high profits in early years; Project II* (below): *high profits in later years*
Accounting rates of return: Project I = Project II
D.C.F. rate of return: Project I > Project II

Provided a consistent assumption is made about the cost of finance, the D.C.F. rate of return and N.P.V. methods will give the same answer to the relatively simple question of whether a proposal is profitable or not. In practice, the N.P.V. method may

occasionally give a different ranking of proposals from the
D.C.F. rate of return method. For example, with highly profitable
projects the N.P.V. method gives a significantly higher weight-
ing to cash flows in the later years of a project's life than does the
D.C.F. rate of return method. This is because the discount factors applied to the cash flows vary in a geometric progression.
The N.P.V. approach can be shown to be superior in choosing
between mutually exclusive investments, and the D.C.F. rate of
return method may produce multiple yields in certain circumstances. When considering *mutually exclusive investments*, the
acceptance of one proposal automatically signals the rejection of
all others. The investments under consideration are alternative
proposals and only one proposal can be accepted. The alternatives may be ranked in one order by the rate of return method
and in a different order by the N.P.V. method. Consider the
situation in Table 6.7: Project Y offers a higher rate of return

Table 6.7

Project	Cash Outlay in Year 1	Annual Cash Flow in subsequent 10 years	D.C.F. Rate of Return	N.P.V. Discounting at 7%
	£	£		£
X	(20,000)	3,986	15%	+7,996
Y	(15,000)	3,220	17%	+7,616
X−Y	(5,000)	766	8.6%	+380

than Project X, but a lower N.P.V. Which alternative should be
accepted? Provided the company is not in a capital rationing
situation, the project which shows the highest N.P.V. is the most
attractive, because this project offers the highest yield over the
cost of capital. This can be proved by examining the *incremental*
cash flows, the additional cash flows that arise if Project X is
accepted. It will be seen that if Project X is accepted it offers a
rate of return of 8.6 per cent on the additional investment of
£5,000. Of course, it is assumed in this calculation that the degree

178

of risk attached to the two projects is the same. If the risks are different it is a question of deciding whether the rate of return on the additional investment is adequate in relation to any additional risks involved. Similarly, if the additional £5,000 investment in Project X would have to be financed by capital costing more than 7 per cent, the higher rate of interest should be used to calculate the N.P.V., and should be compared with the incremental D.C.F. rate of return.

In a capital rationing situation the 8.6 per cent return on the incremental investment would also have to be compared with the return promised by alternative projects. The problem of ranking mutually exclusive alternatives is further illustrated in Figure 13.

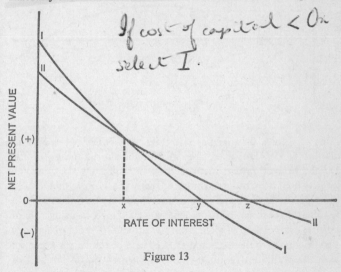

Figure 13

I and II are the N.P.V. curves of two mutually exclusive alternatives. Project II is always preferable using the rate of return method, because it offers a rate of return of 0z compared with 0y for Project I. By the N.P.V. method, however, Project I is preferable if the cost of capital is *less* than 0x.

The rate of return method may produce *multiple yields* when a series of cash flows includes multiple sign changes. The subject is primarily of academic interest and the problem rarely arises in practice.[3] However, it should be noted that the N.P.V. method will always produce a single N.P.V. for such projects and allow a meaningful economic interpretation to be made. The problem is illustrated in Figure 14. It will be seen that the project has two

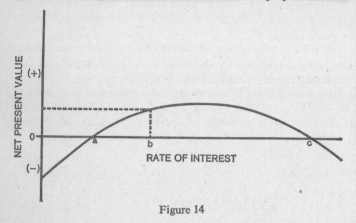

Figure 14

rates of return, $0a$ and $0c$, but only one N.P.V. at a cost of capital of $0b$. However, the theoretical shortcomings of the D.C.F. rate of return method may be sufficient to outweigh its practical advantages compared with the N.P.V. method. In practice, the D.C.F. rate of return method may be preferred for a number of reasons. Management is accustomed to using rate of return as a measure of yield from investment. It is comparatively easy to compare the expected D.C.F. rate of return for a project with the minimum required rate of return based on the cost of capital (discussed in the next section), or with the expected returns from alternative projects. D.C.F. rate of return summarizes expected profitability characteristics into a single percentage regardless of project size. N.P.V. is a £ value which depends in

3. Fuller discussion of theoretical problems of the D.C.F. rate of return method, i.e. choosing between mutually exclusive investments and the possibility of multiple yields, is beyond the scope of this book. Readers are referred to Ezra Solomon (ed.), *The Management of Corporate Capital*, Free Press of Glencoe, Chicago, 1959.

part on the size of the project. This makes interpretation difficult; for example, consider the following statements:

1. 'Sir, Project A has an expected D.C.F. rate of return of 15 per cent, and our minimum required rate of return is 8 per cent.'

2. 'Sir, Project A has an expected N.P.V. of £523 after discounting at our minimum rate of return of 8 per cent.'

It is probably far more difficult for management to interpret the second statement and consider whether the return is satisfactory in relation to the risk and uncertainty attached to the project.

While the D.C.F. rate of return approach may appear difficult and complicated, the trial and error interest calculations are not time-consuming in relation to the main effort of project analysis. Staff can readily be trained to make the necessary calculations easily and quickly. A computer can be programmed to do the calculations in a matter of seconds.

REQUIRED RETURNS

When the D.C.F. rate of return for a project has been calculated, what should it be compared with in order to decide whether the project is financially acceptable? If the N.P.V. method is employed, what rate of interest should be used to discount the future cash flows to arrive at the project's N.P.V.? There are three factors to be considered:

1. The firm's cost of capital;

2. The opportunity cost of investing the capital outside the firm; and

3. The return on alternative projects available.

1. COST OF CAPITAL. The minimum acceptable return from any project is the rate of interest which the firm is paying for the capital invested in the firm, i.e. its cost of capital. A firm draws capital from various sources and each has a different cost. In Chapter 5 it has been argued that it will be to the equity shareholders' benefit if the company obtains some *gearing* in its balance sheet. The objective should be to develop a financing structure which minimizes the firm's weighted average cost of capital. As a standard part of its capital budgeting procedure, a company

should determine at regular intervals its future financing programme, and, on the basis of the proportions of the various forms of finance available, compute the weighted average cost of capital. In calculating the D.C.F. rate of return for a project, it has been shown how account is taken of corporation tax and investment incentives. In calculating the cost of capital, account has to be taken of income tax deductible from dividends and of capital gains tax payable on gains realized on the sale of the shares. A full discussion of the cost of capital concept is beyond the scope of this book. However, it should be noted that there is fairly general agreement on the calculation of the cost of debentures and external equity capital, but there are two schools of thought on the cost of retained earnings. The concept of *opportunity cost* is employed in determining the cost of retained earnings, and the cost of external equity capital. It is argued that the retention of profits is justified only if the company can promise to the shareholder a return on those retained earnings at least equal to that receivable from investing in comparable external equity issues in other companies. The conflict centres on the measurement of this comparable return. One school of thought argues that it is the return the *shareholders* would earn from investing in a comparable company, and suggests that if a company retains £1, the shareholders would receive only £1 less income tax at 8s. 3d. if the profit was distributed as dividend. Therefore, they argue that the company can earn a return lower than that of comparable companies to put the shareholders in the same position as if they (the shareholders) invested in comparable companies. If £1 was distributed as dividend the shareholders would receive £0.5875. If the shareholders would receive 10 per cent return from investing in comparable companies, the company need only earn £0.05875 on £1 retained or 5.875 per cent in order to put the shareholders in the same position.

A second school of thought argues that the opportunity cost of retained earnings should not be measured by the return that the shareholders can earn from investing in comparable companies, but rather by the return the *company* itself can earn by investing in the equity of comparable companies. Cost of retained earnings is higher under this approach, because a company can always obtain a higher net of all taxes rate of return for its shareholders by investing in other companies than can the shareholders by investing themselves. Under the corporation tax system a *company* can escape taxation on investment in other companies if the returns from such investments are distributed to its own shareholders. Income tax is only deductible once. If retained earnings are paid to the *shareholder* he pays income tax on the dividend, and, if he re-invests the net dividend he receives in another company, he pays income tax on dividends received from that company. The shareholder pays income tax twice.

A. J. Merrett and Allen Sykes, leading British authorities on capital budgeting, suggest the following weighted average required returns after corporation tax in *money* terms:

Estimated Weighted Average Required Returns in Money Terms
Returns required in *money* terms with 3% annual inflation

	On normal risk investments		On safe investments	
	Retained Earnings	New Issues*	Retained Earnings	New Issues*
Financing Pattern	%	%	%	%
100% equity	11.5	14.0	8.0	9.5
80% equity and 20% debenture	10.0	12.0	7.5	8.5
70% equity and 30% debenture	9.0	11.0	7.0	8.0

Where the cash flows are in *real* terms the above figures have to be reduced by 3 per cent. This gives minimum required returns after corporation tax ranging from 6 per cent to 11 per cent for normal risk investments depending upon the means of financing. On this

*The required returns which include new issues finance depend on the proportion of net corporate tax profits distributed. The table is based on 50 per cent distribution. Source: A. J. Merrett and Allen Sykes, *Capital Budgeting and Company Finance*, Longmans, London, 1966, p. 35.

basis the Widget project would appear to be acceptable with a 13 per cent D.C.F. rate of return. Merrett and Sykes are in the school that measures the cost of retained earnings by the return the *shareholders* can earn from investing in comparable companies. Two other British authorities, Lawson and Windle, are in the other school of thought and their recommendations on cost of capital will be found in Selected Reading 9 (see p. 196).

2. OPPORTUNITY COST. Regardless of how the cost of retained earnings is calculated, all projects must compete with the return that the company could earn by investing the available finance outside of the business. The risk and uncertainty attached to outside investments must be taken into account. The concept of opportunity cost is considered more fully in Chapter 8.

3. ALTERNATIVE PROJECTS. The ranking of mutually exclusive alternatives has been considered earlier in this chapter. Where the company is in a capital rationing situation, projects will be competing with each other for the limited supply of finance available. Projects may be ranked by magnitude of D.C.F. rate of return as follows:

Project	Capital Required	Cumulative Capital Required	D.C.F. Return	N.P.V. @ 8%
	£	£	%	£
504	10,000	10,000	20	5,382
506	50,000	60,000	18	13,764
501	50,000	110,000	17	12,785
502	35,000	145,000	17	10,743
503	25,000	170,000	17	7,645
505	60,000	230,000	12	12,461
	£230,000			

If the company has £145,000 capital available to finance projects, Projects 503 and 505 would have to be rejected, despite the fact that they promise a return in excess of the company's cost of capital. If the cash flows were discounted at 17 per cent, the return on the marginal project, these two projects would have negative N.P.V.s. If the risk and uncertainty varies between projects, the D.C.F. rate of return may not be the only criterion employed when rationing limited finance to competing projects. The ranking will also become more complex when the projects cover different time periods. A full examination of capital rationing will be found in Selected Readings 2, 9 and 11.

D.C.F. techniques can be used for any combination of cash outlays and cash inflows, i.e. expenditure on fixed assets and working capital in differing proportions in a single year or over an extended period, and for profits generated evenly or unevenly over a period. The information required for a D.C.F. calculation for a proposed expansion investment is:

The amount to be spent and in which years.

The estimated life of the project.

The proceeds of sale of the asset at the end of its economic life.

Profits before depreciation year by year.

Investment grant, taxation allowances, and rates of tax in the country in which the expenditure is to be incurred.

The accuracy of the estimates is likely to diminish for the later years of the project's life, but the discounting procedure gives least weight to these figures; e.g. at 15 per cent cash flows are discounted by one half after 5 years and by three quarters after 10 years. With the traditional 'accounting' methods cash flows in the later years have the same weight as those in the earlier years.

D.C.F. techniques should be employed in the appraisal of all long-run decisions which involve cash flows over *time*, and not simply employed in the appraisal of expansion investments. Two long-run decisions are briefly discussed: replacement decisions and lease or buy decisions.

REPLACEMENT DECISIONS

The main engine of economic growth in a fully employed economy is the introduction of new capital equipment incorporating technical progress. Therefore, the rate of growth of productivity depends primarily on the extent to which today's equipment is an improvement on the old vintages at present in use, and on the rate at which it *replaces* the old vintages. Replacement decisions are important decisions in a mature economy. However, a recent survey by Political and Economic Planning Ltd (P.E.P.) found that in many companies visited decisions to replace machinery were frequently made without a full financial assessment of the consequences. They found an emphasis on using machinery as long as it is still reliable, typified by the following remark of the works manager of a domestic appliance firm:

'Even if the machine was performing well and had been depreciated, there wouldn't be a case for replacement, would there? ... It's earned its keep at work .... There's no case if it is producing effectively to say, "Well, look it's been a faithful servant. We've had it many years. We must get rid of it." I should say "No. If it is a good performer, we'll keep it." '[4]

The appraisal of replacement decisions should be distinguished from the appraisal of expansion decisions. When considering a replacement decision normally the problem is to decide whether to replace a machine at present or at a future date. It is necessary to decide whether *deterioration* and *obsolescence*, which increase with time, have reached the point where the reduction in operating costs resulting from the replacement justifies the net capital expenditure involved in installing the new machine and disposing of the old one. It must be recognized that the cost difference between the old machine and the new machine, which is the profit before depreciation (or cash flow), will tail away and vanish over the life of the new machine at a rate which depends on:

1. The rate at which the operating costs of the new machine rise over its life as a result of physical deterioration; and

2. The rate at which the operating costs on future vintages of machines are likely to decline in relation to costs on today's machines.

In other words, it must be recognized that the replacement machine will have a declining earnings profile.

4. *Attitudes in British Management*, a P.E.P. Report, Penguin, Harmondsworth, 1966, p. 117 (first published as *Thrusters and Sleepers*, London, 1965).

If the new machine was an additional investment, it would be attractive if the D.C.F. rate of return over the life of the asset compared favourably with the company's cost of capital. However, since the timing of a replacement of today's machine influences all subsequent decisions to replace its successors, the correct decision depends, strictly speaking, on minimizing the present cost of the infinite series of replacements that will occur if the present asset is to be repeatedly replaced. Therefore, any replacement formula must be based on the assumption that all subsequent replacements are made optimally.

A further important point regarding replacement decisions is that the return from replacing a machine now rather than later must be calculated by reference to the period for which replacement could really be postponed. Clearly, this is limited by the possible further life of the old machine. To compute the return over the life of the replacement machine would be misleading. The replacement could not be postponed that long: the old machine would probably fall to bits in the meantime. In practice, a one-year period of comparison is normally adequate, since it can be presumed that the relative merits of the old machine will always decline with time. Such a comparison would indicate whether it pays to carry on with the old machine for a further year, or whether replacement now is indicated. If it does pay to carry on, the comparison would be made again a year later.

The D.C.F. rate of return and N.P.V. methods do not enable a replacement decision to be appraised correctly. The D.C.F. rate of return and N.P.V. are not calculated by reference to one year's postponement, but over the life of the new machine. This approach exaggerates the advantages of replacement now. Nor does the D.C.F. literature fully take into account the impact of technological change. Two systems have been developed specifically to appraise replacement decisions using short-cut techniques and incorporating discounting principles. The Machine and Allied Products Institute (M.A.P.I.) system was developed in the United States by George Terborgh.[5] Unfortunately this method is based on United States tax conditions and is not fully applicable in the

5. George M. Terborgh, *Business Investment Policy*, Machinery and Allied Products Institute, Washington, D.C., 1959.

United Kingdom. A، J. Merrett and Allen Sykes have developed the Optimal Replacement Method (O.R.M.)[6] specifically to meet United Kingdom tax conditions.

LEASE OR BUY DECISIONS

In appraising lease or buy decisions discounting techniques must be employed. If an asset is leased a greater sum is paid for the asset over a period of *time* than if it were purchased for cash. A simple illustration, which ignores taxation, provides the best method of examining this type of decision.

XYZ Ltd operates in a tax-free world and is considering the purchase of a machine which will save £4,800 per annum in cash operating costs over its useful life of four years. The machine will have no residual value. The company's weighted average cost of capital is 10 per cent. The machine may be bought outright for £13,000; it is also available on a four-year lease at £4,000 annually in advance. Should the company buy or lease?

At the outset, it should be recognized that the decision is not simply whether to buy or lease, despite the fact that advertisements for leasing frequently describe the decision this way. There are two decisions to be made:

1. THE INVESTMENT DECISION: whether or not to acquire the asset without regard for how the purchase will be financed. The machine promises a D.C.F. rate of return of 17.6 per cent, calculated as follows:

	£
Purchase Price	13,000

[7]Present Value of Future Cash Flows
  Discounted at 17.5% per annum
  £4,800 × 2.7164   13,039 ⎫ By interpolation
                                   ⎬ D.C.F. rate of
  Discounted at 18% per annum   ⎪ return = 17.6%
  £4,800 × 2.6901   12,912 ⎭

6. A. J. Merrett and Allen Sykes, *Capital Budgeting and Company Finance*, Longmans, London, 1966.

7. Where cash flows are constant, Present Value Factor $= \dfrac{1-(1+r)^{-n}}{r}$ and this can be obtained from tables.

The company's weighted average cost of capital is 10 per cent, and the project is therefore attractive. The means of financing the purchase can now be considered.

2. THE FINANCING DECISION: whether to lease the asset or to finance the purchase by borrowing. Leasing is one means of financing the purchase which should be compared with alternative means. By discounting the lease payments back to the cash purchase price of the asset, the cost of using the finance company's money can be determined. The company would be paying the finance company 15.9 per cent per annum if the asset was leased.

	£
Cash Price	13,000
Present Value of Lease Payments	
Discounted at 15.5% per annum	
£4,000 × 3.2644	13,058
Discounted at 16% per annum	
£4,000 × 3.2459	12,984

By interpolation cost of leasing = 15.9%

If the company can borrow money from an alternative source at less than 15.9 per cent per annum, the leasing of the asset is not justified.

The analysis of lease or buy decisions is more complicated in the real world when investment grants, capital allowances, residual values, and corporation tax rates have to be taken into consideration. Further complications arise when the leasing company offers free maintenance or similar inducements. However, the important point is to recognize that a lease or buy decision is a financing problem, and should be appraised separately from the investment decision.

BASIC ASSUMPTIONS

It must be emphasized that any method of expressing the financial implications of a proposed investment is dependent upon the soundness of the basic assumptions. Despite the considerable attention discounting techniques have received in recent years, the assembly of the relevant estimates takes up the vast majority of the total time devoted to the project appraisal. In the Widget Manufacturing Company illustration 95 per cent of the work would probably be concerned with such problems as:

1. The assessment of the demand for the product and selling prices, including estimates of market size, market share, and market growth rate.

2. Estimating and phasing the initial cost of the investment, useful life of the facilities, and working capital requirements.

3. Assessing the rate of output and yield of the plant.

4. Ensuring that the provision of additional services and ancillaries has not been overlooked.

5. Estimating operating costs including assessments of fixed and variable costs.

6. Estimating the rate of corporation tax.[8]

7. Estimating the residual value of the assets.

Usually, there will be imponderables which are hardly susceptible to measurement and evaluation in monetary terms, for example the risk inherent in the particular type of business or in the market to be served. Interpretation and judgement must take over after the calculation stage, however carefully this has been undertaken. It is usually undesirable to calculate one-answer solutions. It is frequently misleading to give the impression that a project promises a return of x per cent. To assist management at the interpretation stage, it is preferable at least to calculate 'optimistic' and 'pessimistic' estimates in addition to 'most probable' results. D.C.F. rate of return, reflecting the whole of the financial life of the project, enables this to be done without overburdening a project report with figures.

A more sophisticated approach is the use of *sensitivity analysis* or *risk analysis* to determine the impact of fluctuations in the basic data on a project's profitability. Sensitivity analysis is an

8. The rate of corporation tax was raised to 42.5 per cent on devaluation of the pound in November 1967 and to 45 per cent in the April 1969 Budget. The Widget Manufacturing Company's accountant assumed the rate would remain at 40 per cent when making his calculations in November 1966.

attempt to show how a project's profitability may be affected by variations or changes in an element of project revenue, operating costs or investment. In risk analysis, probability factors are attached to sales, costs, and other elements of the proposal, and calculations made of the probability of alternative project outcomes. Graphs or tabulations can be presented which array the probable project outcomes according to a scientific combination of possibilities involved. Management may receive a tabulation as shown in Table 6.8, which indicates the probability of achieving a

Table 6.8

Risk Analysis – Project 125

D.C.F. Rate of Return	Probability of Achievement of Return Stated	Probability of Achievement of Return not less than Return Stated
10%	5%	100%
11%	10%	95%
12%	25%	85%
13%	35%	60%
14%	15%	25%
15%	10%	10%

particular D.C.F. rate of return and the cumulative probability of achieving a D.C.F. rate of return not less than a particular return. Table 6.8 indicates that there is a 10 per cent probability that the project will yield a return of 15 per cent, and a 35 per cent probability that the yield will be 13 per cent. The table also indicates that there is an 85 per cent probability that the project will not yield less than 12 per cent and a 60 per cent probability that it will not yield less than 13 per cent. The information in Table 6.8 is presented graphically in Figure 15. A full discussion of sensitivity analysis and risk analysis is beyond the scope of this book, and readers are referred to Selected Readings 5, 6 and 10 (see p. 196). It should be noted that even with a sophisticated probability model *subjective* probability factors have to be attached to the various elements of the proposal.

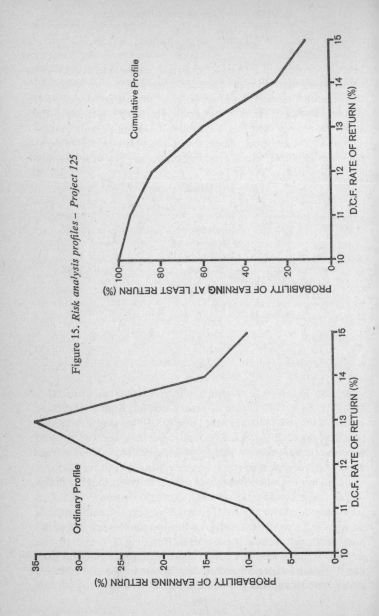

Figure 15. *Risk analysis profiles – Project 125*

BEST ALTERNATIVES

The importance of selecting the best alternatives for investigation and evaluation cannot be overemphasized. If the most advantageous opportunity has been overlooked, this basic omission cannot be overcome by any amount of expertise in other directions. A creative search for investment opportunities is required.

A number of surveys undertaken in recent years of the methods of investment appraisal employed in the United Kingdom have come to the conclusion that companies use methods which are *not* likely to lead to the optimal choice of investment projects. As a result D.C.F. techniques, which have not been widely used in this country, have received considerable publicity. The Government has emphasized the importance of increasing the level of industrial investment. This means that firms should be seeking profitable investment opportunities and correctly appraising them. It has been suggested that many of the 'accounting' methods of investment appraisal now in use tend to lead to under-investment. However, while it is true that D.C.F. techniques accurately reflect the incidence of investment grants and taxation allowances, and the earnings profile of the project, it is doubtful whether the failure to use D.C.F. has been the major cause of under-investment. Where D.C.F. techniques are important is in choosing between mutually exclusive alternatives and between alternative projects in a capital rationing situation. If there has been under-investment, it has not so much been because profitable investment opportunities have been turned down, but rather that:

1. The profitable investment opportunities have not been there in the first place; or

2. If the profitable investment opportunities have been there, they have not been sought out.

In Appendix A to Chapter 4 it has been suggested that corporate profitability, in terms of rate of return on capital employed, has declined seriously during recent years. It is not surprising that firms have been unable to find profitable investment opportunities in certain sectors of the economy. However, the unfavourable economic environment may well be a short-term cyclical problem.

A more serious long-term problem is the failure by many firms to systematically search for investment opportunities, and the conservative and cautious attitude towards investment of some British businessmen.

One has the impression that many firms do not, in fact, look for investment opportunities, but rather wait for capital expenditure projects to present themselves. Organizational theorists have argued that information is not given to the firm but must be obtained, that alternatives are searched for and discovered sequentially, and that the order in which the environment is searched determines to a substantial degree the decision that will be made. In the case of investment decisions it is doubtful whether the environment is properly searched and alternatives discovered. What is required is a creative search for investment opportunities. The realization that, while they provide the most suitable methods of investment appraisal, D.C.F. techniques are not in themselves a panacea for all the country's investment ills may be one important reason for the increasing interest in strategic planning.

Although some of the obvious limitations of any mathematical evaluation of the future have been stressed, the method of expressing the economic worth of an investment is an integral part of the assessment. When a great amount of effort has been expended in investigating the many aspects of a project, it must be worthwhile to ensure that all sides of the financial implications are fairly represented. Although the estimation of future cash flows is at best an inexact science, the data which becomes available should be given its most meaningful expression. In this context the adoption of D.C.F. techniques would seem to be essential if a correct yardstick of economic worth is to be employed. However, it should be recognized that, in evaluating an investment decision, there is a point beyond which financial calculations cannot go and there is a gap left which can only be spanned by managerial judgement. The management accountant's responsibility is to reduce as far as possible the area of uncertainty so that managerial intuition is not overworked.

SUMMARY OF CHAPTER

Capital investment appraisal forms one part of the capital budgeting procedure. It raises problems which are different from the measurement of past performance. The basic object of any investment is that in return for paying out a given amount of *cash* today, a larger amount will be received back over a period of time. Furthermore, the value of a cash payment or receipt must be related to the *time* the transfer takes place. Money has a time value. Discounted Cash Flow (D.C.F.) is based on the cash and time value of money concepts. Discounting, being the opposite of compounding, is used to determine the present value of future cash flows. Traditional 'accounting' rates of return do not satisfactorily take account of the cash and time value of money concepts. The Net Present Value (N.P.V.) method is an alternative application of the D.C.F. principle. While N.P.V. is theoretically sounder than the D.C.F. rate of return method, the latter has strong practical advantages. The D.C.F. rate of return for a project should be compared with the firm's cost of capital, the return on alternative projects available, and the opportunity cost of investing outside of the firm. D.C.F. techniques should be employed in the appraisal of all long-run decisions which involve cash flows over time, including expansion, replacement and lease or buy decisions. Any method of calculating the prospective return from a proposed investment is dependent on the soundness of the basic assumptions. The assembly of the relevant estimates represents the major time devoted to project appraisal. It is usually undesirable to calculate one-answer solutions; at least 'optimistic', 'pessimistic', and 'most probable' returns should be calculated. More sophisticated approaches employ probability analysis to determine the impact of fluctuations in the basic data on a project's profitability. A creative search for investment opportunities is an essential prerequisite for the financial evaluation of alternatives. There is a point beyond which financial evaluation cannot go and managerial judgement must take over.

SELECTED READINGS

1. A. M. Alfred and J. B. Evans, *Discounted Cash Flow – Principles and Some Short Cut Techniques*, Chapman & Hall, London, 1967.
2. Harold Bierman, Jr, and Seymour Smidt, *The Capital Budgeting Decision*, Macmillan, New York, 1966.
3. Joel Dean, *Capital Budgeting*, Columbia University Press, New York, 1951.
4. C. G. Edge, *A Practical Manual of the Appraisal of Capital Expenditure*, Special Study No. 1, Society of Industrial and Cost Accountants of Canada, Ontario, 1964.
5. David B. Hertz, 'Risk Analysis in Capital Investment', *Harvard Business Review*, January–February 1964.
6. R. F. Hespes and P. A. Strassman, 'Stochastic Decision Trees for the Analysis of Investment Decisions', *Management Science*, August 1965.
7. Pearson Hunt, *Financial Analysis in Capital Budgeting*, Harvard Graduate School of Business Administration, Boston, 1964.
8. Institute of Cost and Works Accountants, *The Profitable Use of Capital in Industry*, London, 1965.
9. G. H. Lawson and D. W. Windle, *Capital Budgeting and the Use of D.C.F. Criteria in the Corporation Tax Regime*, Oliver & Boyd, London, 1967.
10. John F. Magee, 'Decision Trees for Decision Making', *Harvard Business Review*, July–August 1964, and 'How to Use Decision Trees in Capital Budgeting', *Harvard Business Review*, September–October 1964.
11. A. J. Merrett and Allen Sykes, *The Finance and Analysis of Capital Projects*, Longmans, London, 1963.
12. A. J. Merrett and Allen Sykes, *Capital Budgeting and Company Finance*, Longmans, London, 1966.
13. National Association of Accountants, *Financial Analysis to Guide Capital Expenditure Decisions*, Research Report No. 43, New York, 1967.
14. National Economic Development Council, *Investment Appraisal*, H.M.S.O., London, 1967.
15. R. R. Neild, 'Replacement Policy', *National Institute Economic Review*, November 1964.
16. W. Scott and B. R. Williams, *Investment Proposals and Decisions*, Allen & Unwin, London, 1965.
17. Ezra Solomon (ed.), *The Management of Corporate Capital*, Free Press of Glencoe, Chicago, 1959.

18. Ezra Solomon, *Theory of Financial Management*, Columbia University Press, New York, 1963.
19. Richard F. Vancil, *The Leasing of Industrial Equipment*, McGraw-Hill, New York, 1962.

CHAPTER 7

Budgetary Control

SINCE resources are relatively scarce and limited, anyone involved in some way in their management is necessarily concerned with the effective utilization of the resources available to him in discharging the economic functions for which he is responsible. In any business, but especially in those where prices are established competitively, costs must be controlled if profits are to be realized year after year. *Control* is concerned with the guidance of the internal operations of the business to produce the most satisfactory profits at the lowest cost. The control process involves three aspects:

1. To *communicate* information about proposed plans.
2. To *motivate* people to accomplish the plans.
3. To *report* performance.

The essential nature of control involves not so much the correcting of past mistakes as the directing of the current and future activities in such a manner as to assure the realization of management plans.

Control involves the making of decisions based on relevant information, which leads to plans and actions that improve the utilization of the productive assets and services available to management.

PLANNING is the BASIS for CONTROL.

INFORMATION is the GUIDE for CONTROL.

ACTION is the ESSENCE of CONTROL.

The results of operations must be expressed as *human responsibilities*, not as abstract concepts:

Men rather than analyses or reports control operations.

To do their jobs efficiently they will need facts.

Supplying the factual basis for control is an important function of accounting.

It is essential that cost centres be planned so that results by responsibilities flow directly from them. *Responsibility accounting*

198

must be employed if effective control information is to be generated by the accounting system. Budgetary control is one of the
most useful accounting tools for planning, co-ordinating, and
controlling the activities of a business. Budgetary control employs the concepts of responsibility accounting.

WHAT IS BUDGETARY CONTROL?

Financial planning is part of the overall planning of the firm
in the long term and medium term, budgetary control is concerned with planning in the short term. The financial plan projects the long-term plans of the company in financial terms. Within the framework of the financial plan, a budgetary control
system should be operated to ensure that detailed plans are prepared for the current year of the long-term financial plan.

When a system of budgetary control is in use, budgets are
established which set out in financial terms the responsibilities of
executives in relation to the requirements of the overall policy of
the company. Continuous comparison is made of actual results
with budgeted results, either to secure, through action by responsible executives, the objectives of policy or to provide a basis
for a revision of policy. Financial limits are allocated to component parts of individual enterprises. Accounting for outlays is
done in such a way as to provide continuous comparisons between,
actual and forecast results so that, if remedial action is necessary,
it may be taken at an early stage or alternatively the objectives
may be reviewed. A manager within an undertaking agrees a
financial limit within which he plans the activities under his
command in accordance with the policies of the undertaking.
The manager must participate in the establishment of the financial limit, since he will be individually responsible for keeping
within the agreed limit.

Thus, the preparation and use of budgets involve the development of a set of estimates of future costs and revenues in a form
which will co-ordinate the activities of the company in accordance with selected objectives, and will serve as a standard for cost
control. Budgets are, therefore, financial and/or quantitative
statements, prepared and approved prior to a defined period of

time, of the policy to be pursued during that period for the purposes of attaining given objectives. A budget may include income, expenditure, and employment of capital.

Budgetary control should assist management in three ways:

1. It provides top management with a summarized picture of the results to be expected from a proposed *plan* of operations. This aids management in choosing between a number of alternative plans and in determining whether a particular plan is satisfactory.

2. Following the approval of the plan, it serves as a guide to executives and departmental heads responsible for individual segments of the company's operations. This aids management in *co-ordinating* the operations by clearly defining the responsibilities and objectives of each segment.

3. It serves to measure performance, since budget deviations reflect either the organization's failure to achieve the planned standards of performance or its ability to better them. This aids management in *controlling* the activities of individuals and the overall performance of the company.

There are a number of basic steps in the design and implementation of a system of budgetary control. The functional structure of the organization must be determined, and the factors which influence the profitability of the business established. Cost and profit centres must be created so that responsibility for the control of each item of expense and revenue can be assigned to individuals. The next step is to define the specific information needs of each managerial position. Working closely with management, the accountant must determine the information requirements of individual managers. Yardsticks for evaluating the actual performance of each manager through the budgetary control reporting system must also be agreed with managers. Having established the information requirements and performance yardsticks for each manager, the control reports each manager will receive can be designed in detail. The accounting system must then be established to generate the information necessary for these reports. This requires a classification and coding system which analyses revenue and expense items in relation to the individuals responsible for their control. Procedures for the development of forecasts, and the preparation and approval of budgets, including the design of forms, must be laid down. Finally, the detailed accounting procedures necessary to generate the control reports when and where they are required must be developed.

It will be appreciated that an effective system of budgetary control requires:

1. A sound and clearly defined organization;
2. Adequate accounting records and procedures;
3. Strong support from and commitment by top management;
4. A continuous programme of education in the development and use of budgets;
5. Continuing study of budgetary and cost control problems, including the motivational aspects; and
6. The revision of budgets when appropriate.

ADMINISTERING THE BUDGETING PROGRAMME

For a budget to be effective in the accomplishment of its end objective, it must be properly developed and utilized. The budgeting programme must be soundly administered. Budgeting is a management function and not simply an accounting exercise; its success depends in no small way on the support given by top management.

Primary responsibility for the administration of the budgeting programme is usually delegated by top management to an executive, variously known as the *budget officer* or budget accountant. He is frequently on the staff of the chief accountant, and this is one reason why budgeting is simply seen as an accounting exercise in many companies. The general duties of the budget officer include:

1. To co-ordinate the efforts of those engaged directly in the preparation of the budgets;
2. To prepare budget reports;
3. To recommend courses of action as may be indicated by the budgets; and
4. To make special studies pertaining to the budgetary control system.

The budget officer is a *staff* officer and as such should exercise no line authority, except over his own staff. Furthermore, the development of the budgets should not be a job delegated to the budget officer but rather one that is supervised and co-ordinated by him. It is a basic tenet of budgetary control that executives develop and accept responsibility for their budgets. The budgets will be the product of the efforts of all levels of management, but these efforts should be co-ordinated and supervised by the budget officer.

In some companies a *budget committee*, composed of executives in charge of major functional areas of the business, may be found to be a useful device for co-ordinating and reviewing the budget programme, particularly as related to general policies which affect the budgets. The budget committee is normally advisory in nature and may be charged with the following functions:

1. To receive and review individual budgets;
2. To suggest revisions;
3. To decide general policies affecting the budgets of more than one department;
4. To approve budgets and later revisions;
5. To receive and consider budget reports showing actual results compared with the budget; and
6. To recommend action where necessary.

The budget committee may become a very powerful group in co-ordinating the activities of the firm and in synthesizing, if not developing, corporate policy. The budget officer will normally be secretary of the budget committee.

It is advisable to develop a *budget manual* which sets forth:

1. The objectives of the business;
2. The part which budgetary control plays in the accomplishment of these objectives;
3. The specific procedures to be followed in the preparation of budgets;
4. The reports comparing budgeted and actual performance to be prepared; and
5. The functions of the budget officer and budget committee, and their relationship with the various levels of management in the development of the system of budgetary control.

DEVELOPMENT OF BUDGETS

Effective planning of one phase of a business is impossible if all other phases are not planned just as carefully, and all phases co-ordinated into a whole. Therefore, a budgetary planning and control system is made up of many individual budgets, but these individual budgets have to be integrated into a master budget. The following steps are normally taken in the development of the individual budgets and the master budget:

1. Preparation of a statement of the *basic assumptions* on which the individual budgets are to be based, including company objectives for profits, growth, and financial position for the budget period.

2. Preparation of a *forecast* of the general economic conditions and conditions in the industry and for the firm. If the company undertakes long-range planning, the basic assumptions and the forecast should flow from the long-range plans.

3. Preparation of a *sales budget* based on the forecast and the productive capacity of the firm. The sales budget will be broken down into areas of responsibility, for example, by salesmen or area sales managers. The sales budget will largely determine how much is to be spent on selling and distribution, and what quantity of goods is to be produced.

4. Preparation of a *production budget* based on and set in conjunction with the sales budget, after making necessary adjustments for planned stock changes. It will also include planning the requirement for materials, labour, and manufacturing facilities, together with the costs of these items. The production budget will be sub-divided into budgets for each production centre.

5. Within each production centre, preparation of budgets for each area of factory *responsibility*, i.e. budgets for responsible departmental managers based on their authority.

6. Preparation of *selling and administrative expense budgets* for each area of selling and administrative responsibility.

7. Preparation of a *research and development budget* analysed into projects and by responsible research staff.

8. Where applicable, preparation of *profit budgets* by areas of profit responsibility and by major product groups.

9. Preparation of a *capital expenditure budget* covering all non-recurring expenditures on fixed assets.

10. Preparation of *working capital budgets* covering all changes in raw material stocks, work-in-progress, finished stocks, debtors, and creditors.

11. Preparation of a *cash budget* reducing all activities into cash flows.

12. Assembly and co-ordination of individual budgets into a *master budget*, that is budgeted profit-and-loss account and balance sheet. From the master budget the budgeted rate of return on capital employed can be calculated, and the management can decide whether it is an acceptable return for the budget period. If the master budget does not achieve the management's objectives, the budget procedure must recommence and a fresh set of budgets based on alternative assumptions must be prepared.

The inter-relationship between the individual budgets and the master budget is illustrated in Figure 16.

The primary responsibility for the preparation of the budgets should rest with the heads of the various departments of the company. For example, the *sales forecast* should be developed by the department charged with the responsibility for market studies. In many firms this may be the sales department, and in others it may be a particular department which specializes in the area, for example the market research department or economics department. However, regardless of the organizational plan, the sales manager should participate actively in the development of the *sales budget*, since he will be individually responsible for the achievement of the sales. This general procedure is equally applicable to every segment of the business and should be vigorously pursued. Considerable frustration will be generated if a departmental manager has laid before him certain objectives to be accomplished, when he is not in sympathy with the programme, and has not had an opportunity to participate in its development. This view is supported by J. O'Neill, Finance Director of Ford of Britain and Ford of Europe. He stresses that 'our experience has been that when we have tried to enforce centrally developed objectives on operating managers, it has been difficult to get

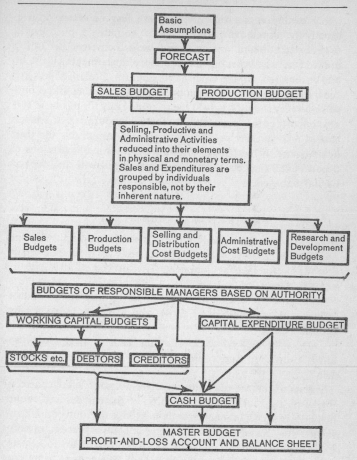

Figure 16. *Steps in development of budgets*

these managers to accept responsibility for performance against these criteria.'[1]

The development of budgets at the departmental level does not

1. Quoted by Robert Heller in 'Ford Motor's Managing Machine', *Management Today*, February 1968, p. 59.

imply to any degree that the budget must be accepted. It is usually the responsibility of the budget committee to review the several departmental budgets, and weld them together into a unified whole, a master budget. Therefore, adjustments will doubtless be required. On the other hand, departmental managers and supervisors are often best equipped for formulating initial budgets and they should be given the responsibility for this task. It is also important that responsibility for the preparation of budgets should rest squarely on those individuals responsible for their achievement. If the budget committee does make alterations to departmental budgets these should be agreed with the departmental managers.

BUDGET ATTAINMENT LEVELS

It has been argued that it is important that responsibility for the preparation of budgets should rest squarely on those individuals responsible for their achievement. This procedure gives rise to two questions[2]:

1. Does the level of attainment incorporated in the budget influence the motivation of those who are responsible for its achievement?

2. Does the method of determining levels of attainment also affect motivation and consequently the usefulness of the system?

The essential nature of control involves not so much the correcting of past mistakes as the directing of the current and future activities in such a manner as to assure the realization of management plans. Therefore, the management control process consists, in part, of inducing people in an organization to do certain things and to refrain from doing others. The control technique may influence both the strength and direction of employee motivation. In particular, the level of attainment incorporated in the budgeting procedure may influence the motivation of individuals responsible for the preparation and achievement of budgets.

2. These questions were first raised by J. R. Small in 'Developments in Management Accountancy', *Certified Accountants Journal*, November 1966, p. 381.

An individual normally acts according to what he perceives to be his own best interests. The budgeting procedure should be designed so that the actions of individuals, which are in part determined by their own perceived interests, are also actions that are in accordance with the best interests of the company. Perfect congruence between individual and organizational goals can never be achieved, but the budgeting procedure should be designed to minimize the difference between individual and company objectives, and between departmental and company objectives. It should not encourage the individual to act against the best interests of the company.

Traditionally, the level of attainment incorporated into budgets is an attainable standard, however this may be defined. It is important that two separate questions are answered regarding this level of attainment in any budgeting system:

1. What will it motivate people to do in their own personal interests?

2. Is this action in the best interests of the company?

The answer to question 1 will depend upon the individual and his position in the organization. Clearly, the management accountant cannot fully answer these questions. An industrial psychologist would have to be consulted. (See Selected Reading 3.) However, these are important questions that are frequently ignored by management accountants and in British accounting literature. Budgetary control involves people and, therefore, it is important that the influence of the system on the motivation of individuals is examined.

FIXED AND FLEXIBLE BUDGETS

Factory overheads include both fixed and variable costs. For control of factory overheads it is necessary to compare actual costs with budgeted costs for each responsibility cost centre. The actual cost must be compared with the budgeted cost for the *actual* level of activity, and this budgeted cost may be derived from a *fixed* or static budget or from a *flexible* budget.

A factory overhead budget which is developed for a specific estimated level of production and operating conditions, and which is used for measurement without change during the budget period, is a *fixed* budget. It is designed to remain unchanged irrespective of the level of activity attained. In most companies operating conditions and levels of activity vary from month to month. Therefore, the fixed budget for a period divided by the months in the period does not provide a fair allowance for overhead for any one month. Neither is it likely that monthly variations in conditions will average out so as to make the fixed budget a fair allowance for the full period. Frequent revision of a fixed budget is necessary to make it a useful control tool, but this is both time-consuming and costly. For these reasons, the flexible budget is more satisfactory and more widely used. A *flexible* budget is a series of static budgets for various forecast levels of activity. By recognizing the difference between fixed, variable, and semi-variable costs, it is designed to change in relation to the level of activity attained. An illustration of a flexible budget is given in Table 7.1. It will be seen that some costs vary proportionately with changes in the level of activity and others are semi-variable or fixed in nature.

Table 7.1

An Example of a Flexible Budget

	Cost Centre 501			Month............19..			
	0hr	200hr	400hr	600hr	800hr	1000hr	1200hr
Capacity	0%	20%	40%	60%	80%	100%	120%
	£	£	£	£	£	£	£
Costs							
Supervision	600	600	600	1,050	1,050	1,050	1,500
Indirect Labour	300	600	900	1,200	1,500	1,800	2,100
Maintenance	100	120	140	160	180	200	220
Depreciation	1,000	1,000	1,000	1,000	1,000	1,000	1,000
Supplies	37	50	62	75	87	100	112
Power	1,073	1,233	1,394	1,554	1,715	1,875	2,036
	£3,110*	£3,603	£4,096	£5,039	£5,532	£6,025	£6,968

*Stand-by cost

Normal overhead rate per direct labour hour:

$$\frac{£6,025}{1,000} = \underline{\underline{£6.025}}$$

It is preferable to ascertain the budget for *actual* activity by interpolation of flexible budget figures, which show the true behaviour of the various items of cost in relation to changes in volume, rather than to attempt to adjust a fixed budget by use of a normal overhead rate. For example, if the actual level of activity for Cost Centre 501 for January 1968 is 1,200 hours and the total actual costs incurred £7,200, using a *fixed budget* the total cost variance would be:

$$£7,200 - (1,200 \text{ hours @ } £6.025 \text{ per hour})$$
$$= £7,200 - £7,230 = £30 \text{ favourable}$$

However, because certain of the cost centre's costs are fixed and semi-variable, the normal overhead rate per direct labour hour is only valid for 1,000 hours normal capacity. If the actual cost is compared with the *flexible budget* for 1,200 hours there is an *unfavourable* variance of £232, that is, £7,200−£6,968. The difference between the fixed and flexible budget of £262 (£7,230−£6,968) is the *volume variance*. The unfavourable variance of £232 is the *controllable* variance for Cost Centre 501 for January 1968, and may be analysed into *cost* and *efficiency variances*. The computation of overhead variances is explained in detail in the next section of this chapter.

The key to the difference between a fixed and flexible budget is that cost performance should be measured by the difference between actual cost and the cost budgeted for actual activity. To obtain a clear picture of cost performance, actual cost at actual activity must be compared with budgeted (expected) cost at actual activity. For purposes of determining standard unit product costs, the budgeted costs for a single level of activity must be used. Hence the calculation of a normal overhead rate per direct labour hour for Cost Centre 501.

OVERHEAD VARIANCES

In Chapter 3, under the heading 'Standard Costing', overhead variances were briefly mentioned, but the computation of the variances was not illustrated. Having explained flexible budgets, we can now consider overhead variances in detail.

An *overhead variance* is the difference between the manufacturing overhead incurred and the standard overhead charged to production (standard hours produced × standard cost per hour) in a period. The overhead variance can be analysed into three general causes:

1. Variances in activity from the normal capacity used for the determination of standard overhead cost per hour, which gives rise to a *volume variance*. The volume variance is the difference between the standard cost of actual hours production and the flexible budget for actual hours production. If actual production is less than normal capacity an unfavourable volume variance will arise, and if actual production is in excess of normal capacity the variance will be favourable. An unfavourable volume variance may be thought of in terms of fixed capacity provided, and giving rise to fixed costs, but not used.

2. Variance of actual overhead incurred from overhead budgeted for actual production, which is called a *cost variance*. The overhead budgeted for actual capacity is determined from a flexible budget. The actual overhead incurred is more or less than the amount that should have been incurred for the actual production.

3. Variance of actual hours from standard hours specified for actual production, which is called an *overhead efficiency variance*. This variance is similar to a labour efficiency variance (considered in Chapter 3). The actual hours required to produce the actual production are greater or less than the standard hours specified for that level of activity.

Assuming all the variances are unfavourable, the various overhead variances may be illustrated as in Figure 17.

The computation of overhead variances is illustrated in Table 7.2. In this illustration the overhead incurred was £470 greater than the standard overhead for actual production based on normal capacity. £74.75 of the £470 unfavourable *overhead variance* arose because the overhead incurred was greater than it should have been for the level of activity achieved, which resulted in an unfavourable *cost variance*. A further £425.25 of this *overhead*

Table 7.2

Computation of Overhead Variances

Overhead Variance = standard overhead for actual production —
actual overhead incurred
May be analysed into:

Efficiency Variance = standard overhead for actual production —
standard costs of actual hours.

Volume Variance = standard costs of actual hours — flexible budgets
for actual hours worked.

Overhead Cost Variance = flexible budget for actual hours worked —
actual overhead.

Example Compute overhead variances from the following data:

Standard Cost Data	£
Budgeted fixed overhead at normal capacity	2,025
Budgeted variable overhead at normal capacity	975
Budgeted overhead at normal capacity	£3,000

Standard allowed hours at normal capacity	1,000
	£
Standard fixed overhead per hour	2.025
Standard variable overhead per hour	0.975
Standard overhead per hour	£3.000

Period Information	
Standard allowed hours for actual production	800
Actual hours worked	790
Actual overhead incurred	£2,870
Flexible overhead budget for actual hours, i.e. £2,025 + (790 × £0.975)	£2,795.25
Standard overhead for actual production (800 × £3)	£2,400

Cost Variance	£
Flexible budget for actual hours worked — actual overhead incurred	
£2,795.25 − £2,870	(74.75)

Table 7.2 – cont.

Volume Variance
   Standard cost of actual hours — flexible budget for
   actual hours
   (790 × £3) — £2,795.25   (425.25)

Efficiency Variance
   (Standard hours — actual hours) × standard rate
   (800 — 790) × £3   30

Overhead Variance
   Standard overhead for actual production — actual
   overhead incurred
   £2,400 — £2,870   £(470)

Note: Figures in brackets indicate unfavourable variances.

variance arose because the actual hours worked (790) were 210
hours less than the normal capacity on which the standard was
based. This gave rise to an unfavourable *volume variance*, because

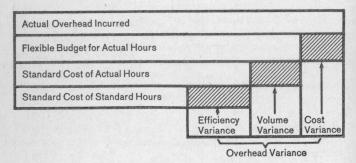

Figure 17. *Overhead variances*

production facilities had been provided but not used. The
unfavourable *volume variance* (£425.25) and *cost variance* (74.75)
were partly offset by the favourable overhead *efficiency variance*
(£30). The company produced 800 standard hours production
during the 790 actual hours worked.

There is no general agreement on how the overhead variance

should be analysed into volume, cost and efficiency variances.[3] One method of calculating these variances has been given. From the manager's point of view it is important that he recognizes that the overhead variance arises from these three general causes. The accountant should clearly explain to management the method of calculating overhead variances he employs.

CONTROL

Having established budgets covering the budget period, budgetary control consists of comparing the estimates of revenues and expenditures in the budgets with the actual revenue received and expenditure incurred. The control embraces every budget, including the cash budget and master budget.

The chief value of a budget as a control device will be realized through the effective use of reports. Reports should be compiled showing the annual and monthly budgets, actual revenue and/or expenditure, the variance between actual and budget, and usually the percentage variance. If the comparisons show 'significant' variations, some comment as to their definite or probable causes should be included in order to assist the recipient in taking action. The accountant's reports should highlight the essentials and point out 'significant' budget deviations and possibilities for improvement. They should:

1. Show the recipient what his costs should have been.

2. Show how closely he came to meeting these costs.

3. Show whether his performance in this respect is improving.

4. Establish a means of explaining the variances so that a knowledge of their causes can be used as a weapon for their reduction.

To be effective reports must be designed with the different levels and types of responsibility of the organization in mind. In good and effective reports each reported fact is in some way related to the authority vested in a single individual or group of individuals. Reports to top management should indicate the overall efficiency

3. For an examination of the various methods of analysing overhead variances, see K. A. Middleton, 'Standard Costing Overhead Variances', *Management Accounting*, February 1968, pp. 60–67.

Table 7.3

MILKY DAIRIES LTD

Bottling Department Operating Statement

Supervisor:..................

Month:..............

	This Month				Year to Date			
	Budget	Actual	Budget Variance		Budget	Actual	Budget Variance	
			£	%			£	%
Output								
Gallons Bottled								
Labour Hours								
Costs	Budget for Actual Gallons		£	%	Budget for Actual Gallons	£	£	%
Controllable Costs	£	£	£		£	£	£	
Bottles								
Closures								
Milk Loss								

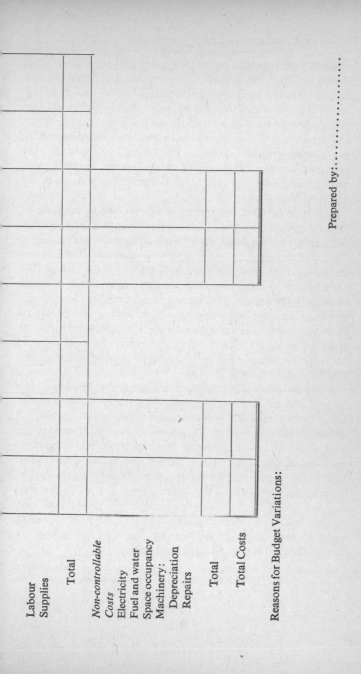

Labour
Supplies

Total

Non-controllable Costs
Electricity
Fuel and water
Space occupancy
Machinery:
Depreciation
Repairs

Total

Total Costs

Reasons for Budget Variations:

Prepared by:.....................

of the organization compared with budgeted performance. They should indicate which departments or functions of the organization require attention or praise on account of the success or failure of their efforts. They should also indicate the trend in the performance of the organization. Reports to functional, sectional, and departmental managers should indicate which elements of performance require attention. They should also comment on good performance. The content of the reports should be kept simple, and limited to data about which the recipient of the report can take action.

Departmental cost variances will be reported in the form of Departmental Operating Statements as illustrated in Table 7.3. A statement will be prepared for each department or cost centre. Costs are divided into *controllable* and *non-controllable* by the individual responsible for that department or cost centre, thus pointing out to departmental managers the extent of their responsibility for costs.[4] This comparison should enable the responsible executive to determine where, how, and why actual accomplishment is not equal to the performance called for in the budget. The comparison should also assist in determining what corrective measures need to be taken to achieve budgeted performance in the future.

It will be appreciated that accounting controls involving both budgets and standards rely heavily upon the 'principle of exceptions', which includes symmetric treatment of favourable and unfavourable variances and a judgement as to whether they are controllable or non-controllable. It is important that the management accountant does satisfy himself that all non-controllable items do in fact lie outside the firm's control. This means that he must be familiar with all the controls operating within the firm, and not simply the accounting ones. There is also the danger, which has already been emphasized in Chapter 3, that, with so much attention being focused on the exceptions, too little attention will be paid to the standards and budgets.

4. There is no general agreement as to whether or not Departmental Operating Statements should include non-controllable costs.

'SIGNIFICANT' VARIANCES

It has been suggested that accountants' reports should highlight the essentials, and point out 'significant' variances from budget and possibilities for improvement. What is a 'significant' variance? Inevitably, variances of different magnitudes will arise randomly from period to period; it is impossible to budget with absolute accuracy. While the interpretation of variances will take into consideration the level of attainment incorporated in the budgets, it is still necessary to decide whether or not a particular variance is 'significant'. For some costs each budget period can be considered in isolation and the judgement as to whether the budget variance is 'significant' can be made without reference to variances of previous periods. The trend of past variances may enable a 'significant' variance to be anticipated, but with this type of cost the variances of one period do not directly influence the variances of subsequent periods. For example, in the dairy industry the budget variances of foil used for bottle closures can be considered independently each period, and a decision can be made as to whether the variance for that period is 'significant' or not. The usage of foil for bottle closures in one period does not directly affect the usage in the next period. Of course, there may be a trend in the past variances which enables the management to anticipate a 'significant' variance. Frequently with this type of cost the significance of the budget variance is measured by expressing it as a percentage of budget. For example, if the variance on bottle closures is in excess of 5 per cent of budget it may be regarded as 'significant' and a detailed investigation made as to the cause. The cumulative variance for the year may not be important.

For many costs the budget will represent the average period cost expected over the whole year, and variances from the budget will arise randomly from month to month. For example, repairs and maintenance costs may be budgeted on the same basis from period to period, but the incurrence of repairs and maintenance costs will probably be uneven during the year. Adverse and favourable budget variances will probably arise randomly from period to period, but they should offset each other over the year so that the cumulative variance is not 'significant'. In this situation it is necessary to determine whether the budget variance in a particular period is simply an expected random deviation or a 'significant' deviation from the budget. Similarly, the cumulative budget variance must be examined to decide whether it is 'significant'. A variance will be statistically 'significant' if it is of such a magnitude that it is unlikely to have arisen purely by chance. It has been suggested that the calculation of budget variances as a percentage of budget, and the detailed examination of variances plus or minus x per cent, does not necessarily tell management whether the variance is statistically 'significant', i.e. whether it is unlikely to have arisen purely by chance.[5] Techniques are available for determining whether a particular budget variance is statistically 'significant' and worth investigating in detail.

The statistical techniques employed are based on applications of probability theory and the normal distribution. It is recognized that certain variations from budget are inevitable and attributable to *chance*, while other important and larger variations are attributable to *controllable* causes. These causes must be traced immediately their presence becomes apparent. Statistical probability tests based on the normal distribution are employed to verify whether variations from budget are attributable to *chance* and not significant or to *controllable* causes and 'significant'.

It is assumed that:

1. The actual costs which are compared with the budget are drawn from a single homogeneous population;

2. The budget is the mean (arithmetic average) of the population, i.e. it is an attainable budget;

3. Any variations from budget arise from chance and not from assignable causes.

If this is true the population of actual costs may be assumed to be normally distributed about the mean. The standard deviation measures the spread of the population about the mean. It follows then that if chance alone causes variances from budget, i.e. the variances are caused by non-controllable random causes, 95 per

5. Lloyd R. Amey, 'Accounting as a Tool of Management', *District Bank Review*, December 1964, p. 24.

cent of the budget variances should fall within the range of mean (budget) plus or minus 1.96 standard deviations and 99.8 per cent within mean (budget) plus or minus 3.09 standard deviations. On this basis 5 per cent and 0.2 per cent control limits can be established for measuring the significance of budget variances. Statistical probability tables are available for establishing other control limits. The calculation of the control limits is dependent upon the estimate of the standard deviation. This is a critical factor and is considered separately at the end of this section. The statistical techniques briefly outlined are fully explained in any standard statistics textbook.

Variance control charts can be employed to present the control limits and the actual budget variances. For example, if the standard deviation for bottle closures is calculated to be 2 per cent of budget, the 95 per cent and 99.8 per cent control limits for bottle closures are indicated in Figure 18. The actual percentage variances from budget are also plotted in Figure 18. It will be seen that 'significant' variances occurred in periods 9 and 10. For costs of the repairs and maintenance type the magnitude of random fluctuations is likely to be greater, the standard deviation should be higher, and the control limits wider. In Figure 19 the control limits are based on a standard deviation of 5 per cent of the budget. It will be seen that in Figure 19 there is a trend of unfavourable variances close to the 95 per cent control limits. If this type of control chart had been in use the upward trend of adverse variances would have been noted, and detailed investigations could have been initiated before the 'significant' adverse variances occurred.

The use of this type of variance control chart enables both significant variances to be isolated and possible future 'significant' variances to be anticipated. The principal indications of 'significant' variances are:

1. The variance is outside the control limits as in periods 9 and 10 in Figure 18.

2. Several variances, especially if consecutive, near the control limit, as in periods 6, 7 and 8 in Figure 19.

3. An undue number of variances above or below the budget. In both cases six of the first eight variances are above budget,

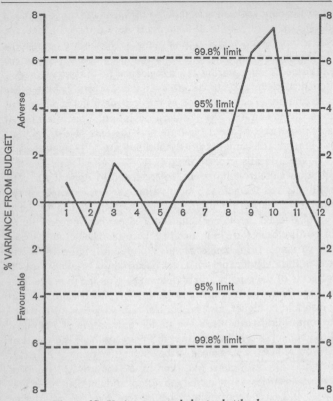

Figure 18. *Variance control chart – bottle closures*

but a 'significant' variance does not occur in both cases until period 9.

4. A trend in the variances, as in periods 5–8 in Figure 19.

Different control limits may be established for different costs. A 3 per cent variance from a budgeted cost of £100,000 is more critical than a 10 per cent variance from a budgeted cost of £1,000. The absolute as well as the percentage variance must be considered when establishing control limits. Ninety per cent control limits (1.64 standard deviations) may be established for major items of costs. On the other hand, for small items of cost 100 per cent control limits (3.9 standard deviations) may be considered satisfactory.

The use of the statistical techniques outlined requires the calculation of standard deviations in order to determine the control limits. It has been suggested that this can be done either by analysing records of actual past achievements, provided the causes of deviation from past expected levels have also been recorded, or by answering such questions as 'what is the budgeted level of expenditure at which there is an even chance that actual expenditure will be greater because of non-controllable causes?'

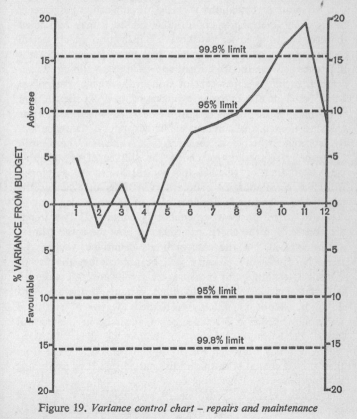

Figure 19. *Variance control chart – repairs and maintenance*

However, it is not simply a question of whether causes of deviation from past expected levels have been recorded, but also whether the past is necessarily representative of the future. If there have been changes in such factors as the method of preparing budgets, plant and equipment, products manufactured, methods of manufacture, organization structure, personnel, managerial policy towards costs, etc., it is doubtful whether the standard deviation of past costs is suitable for establishing control limits for determining whether or not future budget variances are statistically 'significant'. Similarly, if the calculation of standard deviations is based on subjective judgements of the likely level of non-controllable causes, it may be argued that this gives a false statistical sophistication to subjective judgements. It could be argued that there is no important difference between the traditional approach of examining variances plus or minus *x* per cent of standard, with the percentage being based on the *objective* evidence of past experience, and developing control limits based on *subjective* judgements of the chance of non-controllable causes. Neither approach can accurately determine whether a variance is *statistically* 'significant'. However, variance control charts can still be of considerable value regardless of whether the control limits are developed from the calculation of standard deviations or whether the practice of examining variances plus or minus *x* per cent of standard based on past experience is continued. The trends are apparent on the charts regardless of how the control limits are established, but the control limits determine whether the trend is 'significant'. It may well be argued that the use of statistical techniques to measure the significance of variances is 'using a sledge-hammer to crack a nut'. If the standard deviation cannot be reliably calculated the use of statistical techniques implies a false degree of accuracy in the control limits. Furthermore, the cost of employing these statistical techniques may outweigh the additional benefits derived from their use compared with the traditional approach of examining variances plus or minus *x* per cent.

Statistical variance control charts probably offer their widest application in situations which are similar to quality control applications: for example, in the control of physical quantities for which variances are calculated daily or weekly, such as direct labour hours or material usage. Sampling techniques can be employed to determine the confidence limits. The standard deviations are calculated on the basis that a population of means of repeated random samples from a homogeneous population will be distributed in the form of a normal curve, and the standard deviation of the means is proportional to that of the population. The use of statistical variance charts for controlling physical variances which are calculated daily or weekly is fully explained by Horngren.[6] If it is proposed to employ statistical techniques for examining budget variances it is advisable for the accountant to seek the advice of a statistician.

SAME BUDGETS FOR PLANNING AND CONTROL?[7]

In the literature of budgetary control, and so far in this chapter, much stress is laid on the need to ensure that the individual budgets are mutually consistent, in physical and monetary terms. But an important question is: are they consistent with the attainment of the economic objective of the firm as a whole? If only one small part of an organization is looked at and the optimum form of operation for that part found, then whilst this is truly optimum for that part in isolation, it is not necessarily optimum for the organization as a whole. Indeed, acceptance of the apparently optimum solution for one part, i.e. a sub-optimal solution, may force other parts of the organization to adopt policies that lead to the overall solution being far from ideal. It is recognized in team games that an outstanding team is rarely a team of brilliant individualists. Sub-optimizing the parts does not necessarily optimize the whole.

The problem is how to sub-divide the set of operations which make up the firm into proper sub-sets (cost centres or profit centres) in such a manner that each sub-set can be treated as if it

6. Charles T. Horngren, *Cost Accounting: A Managerial Emphasis*, Prentice-Hall, Englewood Cliffs, 1967, pp. 802–15.

7. This section is based on a discussion of this question by Lloyd R. Amey in 'Accounting as a Tool of Management', *District Bank Review*, December 1964.

were a closed system, and every sub-optimizing action for each sub-set will be optimal for the firm as a whole. Thus, the problem is to divide the firm in such a way that, by sub-optimizing the parts, the whole is also optimized. Efforts to maximize profits (or minimize costs) within each cost centre or profit centre should add up to maximum profits for the firm as a whole. Like perfect goal congruence, optimization of the whole and sub-optimization of the part are rarely achieved.

The view most accountants, including the writer, have been brought up on is that the budgets need to be fitted to the organization framework of the firm, so that judgements on past performance match areas of individual responsibility. However, it may well be that, if the object of budgetary control is to assist the management to maximize the profits of the firm by optimizing the parts, the boundaries of budgetary sub-division for planning should not conform to the organization structure. While planning is the basis for control, budgets for planning purposes may be required to be classified in a different way from those for control purposes.

The managerial economist would argue that step-by-step maximization of performance will only in special circumstances yield overall maximization. Similarly, the operational researcher looks across departments and boundaries at systems. In tackling a problem, the operational researcher must first define the area of operations for which optimum solution is required. If the objective of budgetary planning and control is to optimize the profits of the firm, it is permissible to question whether the various attempts at sub-optimization, for example, of stocks are economically consistent with the overall budgetary objective. Does the budgetary planning and control system take account of all economic inter-relationships between the parts of the financial/economic system?

For example, the objective of stock control is, broadly speaking, to reduce the total level of stocks held within an organization to a minimum consistent with the overall objectives of the firm. However, various executives will see sub-optimization of stocks in different ways. Their personal and departmental objectives may be in conflict with those of the firm and with each other.

The production controller may always want to maintain stocks of raw materials and component parts as high as possible, so that production is not delayed at any time through lack of material or components. His interest in stocks of finished goods is probably limited. The sales manager always wants to be able to meet customers' requirements promptly. He will probably press for as high a level of finished goods stock as possible. The management accountant will be conscious that all stocks tie up money in working capital. Clearly the three executives will have different aims and objectives when examining the budget for stocks, and it is this kind of conflict which has to be resolved in attempting to formulate a sub-optimal solution which is consistent with optimizing the whole.

How then are budgets established, and what do they represent? Do they reflect management's best estimate of what is needed if profits are to be maximized, that is, do they optimize the whole? Are they merely attainable targets fixed for control purposes? Usually, one set of budgets serves as both plans and controls. However, a good plan does not necessarily yield a good control, and, likewise, a budget which reflects attainable standards will probably not result in a good plan, that is, one that is designed to optimize the whole. How, then, should budgets be established for control purposes, in order to achieve, as far as it is possible, the objectives of the firm as opposed to those of individuals and departments? It would appear that one set of budgets cannot combine successfully both roles, i.e. planning and control. It would seem that the budgets for planning must be established first. These *planning budgets* would not necessarily conform with the organization structure but would look across departments and responsibility boundaries at systems. They would not necessarily be prepared by a single executive and co-ordinated by a budget officer. They may well be prepared by a planning team with an econometric or operational research bias. A systems analyst would probably be required, as such a team would probably make extensive use of the computer.[8]

8. For example, see K. Knowles, R. M. Tagg, and P. N. Thompson, 'A Heuristic Tree-search Method of Selecting Face Schedules at a Colliery', *Operation Research Quarterly*, Vol. 18, No. 2, pp. 139–48.

Econometrics is concerned with obtaining *quantitative* information about economic systems, and the firm is a financial/economic system. The development of econometrics is changing economics from a largely qualitative to a quantitative science and in the process replacing the hypothetical diagrams of economics textbooks with real-life statistical functions, applicable to actual economies in current problem situations. To date, the work of econometricians on the behaviour of firms has been fragmentary and piecemeal, concentrating on particular issues.[9] However, there is a growing interest among econometricians in the behaviour of firms. Studies have been made and work is currently being undertaken on research and development decisions, production decisions, investment decisions, and financing and dividend decisions.[10] The most sophisticated pieces of operational research are still partial models concentrating on some particular aspect of a firm's activities. However, there is no doubt in the author's mind that the development of highly sophisticated computer-based models for the firm as a whole is not simply a pipe dream. Planning budgets will flow from these models. They should contain the optimal allocation of resources necessary to achieve the firm's short-term objectives. The planning budgets flowing from the computer-based models will be translated into *control budgets* with responsibilities clearly defined by individuals, and agreed with the responsible individuals. The level of attainment may vary between budgets; some may be tighter than others. This would be necessary in order to ensure that every optimizing action by an individual responsible for a control budget would be an optimal action for the firm as a whole. In preparing these control budgets the motivational influences of the different levels of attainment, which have been considered earlier in this chapter, would have to be taken into account.

9. J. Johnston, 'Econometrics: Achievements and Prospects', *Three Banks Review*, March 1967, pp. 3–22.

10. For example, see A. S. Jackson, G. G. Stephenson, and E. C. Townsend, 'Financial Planning with a Corporate Financial Model', *The Accountant*, 27 January, 3, 10 and 17 February 1968, pp. 104–7, 135–8, 167–71, 201–4.

SUMMARY OF CHAPTER

Budgetary control recognizes that it is the people or employees who should be controlled and that by control of people, and proper control of people through their participation in the control system, resource control will be accomplished more effectively. It should always be remembered that management is a human process and involves people:

> *What my Dad does at hp*[11]
>
> You work for *Jack*.
> You sell to *people*.
> You earn money.
> You talk to *people*.
> You work hard.
> And you type too.
> And you talk with *people*.
> And you work hard.
> And you work with *people*.
>
> Liz Combs, aged 6

Budgets are established which set out in financial terms the responsibilities of executives in relation to the requirements of the overall policy of the company. Continuous comparison of actual results and budgeted results is made either to secure through action by responsible executives the objectives of policy or to provide a basis for a revision of policy. Budgetary control assists management in planning, co-ordinating and controlling activities of individuals and the overall performance of the firm. The administration of the budgeting programme is usually delegated to a budget officer. A budget committee may co-ordinate and review individual budgets. It is advisable to prepare a budget manual. A basic tenet of budgetary control is that executives develop and accept responsibility for their budgets. It is important that the motivational influence of the budgeting system on individuals be examined. For control purposes flexible budgets are preferable to fixed budgets. The chief

11. *Measure*, For men and women of Hewlett-Packard, April 1967, p. 4 (*author's italics*).

value of a budget as a control device will be realized through the effective use of reports. It is necessary to decide whether or not a particular variance from budget is 'significant'. Statistical techniques can be employed, but they are often not applicable. It is questionable whether one set of budgets can combine successfully the roles of planning and control.

SELECTED READINGS

1. Lloyd R. Amey, 'Accounting as a Tool of Management', *District Bank Review*, December 1964.

2. Robert N. Anthony, *Management Accounting: Text and Cases*, Irwin, Homewood, Illinois, 1964.

3. C. Argyris, *The Impact of Budgets on People*, Financial Executives Institute, New York, 1952.

4. Robert Beyer, *Profitability Accounting for Planning and Control*, Ronald Press, New York, 1963.

5. Neil W. Chamberlain, *The Firm: Micro-Economic Planning and Action*, McGraw-Hill, New York, 1962.

6. H. P. Court, *Budgetary Control*, Sweet & Maxwell, London, 1951.

7. Harold C. Edey, *Business Budgets and Accounts*, Hutchinson, London, 1966.

8. G. H. Hofstede, *The Game of Budget Control*, Tavistock, 1968.

9. William D. Knight and E. H. Weinwurm, *Managerial Budgeting*, Macmillan, New York, 1964.

10. J. A. Scott, *Budgetary Control and Standard Costs*, Pitman, London, 1961.

11. John Sizer, 'Budgetary Control is Not Obsolete', *The Accountant*, 5 October 1968.

12. D. Solomons (ed.), *Studies in Cost Analysis*, Sweet & Maxwell, London, 1968.

13. A. C. Stedry, *Budget Control and Cost Behavior*, Prentice-Hall, Englewood Cliffs, 1960.

14. W. Thomas (ed.), *Readings in Cost Accounting: Budgeting and Control*, South Western, Cincinnati, 1968.

15. G. A. Welsch, *Budgeting: Profit Planning and Control*, Prentice-Hall, Englewood Cliffs, 1960.

CHAPTER 8

Costs for Decision-making

THE term 'cost' has many meanings in many different situations. Costs suitable for control purposes, which have been considered in Chapters 3 and 7, are not necessarily suitable for decision-making. The relevant decision cost concept to be employed in a particular situation depends upon the business decision being appraised. It is important to understand the different cost concepts available to the accountant for decision-making.

DIFFERENTIAL COST AND INCREMENTAL COST

The process of decision-making is essentially a process of choosing between competing alternatives, each with its own combination of income and costs. Problems of choice include capital expenditure decisions, make or buy decisions, depth of processing, selection of the right product mix, selection of sales areas, selection of distribution channels, adoption of new products, and abandonment of old products. Whatever the decision under consideration the problem can be expressed in similar terms, viz. 'which will be the most worthwhile, alternative A, B, C, ...?' Worthwhileness should be expressed in terms of effect on profitability. Management requires information in a form which enables it to choose correctly which alternative to accept. Management requires information which measures worthwhileness.

Differential costing is concerned with the effect on costs and revenues if a certain course of action is undertaken. The term *differential cost* is generally used by accountants to describe the same costs that the economist calls *incremental costs*. Differential costs may be defined as the increases or decreases in total cost, or the change in specific elements of cost, that result from any variation in operations. Incremental costs have been defined as the additional costs of a change in the level or nature of activity. Any cost that changes as a result of a contemplated decision is a differential cost or incremental cost relating to that decision. Differential cost is therefore a useful cost concept when considering the worthwhileness of different alternatives.

Differential costing eliminates the residual costs which are the same under each alternative, and therefore irrelevant to the analysis. Differential cost is a simple concept, yet it is an essential one in decision-making. However, there are practical difficulties in applying the concept. It is not always a straightforward operation gathering the costs of each alternative in order to determine the differential costs. It is frequently difficult to derive the relevant cost information from an accounting system which employs absorption costing. It has been shown in Chapter 3 that such a system provides average unit cost on a full cost basis, and produces information for control purposes and for valuation of stocks. In making decisions the costs which are of importance are those which will be incurred as a result of the decision, i.e. future costs. Past costs should be ignored. In considering alternatives, past or sunk costs are not relevant to decisions about the future, because these costs have already been incurred. Average unit costs produced by an absorption costing system include such past costs. The relevant costs are future differential or incremental costs – the costs which will be different under each alternative. Similarly, differential or incremental profit consists of differential revenue, based on estimates of future revenue, less differential costs.

Differential costing can be applied to two types of decisions:
1. Short-run or tactical decisions;
2. Long-run or investment decisions.

The essence of the distinction is *time*. Where, in choosing between alternative courses of action, the time factor is important and carries costs or interest with it – the problem is of an investment nature. In this situation the time value of money has to be recognized and discounting techniques employed. Investment decisions have been considered in Chapter 6.

ILLUSTRATION OF RELEVANT COSTS

In the Machining Department of the Odd Job Engineering Company there are two machines, 'A' and 'B', each capable of performing approximately the same type of work. Machine A is a slow-running machine and requires one operator, whereas Machine B, which runs more quickly, requires two operators. The following information is available for the two machines:

	Machine A	Machine B
Expected normal operating hours per annum	2,000	1,800
Hourly rate of each operator	6s.	6s.
Other running costs per hour operated	11s.	16s. 4d.
Fixed overheads – directly allocated per annum	£500	£1,200
Proportion of general factory fixed overheads apportioned to machines per annum	£800	£1,350

A cost clerk prepared a statement (Table 8.1) showing the comparative machine hour rates. It will be appreciated that the

Table 8.1

ODD JOB ENGINEERING COMPANY

Statement of Comparative Machine Hour Rates

	Machine A £ s. d.		Machine B £ s. d.
Operators' Wages at 6s. per hour	6 0		12 0
Running Costs per hour	11 0		16 4
Variable Cost per hour	17 0		1 8 4
Fixed Costs			
Directly allocated (£500÷2,000)	5 0	(£1,200÷1,800)	13 4
Apportioned (£800÷2,000)	8 0	(£1,350÷1,800)	15 0
Total Cost per hour	£1 10 0		£2 16 8

clerk has employed absorption costing principles in calculating the machine hour rates.

Job XYZ can be produced on Machine A at the rate of 30 units per hour, or on Machine B at 50 units per hour. Materials cost 1s. per unit. The management requires a statement of the comparative costs of the two machines for a batch of 300 units (Job XYZ), and recommendations as to which machine should be used. The clerk prepares a comparative cost statement

Table 8.2

ODD JOB ENGINEERING COMPANY

% Comparative Cost of Job XYZ between
Machines A and B

	Batch size: 300 units	
	Machine A	Machine B
Units per hour	30	50
Hours required	10	6
	£ s. d.	£ s. d.
Materials at 1s. per unit	15 0 0	15 0 0
Machine Costs	15 0 0	17 0 0
Total Costs	£30 0 0	£32 0 0

The use of Machine A is recommended.

(Table 8.2), and recommends the use of Machine A because the total cost would be £2 less than with Machine B. However, has the clerk only taken into consideration the differential costs, the costs which differ under each alternative? He clearly has not. His calculation includes material costs which are the same for both machines, and fixed costs which will be incurred regardless of whether the machines are used or not. The fixed costs are sunk costs and are not relevant to the decision under consideration. They will be incurred regardless of which machine is used for Job XYZ. The only costs which vary between the alternatives are the variable machine costs. If Machine A is chosen, it will be used for 10 additional hours at a variable cost of 17s. per machine hour and the *differential cost* will be £8 10s. Similarly, if Machine B is selected, it will be used for 6 additional hours at a variable cost of £1 8s. 4d. per hour, resulting in a *differential cost* of £8 10s. Thus, the differential cost of the two machines is the same, and neither machine has a cost advantage for Job X Y Z. However, if the company is in a limited capacity situation the management would have to consider the alternative work that could be carried out on the two machines. They must consider the *opportunity costs* which are explained later in this chapter. On the other hand the company may be working below full capacity and labour costs may be fixed in the short run (see Chapter 10, p. 316). The company may hoard skilled labour when it is temporarily working below capacity. Different cost concepts are required for different situations.

DIFFERENTIAL COSTING, BREAK-EVEN ANALYSIS, AND MARGINAL COSTING

A knowledge of cost-volume-profit relationships is often essential in differential cost analysis of problems of choice, because the alternatives frequently differ in total volume and in composition of volume. Marginal costing and break-even analysis are concerned with the effect on costs and profit of changes in the volume and type of output. These techniques are considered in detail later in this chapter. It is frequently contended that marginal costing is the same as differential costing or incremental costing.[1] But cost-volume-profit relationships are not the only problems dealt with in differential costing, while marginal costing is essentially a study of the effect of cost-volume-profit relationships based on a classification of costs as fixed or variable. Differential costs and incremental costs include many costs that are normally classified as fixed or semi-fixed, and may be regarded as a general class of which marginal costs are a narrow part, for marginal costs refer to a single kind of increment only, i.e. the addition of another unit to fixed plant.

1. John Sizer, 'The Terminology of Marginal Costing', *Management Accounting*, August 1966, pp. 308-13.

Marginal costing is essentially a short-run concept, and differential costing and incremental costing deal with short-run and long-run problems. The alternatives under consideration frequently involve cost-volume-profit relationships, but this is not always the case, as for example when studying the desirability for a proposed change in material specifications to reduce spoiled work or rework costs. The applications of marginal costing presented later in this chapter are, therefore, examples of the application of differential costing to short-run problems.

OPPORTUNITY COST

Opportunity cost is another important cost concept which should be employed in decision-making. Opportunity cost is concerned with the best alternative forgone. For example:

1. A choice has to be made between three alternatives, and calculations indicate that the three proposed alternatives would increase profit by £10,000, £5,000 and £3,000 respectively. If the first alternative is not accepted its opportunity cost is £5,000, the profit forgone by choosing the next best alternative.

2. If a company retains increased profits to finance growth rather than pay higher dividends to its shareholders, the opportunity cost of this additional finance is the alternative return the shareholders would have earned if the retained profits had been invested elsewhere.

3. If a research and development project is justified on the grounds of potential reductions in production costs if the project is successful, it must still compete with other prospective investments in the business, such as the replacement of machinery, advertising outlays, and new investments. All these prospective investments must justify tying up capital when compared with the alternative earnings from investing the capital outside of the business or the interest cost which would be avoided by not having to borrow.

Thus, opportunity cost should be measured by the profit forgone under the best available alternative. Although it is frequently difficult to measure, opportunity cost is an important concept. It does make the accountant and the management think about the alternatives forgone, which they frequently fail to do.

After considering the concepts of differential cost, incremental cost, and opportunity cost, it will be appreciated that in determining decision-making costs the following are required:

1. A precise picture of the alternatives available;
2. An understanding of different cost concepts;
3. A flexible classification of accounting records on several alternative bases and not a philosophy of absolutism; and
4. Ingenuity and skill in quantitative analysis.

The management accountant must be able to ask the right questions, and be able to select the data which are relevant in answering them.

BREAK-EVEN ANALYSIS

The simplest method of illustrating the relationship between cost, volume of output, and profit is the break-even chart. The *break-even chart* is a graph showing the amount of fixed and variable costs and the sales revenues at different volumes of output. A simple break-even chart is illustrated in Figure 20. It has been described as a condensed master flexible budget showing the normal profit for any given sales volume. It will become apparent that this description overrates its usefulness. Another way of presenting the same information is the *profit-volume chart* (see Figure 21).

A SIMPLE ILLUSTRATION

The XYZ Company's current costs and sales at 100 per cent normal capacity are:

	£'000
Annual Sales @ 100% normal capacity	240
Fixed costs	80
Variable Costs	120

It is proposed to increase the capacity by the acquisition of 33⅓ per cent additional space and plant. Fixed costs will increase by £20,000 per annum. On the assumption that production

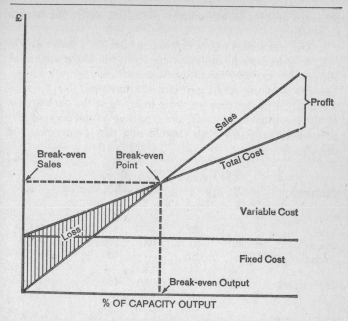

Figure 20. *Break-even chart*

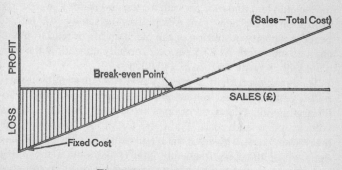

Figure 21. *Profit-volume chart*

efficiency and prices will remain unchanged, determine from a single chart:

1. The break-even points before and after the extension; and
2. At what capacity utilization the profit will be the same as at 100 per cent capacity utilization before the extensions.

The profit-volume chart provides the most suitable form of presentation in this case. In order to arrive at the data to plot on the chart, the sales, costs, and profits at nil and 100 per cent effective capacity for both the old and new plants must be calculated:

% Capacity	Old Plant 0% £	Old Plant 100% £	New Plant 0% £	New Plant 100% £	
Sales	—	240	—	320	+ 33⅓%
Fixed Costs	80	80	100	100	+ £20,000
Variable Costs	—	120	—	160	+ 33⅓%
Profit/(Loss)	£(80)	£40	£(100)	£60	

The loss figures are plotted at 0 per cent capacity and the profit figures at 100 per cent capacity in Figure 22. The lines joining the 0 per cent and 100 per cent capacity points show the loss or profit at different levels of capacity, the break-even points being where the lines intersect the horizontal axis, i.e. 66 2/3 per cent for the old plant and 62.5 per cent for the new plant. The capacity utilization of the new plant which gives the same profit as 100 per cent capacity utilization of the old plant can be read from the chart as indicated. At 87.5 per cent capacity utilization the new plant will generate a profit of £40,000.

The break-even chart is a useful device for presenting a simplified picture of cost-volume-profit relationships as an aid to illustrating the effects of changes in various factors, such as volume, price and costs. However, for profit forecasting the break-even chart with its *static* relationships has serious limitations which its users frequently ignore. Because of the many restrictive assumptions that must be made in order to compute

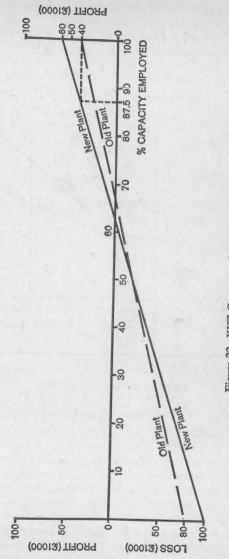

Figure 22. XYZ Company. Profit-volume chart

a break-even chart, the break-even point is only an approximate best. For example, it is assumed that:

1. Costs are either fixed or variable or at least they can be so classified for purposes of break-even charts.

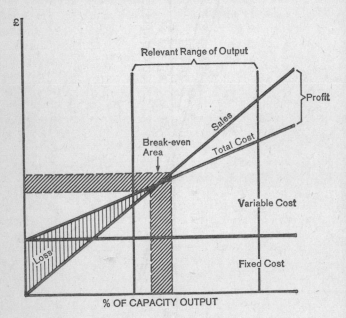

Figure 23. *Break-even area chart*

2. Fixed and variable costs are correctly separated over the whole range of output.

3. Selling price per unit is constant regardless of the level of output, or the demand curve for the product is known.

4. There is one product or, if there is more than one product, a constant sales mix exists over the whole range of output.

5. Production and sales are equal and there is no change in finished products stock.

6. Volume is the only factor affecting costs, and all other factors remain constant.

Since profits are residuals, the profit function bears the full impact of the inaccuracies which arise from the determination of the *static* cost and revenue functions derived on the basis of the above assumptions. Usually the relationship will be valid only within a limited range of activity above and below the level of capacity for which the data is computed. The word *point* carries the connotation of great exactness. A better term would be the break-even *area*, to indicate that the precise location of the break-even point is not known and can be estimated only roughly. To dramatize this point, the cost and revenue lines should perhaps be drawn on the chart as wide bands with intersections over a wide area. It should also be recognized that, because of the many assumptions underlying the break-even chart, the analysis is only relevant over a limited range of output. Outside this range the chart is not meaningful. A break-even chart in the form shown in Figure 23 would be more realistic than that shown in Figure 20 (p. 237).

These limitations of break-even charts do not mean they are completely useless. Provided the assumptions on which the analysis is made are clearly stated, break-even analysis provides valuable information for the guidance of management, and the break-even chart is a simple means of presentation. The greatest value comes from the analysis of the underlying relationships of volume, costs, and profits revealed and *not* from the location of the break-even point.

RATIOS AND BREAK-EVEN POINTS

Information plotted on break-even charts can be summarized in mathematical terms. The *break-even volume*, the *profit-volume ratio*, and the *margin of safety* can all be calculated. The meaning of these terms can best be explained by the use of an illustration.

X Ltd and Y Ltd each anticipate sales turnover amounting to £2,500,000, representing 100 per cent normal capacity. 10 per cent of turnover is expected to be profit if each achieves 100 per cent normal capacity. The variable costs at 100 per cent normal capacity are £1,350,000 for X Ltd and £2,000,000 for Y Ltd.

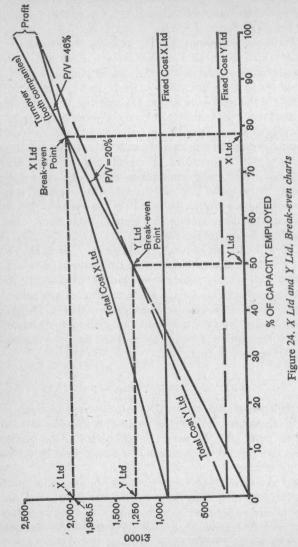

Figure 24. *X Ltd and Y Ltd. Break-even charts*

This information is presented graphically on a single break-even chart in Figure 24.

The *break-even volume* can be calculated as follows:

$$\text{Break-even Volume} = \frac{\text{Total Fixed Cost}}{\dfrac{\text{Total Sales} - \text{Total Variable Cost}}{\text{Units of Volume}}}$$

If the volume is measured in sales value:

$$\text{Break-even Volume} = \frac{\text{Total Fixed Cost}}{1 - \left(\dfrac{\text{Total Variable Cost}}{\text{Total Sales}}\right)}$$

Thus the break-even sales for X Ltd and Y Ltd are:

$$\text{X Ltd} = \frac{900,000}{1 - \left(\dfrac{1,350,000}{2,500,000}\right)} = £1,956,500 \text{ (say)}$$

$$\text{Y Ltd} = \frac{250,000}{1 - \left(\dfrac{2,000,000}{2,500,000}\right)} = £1,250,000$$

As stated earlier, the break-even point itself is of limited significance. It provides neither a standard of performance nor a guide for executive decisions. No business should be conducted in order to break even. The proximity of the break-even point may influence management's attitudes towards costs and risks or towards the urgency for cost reduction efforts.

The *profit-volume ratio* (P/V) is the rate at which profit decreases/increases with a decrease/increase in volume, and is given by the formula:

$$P/V = 1 - \frac{\text{Variable Costs}}{\text{Sales}}$$

or

$$P/V = \frac{\text{Sales} - \text{Variable Costs}}{\text{Sales}}$$

The P/V ratios for X Ltd and Y Ltd are:

$$\text{X Ltd} = 1 - \frac{1,350,000}{2,500,000} = 46\%$$

$$\text{Y Ltd} = 1 - \frac{2,000,000}{2,500,000} = 20\%$$

The P/V ratio represents the slope of the profit line on the profit-volume chart. It makes it possible to determine what change in profit will result from a given change in volume, provided other factors remain *static*. Having calculated the P/V ratios for X Ltd and Y Ltd, what observations can you make regarding the effects of increased or decreased business for each company in the future? With an increase or decrease in sales of £100,000 the profit would increase or decrease by £46,000 (46 per cent) for X Ltd and by £20,000 (20 per cent) for Y Ltd, provided all other factors remain *static*.

Sales in excess of the break-even volume are said to represent a *margin of safety* (M/S).

$$M/S = \frac{\text{Actual Sales} - \text{Sales at Break-even Point}}{\text{Actual Sales}}$$

Thus, if actual sales for both companies are £2,350,000, the respective margins of safety are:

$$\text{X Ltd} = \frac{2,350,000 - 1,956,500}{2,350,000} = 16.7\%$$

$$\text{Y Ltd} = \frac{2,350,000 - 1,250,000}{2,350,000} = 46.8\%$$

244

Since break-even volume depends on the level of fixed costs and on the P/V ratio, margin of safety will change as a result of changes in sales volume, P/V ratio, and fixed costs. If P/V ratio and sales volume are stable, it may be possible to increase the margin of safety by reducing fixed costs. If the P/V ratio and total fixed costs are constant, increases in sales volume will increase the margin of safety.

Break-even point, P/V ratio, and margin of safety are all *static* rather than dynamic concepts. Shifts in volume, particularly downward shifts, are likely to be accompanied by changes in either the P/V ratio or the amount of fixed costs or both. Therefore, such changes affect both the location of the break-even point and the size of the margin of safety. The margin of safety is a rather theoretical concept and is not likely to hold if conditions occur which cause it to be invaded. However, a substantial margin of safety does indicate that a company or a unit of a company is less vulnerable to a decline in sales than one which has a narrow margin of safety.

MARGINAL COSTING

A more useful technique for studying the effects of changes in volume and type of output in a multi-product business is marginal costing.

Marginal costing is an accounting technique which ascertains marginal cost by differentiating between fixed and variable costs. It is primarily concerned with the provision of information to management on the effects on costs and revenues of changes in the *volume* and *type* of output in the short run, although it may be applied to long-run problems. Marginal costing may be incorporated into the system of recording and collecting costs or it may be used as an analytical tool for studying and reporting the effects of changes in volume and type of output. Where it is incorporated into the system of recording and collecting costs, stocks are valued at variable cost and fixed costs are treated as period costs in profit statements.

THE ASCERTAINMENT OF MARGINAL COST

Marginal cost may be defined as the aggregate cost of increasing or decreasing the volume of output of a component, product, or service by *one unit* at a given level of output. The marginal cost of any given unit of output consists of the sum of the additional costs which are incurred as a result of its production and distribution. The additional costs are often the sum of the prime costs and variable overheads resulting from the production of one unit of output. It will be recalled that prime costs are the aggregate of direct material costs, direct wages, and direct expenses, a direct cost being one which can be allocated directly to a cost unit, as opposed to one which has to be apportioned or absorbed by a cost unit. Variable overheads are the aggregate of variable production overheads, variable selling and distribution cost, and variable administration cost. A variable overhead cost is one which tends to vary directly with the volume of output but which cannot be allocated directly to a cost unit. Therefore, in order to ascertain the marginal cost of a given unit of product at a given level of output, the addition shown in Table 8.3 is frequently made. The classification of costs as fixed or variable receives detailed consideration in Chapter 10.

Table 8.3

% Marginal Cost of Product X

Level of Output	5,000 units	
	s.	d.
Direct Material	10	0
Direct Labour	5	0
Direct Expense	1	0
Prime Cost	16	0
Variable Overhead:		
Production	3	0
Selling and Distribution	2	0
Administration		6
MARGINAL COST	21	6

When a system of standard costing is employed the marginal cost calculated will frequently be the standard marginal cost. The use of the prime cost plus variable overhead classification to calculate marginal cost, together with the frequent use of standard costing, tends to lead cost accountants to assume that the cost of the marginal unit is constant over a wide range of output. While marginal cost and variable cost per unit may be the same at a given level of output, the economist clearly distinguishes between marginal cost and average variable cost per unit. Accountants, on the other hand, frequently do not distinguish between marginal cost and average variable cost per unit. If they recognize a distinction in concept, they tend to assume that average variable cost is equal to marginal cost at all levels of output and that both are constant for relevant portions of the output range in which they are operating.[2]

THE EFFECTS OF CHANGES IN VOLUME AND TYPE OF OUTPUT

The use of marginal costing techniques for calculating the effect of changes in volume and/or type of output is now considered. In order to simplify the illustrations the following assumptions are made:

1. Selling price of products remains unchanged with a change in the level of output.

2. Demand for the product is taken as given, i.e. a market price has been accepted, and marginal costing is not being used to determine the selling price. The application of marginal costing techniques to pricing decisions is considered in Chapter 9.

3. Marginal cost is constant for all products over the range of output under consideration.

2. The validity of this assumption and the differences between the economist's marginal cost model and the accountant's marginal costing techniques are discussed in John Sizer, 'Marginal Cost: Economists v. Accountants', *Management Accounting*, April 1965, pp. 138–42.

CONTRIBUTION

The difference between the marginal cost of the various products manufactured and their respective selling price is the *contribution* which each product makes towards fixed costs and profit. Contribution may be defined as the difference between the selling price of a unit and its marginal cost.

In order to determine the effect of short-run changes in volume on the profit of a company, it is necessary to multiply the additional sales of each product by the contribution per unit to arrive at the additional operating profit or reduced operating loss that will result from the increase in volume. This calculation assumes that there is idle capacity and there will be no increase in fixed costs. Any increase in fixed costs can be deducted separately from the additional contribution. For example, if ABC Company received the following order:

Product	Units	Price per Unit
		s. d.
A	800	10 0
B	500	15 0
C	200	8 0
D	1,600	4 0

given the marginal cost per unit for each product, the additional profit can be calculated as follows:

Effect on Profit of Increased Output

Product	Selling Price per unit	Marginal Cost per unit	Contribution per unit	Additional Units	Additional Profit
	s. d.	s. d.	s. d.		£
A	10 0	7 6	2 6	800	100
B	15 0	12 0	3 0	500	75
C	8 0	7 0	1 0	200	10
D	4 0	1 6	2 6	1,600	200
					£385

Any increase in fixed costs which would result if the order was accepted should be deducted from £385.

THE LIMITING FACTOR CONCEPT

Every company has one or more limiting factors, i.e. a factor in the activities of an undertaking which at a particular point in time or over a period will limit the volume of output. It is frequently sales potential, but it may also consist of a certain class or type of raw material or raw materials in general, a specific item of plant, skilled labour, floor space, or liquid resources. It is not a constant; it may vary from time to time within an undertaking and from one firm to another, depending upon the general economic conditions and the specific circumstances applying to the firm.

Where the demands for a company's products exceed its present productive capacity, in the short run, it has to decide which is the best type of output to employ its limited capacity on. The company's aim is to secure maximum profit, which means making the highest possible contribution towards fixed costs. By calculating the contribution which each product makes in relation to the limiting factor, the order of preference in which products should be manufactured can be decided. For example, assuming that the factor which limits the volume of production of X Y Z Company is plant hours, the contribution per hour of plant usage for the five products the company manufactures can be calculated as follows:

Product	Contribution per unit		Limiting Factor Usage (Hours of Plant)	Contribution per hour of Plant Usage	
	s.	d.		s.	d.
R	5	0	4	1	3
S	2	6	2½	1	0
T	3	0	2	1	6
W	3	0	4		9
X	2	6	5		6

Thus, if one additional unit of Product R was produced it would give 5s. additional contribution to fixed costs and profit, and, because it requires four plant hours to manufacture, 1s. 3d. additional contribution per hour of plant usage. In order to produce maximum contribution and maximum profit, X Y Z

Company should first concentrate on Product T. The order of priority after Product T is R, S, W, and finally X.

Assuming the plant capacity is 50,000 hours per month, and the following monthly demand exists for the various products:

Product	Number of Units	Equivalent Plant Hours
R	3,000	12,000
S	4,000	10,000
T	2,500	5,000
W	4,000	16,000
X	3,000	15,000
		58,000

The demand exceeds the plant capacity by the equivalent of 8,000 plant hours production. If fixed costs are £1,000 per month, the most desirable combination of products to produce and the highest attainable profit can be calculated as follows:

Most Desirable Combination of Products

Product	Plant Hours per unit	Units	Total Plant Hours	Contribution per Plant Hour s. d.	Contribution Total £
R	4	3,000	12,000	1 3	750
S	2½	4,000	10,000	1 0	500
T	2	2,500	5,000	1 6	375
W	4	4,000	16,000	9	600
X	5	1,400	7,000	6	175

50,000 Total Contribution 2,400

Less Fixed Costs 1,000

Profit per Month £1,400

The above calculation assumes that it is feasible to market 1,400 units of Product X when the market demand is 3,000 units.

LINEAR PROGRAMMING

In situations where there is a large number of limiting factors and interacting variables, *linear programming* provides an efficient mathematical search procedure for selecting the optimum plan, viz. for selecting the combination which maximizes total contribution. A full examination of linear programming and illustrations of its application to accounting problems is beyond the scope of this book, but basically it involves:

1. Constructing a set of simultaneous linear equations, which represent the model of the problem and which take into consideration all the variable factors; and

2. Solving the equations, usually with the aid of a computer. Simple linear programming problems can be expressed graphically and an example is given below.[3] The role of the accountant is to assist the operational researcher in the construction of the model of the problem. He should assist in specifying the objectives, the constraints, and the variables. The solution of the equations can be left to the mathematician. The accountant should be able to recognize the type of problems which are suitable to analysis by linear programming techniques. He should know when to call in the operational researcher.

X Y Z Company markets two products which are produced in two successive departments. The contribution per unit of the two products and the weekly production capacity of the two departments are:

	Product A £	Product B £
Selling Price	15	16
Marginal Cost	10	12
Contribution	£5	£4

Production Capacity:			
Department Y	150	or	225
Department Z	200	or	200

A further constraint on the production of Product A is that demand is only 115 units per week.

3. For a simple introduction to linear programming and the class of problem to which it is applicable, see M. S. Makower and E. Williamson, *Teach Yourself Operational Research*, English Universities Press, London 1967.

The objective is to determine the combination of products which maximizes the total contribution to fixed costs and profit, taking into consideration the various constraints. This is called the *objective function* and can be expressed in the equation: £5A+£4B, where A and B equal the number of units of Product A and Product B. This equation is subject to the following inequalities:

Production Capacity:

Department Y	$1.5A + B \leqslant$	225
Department Z	$A + B \leqslant$	200
Demand for Product A	$A \leqslant$	115
Because production must be positive	$A \geqslant 0$ and $B \geqslant 0$	

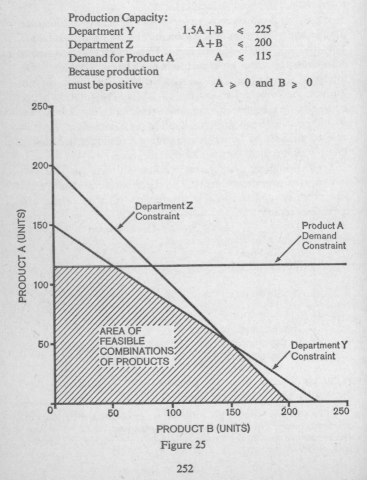

Figure 25

The various constraints on production are shown graphically in Figure 25.

The feasible solution to the problem must be within the shaded area in Figure 25. Within this area the objective function, $5A+4B$, must be maximized. These are quantities of Product A and Product B which lead to the same profit. For example, a total contribution of £400 would be obtained for all pairs of values of A and B satisfying the equation $5A+4B = 400$. This objective function line is shown in Figure 26. Any combination of products on this line will produce a total contribution of £400. The objective function of any other total contribution would be a line parallel to the one drawn for the equation $5A+4B = 400$.

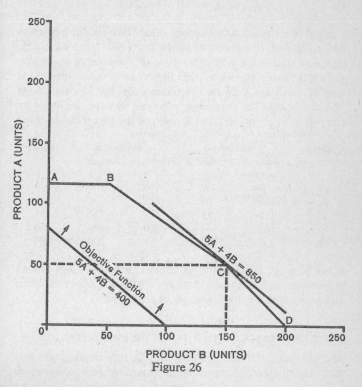

Figure 26

The maximum value of the objective function is determined by finding that line which lies parallel to the objective function line and at the furthest point from the origin, but within the feasible area. This line is $5A+4B=850$ which lies within the area of feasibility at corner C in Figure 26. The combination which maximizes the total contribution is 50 units of Product A giving a contribution of £250 and 150 units of Product B giving a contribution of £600. This combination meets the production constraints and fully utilizes productive capacity of both departments in that

$$1.5A+B=1.5(50)+150=225$$
$$A+B= \quad 50 \ +150=200$$
$$A= \quad 50 \quad \leqslant 115$$

It will be seen that the maximum value of the objective function lies on corner C of the area of feasibility O A B C D in Figure 26, and does not lie on any other part of the area of feasibility. In fact, the maximum value must lie on one of the corners of the area of feasibility because the corners are the furthest points from the origin. The maximum value can therefore be found by computing total contribution at each of the corners as follows:

Corner	Combination		Contribution		Total
	Product A	Product B	Product A	Product B	
	units	units	£	£	£
O	0	0	0	0	0
A	115	0	575	0	575
B	115	53	575	212	787
C	50	150	250	600	850
D	0	200	0	800	800

It will be appreciated that the graphical method has only limited application, and that when there are a large number of variables and constraints a computer must be employed.

MARGINAL COSTING FORM OF PRESENTATION

Marginal costing is particularly effective in providing information and presenting information regarding *cost-volume-profit relationships.* Information of this type is extremely important in selecting products, outlets, markets, etc., and in deciding upon relative emphasis where two or more products are manufactured. In the United States the marginal costing form of presentation is called direct costing.[4]

It has been shown how the contribution per unit each product makes towards fixed costs and profit can be calculated. Similarly, a statement can be prepared to show the total contribution each product class has made towards the recovery of fixed costs. The important point is to determine how much contribution exists, and whether the total contribution from all product classes is sufficient to cover fixed costs and leave an adequate profit. In some cases certain fixed costs, such as annual tooling and product advertising, are so directly involved with each product line that they presumably would be avoided if the product line were dropped. These fixed costs are called *separable* fixed costs. Other fixed costs, such as the managing director's salary and the insurance of his Bentley, are *common* fixed costs and cannot be directly associated with any one product line. A better measure of the profit contribution from each product group may be the profit or loss after deducting any *separable* fixed costs from the total product contribution.

These two points of view can be reconciled, i.e. total product contribution before and after deducting separable fixed costs. Total product contribution *before* charging separable fixed costs is appropriate where the company is already committed to the retention of a product class or is committed to such an extent that the fixed costs directly related to this course of action cannot be saved by dropping the product. When the company is not committed to this course of action, but is merely considering the impact of various alternatives, total product contribution *after* charging separable fixed costs is more appropriate.

The type of statement suggested above for the A B C Company is shown in Table 8.4. It will be seen that Products A and B make the same total contribution to fixed costs and profit, but after deducting separable fixed costs Product B gives the

4. See John Sizer, 'The Terminology of Marginal Costing', *Management Accounting*, August 1966, pp. 308–15.

Table 8.4

ABC COMPANY

Product Profitability 1967

	Product A		Product B		Product C		Total
	Per Unit	Total	Per Unit	Total	Per Unit	Total	
Sales: Units		1,000		2,000		500	
	£	£	£	£	£	£	£
Sales: Value	25	25,000	12	24,000	25	12,500	61,500
Cost of Sales:							
Direct Labour	4	4,000	2	4,000	8	4,000	12,000
Direct Material	5	5,000	4	8,000	5	2,500	15,500
Direct Expense	1	1,000	—	—	2	1,000	2,000
PRIME COST	10	10,000	6	12,000	15	7,500	29,500
Variable Overhead:							
Production	5	5,000	1.5	3,000	5	2,500	10,500
Selling and Distribution	1.5	1,500	.25	500	.75	375	2,375
VARIABLE COST	16.5	16,500	7.75	15,500	20.75	10,375	42,375
TOTAL CONTRIBUTION	8.5	8,500	4.25	8,500	4.25	2,125	19,125
(% of Sales Value)		(34%)		(35%)		(17%)	
Separable Fixed Costs:							
Production		3,000		2,500		1,000	6,500
Selling and Distribution		550		700		1,250	2,500
Administration		450		300		250	1,000
		4,000		3,500		2,500	10,000
Profit (or loss) after Direct Product Costs		4,500		5,000		(375)	9,125

Table 8.4 – cont.

Less Common Fixed Costs:	
Production	3,000
Selling and Distribution	1,000
Administration	1,000
	5,000
NET PROFIT BEFORE TAX	£4,125

highest product profit. Product B's contribution is 35 per cent of sales value while Product A's is 34 per cent, but the contribution per unit is higher from Product A than from Product B. Product C would appear to be unprofitable. Although it produces a total contribution of £2,125, after charging separable fixed costs Product C makes a loss of £375. However, it will be noted that the separable fixed selling and distribution costs for Product C are far higher than for Products A and B. Product advertising and the company's marketing effort have been concentrated on Product C, and sales of this product are expected to increase to 1,000 units per year. Will Product C then be profitable? This question is answered by the following calculation:

Effect of Advertising on Product C

	£
Sales 1,000 units at £25	25,000
Less Variable Costs at £20.75	20,750
Total Product Contribution	4,250
Less Separable Fixed Costs	2,500
Product Profit after Separable Fixed Costs	£1,750

Product C will make a contribution to common fixed costs next year if the product advertising causes the expected increase in sales. Whether the advertising should have been concentrated on Product C is another question. The expected effect of the advertising on the product profit after charging separable fixed costs

Table 8.5

ABC COMPANY

Profitability of Sales Areas 1967

	Area X Units	Area X £	Area Y Units	Area Y £	Area Z Units	Area Z £	TOTAL Units	TOTAL £
Sales:								
Product A	500	12,500	300	7,500	200	5,000	1,000	25,000
Product B	500	6,000	1,000	12,000	500	6,000	2,000	24,000
Product C	50	1,250	200	5,000	250	6,250	500	12,500
		£19,750		£24,500		£17,250		£61,500
	Per Unit							
Variable Cost of Sales								
Product A	16.5	8,250		4,950		3,300		16,500
Product B	7.75	3,875		7,750		3,875		15,500
Product C	20.75	1,037		4,150		5,188		10,375
		£13,162		£16,850		£12,363		£42,375

Total Contribution (% of Sales Value)	6,588 (33%)	7,650 (31%)	4,887 (28%)	19,125
Separable Fixed Costs				
Selling and Distribution Cost	2,000	500	500	3,000
Administration	100	150	250	500
	£2,100	£650	£750	£3,500
Profit (or loss) after Direct Area Costs	£4,488	£7,000	£4,137	£15,625
Less: Common Fixed Costs:			£	
Production			9,500	
Selling and Distribution			500	
Administration			1,500	
				11,500
NET PROFIT BEFORE TAX				£4,125

is shown graphically in Figure 27. It will be noted that Product C will start making a profit after charging direct product costs and, therefore, contributing to the recovery of common fixed costs when sales exceed 590 units. Similar charts could be prepared for Products A and B. The limitations of this type of chart are similar to those of the break-even chart.

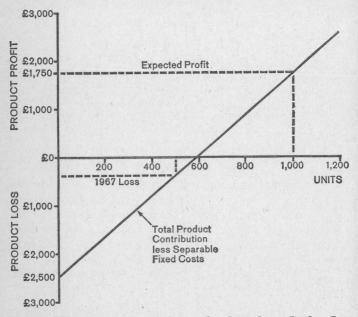

Figure 27. *ABC Company. Product profit-volume chart – Product C*

Statements can also be prepared showing total contribution of different markets, sales areas, outlets, classes of customer, and other sub-divisions of overall company operations. The ABC Company sells in three sales areas and the profitability of each area is shown in Table 8.5. It will be noted that the classification of separable fixed costs is different in this table to that in Table 8.4. The separable fixed costs in this instance are those which would be saved if a sales area was dropped, not a product group. Sales Area Y produces the highest contribution before and after charging separable fixed costs. Sales Area X has the most favourable sales mix in that total contribution is 33 per cent of sales value. It will be seen that the higher advertising on Product C has been concentrated in Sales Area X. If the additional 500 units of Product C are expected to be sold in Sales Area X, the effect on the sales area can be calculated as follows:

Effect of Advertising on Sales Area X

	£
1967 Profit after Direct Area Costs	4,488
Additional Contribution from Product C	
500 units at £4.25	2,125
Expected Profit after Direct Area Costs	£6,613

ABSORPTION COSTING V. MARGINAL COSTING

In Chapter 3 it was suggested that overhead absorption rates are not suitable for calculating the effects of changes in volume and type of output. Marginal costing should be used for this type of calculation. The following simple illustration will demonstrate the dangers of absorption costing and the advantages of marginal costing.

The trading results of X Y Z Manufacturers Ltd for the year 1967 were as follows:

	£	£
Direct Materials		80,000
Direct Wages		
Dept A	20,000	
Dept B	31,500	
		51,500
Variable Overheads		
Dept A	25,000	
Dept B	63,000	
		88,000
Fixed Overheads		77,250
Total Costs		296,750

	£
Trading Profit	13,250
Sales	£310,000

The company manufactures three products, and details of costs, sales, etc. for 1967 were as follows:

	Product		
	X	Y	Z
Sales (Units)	80,000	100,000	12,000
	£ s. d.	£ s. d.	£ s. d.
Selling Price per unit	1 5 0	1 4 0	7 10 0
Costs per unit			
Direct Materials	5 0	10 0	16 8
Direct Wages:			
Dept A	2 0	2 0	3 4
Dept B	3 0	1 6	1 0 0

The company's practice is to absorb departmental variable costs as a percentage on direct departmental wages, and the fixed expenses of the business on the basis of total direct wages.

The cost accountant presents the following information on product profitability for 1967:

	Product X	Product Y	Product Z
	£ s. d.	£ s. d.	£ s. d.
Direct Material	5 0	10 0	16 8
Direct Wages:			
Dept A	2 0	2 0	3 4
Dept B	3 0	1 6	1 0 0
PRIME COST	10 0	13 6	2 0 0

	Product X	Product Y	Product Z
	£ s. d.	£ s. d.	£ s. d.
Variable Overheads			
Dept A	2 6	2 6	4 2
Dept B	6 0	3 0	2 0 0
Fixed Overheads*	7 6	5 3	1 15 0
TOTAL COST	1 6 0	1 4 3	5 19 2
SELLING PRICE	1 5 0	1 4 0	7 10 0
PROFIT/(LOSS) PER UNIT	(1 0)	(3)	£1 10 10
Units Sold	80,000	100,000	12,000
PRODUCT PROFIT/(LOSS)	£(4,000)	£(1,250)	£18,500
TRADING PROFIT FOR YEAR		£13,250	

*150% of Direct Wages.

The results for the year are regarded as unsatisfactory, and as a result of a conference between sales and general management, with the cost accountant's absorption costing information available to them, the following is proposed:

1. As Product X is unprofitable, its sales should be allowed to fall away. It is anticipated that 60,000 units will be sold in the year 1968.

2. Product Y can be sold by additional sales effort and sales can increase by 50 per cent at the same selling price as in the previous year.

3. By reducing the price of Product Z, on which high profits are made, to £6 per unit, sales should be increased by 50 per cent.

It is anticipated that these proposals will lead to improved results in 1968. The cost accountant is asked to prepare a forecast of the probable results for 1968, assuming no variance in manufacturing efficiency, and no change in the total fixed expenses of the business.

The cost accountant asks his newly qualified assistant to prepare the forecast. The assistant, being familiar with marginal costing techniques, prepares the following schedule:

Forecast of Probable Results 1968

	Product X	Product Y	Product Z
	£ s. d.	£ s. d.	£ s. d.
Direct Material	5 0	10 0	16 8
Direct Wages	5 0	3 6	1 3 4
Variable Overheads	8 6	5 6	2 4 2
MARGINAL COST	18 6	19 0	4 4 2
Selling Price	1 5 0	1 4 0	6 0 0
CONTRIBUTION	6 6	5 0	£1 15 10
Units to be Sold	60,000	150,000	18,000
Total Product Contribution	£19,500	£37,500	£32,250

	£
Forecast Total Contribution	89,250
Less Fixed Costs	77,250
Forecast Profit	£12,000

The proposals would result in a fall in profit from £13,250 to £12,000. The assistant cannot understand why this is so; the proposals appeared sound in relation to the cost accountant's schedule of product profitability for 1967. He decides to recalculate the 1967 product profits on a marginal costing basis, and produces the following schedule:

Revised Results 1967

Pro-duct	Units Sold	Selling Price per unit	Marginal Cost	Contribution	Total Contribution
		£ s. d.	£ s. d.	£ s. d.	£
X	80,000	1 5 0	18 6	6 6	26,000
Y	100,000	1 4 0	19 0	5 0	25,000
Z	12,000	7 10 0	4 4 2	3 5 10	39,500
					90,500
		Less Fixed Costs			77,250
		TRADING PROFIT			£13,250

In his calculations the cost accountant had absorbed the fixed costs into products as follows:

Product	Total Contribution	Fixed Costs	Trading Profit
	£	£	£
X	26,000	30,000	(4,000)
Y	25,000	26,250	(1,250)
Z	39,500	21,000	18,500
	£90,500	£77,250	£13,250

The assistant cost accountant now realizes why the proposals had been made and why they result in a forecast of a lower profit. He decides to send his working papers to the cost accountant with the following note:

1. Suggest proposals would result in a fall in profit from £13,250 to £12,000.

2. The following comparison of product contributions to fixed costs can be made:

Product	Actual 1967 Per Unit			Total	Forecast 1968 Per Unit			Total	Change
	£	s.	d.	£	£	s.	d.	£	£
X		6	6	26,000		6	6	19,500	(−) 6,500
Y		5	0	25,000		5	0	37,500	(+)12,500
Z	3	5	10	39,500	1	5	10	32,250	(−) 7,250
				£90,500				£89,250	(−)£1,250

3. Would suggest:

a) Product X is not unprofitable and makes a valuable contribution towards fixed costs and that sales should not be allowed to fall off.

b) The proposed increased sales effort on Product Y is quite profitable but could possibly be better directed at Product X, which makes a greater contribution per unit, depending upon the limiting factors.

c) The reduction in selling price of product Z is not warranted and the present selling price and volume are more satisfactory.

It should be clear from this illustration that the use of absorption costing for providing information to assist management in decision-making can mislead management and result in poor decisions being made.

MARGINAL COSTING, STOCK VALUATION, AND EXTERNAL FINANCIAL REPORTING

Marginal costing may be incorporated into the system of recording and collecting costs or it may be used as an analytical tool for studying and reporting the effects of changes in volume and type of output. The author has argued elsewhere[5] that accountants in Britain have been slow to develop the use of marginal costing techniques for providing management with information for decision-making and control. One possible reason for this delay has been the objection of professional accountants to the use of marginal costing for the external reporting of historical accounting information to shareholders. When marginal costing is incorporated into the system of historical cost recording, stocks are valued at variable cost and fixed costs are charged

5. John Sizer, 'The Development of Marginal Costing', *Accountants Magazine*, January 1968, pp. 23–30.

in the profit-and-loss account as period costs. Traditionally accountants have prepared accounts on an absorption cost basis and have included a proportion of manufacturing fixed costs in their valuation of opening and closing work-in-progress and finished stocks. Differences in stock valuation will arise under the two systems of costing and, therefore, in period profits. This is best understood by studying a simple example.

The XYZ Company manufactures and markets a standard product and the following budget and standard manufacturing cost data was developed for 1967:

	£	Total £	£	Per Unit £
Sales (120,000 units)		120,000		1·00
Production cost of sales:				
Variable	78,000		0·65	
Fixed overhead	24,000	102,000	0·20	0·85
Gross Profit		18,000		0·15
Selling and administration cost (fixed)		8,400		
Net Profit before Tax		£9,600		

It was anticipated that production would be equal to sales, i.e. 120,000 units.

Actual production, sales and stocks in units for 1967 were:

	Quarters 1	2	3	4	Year
Opening stock	—	6,000	2,000	7,000	—
Production	34,000	28,000	33,000	27,000	122,000
Sales	28,000	32,000	28,000	32,000	120,000
Closing stock	6,000	2,000	7,000	2,000	2,000

No price or efficiency variances arose during the year.

Table 8.6

Absorption Costing Approach

| | *Quarters* | | | | |
	1	2	3	4	Total
Sales: units	28,000	32,000	28,000	32,000	120,000
	£	£	£	£	£
Sales: value	28,000	32,000	28,000	32,000	120,000
Production cost of sales at £0·85 per unit	23,800	27,200	23,800	27,200	102,000
	4,200	4,800	4,200	4,800	18,000
Selling and administration cost	2,100	2,100	2,100	2,100	8,400
	2,100	2,700	2,100	2,700	9,600
(Under)/Over absorbed fixed production overhead – volume variance	800	(400)	600	(600)	400
Net Profit before Tax	£2,900	£2,300	£2,700	£2,100	£10,000

Table 8.6 shows the profit-and-loss accounts for each quarter and for the year on an absorption costing basis. Fixed production overhead is absorbed into the cost of the product for stock valuation purposes at the normal level shown in the budget, i.e. £0.20 per unit. It will be noted that the difference between the fixed production overhead charged to production and the budgeted fixed production overhead for a quarter (£6,000) is the *overhead volume variance*. For example, in the first quarter 34,000 units were produced and absorbed £6,800 (34,000 × £0.20) fixed production overhead, the budgeted overhead is £6,000 (30,000 × £0.20), and the *overhead volume variance* is £800 (4,000 × £0.20) favourable.

Table 8.7 shows the profit-and-loss accounts when fixed production overhead is not absorbed into the cost of products for stock valuation purposes, but is treated as a cost of the period and charged against sales. With the marginal costing approach stocks are valued at variable cost and there is no volume variance.

Table 8.7

Marginal Costing Approach

| | | Quarters | | | |
	1	2	3	4	Total
Sales: units	28,000	32,000	28,000	32,000	120,000
	£	£	£	£	£
Sales: value	28,000	32,000	28,000	32,000	120,000
Variable cost of sales at £0.65 per unit	18,200	20,800	18,200	20,800	78,000
Total contribution	9,800	11,200	9,800	11,200	42,000

Fixed costs:	£					
Production	6,000					
Selling and administration	2,100	8,100	8,100	8,100	8,100	32,400
Net Profit before Tax		£1,700	£3,100	£1,700	£3,100	£9,600

The profits produced by the two methods are reconciled in Table 8.8. The difference in the first quarter of £1,200 is represented by the fixed costs included in the closing stock valuation, and in the subsequent quarters by the change in the fixed costs included in the stock valuation.

When a standard absorption costing system is employed, the under/over absorbed fixed production overhead is represented by the volume variance. Students of cost accounting in the 1930s were not entirely satisfied with the techniques of flexible budgeting and the use of volume variances. Volume variances caused confusion, and while accountants understood their meaning they had great difficulty in explaining these variances to management. When there were large fluctuations in the levels of stock, the

Table 8.8

Reconciliation of Profits

| | Quarters | | | | |
	1	2	3	4	Total
Absorption Costing Profit	£2,900	£2,300	£2,700	£2,100	£10,000
Less Change in fixed production costs included in stock valuation:					
Units	+ 6,000	−4,000	+5,000	−5,000	+2,000
at £0·20 per unit	+£1,200	−£800	+£1,000	−£1,000	+ £400
Marginal Costing Profit	£1,700	£3,100	£1,700	£3,100	£9,600

operating management were often very critical of the accountants because of the distortion in reported profits. In the above example sales increased in the second quarter but profit declined under the absorption costing approach (Table 8.6), and in the third quarter sales declined but profit increased. Sales were the same in the first and third quarters but the profit varied between the two quarters with the absorption costing approach. With the marginal costing approach (Table 8.7) the profits vary directly with the sales and are the same in the first and third quarters. This type of criticism was particularly valid in highly seasonal businesses with large variations in stock levels from one period to the next and with a high ratio of fixed costs. Wilmer Wright gives the following example of the experience of one large canning company in the United States:

It was this company's practice to produce and store cans just prior to the packing season because when the season starts it did not have the production capacity to meet demand. Under the absorption costing system, standard costs were set on the average planned level of production for the year. Thus, when production was at capacity for inventory, large volume variance gains resulted and were carried directly to profit and loss. As a consequence, net operating profits could, and sometimes

270

did, exceed net sales. The accountants certainly had trouble explaining that to their directors.[6]

The author has had a slightly different experience with a dairy firm supplying milk and orange drink to holiday resorts along the Lincolnshire coast. Not only were sales seasonal because of the nature of the trade, but in the holiday season they depended upon the state of the weather. Although a flexible budget dealt adequately with the variable elements, the volume variance for the fixed elements could fluctuate violently from quarter to quarter. It was exceedingly difficult to explain to the line management the exact nature of the volume variance.

Direct costing was developed in the United States during the 1930s to overcome the distortion caused by fluctuations in the level of stocks and to eliminate the problem of the volume variance where there are large seasonal variations in the level of sales. Under direct costing only the variable components of cost are charged to products for inventory and accounting statement purposes, and fixed costs are not included in standard product costs. Marginal costing became the term used in Britain to describe the direct costing approach developed in the United States.

Both in Britain and the United States professional accountants have always taken the position that consistency in the method of stock valuation is one of the most important safeguards against the manipulation of the profit reported to shareholders, and rightly so. Unless the method of stock valuation is generally accepted accounting practice, the auditors must qualify their certification of the accounts if such a method results in a material difference in reported profit. 'In the last resort the auditor must decide whether he is prepared to state in his opinion the accounts give a true and fair view; if all the necessary information is not given the auditor is required to qualify his report accordingly.'[7]

'Consistency in the valuation of stocks is one of the well

6. Wilmer Wright, *Direct Standard Costs for Decision Making and Control*, McGraw-Hill, New York, 1962, p. 5.

7. *Report of the Company Law Committee*, Board of Trade, Cmnd 1749, June 1962, para. 334, p. 131.

accepted accounting conventions',[8] and professional accountants in Britain and Canada have been reluctant to accept a change in the method of stock valuation from a full (absorption) cost to a marginal cost basis unless there has been a material change in circumstances. Direct costing is not accepted in the United States for either financial or tax purposes.[9] Professional accountants have been quite agreeable to the use of marginal costing for internal management control, provided the published accounts are adjusted to coincide with the previously accepted method of stock valuation. The result has been that while many companies have gone over to marginal costing for internal reporting, they have maintained their absorption costing methods for external reporting. While for management decision-making and control the value of marginal cost information may far outweigh the work of adjusting figures for external reporting purposes, many accountants either have not recognized this fact or simply have not been prepared to undertake the extra work involved. Thus it may well be argued that the acceptance of marginal costing for external financial reporting has delayed its use for internal decision-making and control purposes. However, marginal costing can always be used as an analytical tool rather than as a system of continuous cost recording involving the valuation of stocks and work-in-progress.

SUMMARY OF CHAPTER

Costs obtained for control purposes are often not suitable for decision-making. Management requires information in a form which enables it to choose correctly between alternatives. To provide this information the management accountant must understand and employ the concepts of differential or incremental cost and opportunity cost. Marginal costing and break-even

8. *Valuation of Stock and Work-in-Progress*, An Accounting Research Study, Institute of Chartered Accountants of Scotland, Edinburgh, January 1968.

9. Accountants International Study Group, *Accounting and Auditing Approaches to Inventories in three Nations: Stock in trade and work-in-progress in Canada, the United Kingdom and the United States*, January 1968, paras. 67–70.

analysis are concerned with the effect on costs and profits of changes in volume and type of output. Break-even analysis can be a useful device provided too much emphasis is not placed on the 'break-even point', and the underlying relationships are carefully examined. The break-even chart can be used as a means of presenting these relationships over a limited range of output. Marginal costing is a more useful decision-making technique in a multi-product business. It relies on the calculation of marginal cost and contribution to determine the effects on costs and profits of changes in the volume and type of output in the short run. Contribution is related to the limiting factor when a company's output is restricted by productive capacity or some other factor. Linear programming provides an efficient mathematical search procedure for selecting the optimum plan when there is a large number of limiting factors and interacting variables. Marginal costing may also be used as a method of presenting information to management regarding cost-volume-profit relationships in a multi-product business. When it is incorporated into the system of recording and collecting costs this gives rise to stock valuation problems. However, marginal costing can always be employed as an analytical tool.

SELECTED READINGS

1. Robert N. Anthony, *Management Accounting: Text and Cases*, Irwin, Homewood, Illinois, 1970.
2. Canadian Institute of Chartered Accountants, *Direct Costing*, Toronto, 1962.
3. Joel Dean, *Managerial Economics*, Prentice-Hall, Englewood Cliffs, 1951, London, 1962.
4. S. Dixon, *The Case for Marginal Costing*, General Educational Trust of the Institute of Chartered Accountants in England and Wales, London, 1966.
5. D. R. C. Halford, *Differential Cost and Management Decisions*, Pitman, London, 1959.
6. Charles T. Horngren, *Cost Accounting: A Managerial Emphasis*, Prentice-Hall, Englewood Cliffs, 1972.
7. Institute of Cost and Works Accountants, *A Report on Marginal Costing*, London, 1961.
8. National Association of Accountants, *The Analysis of Cost-Volume-Profit Relationships*, Research Report Nos. 16–17–18, New York, 1949–50.
9. National Association of Accountants, *Current Applications of Direct Costing*, Research Report No. 37, New York, 1961.
10. John Sizer, 'Marginal Cost: Economists v. Accountants', *Management Accounting* (U.K.), April 1965.
11. John Sizer, 'The Terminology of Marginal Costing', *Management Accounting* (U.K.), August 1966.
12. John Sizer, 'Marginal Costing in the Dairy Industry', *Accountancy*, December 1967.
13. John Sizer, 'The Development of Marginal Costing', *Accountants Magazine*, January 1968.
14. D. Solomons (ed.), *Studies in Cost Analysis*, Sweet & Maxwell, London, 1968.
15. J. Y. D. Tse, *Profit Planning through Volume-Cost Analysis*, Macmillan, New York, 1960.
16. Spencer A. Tucker, *The Break-even System: A Tool for Profit Planning*, Prentice-Hall, Englewood Cliffs, 1963.
17. Wilmer Wright, *Direct Standard Costs for Decision Making and Control*, McGraw-Hill, New York, 1962.

CHAPTER 9

Pricing Decisions[1]

THE determination of selling prices is a major policy decision in the majority of companies. The accountant should make an important contribution to the decision-making process by providing management with costs which are relevant to the pricing decision at hand. Instead, marketing executives often claim that the accountants do not fully understand the importance of competitive pricing, while the accountants frequently contend that marketing executives disregard costs in setting selling prices.

At the root of this conflict is the use of conventional absorption costing (described in Chapter 3), under which the volume of output is fixed or set at an assumed *normal* level, usually for one year, and the product costs are based on that volume. However, product costs based upon *normal* volume and a *normal* mix of facilities do not provide a direct answer to questions which arise in making short-run pricing decisions, because the point at issue is how costs will be changed by differing volumes and mixes of output. It has been illustrated in Chapter 8 that costs which are based on a *normal* volume concept are only valid when the actual volume is the same as the assumed *normal* volume. In making selling price decisions it must be remembered that volume is one of the most important variables. There is very rarely a rigid relationship between selling prices and product costs because competition and the elasticity of consumer demand enter into selling price decisions, as well as product costs. Profits are the result of a satisfactory combination of a number of factors, including price, volume, and product mix, and for this reason volume must be viewed as a variable in assembling cost data to guide management when making selling price decisions.

1. This chapter draws extensively on the author's article, 'The Accountant's Contribution to the Pricing Decision', *Journal of Management Studies*, May 1966, pp. 129–50.

ABSORPTION PRICING

When absorption costing is used and product costs are based on a normal volume concept, unit product costs cease to be a helpful guide in making pricing decisions when the management requires an answer to such questions as:

1. How much more will it cost to produce and sell an additional 1,000 units of Product A?

2. What will this order for 1,500 units of Product B add to the company's overall profit?

The total costs of conventional absorption costing will not give a correct answer to these questions, because they do not represent the *incremental cost*, the additional cost which would result from the change in volume, and they include some fixed costs which are historical *sunk costs* in relation to these changes in volume.

With the conventional absorption costing method of fixing selling prices, the usual procedure is for the manufacturer to calculate the cost of producing a unit of each product at the normal capacity level of his existing plant, and then add to this unit cost what he regards as the most satisfactory profit margin in relation to his competitor's prices. This procedure is illustrated in Table 9.1. The fixed costs have been charged to products using the various overhead absorption rates as explained in Chapter 3.

Table 9.1

ABC COMPANY LTD

Determination of Selling Prices by Absorption Costing

	Production	Fixed Costs Selling and Distribution	Administration
Annual Cost	£30,000	£5,000	£2,000
Basis of Absorption	£60,000	£100,000	£100,000
Absorption Rate	Direct Labour Hours £0.5 per direct labour hour	Cost of Production 5% of cost of production	Cost of Production 2% of cost of production

Suggested Selling Prices

	Product A £ s. d.	Product B £ s. d.	Product C £ s. d.
Direct Labour	4 0 0 (10 hrs)	2 0 0 (5 hrs)	8 0 0 (20 hrs)
Direct Material	5 0 0	4 0 0	5 0 0
Direct Expense	1 0 0	– – –	2 0 0
PRIME COST	10 0 0	6 0 0	15 0 0
Production Overhead:			
Variable	5 0 0	1 10 0	5 0 0
Fixed	5 0 0	2 10 0	10 0 0
COST OF PRODUCTION	20 0 0	10 0 0	30 0 0
Selling and Distribution Cost:			
Variable	1 10 0	5 0	15 0
Fixed	1 0 0	10 0	1 10 0
Administration Overhead:			
Fixed	8 0	4 0	12 0
TOTAL COST	22 18 0	10 19 0	32 17 0
PROFIT MARGIN	2 5 0 (10%)	1 13 6 (15%)	6 9 6 (20%)
SELLING PRICE	£25 3 0	£12 12 6	£39 6 6
MARGINAL COST	£16 10 0	£7 15 0	£20 15 0

There is an evident danger that if these average total costs are
regarded as the benchmark for price making or price taking
actions, business which is going at a price which is less than total
unit cost, but which nevertheless would cover its marginal cost
(or incremental cost) and make a contribution to fixed costs, may

be rejected. This argument is particularly pertinent when business is bad and output is low, for, in conditions such as these, marginal cost will nearly always be *lower* than average total cost, whether the latter is determined in relation to normal output or not. For example, if the A B C Company based selling prices on total cost at normal capacity and received the following order:

20 units of Product A at £20
50 units of Product B at £10
75 units of Product C at £25

they would reject the order because the prices are in each case below the total cost which they have calculated. However, if they accepted the order it would make the following additional contribution towards fixed costs:

Product	Order Price			Marginal Cost			Contribution per Unit			Number of Units	Total Contribution		
	£	s.	d.	£	s.	d.	£	s.	d.		£	s.	d.
A	20	0	0	16	10	0	3	10	0	20	70	0	0
B	10	0	0	7	15	0	2	5	0	50	112	10	0
C	25	0	0	20	15	0	4	5	0	75	318	15	0
											£501	5	0

It is assumed that the company is working at less than full capacity and that there would be no increase in fixed costs.

There is a growing tendency for fixed costs to rise in relation to variable costs.[2] This means that the variable item of unit cost is

2. As the trend develops towards increased automation and higher capital investment per employee, the amount of overhead cost becomes increasingly important. With the continued shift from human to machine production, the decline in the importance of direct labour costs and the increase in the importance of overhead costs becomes more apparent. The introduction of automatic processes results in an increase in the proportion of fixed costs in the total overhead cost. The accountant's definition of overhead cost, as a cost which cannot be allocated directly to a cost unit, may change and resemble more closely the economist's definition of overhead, as a term synonymous with the fixed costs of production.

being replaced by fixed costs which have been allocated to products on the basis of an assumed volume of sales. Total unit costs become increasingly dependent upon the volume of sales assumed, and, in so far as different prices give rise to different sales volumes, unit costs themselves become a function of prices. The increase in the ratio of fixed to variable costs gives the manufacturer far more room to manoeuvre in fixing his selling prices than when variable production costs are high in relation to fixed costs.

The progressive manufacturer operating in a highly competitive industry needs a tool to enable him to take advantage of this room to manoeuvre. For this problem is not the straightforward one of determining his unit costs and then adding on the margin of profit to which he has been accustomed. It is the more complex problem of estimating the sales volume at different prices and calculating his total profits at these different prices and sales volumes.[3]

RATE OF RETURN PRICING

If a standard rate of return on capital employed is established, as suggested in Chapter 4, for a group of companies, a single company, or for individual divisions of a company, this may lead to the introduction of rate of return pricing. As a guide in making pricing decisions, management may wish to know what selling price would be required to produce a given rate of return on capital employed.

With this method of pricing, pricing commences with the establishment of a planned rate of return on capital employed. To translate this rate of return into a percentage mark-up on costs, i.e. to find the profit margin, it is necessary to estimate a 'normal' rate of production, averaged over the business cycle. Total costs of a year's normal production are then estimated, and this is taken as the total annual cost in the computation. The ratio of normal capital employed to the year's total annual cost is then computed, i.e. the rate of capital turnover. Multiplying the rate of capital turnover by the planned rate of return on

3. Gordon Johnson, 'The Pricing of Consumer Goods', *Yorkshire Bulletin of Economic and Social Research*, November 1962, p. 75.

capital employed gives the mark-up percentage to be applied to total unit costs for pricing purposes. The basic formula for this calculation is:

$$\frac{\text{Capital Employed}}{\text{Total Annual Cost}} \times \frac{\text{Profit}}{\text{Capital Employed}} = \frac{\text{Profit}}{\text{Total Annual Cost}}$$

Therefore:

$$\text{Percentage mark-up on cost} = \frac{\text{Capital Employed}}{\text{Total Annual Cost}} \times \text{Planned rate of return on capital employed}$$

For example, if the capital turnover ratio is 0.5 and the planned rate of return is 20 per cent on capital employed, the mark-up is 10 per cent on total cost. In other words, the required mark-up percentage can be obtained by multiplying the desired rate of return on capital employed by the capital turnover ratio, with the latter computed on normal total annual cost.

ILLUSTRATION OF RATE OF RETURN PRICING

The Domestic Appliance Company manufactures and markets a consumer durable. The company's sales volume is strongly influenced by external economic conditions which are outwith the control of the management. The company, over the long run, desires a rate of return of 15 per cent on capital employed. In pursuing this objective, the company has based selling prices on normal production. The existing product is being replaced by a new model, and management require to know the selling price per unit which will produce the desired rate of return on capital employed. The following estimates have been made:

Variable costs	£40 per unit
Fixed costs	£1,000,000 per year
Normal production	50,000 units
Normal capital employed:	
Variable	£10 per unit
Fixed	£1,500,000

The percentage mark-up on cost is calculated as follows:

$$\frac{\text{Capital Employed}}{\text{Total Annual Cost}} \times \begin{array}{l}\text{Desired rate of return} \\ \text{on capital employed}\end{array}$$

$$= \frac{(50,000 \times £10) + £1,500,000}{(50,000 \times £40) + £1,000,000} \times 15\%$$

$$= \frac{2,000,000}{3,000,000} \times 15\% = \underline{\underline{10\%}}$$

The selling price per unit which will produce the desired rate of return of 15 per cent on capital employed is calculated as follows:

	£
Variable Costs per unit	40
Fixed Costs per unit	
(£1,000,000 ÷ 50,000)	20
Total Cost	60
Mark-up on Cost (10%)	6
Selling Price	£66

The calculation of the selling price can be checked by calculating the rate of return on capital employed for 50,000 units:

		£
Sales	at £66 per unit	£3,300,000
Variable Costs	at £40 per unit	2,000,000
Fixed Costs		1,000,000
Total Costs		£3,000,000
Profit		£300,000
Capital Employed:		
Variable	at £10 per unit	500,000
Fixed		1,500,000
Total		£2,000,000

Return on Capital Employed

$$\frac{30,000 \times 100}{2,000,000} \qquad\qquad 15\%$$

The long-run base price that is obtained by applying the percentage mark-up to total unit cost will be altered with short-run changes in costs, such as increases in wage rates or when material prices change significantly, but not for fluctuations in the 'normal' rate of production. During periods when production is in excess of normal, profits will produce a higher than planned rate of return on capital employed, because actual unit costs will be lower than the normal unit costs used as the mark-up base. The fixed costs will be averaged over a greater volume of production, and the unit fixed costs will be lower than at normal production. Similarly, the capital employed will not increase in proportion to the increase in production. It will be seen in Table 9.2 that if the Domestic Appliance Company produces 60,000 units of the new model at a selling price of £66 per unit the rate of return on capital employed increases to 26.7 per cent. In periods of low production the reverse will occur: actual profits and return on capital employed will be lower. If 40,000 units are produced the rate of return on capital employed falls to 2.1 per cent. Thus, as with absorption cost pricing, costs and prices which are based on a *normal* volume concept are only valid when the actual volume is the same as the assumed *normal* volume.

In a multi-product business the percentage mark-up is an average, both among products and through time. Actual prices of specific products will vary from the base price, derived from the long-run mark-up on cost, to meet varying demand conditions and competition for each product. However, if the planned rate of return on capital employed is to be attained over, say, a five-year period these variations must be made to balance so that the weighted average of mark-ups remains close to the planned overall mark-up. The planned mark-up thus provides a benchmark for controlling short-run price making and price taking actions, and appraising the extent to which these actions direct profits away from the planned return on capital employed.

Rate of return pricing is thus a refined variant of absorption

Table 9.2

	Per Unit £	
Selling Price	66	
Variable Cost	40	
Contribution	£26	

Number of Units	40,000	60,000
	£	£
Total Contribution	1,040,000	1,560,000
Fixed Costs	1,000,000	1,000,000
Profit	£40,000	£560,000

Capital Employed		
Variable at £10 per unit	400,000	600,000
Fixed	1,500,000	1,500,000
Total	£1,900,000	£2,100,000
Return on Capital Employed	2.1%	26.7%

pricing. It does build on cost that is 'normalized' for fluctuations in the rate of output, and it develops a profit mark-up that is related to a planned rate of return on capital employed. However, these refinements do not necessarily remove the arbitrary element in setting the mark-up percentage. It may simply transfer the arbitrariness to the planned rate of return. The method does have the advantage of directing pricing at some planned rate of return on capital employed, despite the fact that there is no guarantee that this planned rate of return will be achieved, except when demand and competitive conditions are as anticipated when the mark-up was established.[4] While it might guide short-

4. Varying degrees of sophistication can be introduced into the calculation of the percentage mark-up. In a multi-product business separate mark-ups can be calculated for individual products, but this necessitates the

run pricing decisions there is still the danger that average total costs will be regarded as the rock-bottom price for price making and price taking, and business which is going at a price which is less than total unit cost, but which nevertheless would cover its marginal cost and make a contribution to fixed costs, will be rejected. If the profit margins in Table 9.1 were based on a planned rate of return, the order which gives £501.25 contribution to fixed costs could still be rejected. Thus, it may be argued that rate of return pricing, like any system of cost-plus pricing:

1. Tends to ignore demand and assumes prices are simply a function of costs:

2. Fails to reflect competition adequately;

3. Overplays the precision of allocated fixed costs and capital employed; and

4. Is based upon a concept of cost (full cost) that is frequently not relevant to the pricing decision at hand.

Rate of return pricing would appear to be most suitable in non-competitive situations when selling prices are established on a basis acceptable to the customer. For example, on 26 February 1968 the British Government announced that agreement had been reached with industry for the immediate implementation of new arrangements for placing and pricing non-competitive Government contracts covered by the existing profit formula. It was agreed that the aim of the formula should be to give contractors a fair return on capital employed; that is to say, equal, on average, to the overall return earned by industry in recent years. The yardstick was taken as the average of industry's earnings over the last seven years for which figures were available (1960–66), which gave a figure of 14 per cent on capital employed. It was further announced that given the complex accounting issues involved there would be further urgent discussions with industry. Agreement had to be reached on the difficult problems of bases

---

apportionment of common fixed costs and common capital employed. The time value of money can be introduced into the calculations. Space does not permit a full examination of these approaches, but, regardless of the degree of sophistication, the fact remains that there is no guarantee that the planned rate of return will be achieved.

for apportioning capital employed and overhead costs to contracts. It is interesting to note that agreement was also reached on
a proposal to set up an impartial Review Board, and to secure
acceptance of its rulings by a new contractual condition. Both
sides can refer contracts where profits of 27½ per cent or more
capital employed and losses of 15 per cent or more have been
made, to establish whether any reimbursement or compensation
is justified. If these margins of error in estimating prices are
acceptable for non-competitive contracts, it is not too difficult to
imagine the difficulties of applying rate of return pricing in competitive situations when there is no agreement with competitors
or customers on the basis of determining selling prices.

MARGINAL PRICING

Clearly, the use of conventional absorption costing or the rate of
return variant for pricing decisions has disadvantages, at least in
the short run. Is the marginal cost and contribution towards
fixed costs approach a satisfactory alternative? Marginal techniques can provide better data for pricing decisions that help to
achieve normal capacity levels and optimize profits after normal
capacity is reached. With the marginal approach the question is
not 'Shall we raise or lower our selling prices?', but 'What will
happen to our total profits if we raise or lower the selling prices of
particular products?' In a highly competitive industry where
demand for an individual firm's products is correspondingly
elastic, and the ratio of fixed to variable costs is high, it is
possible to make a wide range of prices which are all economically possible, i.e. each price generates sufficient total sales
revenue to cover total costs and provide some profit. In deciding
these prices, advocates of marginal cost pricing suggest fixed
costs must be omitted from unit costs and selling prices determined on the basis of marginal cost. A pricing decision involves
planning into the future, and as such it should deal solely with the
anticipated, and therefore estimated, revenues, expenses, and
capital outlays. All past outlays which give rise to fixed costs are
historical and unchangeable. They are inescapable, 'sunk costs',
regardless of how they may be 'costed' for financial accounting

purposes, for stock valuation or distribution of profit through time.

With *marginal pricing* the firm seeks to fix its prices so as to maximize its total contribution to fixed costs and profit. Unless the manufacturer's products are in direct competition with each other, this objective is achieved by considering each product in isolation and fixing its price at a level which is calculated to maximize its total contribution. At this point it may be useful to illustrate the discussion with two examples of marginal pricing decisions.

1. *Choice of Contracts.* The Bettermade Electronic Company operates in an area where there is little prospect of increasing its labour force. The firm employs 20 direct operatives whose working week is 40 hours and whose average rate of pay is 3s. per hour. No overtime is worked. On 1 September the company has to choose between two contracts, with A B Ltd or with C D Ltd, each commencing on 1 January and lasting until the end of March. Either contract would fully utilize the company's productive capacity and therefore they cannot be undertaken at the same time. Standard direct costs for each contract, and the best prices that can be obtained, are:

	AB Ltd Contract	CD Ltd Contract
	£ s. d.	£ s. d.
Per dozen:		
Direct materials	4 10 0	1 10 0
Direct wages	1 10 0	3 0 0
Selling Price	10 15 0	13 10 0

The company's standard overhead per week is £300 of which £200 is variable and £100 fixed. Overhead is absorbed by a standard rate per direct labour hour. The managing director asks the cost accountant to:

(a) calculate the total cost per dozen for each contract;

(b) calculate the percentage profit to sales for each contract; and

(c) state which contract he would recommend the company to undertake.

There are no reasons of special policy which favour one contract or the other.

The cost accountant's calculations are shown in Table 9.3.

Table 9.3

BETTERMADE ELECTRONIC COMPANY

Comparison of AB Ltd and CD Ltd Contracts

(a) *Total Cost per dozen*

	AB Ltd Contract	CD Ltd Contract
	£ s. d.	£ s. d.
Direct material cost	4 10 0	1 10 0
Direct wages	1 10 0 (10 hrs)	3 0 0 (20 hrs)
PRIME COST	6 0 0	4 10 0
Overhead at 7s. 6d. per direct labour hour*	3 15 0	7 10 0
TOTAL COST	£9 15 0	£12 0 0

*Overhead rate $\frac{£300}{800}$ hrs = 7s. 6d. per direct labour hour.

(b) *% Profit to Sales*

	£ s. d.	£ s. d.
Selling price	10 15 0	13 10 0
Total Cost	9 15 0	12 0 0
Profit per dozen	£1 0 0	£1 10 0
% of Selling Price	9.3%	11.1%

(c) *Recommendation*

Would recommend the acceptance of contract with AB Ltd. Although the profit percentage on sales is higher in the case of CD Ltd, the total profit for 13 weeks ended 31 December would be more in the case of AB Ltd.

	AB Ltd Contract	CD Ltd Contract
Production for 13 weeks	1,040 doz.	520 doz.

Table 9.3 – cont.

	£	£
Direct material cost	4,680	780
Direct wages	1,560	1,560
PRIME COST	6,240	2,340
Overhead 13 × £300	3,900	3,900
Total Cost	10,140	6,240
Sales	11,180	7,020
PROFIT	£1,040	£780

Another way of looking at the problem is to recognize that direct labour is the factor which limits production and that the objective must be to maximize *contribution per direct labour hour*. In this situation, where the company is operating at full capacity, all costs are fixed costs other than material. The only variable cost in the above calculation is material. The contribution per direct labour hour should therefore be calculated as follows:

	AB Ltd Contract	CD Ltd Contract
	£ s. d.	£ s. d.
Selling price per dozen	10 15 0	13 10 0
Direct material per dozen	4 10 0	1 10 0
Contribution per dozen	£6 5 0	£12 0 0
Direct labour hours	10	20
Contributions per direct labour hour	12s. 6d.	12s.

The additional profit on AB Ltd in 13 weeks would be 10,400 hrs at 6d. per hour = £260.

On the basis of percentage profit to sales the contract with CD would appear to be more profitable. However, it will be seen that when the two contracts are examined more closely AB Ltd gives the higher total profit and contribution per direct labour hour.

2. *Raising or lowering prices.* The XYZ Company is reviewing

Table 9.4

XYZ COMPANY LTD
Revision of Selling Price of Product A

Marginal Cost:
0 – 2,000 units £12 per unit
2,000 – 5,000 units £11.75 per unit
5,000 – 7,500 units £11.5 per unit
7,500 – 10,000 units £11.25 per unit

	Present Price	Alternative Prices					
Selling Price	£18	£17	£17.5	£18.5	£19	£19.5	£20
Estimated Annual Demand	7,600	8,000	7,800	7,400	7,000	5,700	4,200
Contribution per unit:	£	£	£	£	£	£	£
0 – 2,000 units	6.0	5.0	5.5	6.5	7.0	7.5	8.0
2,000 – 5,000 units	6.25	5.25	5.75	6.75	7.25	7.75	8.25
5,000 – 7,500 units	6.5	5.5	6.0	7.0	7.5	8.0	8.5
7,500 – 10,000 units	6.75	5.75	6.25	7.25	7.75	8.25	8.75
Total Contribution	£	£	£	£	£	£	£
0 – 2,000 units	12,000	10,000	11,000	13,000	14,000	15,000	16,000
2,000 – 5,000 units	18,750	15,750	17,250	20,250	21,750	23,250	18,150
5,000 – 7,500 units	16,250	13,750	15,000	16,800	15,000	5,600	—
7,500 – 10,000 units	675	2,875	1,875	—	—	—	—
Total	£47,675	£42,375	£45,125	£50,050	£50,750	£43,850	£34,150

the selling price of Product A, and after carrying out extensive market research has estimated the following annual demands for the product at various prices:

Price	Estimated Annual Demand
£17	8,000
£17.5	7,800
£18 (present price)	7,600
£18.5	7,400
£19	7,000
£19.5	5,700
£20	4,200

Each of these demands can be manufactured with existing productive capacity, and the company has to decide which price will result in the greatest contribution towards fixed costs and profit. The type of calculation the accountant could make is shown in Table 9.4. It will be seen that the greatest profit improvement would result from raising the selling price of Product A from £18 to £19 per unit, provided the market research is accurate and 7,000 units can be sold at the price level of £19 per unit. In establishing the new price, the demand has been taken into consideration, and the cost function is based upon a concept of cost (marginal cost) that is relevant to the pricing decision at hand. It will be appreciated that one of the principal problems associated with marginal cost pricing is that of forecasting the demand curve. This problem is considered later in this chapter.

It is usually assumed in examples of marginal cost pricing that the firm has surplus capacity, and that additional sales can be produced without any increase in fixed costs. It may be argued that if a company is operating at full capacity in the short run, it cannot always take full advantage of demand elasticity and short-term contracts, and that it can therefore rely on the conventional method of fixing its price on the basis of normal cost at full capacity. Is this necessarily so? It is probable that many manufacturers in a highly competitive industry will be working below full capacity and have L- rather than U-shaped marginal cost curves, i.e. they will be operating below the level at which marginal cost starts to rise. In any case if any one or more manufacturers are working below full capacity, they may well be the price leaders when it comes to price fixing. Even if the company is working at normal capacity it can usually increase the output of the existing plant by working it more intensively. This may give rise to higher marginal costs, but this can be taken into consideration when fixing prices. It may be that prices resulting from costs based on normal capacity output are too low. Even when it is necessary to increase plant capacity and pricing becomes a long-run problem, the additional contribution resulting from the difference between the short-run marginal cost and price can be compared with the additional fixed costs which will result from the increased capacity.

THE ACTUAL USE OF MARGINAL COSTS IN PRICING

Despite the apparent advantages of marginal pricing as compared with product prices based on total costs derived from absorption costing, full costs appear to be used by most firms when developing product prices. The results of the author's own research do not cast doubt on the impression obtained from the several empirical studies of product pricing,[5] that the accountant's advice to management is almost invariably based upon full cost at normal capacity in the first stage of price fixing. Marginal costing appears to be used for what might be called 'secondary' pricing decisions, e.g. tenders, by-products, unusual work, export orders, sub-contracting, etc. Full costs usually form the basis of the cost information provided to management for what might be classified as 'primary' pricing decisions, for standard products sold in the home market. 'Consequently, marginal cost is commonly referred to in special pricing decisions where a price close to marginal cost may be appropriate, the original price having been progressively reduced from full cost plus normal margin level.'[6]

The following is an example of the application of marginal

5. For details of the author's, and other empirical research, see John Sizer, 'The Accountant's Contribution to the Pricing Decision', *Journal of Management Studies*, May 1966, pp. 129–50.

6. M. Howe, 'Marginal Analysis in Accounting', *Yorkshire Bulletin of Economic and Social Research*, November 1962, pp. 81–9.

cost data in a 'secondary' pricing decision.[7] The X Y Z Company has invited Milky Dairies Ltd and a number of other dairies to submit quotations for the supply of milk to their Uptown factory and staff canteen, their Downtown depot and their offices. The manager of the Milky Dairies Bigtown dairy has asked the accountant for his recommendations on minimum selling prices and suggested selling prices. The accountant's recommendations are set out in Table 9.5. Dealing first with pasteurized pints, T.T. pasteurized pints, pasteurized bulk and sterilized pints: these are standard lines and additional gallonage can be processed at marginal cost. The milk can be distributed on existing vehicles. It will be seen that to the cost of milk have been added the variable processing and distribution costs to give the marginal cost per gallon. The accountant has then added a minimum contribution of 5d. per gallon to give the minimum selling prices. The suggested prices will be based on his previous experience and knowledge of tender prices to this class of customer. This is a good example of a 'secondary' pricing decision, where the suggested prices have been based on marginal cost data.

It will be noted that, in arriving at his minimum selling price for the half-pint cartons, the accountant has included fixed processing costs for normal capacity output, i.e. he has based his recommendation partly on absorption cost data. Why is this? In the eyes of the accountant this is not a 'secondary' pricing decision; it is closer to a 'primary' pricing decision. Half-pint cartons are not very well established in the British dairy industry, and Milky Dairies have only a very low sales gallonage of this type of container. The present gallonage is not fully recovering fixed processing costs, and the accountant feels that any additional sales must be charged with their share of fixed processing costs, as well as the minimum contribution of 5d. per gallon, in arriving at a minimum selling price.

The probable reason why the full cost basis is used in 'primary' pricing decisions is because they are considered to be long-run decisions. They will in the first instance be long-run prices although they may be increased or decreased in the future to

7. This example is taken from the author's article, 'Marginal Costing in the Dairy Industry' *Accountancy*, December 1967, pp. 789–98.

accord with existing short-run conditions. But when initially deciding the price of standard 'bread and butter' products, firms are thinking in terms of a price which will cover all their costs and give a satisfactory return on capital employed in the long run. Hence the increasing use of the rate of return variant of absorption pricing. Seen in these long-run terms all costs are variable. Therefore, given this long-run attitude, 'once commitments which

Table 9.5

MILKY DAIRIES LTD

Quotations for XYZ Company Ltd, Bigtown

	Uptown Factory (inc. Staff Canteen)				*Down-town Depot*	*Office*
	½ Pint Cartons	*Past. Pints*	*Past. Bulk*	*Steril-ized Pints*	*T.T. Past. Pints*	*Past. Pints*
	d.	*d.*	*d.*	*d.*	*d.*	*d.*
Cost of Milk from Milk Marketing Board	45.375	45.375	45.375	45.375	45.375	45.375
Less Rebate	1.750	1.750	1.750	1.750	1.750	1.750
COST OF MILK	43.625	43.625	43.625	43.625	43.625	43.625
Processing Expenses						
Variable	19.900	1.380	.020	2.410	1.380	1.380
Semi-Variable	.800	.490	.010	.610	.490	.490
Fixed	6.175*	Nil	Nil	Nil	Nil	Nil
	70.500	45.495	43.655	46.645	45.495	45.495
Variable Distribution Costs	3.000	3.000	3.000	3.000	2.000	2.000
MARGINAL COST	73.500	48.495	46.655	49.645	47.495	47.495
Minimum Contribution	5.000	5.000	5.000	5.000	5.000	5.000
	78.500	53.495	51.655	54.645	52.495	52.495

*Normal capacity fixed processing costs per Bigtown Dairy Standard Processing Costs of 1 January 1960.

293

Table 9.5 – cont.

MINIMUM SELLING PRICE per gallon	78.5 (5d. per carton)	53.5	51.5	54.5	52.5	52.5
MAXIMUM CUT per gallon	17.5	10.5	12.5	13.5	15.5	11.5
FULL RETAIL PRICE per gallon	96.0	64.0	64.0	68.0	68.0	64.0
SUGGESTED SELLING PRICE per gallon	80d.	54d.	52d.	56d.	56d.	54d.

entail continuing fixed costs have been made, management wants unit costs for pricing which include a provision for recovery of total outlay according to some systematic plan.'[8] The use of conventional absorption costing with fixed costs included in product costs on the basis of normal capacity offers such a 'systematic' plan. Marginal costing offers no equally obvious plan for the recovery of fixed costs; it merely gives the optimum short-run price-output combination which will yield the largest possible total contribution out of which fixed costs and profit can be provided in the long run. It does not guarantee that all costs will be met and a normal profit will be provided in the long run. On the other hand, full cost pricing only provides this guarantee *if sales volume is equal to or more than normal capacity output.*

ADVANTAGES OF MARGINAL PRICING

What then are the advantages claimed for marginal pricing; is it to be considered superior to pricing under absorption costing?

When making pricing decisions firms have to consider the costs potential competitors would face if they are, or were to commence, producing the firm's products. Will the total costs developed under absorption costing or marginal costs give the best estimate of these costs? In many instances, when the competitor is a multi-product firm with existing production facilities,

8. National Association of Accountants, *Product Costs for Pricing Purposes*, Research Report No. 24, New York, 1953, p. 39.

it is the marginal or incremental cost which the competitor will incur. With marginal pricing prices are never rendered uncompetitive merely because of a higher fixed overhead cost structure, or because hypothetical unit fixed costs are higher than competitors. The firm's prices will only be rendered uncompetitive by higher variable costs, and these are controllable in the short run, while certain fixed costs are not.

Marginal costs more accurately reflect *future* as distinct from present cost levels and cost relationships. When making a pricing decision you are interested in the changes in cost that will result from that decision. Marginal cost represents these changes, while total costs developed by absorption costing include fixed costs which are not incurred as a result of the pricing decision.

When the demand for a product is highly elastic, the price which maximizes contribution, and therefore profits, may be less than (or more than) the total cost plus normal profit margin developed under absorption costing. Many of the prices determined by marginal costing would probably be considered uneconomic if they were simply compared with total costs including fixed overhead based on normal capacity.

Will a policy of rather rigid and uniform pricing, such as absorption costing brings about, be more or less discouraging to actual and potential competitors than a policy which tends to make prices more differentiated and more flexible through time? Marginal pricing permits a manufacturer to develop a far more aggressive pricing policy than does absorption costing. An aggressive pricing policy should lead to higher sales and possibly reduced marginal costs through increased marginal physical productivity and lower input factor prices. However, before entering into a more differentiated and a more flexible pricing policy it would be necessary to consider the impact of unstable prices on customer goodwill.

While marginal pricing is essentially a short-run concept it is probably more effective than absorption costing because of two characteristics of modern business:

1. *The prevalence of multi-product, multi-process and multi-market concerns which makes the absorption of fixed costs into product costs absurd.* The total costs of the separate products can

never be estimated satisfactorily, and the optimal relationship between costs and prices will vary substantially both among different products and between different markets. If markets are to be segmented successfully, it is necessary to know the variable costs and specific fixed costs attributable to each segment. In this type of business one is constantly considering proposals for changing selling prices or terms of sales, for segmenting the market to gain advantage of the different layers of consumer demand, and for selecting the most profitable business when capacity is limited. These are usually short-run problems because the underlying conditions are always changing, and marginal pricing is the most suitable method of short-run pricing.

2. *In many businesses the dominant force is innovation combined with constant scientific and technological development, and the long-run situation is often highly unpredictable.* There is a series of short runs and one must aim at maximizing contribution in each short run. When rapid developments are taking place, fixed costs and demand conditions may change from one short run to another, and only by maximizing contribution in each short run will profit be maximized in the long run. To argue that the normal capacity absorption costing approach is more satisfactory for long-run pricing is to miss the point, for it is doubtful whether it is useful to think in terms of the 'long run' in view of these characteristics of modern business.

It should also be recognized that many branded products cannot be expected to hold a permanent franchise in the market place, whether it be the industrial or retail markets. Many products will have a product life cycle of introduction, growth, maturity, and decline. At the *introduction* stage the product is put on the market; awareness and acceptance is minimal. The product begins to make rapid sales gains at the *growth* stage, because of the cumulative effects of introductory promotion, distribution, and word of mouth influence. However, the rate of sales growth begins to taper off, because of the diminishing number of potential new customers who are either unaware of the product or are aware but are not prepared to purchase. This is the *maturity* stage. *Decline* sets in when sales begin to diminish as the product is gradually edged out by newer or better products or substitutes. In addition to the product life cycle, product obsolescence may arise partly from past mistakes in new product decisions, or from acquisitions of obsolete products through mergers and takeovers. While the product life cycle represents a useful idealization rather than a rigid description of all product life histories, it does make it apparent that different policies are required at different stages of a product's life. There is nothing fixed about the length of the cycle, or the length of the various stages of the cycle. The length of the cycle is governed by a number of factors including the rate of market acceptance, the rate of technological changes, and the ease of competitive entry. With the increasing pace of technological change it may be reasonable to assume that new products' life spans will tend to be shorter than in the past. Of course, products have been known to begin a new cycle or to revert to some earlier stage as a result of the discovery of new uses, the appearance of new users, the discovery of cheap sources, or the invention of new features. The discovery of North Sea gas has led the gas industry in Britain to revert back to the growth stage of the product life cycle. It may also push the coal industry more rapidly into the decline stage. Television sales have reverted to earlier stages in the cycle with the introduction of new sizes of screens, commercial television, and BBC-2. Colour television may well put television sales back into a growth stage. Despite these and other difficulties concerning the concept of the product life cycle, it remains a useful concept in that it reminds marketers and accountants that products have a limited life; that they tend to follow a predictable pattern through the life cycle; and that products require different marketing programmes at each stage in the cycle. Management must be prepared to shift the relative levels and emphasis given to price, advertising, product improvement, product differentiation, etc. during the different stages of the product life cycle. Marketing management requires cost information to assist it in determining the correct combination of price, advertising, product improvement, product differentiation, etc. for each stage of the cycle. They require short-run marginal cost and separable fixed cost data relevant to that stage of the cycle, *not* long-run absorption cost data.

So, while it has to be admitted that marginal pricing is essentially a short-run concept, this is not to say it has no part to play in long-run pricing policy. On the contrary, the consideration of marginal cost and contribution is an essential part of an intelligent long-range pricing policy, especially for multi-product firms. In the long run, cost recovery may be best attained on an overall basis by varying the rates at which 'fixed' costs are reflected in sales prices of different products, or in the sales prices of a product at different stages of its life cycle or in different places. In the multi-product firm a variety of possible combinations must be considered and some products are able to contribute a wider margin over marginal cost than are other products. Products will make different contributions at the various stages of their life cycles. This means setting prices which will maximize contribution in the particular situation, and marginal costs may then be more useful guides. It may be that a range of inter-related products are manufactured and they appeal to the consumer or distributor as a whole range, i.e. there is a demand curve for the whole range rather than for individual products in the range. In such a case each product cannot be considered in isolation, and it will not be possible to think in terms of maximizing the contribution from each separate product. It will be necessary to develop the prices of the products in relation to each other so as to maximize the contribution from the entire range of products. The demand for the whole range of products must be considered rather than the demand for individual products. For example, the Gillette Safety Razor was marketed at very low prices in order to create a market for the very profitable razor blades. In this situation the objective must be to maximize the combined contribution from the safety razor and the razor blades.

Advocates of absorption costing suggest that with marginal pricing there is a lack of information as to whether in the long run in a multi-product business each product is carrying its fair share of overheads, since there is no allocation of fixed costs. With marginal costing the fixed costs can be allocated to products or product groups at least once a year for profit planning purposes. Direct and common fixed costs are distinguished, but they are allocated in total for the planned volume and sales mix; they are never unitized. It is the unitizing of fixed costs on the product cost sheets as in Table 9.1 that makes absorption costing confusing to operating management, because these unit costs are valid only at the assumed *normal* volume and the assumed *normal* mix. By showing the allocation of fixed costs to product lines in total, along with the forecast volume and sales mix, this confusion is avoided. Operating management can see clearly the true interrelationship of sales prices, costs, and volume. This form of presentation has been discussed in detail in Chapter 8. Table 9.6 shows in summary the type of presentation that can be made.

DISADVANTAGES AND SPECIAL CONSIDERATIONS OF MARGINAL PRICING

The terminology of marginal pricing. While marginal pricing may be a better pricing technique it is more difficult to employ than absorption pricing. In order to use the figures it receives as guides in making the most of the opportunities offered by market conditions, it is important that the management understands the nature of the costs and profit margins which it uses in pricing. The executives of a company are usually familiar with the concepts of gross and net profit because they have been widely used for a long time. On the other hand, the breakdown of costs into fixed and variable categories and the use of contribution rather than gross profit are comparatively new developments and many executives are not familiar with these terms. For this reason it will be necessary for executives who have to make pricing decisions to learn the use of this new terminology and the concepts it describes. The accountant, who should be an expert in costing, should be able to undertake this process of education. This is one of the drawbacks to the extended use of marginal pricing; some accountants are not fully conversant with the marginal techniques themselves, and are not therefore capable of explaining their use to management.[9]

9. For an account of the historical development of marginal costing and the extent of its present-day use, see John Sizer, 'The Development of Marginal Costing', *Accountants Magazine*, January 1968, pp. 23–30.

Table 9.6

HIGH QUALITY PRODUCTS LTD

Product Profits Forecast 1969

Product Group	Sales		Variable Cost of Sales	Total Contri- bution	Separable Fixed Costs	Direct Product Profits	Common Fixed Costs	Trading Profit
	Units	Value						
		£	£	£	£	£	£	£
A	2,000	10,000	5,000	5,000	1,000	4,000	1,000	3,000
B	4,000	25,000	16,000	9,000	4,000	5,000	2,500	2,500
C	3,500	22,000	17,000	5,000	2,000	3,000	2,200	800
D	5,000	31,000	24,000	7,000	3,000	4,000	3,100	900
E	8,350	42,000	30,000	12,000	3,000	9,000	4,200	4,800
		£130,000	£92,000	£38,000	£13,000	£25,000	£13,000	£12,000

Note:
Common fixed costs have been allocated to products on the basis of sales value.

The importance of fixed costs. It is important that fixed costs should not be ignored to the extent that they are not covered by contribution. Total contribution from all products must be sufficient to cover fixed costs and leave a balance which is at least a normal profit for that type of business. It is *not* essential that each separate product or market should produce a contribution which is sufficient to cover allocated fixed costs and provide a normal profit. The contribution from an individual product should at least cover the separable fixed costs attributable to that product. Contribution to common fixed costs will vary from one product to another and from one market to another. Another danger in overemphasizing the contribution to fixed overhead approach is that the encouragement to take on business which makes only a small contribution may be so strong that when an opportunity for higher contribution business arises, such business may have to be forgone because of inadequate free capacity, unless there is expansion in organization and facilities with the attendant increase in fixed costs. This is another reason why marginal pricing is a more difficult technique to employ. The management must know its markets and customers, and be able to forecast their future actions.

Marginal pricing and price stability. Is there a danger that with marginal pricing, where prices are fixed at a level calculated to maximize contribution, there will be constant price variations with changes in demand? Will marginal pricing militate against price stability? When there is a temporary expansion of demand will manufacturers raise their prices to maximize short-run contribution and when there is a decline in demand will they lower prices? If a firm is constantly making short-run price changes to exploit changes in demand it may prejudice its long-term interests. In a period of business recession firms using marginal pricing may lower prices in order to maintain business and this may lead other firms to lower their prices. Cut-throat competition might in fact develop. With the existence of idle capacity and the pressure of fixed costs, firms may successively cut prices to a point at which no one of them is earning sufficient total contribution to cover his fixed costs and earn a fair return on capital employed.

With regard to the use of marginal pricing during a business recession three situations can be considered:

1. When there is a short-run recession in the industry, i.e. when there is unused capacity in the industry caused by a temporary fall in demand.

2. When the industry is contracting and there is excess capacity in the industry, i.e. the capacity which if withdrawn from production would bring a rise in prices sufficient to restore normal profits to the industry.

3. When there is a general depression as in the 1930s and there is unused capacity in all industries.

In the first situation, the short-run recession in the industry, the firm can lower its price to take account of the new shape of the demand curve and set a new price which will maximize the total contribution, given this new demand curve. But if the firm considers the recession is only temporary, it may not wish to risk the possibility of a price war with its competitors when there is likely to be a recovery in business in the near future. It may not employ an aggressive marginal pricing policy because of the fear of retaliation. Non-price competition in the form of special offers, gifts, etc. may be more attractive than price cuts, particularly when it is extremely difficult to forecast the new demand curve. However, it may still be possible to engage in an aggressive marginal pricing policy in differentiated markets, e.g. exports, where retaliation is not likely to occur because the firm is not in direct competition with its usual competitors.

In the case of a contracting industry it is a question of the 'survival of the fittest'. The contraction adjustments will tend to take place by means of cut-price competition. The more efficient firms will have lower marginal cost curves and/or lower fixed costs than their less efficient competitors. As the more efficient firms lower their prices to maintain business, their weaker competitors will be eliminated from the industry. Prices will eventually be restored to a level which maximizes total contribution at a figure which provides a normal profit margin. As the more efficient firms lower their prices they attract trade from their weaker competitors, thus increasing their total contribution. Then, as the weaker firms are eliminated, the industry supply curve will rise and so will the price which maximizes total contribution. An aggressive marginal pricing policy by the efficient firms may well speed up the process of contraction.

When there is a general depression in all sectors of the economy, marginal pricing which results in a price lower than the total cost of absorption costing may be necessary to the individual firm, but it may tend to delay general economic recovery. The aggressive pricing policy of the efficient firms may drive the less efficient firms out of business, thus increasing unemployment and reducing income-generating expenditure.

In fact, there appears to be a widespread feeling among accountants that marginal costing is a technique which can be used most advantageously only in periods of business recession. For example, a large steel company stated that marginal costing is not applied to their normal accounting routines. 'However, during the recent trade recession we have applied these techniques in reviewing selling prices of some of our products other than iron and steel'. Thus, when business is buoyant and output is high, average total costs based on absorption costing will be preferred to the accountant's marginal cost as cost data. The typical accountant may assume that marginal cost is always lower than average total costs; that prices should be a function of cost; and he may tend to ignore the fact that prices are also a function of demand. When business is buoyant, he chooses the cost which he believes will give the higher price and therefore higher profits. It may be argued that the cost accountant is in fact honouring the idea that prices are also a function of demand if he considers marginal cost only in recession, and he thinks of the highest price at other times. It is true that the accountant by using marginal cost data does tend to recognize the demand function in a recession, but the use of the total cost data of absorption costing in a buoyant period is not full recognition of the demand function. It does not recognize the fact that profits are maximized at that price which gives the highest total contribution in the short run, and that this is not necessarily the highest price. The price developed by absorption costing will probably not be the price which would maximize total contribution and profits. In the higher ranges of output average total cost may be superior cost data to the accountant's marginal cost, if the accountant assumes that marginal cost is constant in the higher output ranges. But true marginal cost may exceed average total cost as the limit of short-run productive capacity is approached, and marginal cost accurately determined will always be superior to average total cost for short-run pricing decisions.

Will in fact marginal pricing give rise to price instability? It is doubtful in the majority of firms. There are a number of reasons why many firms would be ill advised or reluctant to change prices during short-term cyclical fluctuations, particularly lowering prices during cyclical recessions, regardless of the method of pricing employed:

1. In many industries in the short run it is a very expensive and complicated business altering prices. The benefit to be derived from a small alteration in prices will often be outweighed by the cost of making the price change. If prices are lowered during a cyclical recession it may be difficult to raise them again.

2. In most, if not all, industries some form of imperfect competition exists. If there is price leadership, all the firms large enough to cause the leader concern will probably follow the price leader. Price leadership tends to dampen down the amplitude of cyclical fluctuations. In an imperfect oligopoly situation the firms will have, or will think they have, a kinked demand curve. They will be reluctant to raise their prices because they think their competitors will not do likewise, and they will lose customers to their competitors. They think that if they lower their prices their competitors will do likewise and no advantage will be gained. In other industries, prices are government-controlled: for example in the dairy industry, where competitive pricing will arise principally on tenders and quotations for short-term supplies to schools, hospitals, holiday camps, etc. The earning of additional contribution from products sold or work done in circumstances which would not materially affect the normal markets could be wholly beneficial even though the selling price yields little more than marginal cost. However, a decision to sell at lower prices would be unwise if it might have an adverse effect

upon the undertaking's general level of selling prices in its established markets.

3. Another important factor is the relationship between quality and price in the eyes of the customer. A marketing economist has pointed out:

It has been suggested that to the consumer price is an important indicator of product quality and the satisfaction he can expect from the relevant purchase. The housewife, and the industrial buyer, like, at least socially in the purchasing side of a trade transaction, to 'know where they stand'. Steady price implies steady product quality, makes advance budgeting possible and buying simpler. It reduces the need for 'haggling' or shopping around which tend to be unwelcome chores to the busy Anglo-Saxon purchaser. The seller in the organized market, selling mainly on reputation, his 'brand' image perhaps, in a field where product sophistication makes comparison testing on any scale prohibitive, has no desire whatever to upset his customers in the social activity of buying, or to upset their preconceived notions about the product's quality associated with price.[10]

If one accepts the above arguments then the pricing of consumer goods and mass-produced capital goods will tend to be stable in the short run. Such firms would tend to restrict their aggressive short-run pricing to *secondary* pricing decisions, such as export orders, sub-contracting, supplies to institutions, etc. On the other hand, in a jobbing undertaking, where it is unlikely that any significant degree of repetition of orders for similar products will occur, the objective of maintaining full capacity working and maximizing contribution to fixed costs may only be achieved consistently if the price fixing policy is flexible.

In a competitive industry marginal pricing is more likely to produce price stability by discouraging manufacturers from using every increase in costs as an excuse for raising prices in order to safeguard unit profits. A manufacturer who fully understands the principles of marginal pricing will never increase his selling

10. T. E. Milne, 'Price, Investment Scale and Resource Allocation', in *Essays in the Theory and Practice of Pricing*, Institute of Economic Affairs, London, 1967, pp. 223–4.

price simply because his fixed costs have risen. His existing selling prices should be yielding a maximum total contribution in present demand conditions, and if he raises his selling prices because his fixed costs have increased, he will find himself earning a smaller total contribution than before he increased his prices. The increase in price will be offset by the fall in demand. This does assume that there has been no change in demand conditions. In a period of inflation there will have been a general increase in the fixed costs of all the firms in the industry, and a change in the underlying demand conditions. In this situation an increase will be necessary to maximize total contribution. Any attempt to safeguard profit by raising selling prices because fixed costs have risen will be self-defeating, if there has been no change in the demand function and the selling prices have already been fixed at a level calculated to maximize total contribution.

FORECASTING DEMAND

An important factor which militates against the more extensive application of marginal pricing is the lack of accurate demand information. A forecast of total contribution for any given price depends upon a knowledge of demand at that price. Johnson admits in his paper:[11]

I have been speaking so far as if the price of a product could be varied and as if it were possible to draw up some sort of demand schedule showing the likely volume of sales at different prices. Now although there are various methods of testing elasticity of demand, in the last resort demand schedules must be a matter of judgement based on experience of the particular market.

In fact, locating the position of the demand curve is the major difficulty in the use of marginal pricing. Forecasting demand is a field where commercial judgement is required in the final decisions, but the large firm can remove a considerable amount of

11. Gordon Johnson, 'The Pricing of Consumer Goods', *Yorkshire Bulletin of Economic and Social Research*, November 1962, p. 75.

the doubt by careful and detailed analysis, reducing the error to very narrow limits. Specialists can examine competitors' products and assess their appeal to customers in different markets. Penetration trends in each market can be analysed. Competitors' pricing policies, marketing arrangements, and discount structures can be evaluated. The effect of tariffs and the general economic background of the various overseas markets can be taken into account. Econometric models can be built. Subjective probabilities can be introduced. Although these specialists can remove much of the doubt from demand forecasting there still remains the problem of drawing a demand curve with any great precision. To quote a former Finance Director of the Ford Motor Company[12]:

In a large volume mass production industry a variance of one half per cent in selling price can make a difference of a million or more pounds profit per year. We will pay a very high salary indeed to any economist who can measure the elasticity of demand for a particular motor car within these limits!

If the large firms, who can afford to employ specialists to forecast their demand curves, still find forecasting a major problem, what of the smaller firms who cannot afford specialists? Will the sales department be able to supply the accountant with accurate demand schedules for determining the price which will maximize total contribution?

There is a smaller margin of error with marginal pricing than with full cost pricing, for the price determined by full cost pricing is often higher than that determined by marginal pricing. With the full cost approach, if the rate of output upon which total costs are based is achieved, and if the prices set more than cover the average total costs, then all costs will have been recovered at the end of the accounting period.

12. S. J. Elliot, *Planning and Controlling an Efficient Use of Financial Resources*, British Institute of Management National Conference, 13 October 1960.

SUMMARY AND CONCLUSION

All problems which deal with the future involve risk and uncertainty and the attitude of the decision-maker is conditioned by the degree of risk and uncertainty involved. Accountants by tradition and training are conservative and cautious in their attitude to the future. The full cost approach is attractive to accountants, under these conditions of uncertainty; it provides a starting point from which the process of fixing selling prices can begin. They know that the product cost covers the full cost of production, selling, distribution and administration. Marginal cost on the other hand provides them not with a starting point but a rock bottom price, and not one which will necessarily cover the full cost. Organizational theorists[13] have argued that firms develop a number of simple operating rules and the organization's rules permit the transfer of past learning. Full cost pricing procedures provide such simple operating rules, and this enables the complex problems of pricing involving considerable uncertainty to be reduced to a rather simple problem with a minimum of uncertainty. It is more difficult to develop simple operating rules when marginal cost pricing is employed.

Thus, while it may be persuasively argued that marginal costing principles are superior to conventional absorption costing for developing product costs for price policies and making specific pricing decisions, there is less unanimity and confidence in this area of marginal costing than in others. The conservative and cautious attitude of the accountant, his failure fully to understand marginalist principles, and the problem of forecasting the demand curve have resulted in many progressive, as well as less enlightened, accountants being prepared to rely on the total costs of conventional absorption costing for pricing purposes. As a result, marginal cost data have only been used to supplement the total costs in pricing decisions, and marginal cost pricing has usually been restricted to *secondary* pricing decisions. With these secondary pricing decisions the forecasting of the demand curve is often not very important. While the mechanics of 'full-cost-

13. Richard M. Cyert and James G. March, *A Behavioral Theory of the Firm,* Prentice-Hall, Englewood Cliffs, 1963, p. 104.

plus' pricing may be emphatically and repeatedly rejected in economic theory, for long-run as well as short-run pricing policy, in practice it still forms the basis of the accountant's contribution to the majority of 'primary' pricing decisions.

Of course, it should be remembered that pricing is not simply a process of setting figures at which a company's products are to be offered to the customers, but it is rather a broad and complex field embracing problems of determining characteristics of products to be sold, selecting customers, choosing sales promotion methods, determining channels of distribution, and obtaining a satisfactory volume of business. It is important to keep in mind that estimated costs, whether total or marginal, should be used only as a reference point in determining selling prices.

SELECTED READINGS

1. P. W. S. Andrews, *Manufacturing Business*, Macmillan, London, 1949.
2. R. H. Barbeck, *The Pricing of Manufactures*, Macmillan, London, 1964.
3. Wilfred Brown and Elliot Jaques, *Product Analysis Pricing*, Heinemann, London, 1964.
4. B. V. Carsberg and H. C. Edey (eds.), *Modern Financial Management*, Penguin, Harmondsworth, 1969.
5. Joel Dean, *Managerial Economics*, Prentice-Hall, Englewood Cliffs, 1951, London, 1962
6. André Gabor and Clive Granger, 'The Pricing of New Products', *Scientific Business*, August 1965.
7. Howard Greer, 'Cost Factors in Price Making', *Harvard Business Review*, July–August and September–October 1952.
8. R. A. Gordon, 'Short Period Price Determination in Theory and Practice', *American Economic Review*, August 1965.
9. R. L. Hall and C. J. Hitch, 'Price Theory and Business Behaviour', *Oxford Studies in the Price Mechanism*, ed. T. Wilson and P. W. S. Andrews, Oxford University Press, Oxford, 1951.
10. Gordon Johnson, 'The Pricing of Consumer Goods', *Yorkshire Bulletin of Economic and Social Research*, November 1962.
11. A. D. H. Kaplan, Joel B. Dirlam and Robert F. Lanzillotti, *Pricing in Big Business*, Brookings Institute, Washington, D.C., 1958.
12. Donald F. Mulvihill and Stephen Poranka (eds.), *Price Policies and Practice*, John Wiley, New York, 1967.
13. National Association of Accountants, *Product Costs for Pricing Purposes*, Research Report No. 24, New York, 1953.
14. Philip A. Scheuble, Jr, 'R.O.I. for New Product Policy', *Harvard Business Review*, November–December 1964.
15. John Sizer, 'A Risk Analysis Approach to Marginal Costing', *Accounting and Business Research*, Summer, 1971.
16. John Sizer, 'The Accountant's Contribution to the Pricing Decision', *Journal of Management Studies*, May 1966.
17. D. Solomons (ed.), *Studies in Cost Analysis*, Sweet & Maxwell, London, 1968.
18. Spencer A. Tucker, *Pricing for Higher Profit*, McGraw-Hill, New York, 1966.
19. P. J. D. Wiles, *Price, Cost and Output*, Basil Blackwell & Mott, Oxford, 1961.

CHAPTER 10

The Determination of Fixed and Variable Costs[1]

IN developing costs for control through the use of flexible budgets (Chapter 7), the classification of costs as fixed and variable was important. The segregation of fixed and variable costs is also an essential part of the development of costs for decision-making. It is the essence of marginal costing and the study of cost-profit-volume relationships. In this chapter the determination of fixed and variable costs is considered in detail. In establishing the meaning of the terms 'fixed' and 'variable', the time period is important. Classifications of costs into fixed and variable categories is possible only when the time period to which these concepts are related is specified. If a sufficiently long time period is provided, almost all costs become variable through changes in the scale of the company's operations. In practice, accountants tend to make cost variability studies on the basis of a time period of one year.

In differentiating between fixed costs and variable costs for marginal costing and flexible budgets, it is necessary to consider their variability in relation to volume. A classification of cost according to changes in volume attempts to establish the cost behaviour with respect to the degree of variability. The classification is possible only when specific assumptions are made regarding (1) the plant capacity to be employed; (2) prices; (3) managerial policies relating to the maintenance of an organization; and (4) the state of technology. The cost classification arrived at is a *static* function and is valid only for a specific purpose and a limited period of time. As the underlying conditions change, the classification must be revised.

The differentiation between fixed and variable costs relates generally to a fixed physical capacity situation. In practice,

1. This chapter draws extensively on the author's article 'The Determination of Fixed and Variable Costs', *The Accountant*, 8, 15, and 22 October 1966.

the fixed/variable distinction is generally based on the assumption that volume will move within certain relatively narrow limits (for example, between 60 per cent and 110 per cent of normal capacity) because movements outside this range would be accompanied by changes in the so-called fixed costs.

FIXED COSTS

A fixed cost is one which *tends* to be unaffected by variations in the volume of output. This does not mean that a fixed cost is *always* fixed in amount, for there are other forces, such as price levels, market shortages, etc., which can cause fixed costs to change in amount from period to period. However, in marginal costing, when one is determining how the cost reacts to changes in volume, the other factors are assumed to be held constant. The operation of a business requires facilities and an organization that must be maintained regardless of volume, and this requirement gives rise to fixed costs. Fixed costs are costs of *time* in that they accumulate with the passage of time irrespective of the volume of output. They are frequently called *period costs* because they are costs of time.

Differences of opinion exist among accountants as to the proper definitions of fixed cost. In some cases the term 'fixed' means fixed in amount, rather than fixed in relation to changes in output or volume. Usually, and particularly for marginal cost purposes, it is recognized that fixed costs are fixed in relation to volume, and that this amount of cost can change from period to period but not because of volume, e.g. a change in local government rates. In fact, three basic types of fixed costs can be distinguished:

1. Costs which are not susceptible to any substantial change within the short period, usually a year; for example, certain types of depreciation and other sunk costs.

2. Costs which are fixed for short periods in terms of providing the necessary facilities to produce but which are liable to change if volume changes appear likely to continue in the future: for example, supervision salaries, which although they may be fixed in relation to volume, may be affected by changes in wage rates.

312

3. Costs which are fixed by the management and bear no functional relationship to the current volume of output: for example, pure research and design engineering. These costs have no causal relationship arising from the amount of business actually done. They are usually costs which are covered by the appropriation type of budget and are often incurred with the aim of securing additional sales in the future or to maintain the current position. These costs include some forms of advertising, research and product development, and market research. Some may, in fact, vary with the volume of activity simply because management appropriates more funds on the basis of anticipated sales volume, but this increase is the result of management policy rather than a functional relationship between cost and volume. The change will usually be an annual one when the budgets are reviewed, and therefore the cost still tends to be fixed in the short period. In short, then, managerial policy dictates that these costs are fixed costs, and they may be called *programmed* fixed costs.

VARIABLE COSTS

A variable cost is one which *tends* to vary directly with fluctuations in the volume of output. If a change in volume forces a change in the amount of a particular cost element, then that element is a variable cost. The change in the total amount of the cost may or may not be directly proportionate to the variation in the output. In accounting, straight line or linear relationships are usually assumed, and consequently it is not uncommon to find variable costs defined as those costs which increase proportionately with increases in volume. If this definition is used, the unit variable cost is constant.

While this assumption of linearity may be justified for small changes, if output changes are too large the variable cost may not be linear. This could arise from a change in input factor prices or from increasing or decreasing marginal physical productivity. For example, although a product specification stipulates that a certain amount of material is to be used per unit of product, the efficiency with which materials are used may vary at different outputs. It is therefore preferable to use the word *tends* in the definition of variable costs.

Cost variability in response to changes in volume is not necessarily an automatic one. There are often time lags in the variability of some cost elements, and in other cases control efforts are often necessary to adjust costs promptly where there has been a reduction in volume.

Unfortunately, it is not simply a matter of classifying costs as either fixed or variable. Certain costs, known as *semi-variable* costs, contain both variable and fixed elements. Sometimes a linear relationship can be established when semi-variable costs are separated into their respective elements. In other cases a cost is fixed over large volume ranges but increases in steps at various stages of production. The problems arising from semi-variable costs are considered later in this chapter.

Another point to be remembered is that in some cases one accounting method may make a cost appear variable and another method may make the same cost appear fixed. Within the system of classifying and recording costs which accountants have developed, there are a number of more or less arbitrary conventions; however, these conventions are not always followed consistently from one firm to another. This is particularly so with *depreciation*. The effects of some of the different methods of depreciation are shown in Table 10.1. Occasionally the method of depreciation may give rise to a semi-variable cost. For instance, in a company operating a very large fleet of vehicles the mechanical parts of the vehicle, such as the engine, are depreciated on the basis of 100,000 miles life, while the fixed parts, such as the body, are written off over four years on a straight-line basis. Although depreciation is regarded by some writers as 'the fixed cost *par excellence*', it may in practice be a fixed cost, a variable cost, or a semi-variable cost, depending upon the method used. The businessman, if not the economist, appears to have accepted the accountant's ability to make depreciation a fixed or a variable cost.

Depreciation is a function of time, obsolescence, and wear and tear (deterioration), and the weight to be given to each factor when deciding the method of depreciation differs from

Table 10.1

Effects of Methods of Depreciation on the
Variability of Cost

Method	Fixed cost	Variable cost
Straight-line	*	
Reducing balance	*	
Production unit		*
Production hour		*
Repair reserve	*	
Annuity	*	
Sinking-fund	*	
Endowment policy	*	
Revaluation	*	

one asset to another. Unfortunately, accountants usually apply the same method of depreciation to all assets, or the same method of depreciation to assets falling into a very wide grouping; for example, one method is applied to plant and machinery, another to vehicles, another to office furniture, and probably a final method to buildings. Clearly, the assets within each group are not homogeneous as regards the effects of time, obsolescence, and wear and tear.

In addition, there are the effects of depreciating on a basis of historical cost in a period of rising or falling prices which has already been discussed in Chapter 2. In economic terms, depreciation is the cost of recovering the capitalized value through production and, assuming the business is to continue as a going concern, such recovery must take into account changing technology, rising price levels, etc., if *real* capital of the business is to be preserved. When defined in this way, depreciation is one of the costs associated with a marginal increment of output and is a true part of marginal cost. However, in practice it will scarcely ever be thought of in these terms, and, what is even worse, it is frequently lumped into overheads as a fixed cost. While it may not be possible to calculate the capitalized value consumed by each additional unit of output, some attempt could be made to calculate the average depreciation per unit of

315

output for ranges of output over which the capitalized value consumed per unit is thought to be constant. This average rate per unit of output could then be included in the calculation of marginal cost.

How does the cost accountant set about analysing his costs into fixed and variable elements in order to calculate marginal cost? He normally distinguishes two broad groups of costs: prime costs and overhead costs.

PRIME COSTS

Prime costs are the direct material costs, direct wages, and direct expenses which are directly traceable to a unit of output. Therefore, in theory, all prime costs are variable costs in that their distinguishing characteristic is the very fact that they can be associated directly with particular units of production.

However, before considering overhead costs it is necessary to consider in more detail *direct labour*. The general rule is that direct labour is that which is spent in the actual production of the company's finished products, or which is identifiable with product costs. Indirect labour costs are those which are not identifiable with, or incurred in, the production of specific goods or services but are applicable to production activities in general. The distinction between direct and indirect labour is becoming increasingly difficult to establish. When the company utilizes fully automatic machinery, the worker simply becomes a machine minder. It is the machine which alters the size or shape of the product, the worker merely feeding the machine at intervals and making minor adjustments. The introduction of these new production techniques has led to a reconsideration of what constitutes direct labour. If a man is a machine minder and is tending a productive machine, his labour is as direct as the labour of one producing goods manually. On the other hand, if he is classified as a maintenance mechanic or a set-up man, he may be treated as an indirect worker. Also, a labour item may be direct in nature but for practical reasons it may not be charged directly to a given product, but allocated as direct labour over several products; or it may even be treated as indirect labour. This may happen in the cases of spray painting, inspection, and short operations.

The recent developments in production techniques and employment practices lead one to think that factory direct labour, which is normally regarded as a variable cost, is increasingly assuming the characteristics of a fixed cost. Guaranteed weekly wages and other employment stabilizing devices, combined with increased mechanization and automation, have all tended to reduce the variability of labour costs in response to changes in volume of output. For example, in a large dairy firm, where the rate of production is entirely governed by the processing plant and the workers are merely machine minders, in the short period dairy labour costs are treated as fixed costs. The employees are also on a guaranteed minimum wage. It is only when large variations in output are under consideration that labour cost is regarded as variable. Similarly, in an electronics firm where all the employees are paid fixed monthly salaries, direct labour costs will be fixed for certain purposes and variable for others. When there is surplus capacity and the impact of additional output is being considered, direct labour will be a fixed cost. When choosing between two alternative uses of limited capacity, labour may be a variable cost.

OVERHEAD COSTS

Overhead costs include all production costs, except direct materials, direct labour, and direct expenses, selling and distribution costs and administrative expenses which cannot be traced to specific units of product. Manufacturing overhead also includes some direct costs which are so small in amount that it would be inexpedient to trace them to specific units of production.

The importance of overhead as a component of cost depends on the type and size of business, as well as the type of products manufactured. In the old handicraft industries, overhead cost was not important because of the low capital investment and the limited use of unspecialized indirect labour. The worker was primarily concerned with the conversion of raw materials into finished products, and raw materials and direct labour costs were the principal elements of cost. With the development of large-scale production and distribution, firms have grown in size and this has resulted in increased labour specialization and large capital investments. With increased mechanization and automation many firms have become capital intensive. Firms have also diversified their product lines and in some cases thousands of different types of products are manufactured. All these influences have given rise to a large body of production overheads and distribution expenses. As the trend develops towards increased automation and higher capital investment per employee, the amount of overhead cost will become increasingly important. With the continued shift from human to machine production, the decline in the importance of direct labour costs and the increasing significance of overhead costs will become more apparent. In fact, the introduction of automatic processes will result in an increase in the proportion of fixed costs in the total overhead costs. The accountant's definition of overhead cost, as a cost which cannot be allocated directly to a cost unit, may change and resemble more closely the economist's definition of overhead as a term synonymous with the fixed costs of production and distribution.

Overhead costs consist of three broad groups:

1. *Fixed costs*, which *tend* to be unaffected by variations in volume of output in the short run;

2. *Variable costs*, which *tend* to vary directly with variations in volume of output; and

3. *Semi-variable costs*, which are partly fixed and partly variable.

In computing the variable overhead element of marginal cost in the short run, group (1) can be ignored, group (2) must be included, as must the variable portion of group (3). The determination of the variable portion of the semi-variable costs can be a problem when computing marginal cost. At least four types of semi-variable costs are commonly found:

1. *Fixed and variable element combined*, such as indirect labour when a minimum force is necessary to operate but is easily supplemented when the need arises.

2. *Cost increases in steps* at certain points on the volume-output scale. For example, when increases in volume lead to the addition of a new shift, the hiring of assistant foremen, or other salaried supervisors. One foreman may easily supervise six, seven, eight or even nine workers, but eventually the number of workers will be beyond the control of a single foreman, and the group will be split into two in order to maintain effective supervision. However, with this type of semi-variable cost it is difficult to say with certainty just when the upward 'steps' in the cost pattern will occur, and the downward 'steps' may not occur at the same point for decreases in volume.

3. *Seasonal costs*, when costs tend to be higher during certain months than during others owing to climate (heating and lighting), custom (machine repair, holiday pay), or other reasons not connected with the volume of output.

4. *Cost increases at a fluctuating rate* and the cost curve may have a curvilinear pattern increasing more rapidly at some points on the volume of output scale than others. This is often experienced when a particular department or activity reaches or exceeds its practical capacity, for example, when the maximum demand charge is exceeded for electricity.

With many of these semi-variable costs, the question whether to treat the cost as partly variable depends upon the decision being considered. A cost which remains fixed if volume is changed by 5 per cent may become partly variable if volume is changed by 15 per cent. For example, certain indirect labour costs, such as repair and maintenance wages, may remain the same if an additional order is taken on a once-for-all basis. If the increase in volume is considered to be permanent or likely to continue for an indefinite period, however, additional repairs and maintenance labour may have to be engaged at some later date. In practice, semi-variable costs of the 'step' type and the seasonal type are frequently recorded as fixed costs, while those which are combinations of fixed and variable elements may be broken down and recorded separately as fixed and variable. Semi-variable costs which increase at a fluctuating rate and have a curvilinear pattern may be classified as wholly fixed and wholly variable, or may be analysed into separate elements, depending upon the rate of variability which exists in the output range in which the firm expects to operate. With the curvilinear type of cost, the unit variable cost is often assumed to be constant, i.e. a linear relationship is assumed, so that deviations will be highlighted and subjected to analysis for cost control purposes.

SEPARATION OF SEMI-VARIABLE COSTS

What methods can be used, but often are not used, to separate the variable element from the fixed cost in a semi-variable cost?

1. *Accounts Classification.* A careful examination of the cost code used by the business will reduce the amount of work by eliminating at the outset a large proportion of the costs which tend to be either wholly fixed or variable in direct proportion to the volume of output. Making the decision as to whether a cost tends to be wholly fixed or directly variable requires the exercise of judgement and the result cannot be regarded as infallible. One has to decide whether there is a large variable or fixed element in a cost, which would normally be classified as wholly fixed or wholly variable, to justify further examination to determine the separate fixed and variable elements. Clearly time cannot be expended examining every cost which shows signs of being semi-variable. Any cost element or account classification which cannot be identified as fixed or variable by inspection should be studied by one or more of the methods outlined below.

2. *Estimate Method.* By this method the relationship between the cost and the level of activity is discussed with a person who is familiar with the conditions giving rise to its incidence. He should be asked what expense would result if the department were reduced to an extremely low, or zero, level of activity. His estimate will be checked with the head of the department and other persons familiar with the operation. This estimate is then taken to be the fixed cost and the remainder of the account is assumed to be variable. By this method there is a danger that the fixed cost will be understated in that it may only include the shut-down costs and may exclude the stand-by costs which are also

fixed costs. It is the fixed cost within the normal range of activity levels that is required. Although this method is simple it is not very accurate.

3. *Statistical Methods.* The statistical analysis of historical data utilizes various correlation techniques to isolate the fixed element. However, the existence of a correlation between cost and volume does not necessarily mean that a cause-and-effect relationship exists, and this is sometimes not appreciated. Management policy may dictate that one or more cost elements (for example, advertising and maintenance) may vary directly with volume, even though there is no indication that changes in volume give rise to changes in cost in the technical sense. In the case of advertising for example, the causal relationship may be from cost to volume rather than the other way around. The results of a correlation analysis must be interpreted with considerable caution, as will be illustrated. It should not be used unless there is a strong advance presumption that a cause-and-effect relationship does in fact exist. When the costs are set by managerial policy the *estimate method* is more appropriate than the use of statistical techniques. However, many of these costs determined by managerial policy are fixed in the short run and the problem of separating the fixed and variable elements does not arise. It should also be remembered that in so far as these relationships are based on historical data, these data must be modified to remove the effect of non-volume influences, such as a change in input prices midway through the period being analysed. It is argued later that unadjusted historical data are frequently used and that the results obtained are not very reliable.

The data shown in Table 10.2 will be used to illustrate the different statistical techniques and the different results obtained from their use will be compared.

(a) THE HIGH-LOW POINTS METHOD. This method, like the other statistical methods, establishes a cost-volume relationship on a historical basis. Two extreme points are determined either by past experience or by having the person or persons best acquainted with the conditions estimate the expense that should

Table 10.2

Cost of Lighting

Month	Direct labour hours (000s)	Cost £
January	68	640
February	60	620
March	68	620
April	78	590
May	84	500
June	64	530
July	52	500
August	52	500
September	62	530
October	70	550
November	86	580
December	96	680
	840	£6,840

be incurred at two distinct levels of activity. A linear relationship is assumed to exist between the two points and the rate of change between the two points is assumed to be the variable cost per unit. The total variable cost for one of the points is then calculated, by multiplying the level of activity by the variable cost per unit, and is then deducted from the total cost for that level of activity to give the fixed cost. The calculation is illustrated in Table 10.3. With this method there is often the difficulty of finding two periods which offer the extreme variations in activity required. There is also an assumption that the extreme ranges of activity chosen are representative of the intermediate levels of actual activity.

(b) THE SCATTER CHART METHOD. By this method a line is fitted by observation to a series of data. The slope of the line represents the variable cost per unit, while the fixed cost is the point at which the line cuts the cost axis. Data for a number of

Table 10.3

High-low Points Method

	Direct labour hours (000s)	Cost of lighting £
High point – December	96	680
Low point – July and August	52	500
Variable element	44	£180

Variable cost per direct labour hour:
$$\frac{£180 \times 240}{44,000} = \underline{.982d.}$$

Fixed cost = £500 − (52,000 × .982d.) = £287
or £680 − (96,000 × .982d.) = £287

Cost of lighting = £287 (fixed) + .982d. per direct labour hour (variable)

periods are plotted on graph paper, with activity on the horizontal axis and expense on the vertical axis. By the use of string or a rubber band, the paths of the high and low points are found. A line is drawn between these two paths to fit midway and, at the same time, have as many points above as below. The intention is to draw an approximate line of best fit. The fixed expense can then be read directly from the graph. It is the point where the line intersects the vertical axis. The fixed cost determined by this method is not the amount of expense that would be incurred if the activity were zero, i.e. the shut-down cost, as described under the estimate method. It is the fixed cost that is incurred within the normal range of activity. Provided the basic data is sound, the advantage of the scatter chart method is speed and simplicity, but this may well be at the expense of accuracy. The scatter chart method is illustrated in Figure 28 and Table 10.4.

(c) METHOD OF LEAST SQUARES. The method of least squares assumes that the line is best fitted to a series of data when the sum of the squares of the deviations of the observed points from the line is less than that for any other line which may

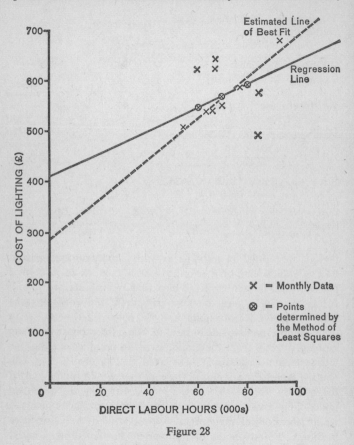

Figure 28

be drawn. While understanding the mathematical development requires a knowledge of differential calculus, the application of the formulae derived from the mathematics is comparatively simple. The method uses the straight-line formula $\bar{y} = a + Bx\bar{x}$, where a is the fixed element and Bx is the degree of variability:

Table 10.4

Scatter Chart Method

Fixed cost = £280 from Figure 28.
Variable cost:
(1) Determined from total cost line in Figure 28.
    60,000 direct labour hours = £525 total cost

$$\text{Variable cost per direct labour hour} = \frac{\pounds(525-280)\times240}{60,000} = .98\text{d.}$$

		£
(2)	Determined from source data	
	Total cost for year per Table 10.2	6,840
	Less fixed costs for year (12 × £280)	3,360
	Total variable cost for year	£3,480

$$\text{Variable cost per direct labour hour} = \frac{\pounds3,480\times240}{840,000} = .994\text{d.}$$

$a = y - Bx\bar{x}$ and $Bx = \dfrac{Cov.xy}{\sigma x^2}$. After the slope of the line (Bx) has been computed, it can be substituted in the formula $a = \bar{y} - Bx\bar{x}$. The numerical figure can then be found for a, which is the fixed cost. The method is illustrated in Table 10.5.

It is important to realize that the method of least squares will give accurate results only if the cost and activity data are secured under controlled conditions. If an abnormal figure appears it will give an unsuitable result. In fact, the result in the example has probably been distorted by seasonal factors. The cost of lighting is the product of direct labour hours and of seasonal effects. The cost will obviously be higher in the winter months than in the summer months, and is notmerelydependent on direct labour hours. The results obtained from the three statistical methods suggested are shown in Table 10.6. Clearly, the result derived from the method of least squares is out of line with the results derived from the other two methods. This is also shown in Figure 28 where the regression line derived from the method of least squares has been fitted. Is there any test that can be applied to the initial data to test its reliability before using the method of least squares?

Table 10.5

Method of Least Squares

Month	Direct labour hours (000s)	Cost of lighting £	Deviation from average of 70,000 hrs (.000)	Deviation from average of £570			
	x	y	$(x-\bar{x})$	$(y-\bar{y})$	$(x-\bar{x})^2$	$(y-\bar{y})^2$	Cov. xy
January	68	640	(—) 2	70	4	4,900	(—) 140
February	60	620	(—) 10	50	100	2,500	(—) 500
March	68	620	(—) 2	50	4	2,500	(—) 100
April	78	590	8	20	64	400	160
May	84	500	14	(—) 70	196	4,900	(—) 980
June	64	530	(—) 6	(—) 40	36	1,600	240
July	52	500	(—) 18	(—) 70	324	4,900	1,260
August	52	500	(—) 18	(—) 70	324	4,900	1,260
September	62	530	(—) 8	(—) 40	64	1,600	320
October	70	550	—	(—) 20	—	400	—
November	86	580	16	10	256	100	160
December	96	680	28	110	676	12,100	2,860
	840	£6,840			2,048	40,800	4,540

$$\bar{x} = \frac{840,000}{12} = 70,000 \text{ direct labour hours} \quad \bar{y} = \frac{£6,840}{12} = £570$$

$$\bar{y} = a + Bx\bar{x} \qquad \text{where } a = \bar{y} - Bx\bar{x} = \text{fixed cost}$$

$$\text{and } Bx = \frac{Cov.\ xy}{\sigma x^2} = \text{variable element}$$

$$Variable\ element = Bx = \frac{4,540}{2,048,000} = £2.21 \text{ per 1,000 labour hours or}$$
.53d. per direct labour hour.

Fixed cost: $a = \bar{y} - Bx\bar{x}$
$$£570 - (£2.21 \times 70) = £415.3 \text{ per month.}$$

Total cost of lighting = £415 + .53d. per direct labour hour.

Test of significance

$$t = r\frac{\sqrt{n-2}}{\sqrt{1-r^2}} \qquad \text{where } r = \frac{Cov.\ xy}{\sigma x \sigma y} = \frac{4,540}{\sqrt{2,048}\ \sqrt{40,800}} = .5$$

Table 10.5 — cont.

$$= \frac{.5\sqrt{12-2}}{\sqrt{1-(.5)^2}} = 1.82$$

t for ten degrees of freedom: 0.05 probability = 2.228
0.01 probability = 3.169

As 't' in test is only 1.82 there is no strong evidence of real positive correlation.

If there is no strong evidence of correlation between the initial data an accurate separation of the fixed cost and the variable cost per unit will not be derived by applying the method of least squares to the data. There are a number of methods of testing the initial data. For example the t-test may be used to measure the significance of the correlation between the direct labour hours and the cost of lighting. The correlation coefficient r has been calculated in Table 10.5 by the formula $r = \dfrac{Cov.xy}{\sigma x \sigma y}$ and then fitted in the formula $t = \dfrac{r\sqrt{n-2}}{\sqrt{1-r^2}}$. The resulting figure has been compared with the statistical probability tables for t. The test shows that there is no strong evidence of real positive correlation for the method of least squares calculation. The least squares calculation has been made before applying the test to illustrate the dangers of using the method of least squares without fully understanding its limitations.

Unfortunately, while many accounting textbooks describe the method of least squares, they fail to mention the importance of testing the reliability of the data with a test of significance. The same conclusion probably applies to many practising cost accountants, that while they are familiar with the method of least squares they are not familiar with the significance tests. With the recent rapid developments in the application of mathematics and statistics to problems of business and industry, it is essential that the accountant of the future should have more than the phrase-book knowledge of elementary statistics which is at present required by the professional accounting bodies in Britain in their statistics examinations.

Table 10.6

Comparison of Results from Statistical Techniques

Method	Fixed cost	Variable cost per direct labour hour
High-low points	£287	.982d.
Scatter chart		
(1) Total cost line	£280	.98d.
(2) From source data	£280	.994d.
Least squares	£415	.53d.

4. *Industrial Engineering Estimates.* Statistical methods are not very useful in cases where there are no historical data available, or the past data are unreliable because of changed conditions, such as a change in the state of technology. In fact, because historical data reflect the effect on cost of a multitude of influences which cannot always be isolated satisfactorily, the underlying relationships between cost and volume will probably appear imperfectly in any analysis based solely on these data. It is therefore necessary to seek the aid of the industrial engineers who, along with members of the accounting department, study each activity or job in an attempt to discover the best methods of performing the function in the short run under the present or proposed methods of production, and establish the cost of performance.

In some instances the engineering methods use historical data like the statistical methods outlined, frequently the same data. However, the engineering approach is more concerned with physical input-output data than with money costs. Industrial engineers attempt to determine the physical inputs necessary to achieve certain levels of output, and then convert these into money costs. Although the engineering methods may apply statistical analysis to historical data, they are generally more flexible than the statistical methods employed by accountants. Engineers are usually far more conversant with statistical and mathematical techniques than accountants. They will be able to apply, for example, multiple regression analysis. On the other hand, the engineering methods are also more time-consuming and costly than the other methods. Not only do they separate the fixed and variable elements, but they also establish efficiency standards for different levels of activity.

These approaches to the separation of semi-variable costs into fixed and variable elements should be used together. There is no one approach which can be said to be fully superior to the others; it is a question of deciding which is the most suitable for the cost under consideration. Where there is strong positive evidence of correlation the method of least squares will probably be the most suitable method. If there is no strong evidence of positive correlation the method of least squares, like the high-low points method and the scatter chart method, will merely produce what is in effect an overhead recovery rate consisting of a fixed and variable element, but not the correct fixed cost and variable cost per unit for decision-making purposes. In these circumstances the industrial engineering estimate may be more accurate, but it is a question of weighing the benefits to be derived from the additional accuracy against the additional cost of using the industrial engineering method.

LIMITATIONS OF USEFULNESS OF VARIABLE AND FIXED COSTS

There are severe limitations on the usefulness of the accountant's fixed and variable cost classification – a classification which is essential to flexible budgetary control, marginal costing, and the study of cost-volume-profit relationships. Most of these limitations arise from the fact that cost is affected by many factors other than volume. The problems caused by these other factors make it difficult to measure variable and fixed costs with any degree of accuracy. The statistical techniques when employed by accountants produce a linear relationship between cost and volume, which may or may not be a good statement of the cost function. When linear relationships are assumed and some method such as simple regression analysis employed, the cost function may be one of volume plus several other factors. This seriously impairs the usefulness of such a function in making volume decisions. Where costs are influenced by more than one factor multiple regression techniques can be used.[2] The assumption that cost-volume relationships are usually characterized by straight lines is a measurement problem and not a shortcoming of the classification itself. It may be true that cost accountants always fit straight lines with the scatter chart and with regression analysis, but if this is so, it is a limitation of the accountant and not the method. Both methods can be used to fit *curves*. For example, quadratic and cubic curves can be fitted to cost data.[3]

There are numerous factors in addition to volume which cause costs to vary. The accountant relies heavily on unadjusted historical data and tends to assume that these other factors are constant during the period to which this data relates. When making a study of cost-volume relationships, he will frequently assume that these non-volume factors affecting costs will also remain constant for the period during which the conclusions from the analysis of the unadjusted historical data are to be applied. Variable costs computed in determining profit may be useful if it is assumed that the present environment will exist in the future. Many cost accountants use the historical data available from the process of determining profit as the basic information for developing cost data more directly applicable to future planning. But the process involved is one of correcting or adjusting historical cost data to the environment which is forecast for the future, and not simply relying on unadjusted historical data. Examples of such non-volume factors which cause costs to vary include:

Changes in plant and equipment;

2. For example, see George J. Binston, 'Multiple Regression Analysis and Cost Behaviour', *Accounting Review*, October 1966, and Eugene E. Comiskey, 'Cost Control by Regression Analysis', *Accounting Review*, April 1966.
3. For a non-technical description of these cost functions, see Milton H. Spencer and Louis Siegelman, *Managerial Economics*, Irwin, Homewood, Illinois, 1964, Ch. 9, pp. 301–52.

Changes in products manufactured, methods used, or methods of manufacture;

Changes in organization, personnel, working hours, or conditions of efficiency;

Changes in managerial policy towards costs;

Changes in prices paid for cost factors;

Lags between incurrence of costs and reporting of production;

The inclusion of materials and depreciation on a historical cost rather than a replacement cost basis;

Random influences such as strikes, weather and wars.

The concurrent operation of these non-volume factors on a cost tends to obscure the fluctuations due to volume alone. It will usually be necessary to make some adjustment or selection of data before the rate at which a cost should vary with volume can be established. However, in practice accountants frequently fail to make such adjustments; they are quite happy to use unadjusted historical data. Possibly this is because the additional accuracy achieved is far outweighed by the additional cost incurred in achieving it. Marginal costing and differential costing are essentially tools for decision-making, and decision-making is concerned with the future; unadjusted historical data can only be a guide to what will happen in the future. However, they have often proved a poor and inadequate guide, even though at the time the unadjusted historical data seemed reliable.

Another fault with some accountants' classification of costs into fixed and variable is their *philosophy of absolutism*. The whole procedure of breaking down costs into fixed and variable elements may suggest an accuracy which is misleading. They frequently make a once-for-all classification of costs and then consider that it will be true for all purposes and under all conditions. They often fail to realize that whether a cost is variable depends on the problem or the decision at hand; that there is *no* single division of costs into fixed and variable classifications which will serve all purposes. The accountant attempts this once-for-all classification of costs within the period of his own accounting system. Having made this classification he will maintain his distinction between fixed and variable costs for the rest of the budgetary period, which is usually one year. And even when he comes to revise his budgets he will nòt look very closely at his existing classifications. What is required is a flexible classification of accounting records on several alternative bases, and not a philosophy of absolutism. The increasing use of the computer should make this possible.

These limitations on the usefulness of variable and fixed cost classifications are not limited to marginal costing; they are common to the whole field of cost accountancy and particularly to those techniques which rely on cost-volume-profit relationships. However, these limitations are, in part, of the accountant's own making because of his failure to adjust historical data, his habit of making a once-for-all classification of costs, and his inability to make use of modern statistical and mathematical techniques. While it is true that in some instances a more accurate cost classification would be far too expensive, many accountants have never tried to make a more accurate classification and probably would not know how to do so. It is appreciated that cost accounting is not and can never become an exact science because of the inherent element of judgement, but surely there is considerable scope for improvement in this branch of the discipline. It is not suggested that absolute accuracy is necessary, but when these estimates are made some measure of the possible margin of error involved should be given.

SUMMARY OF CHAPTER

The segregation of costs into fixed and variable categories is an essential step in the development of costs for both decision-making and control. It is important to appreciate that whether a cost is fixed or variable depends on the problem or decision at hand. A fixed cost is one which tends to be unaffected by variations in volume of output, and a variable cost one which tends to vary directly. Recent developments in production techniques and employment practices lead one to think that factory direct labour is increasingly assuming the characteristics of a fixed cost. The determination of the variable element of a semi-variable cost can be difficult. Some accountants treat semi-variable costs as wholly fixed or wholly variable. Many of the methods which are used by accountants to separate the variable element are open to criticism. There is no one approach which is clearly superior to others; it is a question of deciding which is the most suitable for the cost under consideration. The approach of some accountants is too rigid and inflexible. They tend to make a once-for-all classification of costs as fixed or variable, and frequently use unadjusted historical data. The management accountant must recognize that different costs are required for different purposes.

SELECTED READINGS

1. Robert N. Anthony, *Management Accounting: Text and Cases*, Irwin, Homewood, Illinois, 1970.

2. J. G. Birnberg and N. Dopuch, *Cost Accounting Data for Management Decisions*, Harcourt, Brace & World, New York, 1969.

3. Charles T. Horngren, *Cost Accounting: A Managerial Emphasis*, Prentice-Hall, Englewood Cliffs, 1967.

4. J. Johnston, *Statistical Cost Analysis*, McGraw-Hill, New York, 1960.

5. National Association of Accountants, 'Separating and Using Costs as Fixed and Variable', Accounting Practice Report No. 10, *N.A.A. Bulletin*, June 1960, Section 3.

6. John Sizer, 'The Determination of Fixed and Variable Costs – A Critical Appraisal', *The Accountant*, 8, 15 and 22 October 1966.

7. D. Solomons (ed.), *Studies in Cost Analysis*, Sweet & Maxwell, London, 1968.

MORE ABOUT PENGUINS
AND PELICANS

Penguinews, which appears every month, contains details of all the new books issued by Penguins as they are published. From time to time it is supplemented by *Penguins in Print*, which is a complete list of all books published by Penguins which are in print. (There are well over three thousand of these.)

A specimen copy of *Penguinews* will be sent to you free on request, and you can become a subscriber for the price of the postage – 30p for a year's issues (including the complete lists) if you live in the United Kingdom, or 60p if you live elsewhere. Just write to Dept EP, Penguin Books Ltd, Harmondsworth, Middlesex, enclosing a cheque or postal order, and your name will be added to the mailing list.

Some other books published by Penguins are described on the following pages.

Note: *Penguinews* and *Penguins in Print* are not available in the U.S.A. or Canada

A HISTORY OF MONEY

E. Victor Morgan

REVISED EDITION

Adam Smith regarded 'a propensity to truck, barter and exchange one thing for another' as one of the basic ingredients of human nature. Certainly in the growth from the earliest exchanges of rice and honey to the complexities of modern international monetary systems, the invention and development of money ranks with the great dynamics of world civilization, the domestication of animals, the culture of land, and the harnessing of power.

Dealing with money only in its broadest sense, Professor Morgan surveys the ideas, concepts, and institutions associated with it and ranges the whole diversity of this fascinating subject, from money and other means of holding wealth to banking, the money market, the origins of accounting, and the system of 'double entry'. The meaning of 'capital' leads to an impressive analysis of the relationship between government and money, ranging from government finances in Athens to the International Monetary Fund.

Two final chapters survey monetary theory and policy, making clear the relationship between money and fluctuations in business, employment, and prices. Professor Morgan ends a description of the modern British monetary system with a discussion of the highly contemporary problems of full employment and inflation and shows how governments have tried to control money as part of the effort to secure stable economic growth.

PROGRESS OF
MANAGEMENT RESEARCH

Edited by Nigel Farrow

Management research, writes Nigel Farrow, is science's
Oliver Twist: a delicate and neglected infant of obscure
parentage, it has been suddenly claimed by various competing godfathers for reasons ranging from disinterested charity
to commercial exploitation.

This volume in the Pelican Library of Business and
Management contains ten articles which originally appeared
as a series in *Business Management*. It is a sign of the fluid
state of management studies that the contributors include
professors of marketing, business administration, industrial
psychology, operational research, and industrial and
management engineering, as well as economists and consultants. Covering the functional areas of production, personnel,
finance, and marketing, they indicate the debt owed by
business research to economics, mathematics, psychology,
and sociology.

It remains a question whether management research does
better to be wide, general, and abstract (a pursuit for academic cloisters); or specific, local, and concrete (an exercise
for the oil-grimed shop). But in any case the recent research
outlined in these essays is constructive and practical and
never loses sight of the manager on the spot.

COMPUTERS, MANAGERS
AND SOCIETY

Michael Rose

Computers, Managers and Society is an account, part technical, part sociological and part philosophical, of the computer revolution.

After a general survey of the development of computer-controlled data processing, Michael Rose examines the complex effects of the computer upon the clerical worker – the new opportunities, the dangers of alienation, the threat of technological unemployment. He then focuses upon the fast-developing problems of managers. Many of the standard managerial functions can already be programmed. But should executives delegate qualitative decisions to a machine? And if so, how far can and should these changes go?

'Computerization' presents managers with new opportunities on a structural scale unmatched since the Industrial Revolution. Do they really understand the new situation? Can they, when it is transforming itself so rapidly? And are we enough aware of the effects of the computer upon an even larger social group – society itself – now faced with the need to clarify its whole attitude to technological change?

MATHEMATICS IN MANAGEMENT

Albert Battersby

Sophisticated methods of planning, control, and decision-making, together with the advent of the electronic computer, have already brought mathematics well to the fore in modern industry and commerce. At the present rate of advance, mathematics will soon be an indispensable tool of the intelligent manager.

Mathematics in Management has been specially written, for managers and others, to provide a sound basis of knowledge about the methods of operational research now being applied in public industries and services, to save resources and prune expenditure. Some such account is urgently needed, since general education has not kept pace with advances in this field, and mathematicians have difficulty in 'talking' to managers.

Among the particular topics covered by Albert Battersby in this new Pelican are network analysis, simple functions, linear programming, simulation, and electronic computers. The author employs a minimum of mathematical notation in his text and, wherever possible, makes his points with the help of drawings. He has also included a set of exercises with full solutions.

Also available

Sales Forecasting